PRAISE FOR BRANDON MULL'S BOOKS

"Brandon Mull is a wizard with words. With Beyonders,
he has conjured one of the most original fantasies I've read in
years—an irresistible mix of adventure, humor, and magic."
—RICK RIORDAN,
author of the Percy Jackson series, on
A World Without Heroes

"The Fablehaven books . . . kept me turning the pages until 4:40
in the morning. Each book was better than the last!"
—CHRISTOPHER PAOLINI,
author of the Eragon series, on Fablehaven

"Like Harry Potter, Fablehaven looks like a book for kids,
but, like Harry Potter, Fablehaven can be read aloud in a family with
as much pleasure for grown-ups as for children."
—ORSON SCOTT CARD,
author of *Ender's Game,* on Fablehaven

BEYONDERS

CHASING THE PROPHECY

BEYONDERS

CHASING THE PROPHECY

✦ BOOK THREE ✦

BRANDON MULL

Aladdin

NEW YORK   LONDON   TORONTO   SYDNEY   NEW DELHI

ALADDIN

An imprint of Simon & Schuster Children's Publishing Division

1230 Avenue of the Americas, New York, NY 10020

First Aladdin paperback edition February 2014

Text copyright © 2013 by Brandon Mull

Cover art copyright © 2013 by Jason Chan

For information about special discounts for bulk purchases, please contact Simon & Schuster Special Sales at 1-866-506-1949 or business@simonandschuster.com.

The Simon & Schuster Speakers Bureau can bring authors to your live event. For more information or to book an event contact the Simon & Schuster Speakers Bureau at 1-866-248-3049 or visit our website at www.simonspeakers.com.

Designed by Lisa Vega

The text of this book was set in Goudy Old Style.

Manufactured in the United States of America 1213 OFF

2 4 6 8 10 9 7 5 3 1

The Library of Congress has cataloged the hardcover edition as follows:

Mull, Brandon, 1974

Chasing the prophecy / Brandon Mull. – 1st Aladdin hardcover ed.

p.cm. – (Beyonders ; bk. 3)

Summary: Jason and Rachel's adventures and friendships have made Lyrian more of a home to them than they could have imagined, so no, armed with the prophecy of a dying oracle, they are ready to become Lyrians's heroes whatever the cost to themselves.

[1. Space and time –Fiction. 2. Prophecies—Fiction. 3. Revolutions—Fiction. 4. Wizards—Fiction. 5. Magic—Fiction. 6. Heroes—Fiction. 7. Fantasy.] I. Title.

PZ7.M9112Ch 2013 [Fic]—dc23 2012035223

ISBN 978-1-4169-9796-2 (hc)

ISBN 978-1-4169-9797-9 (pbk)

ISBN 978-1-4169-9800-6 (eBook)

This book is dedicated to you, my reader.
I hope you find it rewarding!

A HERO FALLS

Nearly Twenty Years Ago . . .

An arrow hissed out of the night and thudded near the embers of the shielded campfire. Always a light sleeper, the young squire jerked awake. This close to Felrook it was a wonder he had dozed at all. Nedwin stayed low, holding his breath, and stared out into the darkness, scrutinizing the shadows beyond the shelter of their modest encampment. All was dark and still. Some of the men around him whispered and stirred.

Prince Galloran had posted two sentries up in trees. The angle of the arrow showed that it had come from Malak. Nedwin regretted having glanced directly at the arrow, because the nearby embers from the fire had dulled his night vision. Listening intently to the quietness, he tried to will his eyes to penetrate deeper into the gloom.

Malak would not have launched an arrow into camp unless enemies were almost upon them. Such an arrow was reserved as their most urgent distress signal, and Malak was no jittery novice. Quite the opposite. The twenty men Galloran had handpicked for this final mission were among the most seasoned and intimidating warriors in all of Lyrian. All were veterans of daring campaigns, all had shown an ability to prosper against incredible odds, and all were despised by the emperor.

Nedwin grimly reflected that he was the sole exception. As squire to Galloran, he had been thrilled and honored to learn that he would join this noble company as the only participant who had not yet reached full manhood. He was no great soldier, no master woodsman—his only real specialty was that he knew how to sneak.

Although Nedwin was scarcely thirteen years old, Galloran had already used him as a spy for years. Nedwin possessed a knack for quietly ferreting out information. He understood where to stand in a crowd, how to position himself where a conversation could barely be overheard, how to use his expression and posture to appear inattentive. He had a sense for when to hide, when to run, and when to appear obliviously engaged in some mundane task. At first Nedwin had brought Galloran unrequested information—suspicious murmurs overheard at court. As Galloran began to recognize his talent, he gave Nedwin secret assignments, and Nedwin had faithfully delivered.

Despite his useful history, Nedwin would not have expected to be included on a campaign like this or to be entrusted with a secret like the one Galloran had privately shared. Faced with the sudden prospect of approaching enemies, Nedwin was relieved to find that he was not particularly afraid for his life. His main worry was disappointing his master.

A strangled cry interrupted the silence. The voice might have been trying to shout "Flee!" or "Fly!" Nedwin listened intently as Malak's unseen body crashed through branches on the way to the forest floor.

While men around him staggered to their feet, drawing swords and fumbling with bows, Nedwin scurried away from the encampment. He moved using his hands and feet, springing more than crawling. Haste was so crucial that he allowed himself to make a little noise. Finally, he paused behind the trunk of a knobby old tree, wedging himself between a pair of thick, gnarled roots.

The half moon came out from behind a cloud, spreading soft silver radiance over the scene. Before sunset, Galloran had chosen to bed down in the remains of a hall of an ancient warlord. The walls had tumbled down long ago; a few jagged remnants jutted up like haphazard tombstones. Lawson had built the modest fire in the ancient hearth, shielding the flames and trusting the darkness to hide the wispy smoke. Although the timeworn ruins were all but forgotten, and far from a path, they were still something of a landmark. Nedwin would have preferred a more anonymous campsite.

By the ghostly moonlight Nedwin watched a barrage of arrows whisper out of the night, thunking against shields, clanging off armor, and also finding flesh. After three heavy volleys, armored swordsmen rushed into the camp. Galloran's men raced forward to engage the attackers.

Nedwin gaped at the masterful assault. Clouds had obscured the moon all night. How had their enemies synchronized the attack so perfectly? Darkness had disguised their approach until Malak had issued a late warning. Then the moon had come out just in time to help the enemy archers find targets and to make escape into the murky forest more difficult. Could such impeccable timing be ascribed to luck?

Nedwin noticed a pair of bodyguards ushering Galloran away from the oncoming foes. Galloran appeared to be resisting, and Nedwin had to clap a hand over his mouth to prevent himself from yelling for him to run. If Galloran fell, all would be lost. The other men understood this—all were ready to die for him.

Tursock of Meridon, a bear of a man who wielded a huge war hammer in each hand, charged the onrushing attackers. Lesser fighters would have struggled to employ either of his hammers using both hands, but Tursock's strength was legendary, and he began to send opponents flying, crushing shields, helms, and bones. Other comrades of Galloran followed Tursock into the fray, each a champion capable of singlehandedly turning the tide of a battle. The overmatched attackers quickly succumbed to sword, ax, and spear.

In the brief lull that followed, a fresh volley of arrows hissed from various angles. In a flash Nedwin understood that the foot soldiers had been a sacrificial ploy to draw Galloran's men away from cover! Many of the archers had sighted on Tursock, who staggered and then dropped to his knees, the dark form of his bulky body suddenly imitating a pincushion.

As shields were raised and Galloran's men sought cover, manglers—huge creatures encased in spiky armor and fitted with a deadly variety of whirling blades—appeared out of the darkness. Elite soldiers—conscriptors and displacers—joined them. And arrows continued to fly with fatal accuracy.

Galloran and his bodyguards had retreated into the woods out of view. Nedwin knew how hard it must be for his master to run while others fought to defend him.

Tursock struggled to his feet as the manglers approached. With a tremendous clang he toppled the nearest one, denting its iron shell. A clamor resulted as his hammers battered another, even as a multitude of merciless blades penetrated his furry robes. As the manglers plowed into the other defenders, it became clear that many of the men lacked their full armor. Nedwin's eyes widened in horror as men he had idolized his entire life began to fall.

He tore his gaze from the grisly battle. He had to hide! Galloran had entrusted him with crucial information. His position behind the tree would not suffice. Scanning the vicinity, he spotted a hollow log. He was small enough to squirm inside. But the best hiding places had to be unpredictable. He glanced up. If all else failed, he could climb a tree. He knew how to do so quietly, creeping up to limbs that would seem unreachable to most. No, he wanted something better.

Some distance away Nedwin observed a minor tangle of dead branches on the ground. Perfect. The branches did not appear to offer terrific cover, but if he wormed deep beneath them, took advantage of the shadows, and camouflaged himself using the surrounding foliage, he could become virtually invisible.

Despite the distracting uproar of the battle, Nedwin stayed low and moved silently. There was no way to be sure who else was lurking in the woods. Since he had watched the arrows fly, he did not believe an archer was near his current location, but he had no guarantee.

No armor slowed him. When stealth is your best advantage, armor and cumbersome weaponry become more a hindrance than a protection. He carried only a knife, a small crossbow, and one of the precious explosive spheres that Galloran had entrusted to his care.

Nedwin made it to the deadfall and squirmed underneath, dry twigs crackling despite his best efforts. He brushed leaves and moist dirt over himself, moving efficiently. His position still provided a partial view of the skirmish. Breathing softly, he watched as archers converged on the remaining combatants, bows drawn, led by a very tall conscriptor who held a heavy iron rod.

"Hold!" the tall conscriptor bellowed.

Amazingly, the fighting stopped. Only five of Galloran's men remained standing, winded and injured. Several manglers had fallen, as had many enemy soldiers. But plenty remained.

"You are surrounded!" the tall conscriptor asserted, leaning on his metal war bar. "This is over! Throw down your arms!"

Nedwin bit his bottom lip. The conscriptor was right. The archers were now near enough that they could easily eliminate the remaining defenders.

"Stand down, lads," Lawson growled, dropping his short sword.

Nedwin scrunched his brow. Then he realized that taking five live prisoners would cost the attackers more time than five speedy executions. The current priority was to buy Galloran time to escape.

The other defenders surrendered their weapons.

"Where is Galloran?" the tall conscriptor asked, his deep voice carrying.

"You're misinformed," Lawson replied. "He was never with us, Groddic. You'll have to settle for us as your prize."

Nedwin felt his jaw dangling. The tall conscriptor was Groddic? He was the emperor's right hand, the commander of the conscriptors. No wonder the attack had been so flawlessly coordinated!

Groddic turned to face the woods, raising his powerful voice. "I am willing to wager that Galloran can still hear me! Furthermore, I expect he will not be content to cower in the woods as I execute his men one by one."

A jolt of panic coursed through Nedwin. Apparently, this conscriptor knew Galloran well. Nedwin wished Jasher were here. He and two other seedmen had gone ahead to scout the rest of their path to Felrook. Jasher might have been able to restrain Galloran or, that failing, might have successfully attacked Groddic himself. Could Groddic know that Jasher was currently absent? He had known when the moon would emerge. . . .

"Surrender yourself, Galloran!" Groddic demanded. "Come

forth now, and I swear that your men will survive. Do not force them to pay for your inept leadership!"

Nedwin found a hand straying to the crystal globe Galloran had given him. What if he burst from hiding and threw the sphere at Groddic? No. He could not defeat the remaining foes alone, and if they caught him, they would have even more leverage to lure Galloran out of hiding.

"Don't listen!" Lawson cried. "Honor us by succeeding! We are proud to die for this cause!"

Groddic made a small gesture, and multiple arrows pierced Lawson. The woodsman kept silent as he collapsed.

"As he requested, your companion has died honorably!" Groddic called. "You can still save the other four. Do not hide behind the corpses of your friends! We will track you and find you either way. Torivors are aiding us. No man can escape them."

Groddic waited. His prisoners remained silent. Nedwin hoped his master was hurrying away.

"I am not a patient man!" Groddic bellowed. "Time for another of your comrades to perish."

A blazing white flash suddenly brightened the night, followed by a thunderous boom. Nedwin closed his eyes and listened to the subsequent explosions. Galloran had taken the bait and was hurling explosive spheres at his enemies.

After the explosions ceased, Nedwin opened his eyes, blinking in an attempt to dispel the afterimage of the initial flash. Those explosions must have destroyed several manglers and soldiers and left the survivors temporarily dazzled.

As his vision returned, Nedwin saw his master engaging the enemy. He and his bodyguards would have shielded their eyes as they threw the spheres. They were seeing clearly while the others were half blind.

One of the bodyguards, Alek, had taken up a position atop a heap of worn stones, and he now fired arrow after arrow with lethal accuracy. The other bodyguard used his battle-ax to protect Galloran, who stalked implacably among his enemies, slaying them at will.

Nedwin could not see Groddic. Could the initial explosions have slain him? Could they have been so fortunate?

Galloran's captured men were resisting, but as the enemy soldiers recovered from the initial surprise, the rebellious prisoners began to fall. There were too many enemies! Alek went down, injured by a projectile. Galloran and his remaining bodyguard ended up back-to-back, fighting for their lives.

When his bodyguard fell, Galloran charged forward, whirling and dodging and slashing, somehow carving a path through the crowd of opponents. Nedwin had never seen a man dispatch foes so efficiently. Against all odds, having rescued no men, Galloran might cut his way free. If he could just carve a path to the woods, he could leave behind not more than fifteen disorganized enemies. Galloran raged forward, his matchless sword cleaving helms and shearing through armor. He was going to escape! As had happened so many times before, despite his ill-advised bravado, Galloran would live to fight another day.

"Face me, coward!" a deep voice bellowed. Limping toward Galloran, Groddic shoved his own men aside. He wore no helm, and it was clear that part of his face had been charred.

"No," Nedwin whispered. "Go."

Groddic continued on a course to intercept Galloran. If Galloran turned away from the towering conscriptor, he only needed to fight his way past a few more men, and he could be running through the woods.

"Make way!" Groddic demanded, and those between him and Galloran hastened to comply.

Run, Nedwin mouthed, willing his master to flee.

Galloran hurled a knife at Groddic, which clanged off his rod. "Let's see if you can give me more of a fight than your men did!" Groddic roared.

Galloran charged.

His sword glinting in the moonlight, Galloran pressed Groddic back. The conscriptor was barely quick enough to defend himself as the sword chimed against his war bar. Nedwin felt some of the tension leave his body.

Galloran slashed Groddic across the waist. The conscriptor tripped and fell. As Galloran sprang forward to issue the killing stroke, Groddic flung what looked like a handful of dust into his face. Galloran staggered backward, his sword falling from his hands as he pawed at his eyes.

Nedwin squeezed a branch as Galloran tumbled to the ground. What could Groddic have thrown at his master? Galloran was reacting like his face was on fire.

Using his war bar like a crutch, Groddic rose to his feet. His men surrounded Galloran, poised to pounce. The tall conscriptor gestured for them to wait.

"You're finished," the conscriptor told the fallen prince, a gloved hand cradling his bleeding abdomen. "Surrender and I can cool the burning."

Rolling sideways, Galloran grabbed his sword, rose to a crouch, and lunged, stabbing blindly toward Groddic. The conscriptor sidestepped the thrust, then used his rod to knock the sword from Galloran's grasp. Enemies surged forward and forced Galloran to the ground.

Nedwin averted his eyes. He could not bear to witness this private moment of shame. Galloran, the hope of all Lyrian, had finally been bested.

Nedwin considered the explosive sphere in his hand. He looked back at Groddic and his soldiers. Barely fifteen remained, and more than a few seemed wounded.

Bowing his head, Nedwin closed his eyes. Galloran had given him specific instructions. He could remember his master's sober expression as he spoke the words.

"I have learned a precious word of power. Few know that I have been searching for it. Fewer know that I now possess it. This word is vital to our resistance of the emperor. Three syllables are now inscribed in locations known to my allies. I will tell you three others, which you must take to Nicholas of Rosbury. You must never divulge these syllables or let others know I shared them. Our lives, and the fate of Lyrian, depend on it. Should I fall, you must abandon the company and make your way home to Trensicourt with this knowledge. This is why I brought you with us, Nedwin. I regret bestowing this burden on one so young, but you are the most likely to succeed. Should I perish, you must not fail me on this last assignment. I need your word."

Nedwin had given his word. He remembered the syllables and was committed not to speak them aloud until he could do so privately to Nicholas. Galloran had known he could keep a secret. Galloran had known he could sneak away if everything went wrong. And Galloran had known that others would not imagine he had entrusted this vital intelligence to one so young.

Nedwin opened his eyes. Galloran had been captured, not killed. He was alive. He had not yet truly fallen.

Groddic knelt beside Galloran, applying salve to his face. Two men held him down, but he no longer struggled. The other men loitered nearby, evidently awestruck that their unconquerable adversary now lay helpless before them.

Groddic stood up, his back to Nedwin. An owl hooted.

Nedwin hefted the globe. If he could hit the conscriptor high on the back with an explosive sphere, most of the surrounding men would feel the blast. Groddic's body should shield Galloran from the worst of it. All Nedwin had besides the sphere were a small crossbow and a knife. But with the men newly blinded and injured from the explosion, the knife and crossbow might be enough.

Nedwin tried to muster the courage to burst from hiding, but doubts restrained him. What if he failed and got captured? The precious syllables would be lost. With Galloran in custody, Groddic and his men already had their prize. Nedwin felt confident that if he held still and kept quiet, he could eventually make his way back to Trensicourt and successfully deliver the essential message.

He hesitated. The word of power might be important, but what would become of the resistance without Galloran? Nedwin tried to imagine living with himself if he did nothing to intervene.

Galloran understood how much he mattered, both as a leader of the resistance and as a symbol of hope for all of Lyrian. But when his men had faced execution, he had put himself at risk. Didn't he deserve to have his squire show similar courage?

Nedwin silently eased himself out of his hiding place. If he failed, Galloran would regret having put his trust in him, and the cause he had fought for his entire life would be irreparably damaged. If he succeeded, Galloran could finish his mission and bring down the emperor. So Nedwin only had one option. He had to succeed.

He ran forward swiftly and quietly. As he left the cover of the trees, a couple of heads turned toward him. Groddic still faced away from him, standing over Galloran. Nedwin was not as close as he would have preferred, but Groddic was about to turn, and his men were about to scramble.

Nedwin threw the sphere with all his might. It flew true, straight at Groddic. But the conscriptor reacted to the stares of his men by turning and then catching the sphere in his right hand with an almost casual motion.

Nedwin skidded to a halt.

In order for the sphere to explode, the crystal casing needed to rupture. Groddic had caught it lightly.

Raising his undersized crossbow, Nedwin sighted at the sphere, but an arrow hit Nedwin in the shoulder, and his shot went wild. As he fell, other arrows whizzed past him. On his back, the feathered shaft protruding grotesquely, Nedwin felt despair flooding over him. His master remained an injured prisoner, no vengeance had been achieved, and the invaluable secret Galloran had shared would never reach Nicholas! Enemies gathered around him. Burning with frustration and shame, Nedwin closed his eyes and waited for death.

CHAPTER 1

ACOLYTE

Rachel . . . help me . . . Rachel, please!

Rachel awoke, clutching her covers. She sat up on the soft mattress. Shadows shrouded her bedchamber. The telepathic voice in her head was unfamiliar. The female speaker was not Corinne, and not Ulani, who had recently learned to transmit simple thoughts over short distances.

Who are you? Rachel conveyed with all her will.

Rachel! I can't hang on much longer. . . . Come now . . . please hurry!

Despite the urgency behind the message, the mental outcry was fading. Rachel had worked with several of the acolytes on speaking in silence, but so far only Ulani had succeeded. Was it possible that in a desperate moment one of the girls had unlocked the ability? Rachel slept in the area of the temple set apart for the acolytes. They were all relatively near. Who else at Mianamon would be able to contact her like this?

Apart from the words in her mind, the night was still. No sounds intruded from outside her room. Mianamon was not under attack. So what was the problem?

Who is this? What's wrong?

The words came weakly, the mental equivalent of a whisper. *Kalia. Training room. I tried a strong command. Failed. I hurt all over. . . . Don't tell the others. . . . Please help me.*

Kalia. Rachel had trained with the acolytes for months. Most had only a hint of Edomic talent. None had a natural ability like Rachel, but Kalia was among the more promising. On more than one occasion Rachel had tried to teach her to speak in silence.

Hold on. I'm coming.

Speaking an Edomic word, Rachel lit a bedside candle, then rose and shrugged into her acolyte robe. Kalia must have slipped down to the training room in the night for some extra practice. She must have attempted something too ambitious and lost control of the command. Rachel knew firsthand how debilitating the consequences of a failed Edomic directive could be.

If Kalia could still find the strength to call out mentally, she probably wasn't fatally injured. But that didn't mean she might not *feel* like she was going to die.

Rachel spoke another command, igniting a clay lamp. Picking it up, she unlocked her door and stepped into the hallway.

Darkness awaited beyond her lamplight in both directions. Rachel was not accustomed to roaming the Temple of Mianamon after-hours. She and her friends had been here for the whole winter, but she had never walked these stone corridors when all was dark and empty. The familiar passage suddenly seemed ominous.

Still there, Kalia?

No response came. The acolyte could be unconscious. Or she might simply lack the energy to send another message.

Rachel passed several doors. No life could be heard behind them. No light seeped through the cracks. After rounding a corner, she reached the stairway that led down to the training room. Beyond the bubble of light from her lamp, all was silent shadow.

Rachel knew that outside the section of the temple reserved for acolytes, she could find the human guards who protected their privacy at all hours. She also knew where she could find Jason, Drake, or her other companions. Or she could call out mentally to Galloran or Corinne.

But the painful experience of a failed command was best kept private. Kalia would not appreciate others seeing her in an injured, weakened state. Straightening her shoulders, Rachel started down the stairs. She arrived at the bottom and moved along a broad hallway.

The darkness retreated from her approach until Rachel reached the door to the main training room. It was slightly ajar. Rachel nudged it open and stepped inside.

"Kalia?"

A vehement Edomic command answered her inquiry. The words demanded that Rachel hold still. As requested, her muscles locked up, leaving her temporarily immobilized.

Rachel knew this command! The acolytes of Mianamon practiced an Edomic discipline that enabled them to issue directives to people. Upon her arrival at Mianamon, Rachel had known how to use Edomic to get some animals to heed certain instructions, but she had never guessed that she might be able to use similar tactics on humans.

Commanding inanimate matter with Edomic was straightforward—all matter and energy understood the language. You simply needed to accompany the proper words with enough focused willpower to demand compliance. If you tried to accomplish too much, you would fail and face a backlash of physical and psychic traumas.

With animals it was trickier. Edomic did not work well on living things. Instead of compelling animals, you had to make suggestions that they could either heed or disregard. Ask too gently and the animal would ignore the directive. Push too hard and you risked the consequences of a failed command.

Humans were even more complicated. You couldn't really use Edomic on the mind. You couldn't implant a complex idea. It was more like speaking to the spine, suggesting a reflexive response that the mind would counter once it caught up. Rachel now knew roughly fifty suggestions that might work on a human, most of them at the level of dog commands: stay, lie down, turn around, jump. In a moment of distress, Rachel knew, the ability to cause an enemy to temporarily freeze or flop to the ground might prove very useful.

Rachel had practiced this discipline for months. None of the acolytes could match her skill at it. For instance, most of the girls could not demand any form of compliance from Ulani, but Rachel could freeze her with a word. Conversely, even the most capable acolytes couldn't make Rachel do much more than twitch.

Except now she couldn't move!

The command had been uttered with power and expertise. It held her like no command had since her first day of training. Was her guard down because of fear? Sure, she was scared, but she was resisting the mandate the same way she had practiced. It just wasn't working.

Rachel heard another muttered command. A black metal spike streaked toward her chest, gleaming in the light of her lamp.

Rachel still couldn't move. Instead, she spoke in silence. Rachel had lots of practice moving physical objects. She telepathically ordered the spike to hold still. It stopped just over a foot from her chest, quivering in midair.

More words issued from the shadows beyond her lamplight. A robust will contended with hers, inching the spike toward her.

Rachel had regained control of her body, but she didn't want to advertise her recovery to her enemy. Instead, Rachel bore down and pushed the spike away. The will of her enemy broke, and the spike went sailing into a wall.

Rachel knew the location of many torches, cressets, and lamps in this room. With a word she illuminated several at once. The light displayed Kalia charging toward her, a knife in one hand, a long needle in the other.

Rachel commanded Kalia to fall to the floor. The acolyte obeyed, losing hold of her knife. Kalia tried to compel Rachel to freeze again. The expertly phrased directive worked for a fraction of a second, but Rachel was ready this time, and promptly reasserted control. She then countered by commanding Kalia to be still.

"What are you doing?" Rachel spat.

Kalia remained immobile for barely a second. The girl rolled over and looked up, red spittle leaking from one corner of her mouth. Rachel realized that when Kalia had lost control of the spike, the resulting failure must have injured her.

Kalia growled a command, and the knife darted at Rachel. Ducking to the side, Rachel seized control of the knife and put it to the throat of the acolyte. Holding it there took great control, but Rachel had practiced manipulating physical objects more diligently than any other Edomic discipline.

"Why?" Rachel demanded, panting.

Kalia spat blood. Sweat dampened her face. Her feral eyes were panicked and angry. Kalia was among the younger acolytes. Although she looked to be in her twenties, she was actually closer to fifty. Acolytes employed routine Edomic meditation to slow the aging process.

"Why?" Rachel repeated.

Kalia spoke a command, trying to seize control of the knife, but Rachel countered with a stern mandate, and Kalia's effort dissolved, crushed by a superior will. Rachel angled the knife away as the acolyte doubled over, writhing in pain. The failed commands were taking a heavy toll.

"When did you get so good?" Rachel demanded. "You never moved objects."

I never spoke in silence, either. The furious words burned in Rachel's mind. *He should have given the order earlier, before you had so much training. I could have taken you when you first arrived. I know I could have!*

Who ordered this? Rachel pressed.

Use your imagination, Kalia communicated, her rage diminishing. *My only solace is that he'll get you yet. I chose the winning side. He asked too much of me at the wrong time. Bad for me. But it won't save you. Mark my words. He'll get you all.*

You work for Maldor?

He'll kill every last one of you!

Galloran burst into the room, his blindfold off, his torivorian sword drawn, several treefolk and human guards following in his wake. He looked from Rachel to Kalia. *I sensed a great deal of Edomic in use.*

Kalia jabbed the long needle into her thigh.

What have you done? Rachel asked.

Another inane question! How does such a simpleton access so much power? It's infuriating! It's disgusting! Kalia began to convulse. Red foam frothed from her lips.

"She tried to kill me," Rachel explained, turning away in horror and disgust.

Galloran took her lamp, set it aside, then wrapped his arms around her. Rachel felt embarrassed that he must feel her trembling. But she was not embarrassed enough to reject the comfort. *I'm so sorry, Rachel. I never would have guessed Maldor could have planted an assassin at Mianamon.*

Where can't he come after us? This is the one place in Lyrian where I felt safe!

The sad truth is that no place in Lyrian is secure anymore, no matter how remote. And the problem will only worsen. We've been planning to leave soon. Let's make it tomorrow. We have stood still for too long.

Rachel clung to Galloran, wishing she could disappear. Kalia had set a trap and tried to kill her!

A man covered from head to toe in moss brought the knife and the iron spike to Galloran. "Both poisoned. Giantsbane. Just like the needle."

"Later," Galloran said. He waved a hand. "Leave us."

The men and treefolk exited the training room.

"I'm so sorry, Rachel," Galloran said again, still holding her.

Rachel felt bad for the amount of pain in his voice. "It wasn't your fault. Thanks for coming so quickly."

"I was a fool for allowing you to room so far from the rest of us. I should have foreseen this possibility. Thank goodness you saved yourself. I could feel the strength behind her commands. This traitor was no novice. I did not know that any Edomic adepts of her ability remained. She must have hidden here for a long while."

"More than thirty years," Ulani said, entering the room. She glared bitterly at the fallen acolyte, then shifted her attention to Rachel. "Are you all right?"

"I'm all right," Rachel managed. "It's all right."

Galloran continued to hold Rachel close. "Maldor must have known we were preparing to leave. He wanted to strike before we departed."

Rachel scowled a little, pulling back from the embrace. "Why didn't the oracle know about her? Why didn't Esmira see this coming?"

"I wish she had," Galloran said.

"I never sensed any evil in Kalia," Ulani said. "Nor did I perceive unusual power. Potential, yes, but unrealized. Perhaps Kalia knew how to shield her mind from scrutiny. Perhaps Maldor only got to her recently. We may never know. Esmira saw many things, but I can't imagine she spent much time looking for traitors among us. We were too isolated, too united against the emperor and all he stands for."

"He tried to kill me," Rachel said in a small voice.

After a final hard look at the body on the floor, Galloran tied his blindfold in place. Apparently, he didn't want any more details to reach Maldor through his displacer eyes. "Maldor would have rejoiced at your death. But he has some idea of your abilities. He should have recognized that this Kalia, although talented, was probably not up to the challenge. This attack may have simply been a test."

Rachel huffed softly. "Rough test."

"Maldor knows no gentle games." Galloran put an arm around her shoulders. "Try not to let this rattle you. Take solace that you rose to the occasion. Thankfully, we've kept the details of the prophecy from all at Mianamon save Ulani. Even so, Maldor knows exactly where we are and may have deduced some of our intentions. As we embark on our quests, we'll all have trials to face in the coming days. I fear this is only the beginning."

CHAPTER 2

MIANAMON

From his perch hundreds of feet above the temple floor, Jason watched a pair of apes circle each other, quarterstaves held ready. The simian combatants stepped gingerly, slender torsos hunched, long limbs coiled. The taller of the white gibbons stood roughly the same height as Jason. Screeching and hooting, they rushed together, elongated forms wielding the staffs with fluid agility. Many other apes watched the duel, close-set eyes fixed on the fiercely clacking rods.

The white gibbons had been engineered by Certius, the ill-fated wizard who had made his home in the southern jungles of Lyrian. Although the gibbons lacked the power of speech, they had surprising intelligence, and communicated with humans using hand gestures.

Iron lattices covered many of the higher walls and ceilings within the Temple of Mianamon. The gibbons could travel across the framework with careless grace, leaping and swinging, dangling from hands or feet, heedless of the potential fall. They mostly resided on lofty shelves near the summit of the temple. Jason had made it up here using a cramped system of tunnels, stairways, and ladders.

Observing the apes was one of his favorite pastimes at Mianamon. He had taught them to hold batting practice using quarterstaves and citrus fruit. He could seldom get an ape to strike out. Changeups worked best.

Today the brawling apes failed to distract Jason. Rods cracked, gibbons hooted, but he watched from a distance, alone, his mind far from the playful sparring. After several months, this would be his last day at Mianamon. Within hours he would part with Rachel and Galloran and many of his other friends. Their season of rest and preparation had been shattered when Rachel was ambushed last night. With little warning, suddenly they had to leave.

Jason watched the skillful apes without any pleasure at all. So why was he here? Had he thought the apes might hold solutions to his troubles? Of course not. Then what was he doing? Sulking? Hiding?

Jason had spent more days at this tropical temple than the rest of his time in Lyrian combined. He had turned fourteen at some point, though he couldn't be certain which day, since the passage of time between his world and Lyrian was out of sync. Further complicating matters, the calendar in Lyrian had ten months, each with thirty-eight days.

Winter in the jungle had never grown cold. The days had gotten a little shorter, the air less warm on occasion, the rainfall more persistent, but Jason had never needed a heavy cloak. He had spent much of the winter training with weapons. Ferrin, Drake, Aram, Corinne, and Jasher had been working directly with Galloran, and they had in turn provided instruction to Jason, Tark, Nia, Io, and Farfalee.

Jason was a much improved swordsman. He could now make a respectable showing against Ferrin or Drake on the practice field. Farfalee had helped him with archery, Nedwin had offered lessons in knife work, and Io had tutored him in wrestling. For the first time, Jason felt he might be able to contribute in a fight, rather than desperately hope to survive until the others got the job done. In theory he would be more useful than ever. Could his new combat skills be part of the reason the oracle had placed so much importance on his participation in the upcoming quest?

"Catching one last ape battle?" a voice asked, making Jason jump and turn. It was Rachel, looking mystical in her acolyte robes. He hadn't seen her since the incident, and although Galloran had reassured him that she was fine, it was a relief to see she truly looked unharmed.

"Some people build model ships. Some pop bubble wrap. I'm more into dueling gibbons."

"Ferrin was looking for you."

"I was going to come down. Eventually." He tried to think of a smooth way to bring up the attempt on her life. "Hey, are you okay?"

"I didn't get stabbed. I'm about how you'd expect."

"I'm so sorry that happened."

"I talked to Galloran. He helped. I'd honestly rather not dwell on it." Rachel sighed, eyes on the apes. "Can you believe we're leaving?"

"Not really. I knew it was coming, but still . . . I wish I felt more ready."

"How do you get ready to save the world or die trying?"

"I guess that's the problem." Jason stood, stretching his arms and legs. It felt good. He must have held the same position for longer than he had realized. "Are you wearing those robes out of here? Planning to do some trick-or-treating?"

Rachel chuckled, looking down at herself. "I'll wear Amar Kabal robes for the road. But I'm bringing these, too. Galloran thinks they make me look more wizardly."

"Don't dress for the job you have—dress for the job you want."

"I guess that's the idea. Maybe I should dress up as an innocent bystander."

"Too late for that." Jason stared down at his feet. He was going to miss her. Rachel's hand clasped his and he glanced up. Her eyes looked a little misty. He scowled. "Don't get all sentimental."

"I hate that we have to split up."

"If you can't trust an old lady packed in clay and dipped in perfume, who can you trust?" With her dying words, the oracle had established that Rachel, Galloran, Io, Ferrin, Nedwin, Nollin, and Tark had to depart on one quest while Jason, Farfalee, Jasher, Drake, Aram, Corinne, and Nia left on another. While Rachel was off trying to raise an army to attack Felrook, Jason would be seeking crucial information from an ancient seer. According to the oracle, both quests needed to succeed in order to defeat Maldor.

"That really is what we're doing," Rachel sighed. "We're placing our lives in the hands of some old lady packed in clay."

"I didn't mean to insult her," Jason amended. "Everyone says she was a true oracle. She seemed legit."

"She's the same lady who sent Galloran on the quest for the Word. Look how that ended up! He suffered so much based on a false hope!"

Jason shrugged. "Do you have a better idea?"

"Not really. But just because the oracle proposed a plan doesn't necessarily make it perfect. One of her people tried to kill me! How'd she miss that? I've been working with the top acolytes. They've taught me some Edomic words, but I can already use the commands better than any of them. I wouldn't trust most of them to foresee what I'm having for breakfast tomorrow. What if the oracle wasn't as wise and magical as everybody thinks? Or what if she went crazy? Farfalee told us that Darian the Pyromancer lived ages ago. He should be dead. What if he is? And Felrook seems invincible. What if we're all marching to our doom, thanks to the desperate ramblings of a dying crackpot?"

The possible validity of her doubts made Jason uncomfortable. "You're probably just spooked because of last night."

"This isn't just about that," Rachel said. "I've been getting more stressed ever since the oracle spoke. I wanted to believe her. She seemed confident and sincere. She gave us hope. I've tried to be positive and to focus on my training. But with us about to actually leave, I feel less certain than ever. I needed to tell someone."

"And you picked me? I'm honored."

"I was thinking maybe we could go talk to Galloran."

"We? When did I sign on as a doubter?"

Rachel scowled skeptically. "You aren't nervous?"

"Sure, I'm nervous! But that's not the same as deciding it's a mistake." Jason paused. He wasn't ready to do cartwheels of joy at the prospect of leaving Mianamon, but in spite of his insecurities he found he really did feel they were doing the right thing. That was something, at least. "You really want to bug Galloran with this on the day we're supposed to leave?

"Maybe," Rachel said uncomfortably. "I'd hate to be part of a train wreck just because I was too scared to speak up."

"Getting attacked in the middle of the night would freak out anybody. I can understand how it could make you question the oracle."

"That's only part of it. I worry that we're betting everything on this one opinion. Are we really sure she got it right?"

Jason glanced at a hooting gibbon as it triumphantly raised its quarterstaff in the air. "Tell me what you would tell him."

"Not if you're just going to watch the gibbons."

"Sorry. I like how they celebrate. Go ahead. This is actually a great place for a private talk. I'm paying attention."

Avoiding his gaze, Rachel tugged self-consciously on her sleeves and cleared her throat. "Okay. Galloran, I'm worried that the oracle may not have made an accurate prediction. I mean, she sent you after the Word, and that didn't turn out so great. She didn't know that one of her students was an assassin. She was dying when she spoke to us. What if her mind was foggy? What if she was just desperate?"

"You're worried that Felrook can't be taken?" Jason checked.

Rachel shrugged. "I know we have an opportunity. Maldor's main armies are in the east, fighting Kadara. Since Maldor isn't worried about anyone attacking him, Felrook isn't heavily defended. But what if he's right not to worry? Nobody thought Felrook could be taken until the oracle told us to do it. If she was wrong, the last armies resisting Maldor will be crushed! And the other group won't have it any easier."

"We have to do impossible stuff too," Jason agreed.

"What if this is like the Word? What if we're heading down a false trail?"

"We'll all die," Jason said honestly.

"And you're okay with that?" Rachel blustered.

"I'm not okay with dying," Jason said. She clearly needed reassurance. It was hard to tell what would help her. He had plenty of his own concerns, but at least he felt convinced that their quests were necessary. "Normally, I wouldn't risk my life for anything. But these aren't normal circumstances. I get that we really could die—we've already lost people we know. The oracle never promised we'd make it. She didn't promise we'd succeed, either. But she did say that our only chance for winning would be to follow her instructions. Her words were good enough for Galloran. They were good enough for the drinlings. They were even good enough for the Amar Kabal, and you know how careful they are."

"But how do *I* know the oracle got it right?" Rachel asked, almost pleading.

Jason considered her question. "You know better than anyone how Galloran can look into minds."

"We talk without speaking all the time," Rachel said. "He even sometimes does it when I'm not communicating with him on purpose."

"Don't you think he was making sure the oracle was being straight with us?" Jason asked. "Don't you think he was watching her mind the whole time? You know how smart he is, how cautious. He's been burned before. And he's convinced."

"True," Rachel admitted.

"You spoke with the oracle, just like the rest of us. She knew things about us that she couldn't have known unless she was the real deal. She was the oracle here for a long time. Everybody accepted her as authentic. She didn't promise we'd win, but I'm sure that what she told us is true. Basically, if we want to save Lyrian, we have to do this, even though it'll be brutal."

"She warned that even if we won, many of us wouldn't make it," Rachel reminded him. "And she told us that we would probably fail."

"True," Jason said. "But we fail for sure if we don't try."

Rachel nodded thoughtfully. She looked into his eyes. "You're convinced?"

Jason found himself turning inward, taking her question seriously. Sure, he had been looking for arguments to reassure her, but it was more than just that. He realized that he really believed what he was saying. This needed to happen. It felt true in his gut, in his bones, right down to his core. "Yeah, I am."

"So I shouldn't bother Galloran?"

"Depends why you want to talk to him. If you need reassurance from him, go ahead. But you're not going to point out any doubts he hasn't already considered. He knows the stakes, and he made his choice."

Rachel sighed, her whole body sagging. "Maybe you're right. It isn't like I realized some specific danger that everyone overlooked. I guess I'm mostly nervous about leaving, and I let that make me paranoid."

"You're not alone. I get worried too. At least you've become the ninja wizard girl. You'll probably make a big difference out there."

"And you won't?"

Jason shrugged, trying not to let his worries show. "I hope so. I'm just not sure how."

"You've done so much. I can't picture you very nervous."

Jason smiled. "I'm glad you can't imagine me that way. But I'm all wound up, too. Why do you think I'm hiding out up here when I should be packing? Just because these quests are the right thing to do doesn't mean they won't be hard."

"Or maybe even impossible."

"We can't think that way. We'll psych ourselves out."

Rachel nodded. "All right. I guess you've talked me off the ledge."

Jason glanced at the enormous drop to the temple floor. "Were you going to jump?"

"I didn't mean literally. Wanting to die isn't my problem."

"Good. The slow way down makes a lot more sense. You sure you're okay?"

Her smile looked a little forced. "Depends what you mean by okay. Am I looking forward to leaving? No. Do I wish I could go hide under a rock? Yes. Will I do my duty? I don't really have another choice. I can't abandon everybody, and I can't deny that this is the right thing to do."

Jason nodded. "That's what it comes down to. Difficult or not, scary or not, it's the right choice. Our friends need us. Lyrian needs us. We have to keep going."

Her smile became sweeter, more natural. "Thanks, Jason. I needed this. You can be pretty impressive sometimes. Now I don't have to embarrass myself by bothering Galloran. I'll find a way to keep it together. Are you done up here? Should we head down?"

"I guess." Following her to a ladder, Jason turned to look back. "So much for my farewell ape fights."

While descending from the heights of the temple, Jason and Rachel found Ferrin awaiting them near the base of a long ladder. Dressed for travel, he leaned against the wall, balancing his dagger on his fingertip. "Jason," the displacer greeted, sheathing the knife. "I was beginning to worry you had been made an honorary gibbon."

"I heard you were looking for me," Jason replied.

"Can we take a walk?"

Jason looked to Rachel.

"Go ahead," she said. "I have some things to gather. I'll see you when we meet up to leave." She started down a nearby flight of stairs.

Ferrin led Jason to a high terrace that wrapped around the outside of the temple. They walked beside a waist-high parapet, the jungle spread out below them. Under the direct sunlight, the temperature climbed from uncomfortably warm to hot. The humid smell of vegetation filled Jason's nostrils. "Seems to be getting hotter every day."

"Spring will do that," Ferrin replied. "Winter is ending."

"What's up?"

Ferrin winced. "We're about to go our separate ways."

"I know. Part of me never wanted this day to come. It's been nice to spend some time without death and destruction around every corner."

"It's been there waiting all along. But I know what you mean. Mianamon has provided a welcome season of relief. I've enjoyed the chance to observe your nature when you're not under duress."

"That makes me feel like the subject of an experiment."

Ferrin shrugged. "If you were, the experiment was a success. You're a good person, Jason. A true friend."

Jason felt unsure how to respond. He had never heard Ferrin give compliments lightly. "Thanks. You are too. You'll keep an eye on Rachel?"

"The one I have left," he said, tapping his eye patch. "Do you realize what awaits you at the Celestine Library?"

"I've heard the basics. Zokar placed a guardian there."

"Right. I went over this with Galloran and Farfalee, and I know they've spoken with you, but I want to make sure you fully understand. Zokar was obsessed with the torivors. Rightfully so— they're probably the most powerful beings in Lyrian. He spent years attempting to create a race of similar prowess. The results became known as his Abominations."

"And one of them protects the library."

"Zokar never felt he had perfected his Abominations. There were three, each unique, each less governable than he desired. He never turned them into races because he feared they would usurp his power. One was a sinister being with an extraordinary gift for invading thoughts and dreams. It was dubbed the Visitor, and Zokar eventually destroyed it. Some historians cite evidence that

Zokar was never the same after besting the Visitor, and argue that the confrontation may have permanently disrupted his sanity."

"I wish I were an evil wizard," Jason complained. "They have all the fun."

"The second creation was a shape-shifter. It was called the Wanderer. Zokar tried to eliminate it, but the shape-shifter escaped and vanished. None know its fate."

"And the third?"

"It was known as the Maumet. In form it was like a torivor, but considerably larger. The Maumet can transform itself into any material it touches. Zokar successfully imprisoned the Maumet on Windbreak Island."

"The same island as the Celestine Library."

"Correct. None have entered the library since that time. Many have tried. Eldrin was not one of them."

Jason frowned. "But after Eldrin defeated Zokar, didn't he go on a rampage destroying books?"

"Good memory," Ferrin approved. "Eldrin decided to rid Lyrian of wizardry, and sought to destroy all the books that taught Edomic. Of the great storehouses of learning, only the Celestine Library remained untouched. Even the legendary Eldrin chose not to confront the Maumet. What does that tell you?"

"The Maumet is tough."

"It intimidated the most powerful wizard Lyrian has known. It got between him and his mission, and he let it stay there."

"He might have figured the Maumet would be able to guard that information forever," Jason said.

"All indications have shown that he would have been correct," Ferrin said. "Maldor has sent several teams to retrieve information from the Celestine Library. None have succeeded. I've heard that the only way to harm the Maumet is to chip off pieces.

Sort of the opposite of me." He casually detached one hand at the wrist, flipped it into the air, then caught it on the stump at the end of his forearm. The hand fused seamlessly back into place.

"So if we chop off an arm, the arm is gone."

"Supposedly, the Maumet never regenerates lost material. But this is all speculative. Nobody has ever severed a limb. To my knowledge nobody has ever seriously harmed it."

Jason stared out over the steaming jungle. "And we need to find a way."

"The oracle tasked Galloran with regaining control of Trensicourt, raising an army, and mounting a direct assault on the emperor's impenetrable stronghold. If you ask me, Galloran has the easy job."

"Rachel seems pretty nervous," Jason said. "She was worried the oracle might have been wrong."

"I don't think the oracle was wrong."

"No?"

"No. She was authentic. I expect that her prediction was valid. Remember, she wasn't promising victory. She was looking for any possible route to victory, no matter how faint. I'm sure if you can somehow access the library, there is a chance of finding a way to contact Darian the Seer, even though he is supposed to be dead. Those strong enough in Edomic have found methods to achieve astonishing life spans. And it is conceivable that the famed pyromancer could provide some arcane information that might help an attack on Felrook succeed. I can't begin to imagine what that information could be. And I doubt that any knowledge could make such a victory likely."

"This isn't sounding good," Jason said, dread pooling in the pit of his stomach.

"We asked if, among all the possible futures, there might be a one-in-a-billion chance of turning the tide and dethroning Maldor. I'm sure the oracle found what Galloran sought: a theoretically possible, but highly unlikely, path to victory."

Jason rubbed his wrist anxiously. "In other words, we won't just probably fail—we'll almost certainly fail. You're still willing to go along with it?"

"If Maldor ever apprehends me, my fate is certain. Just like you and Galloran and the Amar Kabal, I'd take a minuscule chance at victory over certain doom. If we fail, I can still try to jump ship and hide in the wilderness for the rest of my life, which is my only other current option."

Jason shifted uncomfortably. "You're warning me that my quest probably ends with the Maumet."

"I want you to appreciate what you're up against. You will have to succeed where multitudes have failed. You'll have to accomplish something that the mightiest wizard in the history of Lyrian didn't dare to attempt. You've pulled off some shocking upsets in the past, but only a fool would bet on you this time. So I will." Ferrin detached an ear and held it out to Jason.

"You're betting an ear?"

"I'm betting that not only will you find a way past the Maumet, but that you will locate Darian the Pyromancer and need to offer us crucial information from a great distance. If you perish, I'll just have to get used to life with one eye and one ear."

"Farfalee is bringing messenger eagles," Jason reminded him.

"I know, and they will serve as an important redundancy, but nothing beats sure, instantaneous communication."

Jason accepted the ear. It represented a great deal of trust. Too much trust, maybe? Could Ferrin have other motives? They had spoken frankly about his allegiance issues on other occasions. "What if you betray us?"

Ferrin flashed a crooked smile. "The oracle had the same concern."

"She did?"

"In our private conversation. She told me that I could be either a vital asset or a crippling traitor. She assured me that Maldor would never accept me, that any treachery would end in my ruin, things I already know. Things she needed me to believe."

Jason held up the ear. "This is your attempt to help us?"

"Part of it," Ferrin said. "If we mount an attack on Felrook, I have a lot of information that could prove advantageous. Assuming Galloran can muster his army, and you can accomplish your role, I'll help see this through."

"Are you sure?" Jason asked. "Are you really on our side? Totally?"

Ferrin raised his eyebrows. "It's possible that you would learn a vital secret, speak it to my ear, and I would take the information straight to Maldor in search of forgiveness. Such an act of betrayal could enable the emperor to counter whatever secret tactic Darian might suggest, even if the messenger eagles still deliver the information to Galloran."

Jason resisted an impulse to fling the ear into the jungle. "I know you think like that. Do you have to be so open about it?"

"Would you prefer I kept those thoughts private?"

"I wish you'd quit having those thoughts at all. It's a scary sort of honesty when you openly admit you might betray us."

Ferrin lifted his hands apologetically. "I've plotted like this my entire life. I like you enough that I try to be candid."

"It's not just that you have those urges. I know you're capable of carrying them out."

Ferrin laughed darkly. "Makes me a lousy teammate. But the oracle indicated that we need to stand together or else none of this will work. Doesn't that mean you have to rely on me?"

"I want to count on you. You've picked us over Maldor before."

Ferrin held up a finger. "Back before I really knew the stakes, I picked you over the chance of upsetting Maldor if I got caught. Then the situation spiraled out of control. But I see what you mean. If I wanted to ruin your cause, I could have already done so."

"True," Jason said, "but that gives us no guarantee about what you might do tomorrow. I'd feel better if you promised me you won't turn on us."

"Haven't you heard? The word of a displacer is worthless. There is a whole family of jokes on the subject."

"I can't judge the other displacers," Jason said. "I've barely known any. You're the only one I really know. Ever since Whitelake, you've been really honest with me. Even when you turned in me and Rachel, you were open about it. You've stuck your neck out for me. Your word means something to me."

Turning to gaze out at the horizon, Ferrin gave a slight nod. "Very well, Jason. I swear that I will continue to support this rebellion. I gave part of my carotid artery to Galloran in token of my sincerity, and part of my brachial artery to you. With that ear, I'm running out of body parts to spare."

Jason pocketed the ear. He would put it in the same pouch as the artery. "The ear will be good to have. Imagine if something happened to the eagles!"

"The possibility had crossed my mind."

"This will be one-way communication," Jason realized. "I won't be able to hear from you. How will I know you're listening?"

"I'll be listening," Ferrin assured him. "Unless I die, in which case the cross-dimensional connection will be severed, and the ear will leak blood and grow cold. It would be hard to miss."

"Right. Hey, speaking of broken connections, I have a displacerly question."

"Then I probably have an answer."

"Two displacers gave Galloran their eyes," Jason established.

"Yes."

"What if they die? Would his eyes rot?"

"A fair question," Ferrin said. "Can Galloran see out of those eyes?"

"Of course."

"And the displacers can too, which means he has a shared grafting. In a shared grafting, the mutual body part is simultaneously supported by both organisms. If Galloran dies, the eyes can draw from the displacers to remain alive and functional. If the displacers die, the eyes will lose their cross-dimensional connection and become the sole property of Galloran. They should remain healthy and serviceable. Displacers have been hunted and killed so a person could become the sole owner of a grafting. It makes our kind think twice before we share a body part."

"That's good to know," Jason said. "I was kind of worried about him."

"There are plenty of reasons to worry about Galloran," Ferrin replied. "Rotten eyeballs is not one of them."

"Thanks for the info." Jason realized that this might be the last time he spoke to Ferrin in private before parting ways. "Take care of yourself."

"I always do." Ferrin placed a hand on Jason's shoulder and looked him in the eye. "Jason, I wasn't joking that I'm betting on you. I'm wagering everything. This will be tough all around. Find a way to get your part done. I believe in you."

Jason swallowed. He didn't want to ask the question, but he couldn't resist. "Why?"

"Excuse me?"

Jason looked away, toward the carved wall of the building.

"Nothing. I've just been stressing out lately. I don't get why the oracle would count on me so much."

Ferrin nodded reflectively. "I'm glad you feel that way."

"What do you mean?"

"The odds are against you. You'd be a fool if you went into this feeling overconfident."

"So why would you bet on me?"

Ferrin looked at Jason shrewdly. "For my part in this to succeed, your part must succeed. The odds are against us, but even if the chance is minuscule, we still have one. You've accomplished some amazing things. You've performed well under pressure. You've shown conviction and integrity. Maybe it's not realistic, but it's bold, and necessary, so I'm willing to believe you can pull this off."

"Okay," Jason managed, his throat thick with emotion. "I'll believe in you, too."

CHAPTER 3

DEPARTURE

Rachel stood before a full-length mirror in her room. Turning left and right, she supposed her acolyte robe did look kind of like a Halloween costume, but not a cheap one. Made of fine material, the robe felt silky and comfortable, and it gave off a faint shimmer, as if silver threads had been woven into the dark-gray fabric. Light and billowy, the robe stayed surprisingly cool considering how much of her body it covered.

She shed the fine robe, folded it neatly, and began dressing for her upcoming journey. Though less silky, her Amar Kabal robes were also comfortable. The acolyte robe was great for roaming enclosed hallways, but would prove restrictive for running or riding. The more rugged Amar Kabal robes made much more sense for travel.

A soft knock made Rachel turn. "Come in."

The door to her bedchamber opened, and Ulani entered, wearing a gray acolyte robe accented by a silver mantle, which designated her as the future oracle. Few people made Rachel feel tall, but Ulani was one of them. Short and slight, the woman looked to be about forty, although Rachel knew that her real age was closer to a hundred. A circlet of violet blossoms ringed her head.

Ulani spoke a brief Edomic phrase. Rachel's initial reaction was to flinch, but the words were an appeal for Rachel to stay, and carried many subtle nuances. Rachel belonged with them, had a promising future with them. Her departure would wound many hearts and lead her into perilous circumstances. Sometimes Rachel wished that Edomic weren't quite so expressive.

"I don't want to leave," Rachel apologized in plain English. "I've enjoyed studying and training here. You of all people should understand why I have to go."

Ulani nodded. "Your departure was ordained by the oracle. She also privately wished for you to return."

Rachel paused. "I might."

Ulani narrowed her gaze. "I do not foresee it."

"Have you . . . looked?"

"Not prophetically. I would never be able to see beyond the upcoming conflict with Maldor. I simply realize that you yearn for your home more than you aspire to serve with us here."

"I don't really belong to this world," Rachel apologized. "I know my parents are worried about me. They may have given up hope by now."

"For decades I have toiled to develop my talents," Ulani said. "I was disciplined. The oracle tutored me. And in a few short months you have surpassed all that I accomplished. You have the innate gift. You could become a true prophetess, perhaps greater than Esmira."

"That's too much praise," Rachel replied. "I was never tested to discover if I could see beyond the present."

"Only because Galloran forbade it," Ulani said. "Not without reason. The test can be fatal. But you display every indication of one who would more than excel. The oracle herself sensed your potential. You've already mastered everything else we could teach you."

"I'm no master," Rachel corrected.

"You're much better at our disciplines than those of us who have studied them our entire lives," Ulani insisted. "I think you're already even more adept than the oracle was."

The praise made Rachel blush. "I'm very grateful for all I've learned."

"It was our privilege to host you." Ulani lowered her gaze. "I'm very sorry about Kalia. She brought shame upon us all. This should have been a haven for you."

"It wasn't your fault," Rachel said. "Maldor finds ways to harm whoever he wants, wherever they are."

"It was our duty to protect you. Instead, you had to defend yourself against one of our own. It's inexcusable."

"I don't blame you." Rachel took Ulani's hand. "Everything else has been wonderful. These have been the best weeks I've spent in Lyrian."

Ulani nodded and offered an apologetic smile. "It will be lonely here without you."

Rachel knew that Ulani felt trapped. She had nowhere near the raw ability that the previous oracle had possessed. Yet everyone expected her to become the next great prophetess, to guide the children of Certius through the troubled years to come, and to keep the peace among the different factions of treefolk.

"You have a lot to deal with," Rachel said. "Don't underestimate yourself. You'll do great."

Tears brimmed briefly in Ulani's eyes. The head acolyte replied with a slight nod that showed little confidence. "We each have our duties."

Rachel rested a finger beside her temple. "I see lots of walking in my future."

Ulani smiled. "I hardly know you in those barbaric clothes."

"Function before fashion. I'll miss you."

Ulani's mouth twitched. No words came out. She nodded again, turned, and left the room.

Rachel swiveled to face the mirror. Ulani had finally voiced what many of the other acolytes had hinted at for weeks. After months spent practicing together, they knew how quickly Rachel learned, and regarded her with wary awe. Even the most jealous ones seemed to recognize Rachel as the greatest among them. Uncertain times were looming. The acolytes did not want to lose her. She had never felt so needed.

Did anyone rely on her like this back home? Her parents loved her, and certainly missed her, but did they *need* her? Not the way the people in Lyrian needed her. As her abilities increased, her role here in Lyrian would only grow more significant.

Are you busy? The words reached her mind as clearly as if spoken.

Come in.

The door opened and Corinne entered, honey-blond hair tied back, her robes fitting like she had been prepped for a photo shoot. *I saw Ulani leave.* Corinne's room was not far down the hall.

She was saying her good-byes. What have you been up to today?

I was helping Father, Corinne conveyed. *We were sending messages to our allies. We won't have easy access to messenger eagles again until we reach Trensicourt. I'll miss them. They're such intelligent, impressive birds. How are you feeling?*

I've been tense, Rachel admitted. *I had a good talk with Jason. It helped.*

We live in very difficult times, Corinne conveyed. *None would envy us.*

I'm not looking forward to the good-byes, Rachel expressed.

Corinne closed her eyes. The words came clearly to Rachel,

laden with heartache. *I understand, Rachel. I'll miss you too. And the others. I have grown comfortable here. Resting. Sparring. Socializing. I may never see my father again after today.*

I can't think about all the separations, Rachel replied sympathetically. *It's too much. I've been dreading this. I don't feel ready.* Not only was she going to miss her friends, but many parts of the prophecy left her full of unsettling doubts and questions.

Corinne opened her eyes. *I know! Why do oracles have to be so cryptic?*

I didn't share that on purpose, Rachel responded. Like her father, Corinne was growing increasingly adept at perceiving unshared thoughts.

Sorry, Corinne apologized. *I couldn't help sensing your attitude. I know that Father has puzzled over every word. For example, what servant will betray what master? Could be almost anyone.*

Rachel nodded. *I can't resist searching for clues in her final words. She said our hope would be red like the blood of heroes, black as the bowels of the earth, and white like a flash of orantium. Is there some hidden message we need to deduce from that? Or was she just confirming that some of us will die and orantium will help in our battles?*

It could be worse, Corinne comforted her. *Some prophecies can be hopelessly vague. At least we know a few things for sure. We know that we have to split up. We know who goes where and generally what they must do. As for the rest? Good luck figuring out which secret from the past will ransom the future.*

Maybe we'll know it when we come across it.

Let's hope so. Do you need more alone time?

Rachel scanned her room, realizing that it truly felt like *her* room. It was the only space in Lyrian over which she had ever felt a real sense of ownership. She sighed. The plan had never been to stay here. Her belongings were packed. "I'm ready."

* * *

Rachel and Corinne caught up to the others on the main floor of the temple. A variety of treefolk mingled with Rachel's companions. Certius had engendered the treefolk, humanlike races covered with foliage, most with moss or ivy, some with vines or thorns. Treefolk guides would be escorting both of the departing groups out of the jungle.

Galloran, his blindfold in place as usual, stood conversing with Nollin, Kerick, and Halco. The amars belonging to Kerick and Halco had been planted in a fertile patch of soil shortly after their arrival to Mianamon, and they had been reborn barely ten weeks later. The three seedmen would be accompanying Galloran's group—Halco meant to split off and rejoin his people, while Kerick and Nollin would proceed to Trensicourt. Kerick and Halco appeared to be in good spirits as they chatted with Galloran, while Nollin seemed to brood.

Of all the members of the delegation who had set out from the Seven Vales, Nollin had liked the prophecy least. Although he had kept in contact with influential seedfolk, sending many messages by eagle proclaiming his doubts and misgivings, to his credit the dour seedman had confirmed that the oracle had indeed foreseen at least a small chance at victory if Galloran and his remaining allies took the offensive. Since the prediction contradicted Nollin's personal expectations and politics, his affirmation lent needed credibility to the report.

Galloran had shaved his beard and trimmed his hair short. His face looked younger than the gray hair and whiskers had hinted—middle-aged, with chiseled features and a strong chin.

Jason waved at Rachel, and she trotted toward him. He looked good in his clean traveling robes. On the floor beside him sat a pair of covered buckets.

"What's in there?" Rachel asked.

"Galloran is sending us with most of the extra orantium," Jason explained. "Twelve globes. He's only taking three, since the Amar Kabal have hundreds in reserve for the assault on Felrook. They promised to resupply him early by sending fifty to Trensicourt."

"You're carrying the spheres in buckets?"

"Check it out," Jason said, prying off one of the lids. Inside, six crystal orantium globes floated in clear gel.

"What's with the goo?"

"I was just asking the same thing," Jason said. "The wizard Certius invented it specifically for transporting orantium globes. I guess they still have a decent stash here."

"I thought that hardly any orantium had survived except for what we found in the swamp."

"Right. But Mianamon is old. They have more left here than any other place besides the Sunken Lands. Like, twenty globes."

Rachel dipped a finger in the goo. It came out coated in glossy syrup. "So the goo keeps the globes from smacking together and cracking?"

"Partly. Also, if a sphere breaks, supposedly the mineral won't explode."

Rachel rubbed her thumb against her slick finger. "I get it. Orantium combusts when exposed to air or water. But not this stuff."

"It lets us transport orantium with less fear of blowing ourselves apart."

Rachel wiped her hand on her robe. "I wonder if they used something like this to mine orantium in the first place."

"Maybe," Jason said. "The people who would know are long gone, along with the mine."

"You could always check at the Celestine Library," Rachel suggested.

"That's totally what we'll do there. Ancient mining research. Either that or we'll find the location of Darian the Seer and save the world."

Galloran raised his hoarse voice. "I believe we're all assembled." All other conversation stopped as everyone turned to hear him speak. Many acolytes and treefolk had gathered to see them off. "I would like to thank the inhabitants of Mianamon for their generous hospitality over the past months. You have proven yourselves friends and allies in times of hardship."

The compliment earned scattered applause.

Galloran went on. "We now embark on missions prescribed by your most recent oracle. I thank the treefolk for providing us with safe passage through the jungle. Troubled times await us all. I will remain in communication via eagle whenever possible.

"The future of Lyrian has never been more precarious. Remain vigilant. Hope for the best, but prepare for the worst. I salute Jason and my friends, who now embark on a hazardous quest to a secret destination. Together they form one of the finest teams ever assembled in the history of Lyrian. If they counsel wisely and work as one, I expect there is little they cannot accomplish."

Nollin started laughing derisively.

"Is something humorous?" Farfalee asked.

"I'm simply amused by this brave talk of victory," Nollin said. "Can we be just a touch more realistic?"

"Enlighten us," Galloran offered. Rachel could tell he wasn't thrilled with the interruption.

"We're not going to accomplish anything," Nollin said simply. "I'll do my best alongside you, but we're chasing a phantom triumph. A fool's mirage. The oracle made it clear that victory was all but impossible."

"What would you have us do?" Drake challenged.

"I would tell the good people of Mianamon to expect word of our failure," Nollin replied. "I would encourage them to withdraw deep into the heart of the jungle, to promote the breeding of ferocious beasts, and to erect whatever defenses they can contrive. After our nations fall, this will be the last vestige of free civilization on the continent. They should take every measure to protect it."

"You can't write us off like that," Jason argued.

"Can't I?" Nollin asked innocently. "The oracle did. She made it abundantly clear that this venture has virtually no chance of success. It will end in our ruin."

"Then why are you participating?" Farfalee asked.

Nollin faced her. "If we're already doomed, why not chase one last pleasant illusion? This was the decision of my people, and I will hold true to it. But the rest of Lyrian should brace for disaster."

Rachel noticed the treefolk murmuring and shifting uncomfortably.

"If we think like that, we probably will fail," Jason said resolutely. "The oracle told us that we still have a chance to beat Maldor. We need to focus on that."

"You're free to dream however you wish," Nollin teased. "But don't ask the rest of us to share your unrealistic—"

"Then don't ask us to share your weakness!" Jason interrupted.

Nollin seemed taken aback.

Jason plowed forward. "This isn't really my fight. It's not my world. I'm not helping because my people obligated me. I'm helping because Lyrian needs to be saved. It's a good place with good people. There's so much potential that will be lost if Maldor wins! I've met him. He wants to control all of Lyrian. He wants to rule it completely, for as long as he can, and since he could live hundreds of years, that could add up to a really long time. If he wins, Lyrian will become a terrible place. He barely even tries to hide that. Stopping him is the right thing to do."

"Nobody is arguing that we should embrace Maldor," Nollin said soothingly.

"You're arguing that stopping him is unrealistic," Jason said. "But don't you get what Galloran was saying? You're with people who do unrealistic things. He's killed three torivors! I spoke the Word to Maldor and then escaped Felrook. Rachel killed Orruck and we took his orantium. We all made it through Ebera. We've done lots of unrealistic things. Why not try for a few more?"

The assemblage cheered. Rachel wanted to hug Jason. The mood in the room had gone from gloomy to jubilant in a matter of moments. Nollin surveyed the surrounding reactions with a condescending smile. He shook his head a little and raised his hands in surrender. The gesture reluctantly gave permission for the others to enjoy their delusion. They took him up on the offer.

"Well said, Lord Jason," Galloran approved, motioning for the crowd to quiet down. "This is not an hour for doubt or fear." The blindfolded king drew his sword. The sleek blade flashed like a mirror. "I have in my custody four swords of torivorian make, won by besting lurkers in battle. I have owned two others, but they were lost when I was taken by Maldor. I will keep one of the four swords. My daughter Corinne will retain another. A third will travel into peril with Lord Jason of Caberton."

"Me?" Jason blurted.

Rachel glanced at his shocked expression.

"I wish I could give more," Galloran apologized.

"But I'm not the best swordsman in my group," Jason protested. "Far from it. How about Jasher? Or Drake?"

"According to the oracle, you must survive to reach Darian the Pyromancer," Galloran said. "You must live to receive the vital information. Therefore you should be the best equipped of your party."

Jasher nudged Jason. "Go accept it," the seedman whispered.

Rachel nodded her agreement.

"Okay," Jason said, walking to Galloran. "Thank you—I can't believe it. I'll do my best."

Jason strapped the sword about his waist. Despite his height, he looked young.

Tark began the cheering. Others noisily joined him, and the approval quickly swelled to a wholehearted level that surprised Rachel. She found herself caught up in spirit of the moment, whistling and clapping.

Jason smiled bashfully. The cheers subsided. Jason stepped away from Galloran, who produced another torivorian sword. "The fourth sword will travel with me to Trensicourt, borne by Ferrin, son of Baldor."

Mutters rippled through the crowd, not all of them approving. Rachel glanced at the displacer, his expression a study in surprise and disbelief. He walked over to Galloran and knelt before him. "This is too kingly a gift."

"The blade comes with a price," Galloran said. "You must wield it in defense of our cause. If you do so, you will more than earn it."

Ferrin bowed his head. "I'm deeply honored, Your Majesty."

"More honor awaits if you see this through," Galloran rasped softly.

Io handed Ferrin the sword. The displacer belted it on.

Considering Ferrin, Rachel decided that Galloran was wise to entrust him with the torivorian weapon. She knew Ferrin viewed the fine swords with an almost religious awe. Any gesture that might help cement his loyalty would give them a better chance for success.

Galloran raised his voice again. "Nedwin left weeks ago to prepare the way for us at Trensicourt. Nia did likewise for Jason and his party. The day wanes. The hour for farewells is almost past. Let us make ready to depart. Know that with every remaining moment of my life, with every opportunity I can seize and every resource I can borrow, I will devote myself to bringing down the emperor!"

This earned a final rousing cheer from the assemblage. Rachel found herself clapping and yelling along with the others. At the same time, she felt a little distant. Soon this moment would be a memory, as would the protective walls of Mianamon. Before long she would be separated from her two best friends in Lyrian, perhaps never to see them again. No more cheering. No more rest. No more jokes. Just a parade of unpredictable difficulties and dangers.

Corinne took her hand. Rachel looked up at her. *Are you in my mind?*

We'll see each other again.

Do you really think so?

At times like this, it's the only thing we can let ourselves believe.

A cynical part of Rachel wondered how much Corinne could possibly understand about times like this.

When I stood outside that tree in the swamp, Corinne conveyed gently, *all I clung to for years was a hope that my father would return for me. Long after I might have stopped believing, he finally came. And here I am.*

Rachel hugged her. *Be safe. Watch out for Jason.*

I'll protect him with my life.

Rachel looked up, startled by how earnestly Corinne had conveyed the sentiment.

I'll do my best to stay alive too, Corinne assured her.

"Bye, Corinne."

"Safe travels."

Everyone was checking gear and shouldering packs. They were really leaving! Rachel hurried over to Jasher and hugged him. "Be safe."

"You too."

She turned to the half giant, Aram, who would remain small and unremarkable until sundown swelled him into a tall, heavily muscled warrior. "Take care of yourself."

"Don't fret about me," Aram said. "I'll do my best to watch out for the others."

Drake was walking away, following a treeperson draped in heavy vines. Rachel jogged to him and placed a hand on his elbow. The seedman stopped, turning somewhat, not fully facing her. The profile view of his face emphasized his flat features. "I suppose there was no escaping you."

"What? You wanted to just wander off without a word?"

"It can be easier that way."

"Don't be silly. You come back. You survive. I want to see you after this. I want you to show me your private valley in the mountains."

"It wouldn't be private anymore." A small grin bent his lips as he rubbed the back of his neck, the place where his amar had failed to grow correctly after his last rebirth. "But I suppose I could live with that. Stay close to Galloran. He'll keep you from harm."

Rachel threw her arms around him. They had not been parted since Drake had guided her away from the torivor for weeks in the wilderness. "Take care."

"I'll try. Have a safe journey, Rachel."

"I'll miss you."

He gave a stiff nod and strode away. She thought he might be near the brink of showing emotion. Her heart squeezed painfully at the thought of parting from him and so many of her other friends. She tried to draw strength from his example.

Rachel caught up to Jason, who already had a pack on his back and a bucket of orantium in one hand. He set down the bucket and hugged her. He felt solid. Consecutive months of good eating and intense physical training had paid off.

"Are you trying to speak with your mind?" he said after a moment. "I can't do that."

She pulled away from the embrace and looked into his eyes. "Don't give up."

"There goes my plan."

"I'm serious. Even if things look bad, find a way. You're good at that. The oracle saw a way that we could win. Find it."

"You too," Jason urged. "Within reason. Don't try some huge Edomic command and blow yourself to pieces."

"There goes my plan."

"You stole my line." Jason glanced at the others departing.

"I know we have to hurry," Rachel said. "But this is it. We're taking different paths." She took a breath and put conviction into her words. "We'll see each other again."

Tark came up to them. "This is wrong, Lord Jason, letting them part us."

Jason turned to the stocky musician. "Sorry, Tark. The oracle is calling the shots on this one."

"I remain your pledged man," Tark avowed, touching a fist to his chest. "What are your orders?"

"Do your best to help Galloran win his war."

"I swear it."

"And keep an eye on Rachel. See if you can get her to stop telling me she's going to see me again. I think she's jinxing us."

Rachel punched Jason's arm.

Tark eyed Rachel uncertainly. She saw a hint of disapproval in his gaze, along with a little wariness.

Jason smiled. "That's assault. Tark, take her out."

The musician grinned, but not with his eyes. "You better handle this one."

Chuckling, Jason picked up the bucket of explosives.

Rachel felt the moment slipping away. There was so much she wanted to say. What if something happened to him? What if she never told him how much she appreciated his coming back to Lyrian for her? How much she cared about him? There were too many feelings to translate into words. "See you later," she managed.

"Not if I see you first," Jason said, starting toward the main doors of the temple.

She watched him walking away. Were those the last words he would say to her? She stalked after him. "You can't leave with a joke."

He glanced back. "Why not?"

"What if I die?"

"Then at least I cheered you up before the end."

"That wasn't a cheerful joke. It was a teasing joke. And not even a very good one."

"Fine. Why did the baby cross the road?"

"No jokes," Rachel complained, striding along beside him.

"I guess it's more fitting that we should end with an argument."

"I just mean there are certain times when jokes aren't appropriate."

"Which makes them more needed and funny."

She grabbed his arm and tugged him to a halt. "You have your way of coping, and I have mine. You're amazing. You're inspiring. You're so brave. I'll miss you and I appreciate you. Everything about you."

"Even my humor?"

"Almost everything. Don't die."

"It might help if you stop giving my eulogy. You don't die either. I'll miss you too. I have one last question."

"What?"

"Are you going to bring your pack?"

Rachel started. She had left it back where she had been talking with Corinne.

"Never mind," Jason said, looking over his shoulder. "Your acolyte worshippers are grabbing it for you. Do you have a pen? You should really sign some autographs for them."

Rachel banged her forehead with the heel of her hand. "You know what I still have? My camera! I've been meaning all winter to get a group shot."

She rushed over to the acolytes, retrieved the camera from her pack, and hurried back to Jason, who stood waiting.

"You really are an optimist," Jason said. "You realize you'll have to get back home before you can develop any photos?"

"At least I can do it myself," Rachel said. "I've done it lots. If this camera were digital, I'd probably be out of batteries by now."

Jason helped her round everyone up for a group shot on the temple steps. Rachel showed Ulani how to work the camera. Jason explained that the device would capture and preserve the image, along with their souls. Rachel explained that he was joking. Once Ulani had taken a couple of shots, Rachel let Tark have a turn as photographer with Ulani in the picture. Then Rachel snapped an extra one herself for good measure.

After stowing her camera, Rachel gave Jason a final hug goodbye. And then they left by separate trails into the muggy jungle.

CHAPTER 4

THE JOURNEY NORTH

Even with the expert guidance of the treefolk, Jason found jungle travel exhausting. In the gloom beneath the dense canopy the humid air stayed oppressively hot and still. Hidden by the ferny undergrowth, roots and creepers crisscrossed the uneven ground, ready to catch a toe or turn an ankle. At times the group would take to the trees, moving along massive limbs or traversing camouflaged bridges fashioned from vines.

The way proved challenging at its gentlest—without the guides the pathless journey would have been hopeless. The tree-folk navigated around endless thickets of impenetrable vegetation without ever needing to pause or double back. They avoided numerous carnivorous plants: huge, quivering mouths on nimble stalks; squidlike, thorny tendrils that attacked from above; bulging bulbs poised to emit poisonous spores; and sticky mats ready to enfold the unwary. Dangerous snakes, centipedes, and spiders were identified and eluded. Twice, the treefolk waited silently with the group, high in a tree, while a jungle cat the size of a horse prowled down below, great bunches of muscle churning beneath a glossy pelt.

At times the abundant plant and animal life distracted Jason from the taxing terrain. With the mild winter waning, blossoms flourished throughout the jungle, from elaborate trombone-shaped flowers to glorious blooms on corkscrew vines to delicate orchids of infinite color and variety. Exotic birds with vibrant plumage and monkeys of all description populated the trees. After they happened across a large family of obese, blue-gray apes, the others had to drag Jason away. He would have contentedly watched the shaggy brutes toddle about on their stumpy legs for the rest of the afternoon.

The treefolk foraged most of the food for the group. Diverse fruit, rich nectar, savory mushrooms, peculiar nuts, and crunchy grubs made up the majority of their meals. Jason enjoyed the unusual diet and seldom craved hot food in spite of its absence.

One steamy morning Bahootsa, the thorn-encased leader of the eight treefolk escorts, announced that they were approaching the northern perimeter of the jungle, where imperial soldiers had been known to venture. When he suggested a break for the day to allow five of the treefolk to scout ahead, nobody complained.

They stopped beside a swift brook with banks of dense red clay. Trees and shrubs didn't crowd the stream, which created a clearing of sorts—a rare sight in the heavily vegetated region.

Wandering along the brook away from the group, Jason drew the torivorian sword Galloran had given him. The elegant weapon felt lighter than it looked. He held the blade horizontally in front of his face, staring at the clear reflection of his eyes in the burnished metal, and saw Corinne approaching from behind. Jason turned.

"Isn't it beautiful?" Corinne asked.

Jason thought *she* was easily the most beautiful thing in sight.

The realization made him embarrassed, so he looked around, trying to appreciate what she meant. Tall palm trees with broad fronds screened the morning sun. Bright birds flapped and perched overhead. The aroma of tropical blossoms filled his nostrils. "It's like paradise."

Corinne smiled. "I meant the sword." Her hand rested on the hilt of her matching blade.

"Right." Jason swished it through the air, trying to look heroic. "It feels so light."

"Mine too," Corinne said. "But don't worry. The sword will feel plenty heavy to your enemies. Father explained that the blades contain more mass than the wielder feels."

"I guess that makes sense," Jason said, holding the sword vertically. "At the Last Inn, Galloran slashed through helmets and armor like they were made of paper."

"You should practice with the sword," Corinne urged. "Get used to how it differs from other weapons. The shock of impact feels dampened. The blade swings light but strikes heavy." She drew her sword and stabbed it through the trunk of a palm tree with an easy thrust. The tree was nearly a foot thick, but the sword penetrated the wood effortlessly, the polished blade protruding from the far side. Corinne withdrew the sword.

Jason swung his sword back and forth a few times, then approached the same trunk Corinne had stabbed and hacked at it with the edge. He swung hard and expected the blade to bite deep, but he was surprised when the sword passed clean through the tree without too much resistance. Jason skipped aside as the palm tree toppled in his direction.

"Careful," Corinne laughed after the tree had crashed down parallel to the brook.

"That's what I call sharp," Jason said, inspecting the blade with new respect. Passing through the trunk had left no stain on the reflective surface. "We should become lumberjacks."

"Maybe someday," Corinne said wistfully. "I'd rather chop trees than people."

"Don't get all serious on me," Jason complained. "You're as bad as Rachel."

"You miss her."

Jason shrugged, looking away. "It was nice having her around. I worry about her. I try to remind myself that she's in good company. I bet you miss the mental chats. With Galloran and Rachel gone, you're the only telepathic person around."

"I'm not sure I appreciated how much I relied on speaking in silence until the option was taken from me. I've tried several times to reach out to them over the great distance, but with no hint of success."

"You guys never could make it work over more than a mile or so."

"And only that far with considerable effort."

"Well, it'll be good exercise for your lips."

"It'll be good exercise for your lips," Jason's voice repeated from behind him. Jason whirled, sword ready, baffled by the perfect echo. He glanced over at Corinne. "Did you hear that?"

"Did you hear that?" replied a voice not far off in the jungle. Once again the speaker managed a perfect impersonation of Jason. Taking a few steps in the direction of the impostor, Jason found himself staring at a creamy parrot with a frill of orange feathers around its head.

Corinne stepped toward Jason, sword in hand. "It sounded just like you."

"It sounded just like you," the bird repeated in Corinne's voice. It flitted from the branch it occupied to a perch farther from the brook. "Did you hear that?" the parrot asked in Corinne's voice.

"It sounded just like you," the bird replied as Jason.

"No way," Jason said, pushing past ferns to get a closer look at the parrot.

"No way," the bird responded in Corinne's voice.

Something came charging recklessly through the shrubs from off to one side. Jason pivoted to see Bahootsa racing toward him, a knife in one hand, the other thorny arm flailing, waving Jason back toward the brook.

Jason looked from Bahootsa to the bird. Could it be danger-ous? As he backed away uncertainly, the parrot took flight, and the shadows behind it came to life as a gargantuan jungle cat sprang out of the gloom. Bahootsa intercepted the monstrous feline mid-leap, tackling it sideways, altering the trajectory of the jump enough that the outstretched claws whooshed through the air beside Jason, narrowly missing their target.

The jungle cat shook off Bahootsa. Numerous gaping wounds opened as unforgiving thorns shredded its glossy hide. Bristling and falling back, the huge cat roared, a ferocious sound that sent dozens of the surrounding birds skyward. Jason stared numbly at its long white fangs, yellowed at the base, and held his sword ready. No lion or tiger was ever half the weight of this huge alpha predator.

Bahootsa was back on his feet, shuffling to position himself between Jason and the great cat, crimson blood dripping from his thorns. Sword held defensively, Jason backed out of the vegeta-tion to the bare red clay of the stream's bank. He sensed Corinne behind him and stopped retreating. No way would he let the jungle cat get to her. The thought made him braver. If his sword could cut through a tree, it could tear through an oversized cat skull. He would need to time it right.

As the jungle cat crouched low, wads of muscle bunching in

the shoulders, one of its green eyes vanished, a feathered shaft suddenly protruding. Yowling fiercely, the great cat whirled and darted away into the trees.

Swiveling, Jason saw that Farfalee had already set a second arrow to her bowstring and drawn the feathers to her cheek. She stood no less than thirty yards away. How she had threaded an arrow through all that foliage and into the eye of the cat was mind-blowing. She remained ready to release the second arrow as Bahootsa joined Jason and Corinne.

"We call the mimicking bird a sonalid," Bahootsa said, the words coming out heavily accented. "They often hunt in tandem with a dagamond. The sonalid lures the prey into danger. While the cat eats, the sonalid picks parasites from its pelt."

Heart thudding, Jason nodded woodenly. The shock had barely begun to fade. "Are you okay?"

Bahootsa grinned. "My thorns are harder than stone. I am not easy prey. Worse predators than dagamonds prowl the depths of the jungle."

Jason had never fully appreciated how well the serpentine briars and abundant black thorns of the prickly treefolk functioned as armor. Bahootsa was walking around in his own portable shark cage.

"You saved my life," Jason said as Farfalee, Jasher, and Drake approached.

"I pledged to see you safely to our borders," Bahootsa replied. He gestured at the others. "We save your lives many times each day. This time was just a close call. It was a wily old dagamond. I did not sense it stalking us." He faced Farfalee. "An expert shot."

"I try to be useful," she replied, the arrow no longer on her string but still in her hand. Her eyes studied the jungle.

"It is gone," Bahootsa said. "The dagamond got more than it

bargained for. Plenty more. It prefers to surprise its victim, make an easy kill. It isn't accustomed to a challenge. It has little experience with pain."

"Are you all right?" Corinne asked, placing a hand on Jason's arm.

"I'm fine," Jason replied. "My heart rate might be a little high. For a second there I thought I was panther chow." He sheathed his sword.

"Predators love stragglers," Bahootsa said. "We should remain together."

Over the next several days the jungle began to feel more sparse, the air less humid, and the nights chillier. Animal sightings became less frequent, and the need for the treefolk guides diminished.

Atop a low bluff, with grassland stretching out before them, Jason and his companions bid farewell to Bahootsa and the treefolk. The sun went down, and Aram expanded from puny to formidable. After their guides melted away into the twilight, the others sat in a loose circle. Jason appreciated the chance to rest. Without the treefolk the group felt small.

"We'll miss those guides," Drake commented, biting into a succulent piece of fruit. "Having them around almost made this a holiday."

"The jungle is their domain," Jasher replied. "They're uncomfortable abroad. And with stealth our greatest need, their presence would prove a liability. Every pair of eyes would linger on them."

"More treefolk should roam the kingdoms," Drake groused. "At least in the south. If they left their jungle from time to time, they might not stand out so much in a crowd."

Jason gazed ahead at the grassy expanse they would have to cross. Maldor would be hunting for them, and he saw no place to hide. At least with the treefolk along they could have fought off greater numbers.

"Nia was going to provide horses?" Aram asked, his voice a low rumble.

"Ideally, yes," Farfalee replied. She sat near Jasher, petting the eagle that perched on her forearm. "Her first priority is to recruit enough drinlings to man a ship. After that, if possible, she will endeavor to send horses and an escort to the woods north of a hamlet called Hilloby."

"Let's hope she succeeds," Drake said. "It's a considerable walk to the Inland Sea."

"How far to Hilloby?" Corinne wondered.

Jasher squinted at the sky, then scanned the horizon. "Maybe three days on foot."

"Not much cover out there," Jason observed.

"We'll travel at night," Jasher said. "Hide during the day."

"The comforts of life as a fugitive," Drake sighed. "Stumbling about in the dark without mounts."

"It beats capture and torture," Farfalee said shortly.

"Granted," Drake agreed. "No need to take offense."

"No need to emphasize obvious discomforts," she replied. The eagle spread its wings and gave a shriek.

"You're upsetting the bird," Drake accused.

"*I'm* upsetting . . . ," Farfalee repeated in a huff. She compressed her lips, clearly making an effort to restrain her temper.

"They can sense bossiness," Drake warned matter-of-factly.

Jason worked to keep his expression composed. He didn't look toward Corinne, who also seemed to be resisting her amusement.

Jasher leaned close to Farfalee. "Don't let him get to you," he said gently, touching her elbow.

Farfalee shrugged away from her husband's touch. With a

measured motion of her arm she sent the eagle into the sky. Many stars were now visible. The eagle soared away.

"I can't believe it can find its way back to you," Jason said, eyes skyward, hoping to change the subject.

"Eldrin was no amateur," Farfalee said, her tone kinder. "He engineered this breed of eagles to be ideal messengers. Once they bond with a person, the eagles can find them no matter how separated they become."

"The three we have are also bonded to Galloran?" Jason asked.

"And Tark, and Io, to be safe," Farfalee said. "Once we learn what Darian has to tell us, I have but to command, and the eagles will carry the message to our friends."

"And until you send a message, they keep returning to you," Jason said.

"Correct. I have worked with messenger eagles for centuries. I spent many days at Mianamon's aviary selecting the most reliable birds and prepping them. Until we need them, they should remain self-sufficient—hunt their own food, find their own shelter. They'll return to me every couple of days."

"An expert tracker might follow them to us," Aram cautioned.

"Possibly," Farfalee conceded. "But that's a chance we have to take."

"Jason has Ferrin's ear," Drake reminded everyone.

Farfalee glared at her brother. "Which is a welcome redundancy, even if the displacer might only be interested in spying on us."

"He might be able to hear you," Drake muttered.

"I hope he does," Farfalee said. "I won't trust that scoundrel until this is over and he's done his part. And I don't mind him hearing it."

"He won't hear much," Jason said. "I keep the ear heavily bundled, deep in my bag."

"Probably for the best," Farfalee said.

Somewhere overhead, an eagle let out a piercing cry. Jason tilted his head back but couldn't spot the bird in the darkening sky. He didn't like the idea of enemies tracking them using the messenger eagles. Unfortunately, Farfalee was right—they couldn't afford to place all their trust in Ferrin.

Drake stretched, fists extended, back arched. "What if some accident should befall you, dear sister? Would the eagles come to your seed? Are they bonded to any of the rest of us?"

"They're also bonded to Jasher," she replied. "They would also come to Corinne."

"Jasher?" Drake challenged. "Jasher dies all the time! He has too many lives to spare. Why not Jason?"

"I'm allergic to eagles," Jason joked, trying to keep out of it.

"Then why not Aram? He strikes me as a survivor."

Aram grunted. "The survivor suggests that if we need darkness to travel, we take advantage while we have it."

Drake extended a hand toward the half giant. "See? Forget bonding the bird to him. Why isn't he the leader?"

"I've sampled that role," Aram chuckled. "Too much responsibility. Too much accountability."

Drake shook his head. "Mark my words, he'll outlive us all."

"Aram certainly has a point," Jasher said. "We should get underway."

"Are you the leader?" Drake asked with mock curiosity, eyes on Jasher, then glancing at Farfalee.

Jason noticed Corinne shift uncomfortably. She didn't like conflict, and when Drake got in a mood to bother his sister, there was always plenty. At least Farfalee looked like she was trying to remain patient.

"Jasher is in charge of tactics," Farfalee sighed. "Aram is the muscle. Jason has the ear. Corinne has her sword. You're the pest. And I'm the leader."

"I can live with that," Drake said. "Leaders draw a lot of attention. The pest sometimes survives."

"We're all going to survive," Farfalee affirmed.

"Not according to the oracle," Drake reminded her.

"Maybe the casualties will be with the other group," Aram speculated.

"That's the spirit!" Drake praised, clapping the big warrior on the back. "Friends, if we watch Aram, we might have a chance. Dodge when he dodges. Duck when he ducks."

"I feel a headache coming on," Farfalee deadpanned. "Drake, why don't you scout ahead?"

Drake glanced at Aram. "What do you say? Will I survive the assignment?"

"I give you better odds than if you keep needling your sister."

"Good enough for me," Drake declared, rising. "Try to keep up."

The next three nights were spent covering as much ground as possible, with the secondary mission of finding concealment before sunrise. Aram toted his heavy sword and armor as well as the two buckets of orantium. The first day they hid in the middle of some bushes. The second day was spent in a shallow ravine. During the third day they huddled against a steep hillside.

Not long after sunset on the fourth night, Jason and his companions came within sight of Hilloby. There were no more than twenty buildings in the humble hamlet, and not all of them had lit windows. Scattered farmhouses added somewhat to the community. The modest village represented the first evidence of other people Jason had seen since leaving the jungle.

"Who checks the woods north of town?" Drake asked.

"We could all go," Jason said.

Farfalee shook her head. "We expect to find drinlings with horses, but the drinlings could have been followed. Anything could await us in those woods. We should send a pair to scout."

"I'll go," Jasher said. "And Drake."

Farfalee gave a nod, and the two seedmen departed.

Jason found a seat beside Corinne on a flat boulder. The night was cool but not cold. Half a moon hung in the sky. He had grown used to sleeping during the day, so he felt wide awake.

He still couldn't converse with Corinne privately without feeling a flutter of nervous excitement. It wasn't just because she was ridiculously pretty. She was also grounded and smart and sweet and . . . ridiculously pretty.

"How are you holding up?" Jason asked.

It took her a moment to respond. She shivered and rubbed her elbow. "Honestly? I'm kind of worried. I've had this persistent feeling of dread lately. Like something bad is coming."

"Tonight?"

Her brow furrowed as she looked up at the moon. "I'm not sure. I hope not."

"Might just be the prophecy," Aram said, joining the conversation unexpectedly. "I've felt unsettled ever since it was spoken. Nobody wants to hear that the odds are stacked heavily against them. It's one thing to suspect it. Another thing to know it."

"That's probably it," Corinne said, looking up and back at Aram.

"We should be fine for a while," Jason said. "Nobody has seen us. Even among the others at Mianamon, nobody knows where we're going."

"Maldor must have been furious when we fled into the jungle," Farfalee said, approaching and placing a foot on the edge of the boulder beside Jason. "It is one of the few places where he holds little influence. He'll be watching for us to emerge all along the border."

"He knows we were with Galloran," Aram said. "He'll pay special heed to the roads leading to Trensicourt."

"Perhaps," Farfalee conceded. "Jason is correct that stealth remains our best asset for the present. I'm going to take a look around." Farfalee strolled away into the shadows.

"The eagles," Aram muttered once she was out of earshot. "I could do without the eagles. If a tracker knew his trade, those eagles could lead him straight to us. Otherwise I can't imagine how the emperor—"

"Lurkers," Jason interrupted. "He's used them before." Jason fingered the strand of beads and bone around his neck. "I still have the necklace Rachel brought me from the charm woman. But since Drake gave his to Galloran, the rest of our minds are open to them."

"I'd sense a lurker," Corinne said. "I could hear the one that attacked Father. If one reached for us mentally, I'd know."

"Best not to discuss such things," Aram said with an air of superstition. "The less our thoughts turn their way the better."

Jason decided not to add that the best way to get him to focus on something was to tell him not to think about it.

The moon slowly moved across the sky. Corinne leaned back and closed her eyes. Jason tried not to stare at her. Weird that she could totally take him in a swordfight. He had seen her practicing with her father, and she was out of his league.

Jason folded his arms. He glanced at Aram, who had settled on the ground, his broad back to the boulder. Hypothetically, would he have a chance against Aram in a duel? No way. The half giant had such a long reach and swung so hard. What about Jasher? Or

Drake? Not if they were really trying. He could spar with them, but if it came down to it, life or death, they would certainly beat him. What if he was using his torivorian sword? No, not unless it shattered Jasher's blade, and then the seedman tripped or something. Farfalee had never taken a big interest in hand-to-hand combat. Jason thought he might have a chance against her if she didn't put an arrow through him from a mile away.

Corinne breathed softly, her elegant features bathed in moonlight. Jason shifted around, trying to get more comfortable on the boulder. He was definitely a better fighter than he used to be, but if every member of his team could defeat him in combat, didn't that make him the weakest link? When things got bad, what was he supposed to contribute?

He understood how Rachel would help. As her Edomic abilities increased, her value grew exponentially. He remembered her sending that flaming table across the main room at the Last Inn. That was some serious power. He could picture her making a difference on her mission. He just didn't understand why the oracle had paid so much attention to him.

Maybe he was stressing too much. Maybe he just needed to relax. Hopefully, if he stayed ready and tried his best, he would manage to make himself useful when the time came. Why did he feel like he was totally kidding himself?

Aram began to snore. Farfalee, obviously restless, came and went a few times. And then the sound of approaching hoofbeats brought Jason, Corinne, and Aram to their feet.

"That has to be good, right?" Jason said. "Horses?"

"I don't sense anything bad," Corinne said, wiping her eyes.

"They're coming right at us," Aram whispered. "Jasher or Drake would never have given us up. Let's take cover just in case." He drew his enormous sword, from pommel to tip about as long as

Jason was tall, the blade heavy and sharp. Aram held it casually in one hand. Most grown men would struggle to heft it with two.

The threesome ducked into the cover of some bushes. Farfalee joined them after a moment, an arrow nocked and ready. Aram pried the lid off one of the buckets of orantium.

Eight horses with six riders trotted into view. Four of the riders were drinlings. "All clear," Jasher called from astride his mount.

Jason and the others emerged from hiding.

"We made four new friends," Drake said. "They're well provisioned."

"I only count two spare mounts," Farfalee observed.

"Two of us will now make our way afoot," said one of the newcomers, his words accented.

"We'd hate to strand you," Aram said.

The drinling speaker smirked. "If we raced to Durna, the two of us on foot might beat you. Horses need rest. We don't. A drinling can cover a lot of ground running at a full sprint day and night. All he needs is food."

"Helps when he can eat dirt," Jason said. "Or grass, or squirrels, or pinecones."

"Sounds as though you know our ways," the drinling said.

"Nia never fails to amaze me with what she can eat," Jason said.

"She may amaze you again with the team she assembled," the drinling replied. "Good people. We drinlings will get you on the water. We'll defend you as best we can. The rest is up to you."

Jason glanced at Corinne. She looked relieved. Hard times might be coming. But maybe not tonight.

CHAPTER 5

A PRIVATE MEETING

A cold rain sheeted down relentlessly, pattering against the roof of the old storage shed and making the puddles outside appear to boil. Seated on a wooden cask, Rachel drew her cloak closer about herself to help against the chill. Across the yard three lanterns hanging under the eaves of the stable brightened the rainy night.

Beside her sat Galloran, blindfold in place, his sheathed sword resting across his knees. At her other hand crouched Bartley of Wershon. Yesterday the husky viscount had been full of blustering bravado. Today he was much more subdued, rubbing his lips regularly as he stared soberly outside.

Rachel noticed her fingers trembling. Was it the cold or her nerves? She tightened her hands into fists. Weeks of travel and anticipation had led to this night. Much time and effort could be saved if the meeting went well.

"They're late," Bartley whispered.

Rachel had only seen the viscount briefly on the day when Jason had faced Chancellor Copernum in a battle of wits. But she knew that he had helped Jason. And according to Brin and Nicholas, he had quietly proven very useful ever since Jason had departed Trensicourt months ago. At present he had really stuck his neck out, offering his estate as the location of the upcoming meeting.

"Tardiness is probably a good sign," Galloran said. "If this were an ambush, they would have taken care to be prompt."

"Instead they elect to insult us?" Bartley asked softly.

"The weather is harsh tonight," Galloran replied calmly.

Tark suddenly ducked into the storeroom, water streaming from his cloak. "I saw the signal. Three quick flashes, evenly spaced."

"Then our guests approach as requested," Galloran replied. "No evidence of foul play."

"Aye," Tark confirmed, and slipped away into the darkness.

Rachel knew that Nedwin, Ferrin, Brin, and Nollin were scouting the area. Tark and Io were stationed in a neighboring outbuilding with horses ready for a getaway. They had worked hard to defend against a potential ambush. The visitors thought the meeting was taking place up the slope at the manor. At the last moment one of Bartley's sentries would divert them to the lower stable, where Kerick awaited to greet them.

After riding hard from the jungle's edge to the outer boundaries of Trensicourt, Rachel had spent two days living in a remote barn while Nedwin arranged the particulars for this meeting. Yesterday morning, before sunrise, she and her friends had arrived at the Wershon estate to temporarily take up residence in a large mill at one corner of the property. If this meeting went well, she might sleep in comfort before much longer.

"You're sure you want me at the meeting?" Rachel asked.

"Certain," Galloran replied. "These are men accustomed to solving problems through negotiation, but they will not be eager to surrender the kingdom. We must appear strong. A talented Edomic adept is a unique and intimidating weapon. Remember, if the opportunity arises, show your power by exerting control over them. Petrify them, put them on the ground—anything to make them feel vulnerable. The talent to command men is extremely rare and bespeaks a deep reservoir of power."

"All right," Rachel said, trying to sound like somebody he could rely on. Did Galloran suspect how terrified it made her to think that the outcome of this meeting might depend on how intimidating she seemed? Was he hearing her insecurities as she thought them? Maybe his attention was elsewhere. Or maybe he was kind enough to pretend he couldn't sense her anxiety.

Rachel noticed Bartley warily eyeing her acolyte robe through the gap in her cloak. At least they seemed to have an effect on him. He turned his attention back out the door and softly cleared his throat. "A lone rider approaches."

"We invited three guests," Galloran said. "Have they only sent a messenger?"

Rachel watched the hooded rider pull up to the stable, dismount, and lead his steed below the overhanging eaves. Not far from one of the dangling lanterns, Kerick approached the man and engaged him in conversation. After words were exchanged, Kerick took the reins and gestured for the man to enter the stable. He then faced away from the storage shed where Rachel hid and waved his arm twice over his head.

"There's the signal," Bartley whispered. "I suppose this means at least one of them came."

"How could they resist?" Galloran asked. "Trensicourt is currently run by strategists and compromisers, not men of action. Strategists need information. Compromisers require meetings. They had to send someone."

"Strategists also like traps," Bartley added. "These compromisers have an untrustworthy reputation."

Galloran gave a nod. "We'll remain on guard. Rachel, at the first sign of trouble, don't be afraid to use force."

Rachel told herself that she had trained for this. She had used Edomic in dicey situations before. But she had only commanded a person under pressure the night Kalia had attacked. Those commands had been urgent and reflexive. This would be a different sort of challenge: commanding a powerful enemy to prove a point. Would she be able to get it right?

Rachel raised the hood of her heavy cloak and took Galloran by the hand. She led him out into the downpour, with Bartley close behind and Io joining them. Rachel kept her eyes on the stable, but there was little to see. Kerick and the visitor had disappeared inside. Rain drummed against her hood. She tried to help Galloran avoid the worst puddles. By the time they reached the overhanging roof of the stable, their boots were caked with mud.

As Rachel led Galloran through the entryway, she got her first clear look at the visitor. An open area before the stalls had been swept, and a large table had been brought in. Food awaited, and drink. The smell of fresh rolls mingled with the inevitable odors of pent-up horses.

The visitor stood near the table. Tall and thin with stooped shoulders, he had a prominent, bony nose and wore a stern expression. A dagger hung from his belt, but no other weapon was apparent. He had hung his cloak on a peg and had replaced his hood with a large tricornered hat.

"Who has come?" Galloran whispered.

"Chancellor Copernum," Bartley and Rachel murmured in unison.

Kerick had led Copernum's large steed into a stall and was now rubbing it down. Copernum regarded the four newcomers in silence, his body still, his alert eyes in constant motion.

His gaze made Rachel uncomfortable. He was renowned for his clever mind. He had tried to have Jason killed.

"Welcome, Chancellor," Galloran said, doing his best to sound upbeat with his raspy voice, ruined by the same caustic powder that had blinded him. "Thank you for accepting my invitation."

"How could I ignore an opportunity to meet the renowned heir to Trensicourt?" Copernum replied dryly. "Bartley, good of you to host the evening, although the accommodations leave something to be desired."

"Lay the blame on me," Galloran insisted as Rachel led him to the table. "The viscount offered his home. Considering the purpose of our discussion, I opted for discretion over comfort."

"An option to which you have undoubtedly grown accustomed," Copernum replied.

Io took Galloran's wet cloak. Galloran sat down, and Copernum mirrored him on the far side of the table. "I have endured some trying years," Galloran agreed amiably, as if missing the condescension behind the remark.

"I'm afraid I don't know your companions," Copernum said.

Io collected Rachel's cloak.

"This is Rachel, a Beyonder and a skilled Edomic adept," Galloran said.

Copernum turned his shrewd eyes to her with sudden interest. "She wears the robe of the oracles."

Galloran had suggested she wear the fine robe because it might make her appear more impressive. She hoped she wouldn't come across as an imposter instead.

"Rachel has trained with multiple masters," Galloran said. "The man hanging our cloaks is Io, future chief of the wild clan of drinlings. And you met Kerick, of the Amar Kabal, who is tending to your horse."

"You travel with quite a menagerie," Copernum said.

"You came alone," Galloran replied.

Copernum nodded, picking up a dark roll and cracking it open. "The invitation did not allow for bodyguards. The Grand Duke of Edgemont sends his regards, as does the regent." He took a bite.

"Was the weather too much for them?" Galloran asked.

"They have empowered me to speak on their behalf," Copernum answered. "You have a reputation of impeccable honor, but years in Felrook have been known to alter a man. The duke and the regent did not feel it was prudent for the three of us to meet unguarded in a place of your choosing."

"Regrettable, but I understand," Galloran said.

Copernum poured himself a drink and took a sip. "Tell me: Why, after all these years, has the Blind King decided to come out of hiding?" The comment was clearly meant to imply that Copernum had known all along that Galloran was concealed in plain sight as the Blind King. Rachel supposed it was possible, since Maldor had known, and Copernum reportedly had strong connections with Felrook.

Galloran touched his blindfold. "I did not wish to emerge from exile until I felt whole and ready for the responsibilities ahead of me."

"Are you whole, then?" Copernum asked.

"As close as I can ever expect to be," Galloran replied. He half turned in his chair. "Rachel, Bartley, Io, please relax and be seated."

Rachel realized that she still stood near Galloran's chair, riveted into stillness by the tension underlying the conversation. She sat down to one side of Galloran; Bartley sat on the other. Io claimed the seat at the end of the table near Rachel.

Across the table Copernum set aside his roll. He leaned forward, narrow shoulders hunched, eyes intent. "What do you propose?"

"I am here to claim my birthright," Galloran said. "For years you and Dolan have managed Trensicourt in my absence. You have my gratitude for keeping Trensicourt independent. Now, for the good of the kingdom, I hope you will help make this a smooth transition."

Copernum folded his hands. "Do you believe that your ascension to the throne will benefit Trensicourt?"

"Who else could properly fill the role?" Galloran asked. "No other sons of Dromidus remain. I am the undisputed heir."

"If you are the rightful king, I don't see why you need my permission."

"Don't play the fool with me, Copernum," Galloran said. "We never knew each other well. As I recall, the former Marquess of Jansington was a distant cousin of yours. Lacking heirs, he bequeathed his title to you over his nephews. You and I only met briefly during the latter years of my father's reign. Yet I have observed you from afar. You combine a scholarly background with a knack for deft political maneuvering. You and Dolan have nearly rid the nobility of all who openly speak against Felrook. Nobles who hope to appease the emperor will be reluctant to install me as their new monarch."

"Would they be right to worry?" Copernum asked.

"I don't intend to court the emperor," Galloran said flatly. "I will not pay him tribute. I will not let him dictate policy. I will not ignore his aggressive expansion. I will not enter into lopsided compromises. Those kingdoms who have tried to appease Felrook have all fallen. A gentle approach toward the rising empire will inevitably bring an end to our sovereignty."

"Have you considered that perhaps you are a decade too late?"

Copernum asked. "Have you recognized that the only remaining option besides aligning ourselves with the emperor is obliteration?"

"I will never submit to Maldor," Galloran stated.

"Interesting. I have been led to believe that you no longer require that blindfold."

"I accepted eyes from Maldor," Galloran admitted assertively. "He offered them years ago. I finally claimed them. But I made no pledge of fealty."

"And yet some of his top spies now share your eyes," Copernum chuckled. "How do you intend to resist an enemy who can watch your every move?"

"With a blindfold in place."

"Then why accept the eyes?"

"For those moments when I need to see in order to kill."

"Very dramatic," Copernum approved glibly. "Tell me, why are you wearing the blindfold now?"

"Partly as a courtesy," Galloran said. "I was unsure whether you would want the emperor to know we had conversed."

"You told me not to play the fool," Copernum said. "Let me be direct. The emperor is not my foe. I have kept Trensicourt intact by maintaining positive relations with Felrook. I have nothing to hide from Maldor. If the emperor cares to know, I would happily divulge all we discuss this night. I would not do so out of disloyalty toward Trensicourt. I would do it to protect Trensicourt. I would do it so that men who care about Trensicourt might be permitted to run this kingdom rather than callous imperial governors."

Galloran began untying his blindfold. "By your description, are you not becoming an imperial governor yourself?" Galloran removed the blindfold, revealing one brown eye, the other blue. His gaze was hard.

Rachel did not appreciate the reminder that agents of

Maldor were observing all that Galloran saw. She loved and trusted Galloran, but the thought made those mismatched eyes seem sinister. At least they weren't focused on her.

Copernum looked mildly disconcerted by the stare. "Dolan does not take orders from Felrook. Neither do I. We make certain allowances to preserve the peace."

"I know plenty about the allowances you have made," Galloran said. "More than enough to label you a traitor and have you hanged."

Copernum bristled, but he held his tongue for a moment. He took a bite from a fat wedge of cheese and chewed thoughtfully before responding. "I wondered how long it would take before this discussion turned unpleasant. You have not yet been crowned, sir. In fact, you have left your alleged right to the throne unclaimed for years. Currently, Dolan is custodian of this kingdom and holds the highest legal authority."

"Are you insinuating I will have to take Trensicourt by force?" Galloran asked.

Copernum shrugged casually. "Do I think you could? Possibly. Martyrs tend to win the best reputations. As far as this kingdom is concerned, you have been dead for more than ten years. Your repute has grown accordingly. You have been aggrandized into a folk hero, more legend than man. Your agents have whispered rumors foretelling your return for months, and the rumors have taken hold. The city is waiting for you, watching for you, many not believing, but most hoping. I expect you could rally many to your cause."

"Not enough?" Galloran asked.

"That depends. As of yet I have refrained from planting rumors of my own. Rumors that Galloran sold his eyes and his loyalty to the emperor to buy his freedom. Rumors that Galloran has been living in imperial luxury while the people of Trensicourt have toiled in doubt and fear. Rumors that Galloran lost his mind at Felrook, leaving him driven to fight Maldor at all cost, even if it means destroying the kingdom in a hopeless war. These and many other stories could be circulated. In Trensicourt nothing moves faster than rumors."

"Why have you refrained?"

"I was not yet sure whether you were my adversary. We do not have to be enemies. It is likely that you could lead Trensicourt far more effectively than Dolan. Of course, if we become enemies, I will have to remind you that many of the best fighting men of Trensicourt are unswervingly loyal to their liege lords, the nobles. And the nobles are loyal to Dolan. And to me. Naturally, if we needed imperial aid to maintain control of Trensicourt, Felrook would gladly intervene."

Galloran finally began to lose his temper. "If you bring imperial troops into Trensicourt, they will never leave."

"We have never allowed an imperial host into the city for that precise reason," Copernum hurriedly agreed. "We would only consider such rash action if our government were threatened." He grinned like a shark.

Galloran gave a nod. One nostril twitched. His whole body looked tense, ready to snap. He almost managed to keep his tone conversational. "You have spoken plainly. Let me be equally clear. I have already been in communication with many of the lesser lords, as well as some key members of the upper aristocracy. You might be surprised how many of the blue bloods remain loyal to the crown. If you force my hand, tomorrow I will offer an ultimatum to the nobles of Trensicourt—side with their king or perish as traitors. I have no intention of waging open war to reclaim my kingdom. My foes will be eliminated, and we will see where their leaderless minions stand afterward. There are insufficient imperial troops to reach this region in time to hinder me. If you were foolish enough to try to summon them, even your most stalwart supporters would abandon you. A revolution won't take months or weeks. It will require three days."

"Well spoken," Copernum conceded. "A skeptic might wonder how you propose to collectively assassinate the most powerful men in the kingdom."

Galloran glanced at Rachel. With a jolt of panic she realized he was asking for a demonstration. Something to intimidate Copernum. The tension in the room was palpable, both sides trying to seem calm and in control, each side wondering how much the other was bluffing. The negotiation could go either way. A lot was riding on how she performed.

Rachel told herself that she had practiced these techniques for months. But what if she pushed too hard and the suggestion failed? What if she didn't push hard enough? Copernum was a cunning man. What if he had studied how to resist Edomic suggestions? What if he was immune?

The moment was passing. Doing nothing would be the same as failure. Mustering her will and relying on her training, Rachel spoke a pointed Edomic suggestion. Copernum flopped to the floor, striking his cheek on the edge of the table on his way down. Relieved that the directive had worked so well, she spoke again, and his body went rigid. Io crouched beside him and ran a forefinger across his throat.

Rachel briefly met eyes with Galloran. His glowing approval reflected her quiet elation, reinforcing the feeling of triumph. Then she thought about displacers watching her little display through those same eyes, and the emotion was tainted.

Copernum remained immobile for longer than normal. A full

ten seconds elapsed before he arose, looking pale and shaken, a bruise starting to form on his cheek. "A compelling exhibition," he sniffed, letting his worried gaze dance between Rachel and Galloran. He reclaimed his seat, brushed off his sleeves, and tried to regain his composure.

"I invite skeptics to doubt my capabilities," Galloran said, his voice iron. "But any skeptic would have a poor knowledge of Trensicourt if he hoped to stand against the tide of humanity that will rise up to welcome their king home."

"What do you expect from me?" Copernum demanded.

"I don't want my kingdom in an uproar," Galloran said. "I want my kingdom united. I am willing to concede that, however misguided your dealings with Felrook have been, you may have had the best interest of Trensicourt at heart. My kingdom remains independent, at least in name, and for this I am grateful. If you, Dolan, and the nobles you influence welcome the return of your king and support a quick, smooth transition, you will retain your titles and holdings. You will enjoy a full pardon for any past misdeeds, and need only look to your future behavior with any fear of reprisal."

"That is your offer?" Copernum asked.

"In essence."

"Am I to believe that I will remain chancellor?"

"Another presently has claim to that office," Galloran said.

"Lord Jason abandoned his post," Copernum reminded gently.

"Lord Jason never resigned," Galloran corrected. "He has been on errands with me. You will continue to serve as chancellor until Lord Jason returns. Once Jason rejoins us, you would be welcome to challenge him for the position. Your other titles and holdings will remain as they stand."

Copernum leaned forward. "You will confirm our titles and

holdings in writing? You will document an unconditional immunity regarding any perceived injustices of the past?"

"Indeed. In return I will require full cooperation. Not just assistance arranging my prompt coronation, but also support of my strategies going forward."

Copernum narrowed his eyes and nodded slightly. "As a future collaborator, might I be entitled to a preview of your intentions?"

"It is no mystery," Galloran said. "I will stand firmly against Felrook. More firmly than Trensicourt has ever stood."

Copernum glanced around the room. "Are those present meant to imply you have support from the Amar Kabal, the drinlings, and the children of Certius?"

"Trensicourt will not stand alone against Felrook," Galloran replied. "Time is precious, Copernum. You have tonight to confer with your cohorts. I expect an unambiguous response on the morrow. Anything less will be deemed an act of treason against your rightful king, punishable as such."

Copernum bowed his head in thought. "The emperor will be sorely displeased."

Galloran straightened in his chair. "I vow to do much more than displease him."

Copernum looked up. "I applaud your nerve. If I seem less than ecstatic, please understand, my reluctance does not grow out of a love for the emperor. A tenuous peace has been cultivated with Felrook for years, which has enabled us to prosper while other kingdoms crumble."

"What you call peace the emperor calls postponement," Galloran said. "Aside from the Seven Vales, we are the best-defended sovereignty in all of Lyrian. He would rather wait to crush Trensicourt until he can focus all his clout on the task. That day is not far off. It will come after Kadara falls. We must take action before we become the last kingdom of men to topple."

Copernum folded his hands on the table. "I comprehend your terms. How shall I deliver the reply?"

"I will station representatives at the covered bridge over Cobble Creek. Your response should arrive by noon, carried by no more than two riders. Thereafter, we will confer accordingly."

Copernum rose. "I expect all will be as you hope, my prince. You seem as capable and committed as your reputation warrants, undiminished by your past hardships. By way of explanation for my adversarial conduct tonight, there was concern that Felrook could have left you unbalanced. Rightful heir or not, Dolan and I had no intention of handing Trensicourt over to a madman or to a broken exile who had clearly been corrupted by the emperor. These times demand a watchful eye and a steady hand. You have more than allayed my concerns. I look forward to serving with you once we take care of the formalities." He bowed deeply, removing his hat and pausing for a beat with his head down.

Galloran stood, as did the others around the table. "If all proceeds as you describe, I look forward to our partnership leading Trensicourt into a brighter future."

Copernum nodded at the others in turn, his gaze lingering longest on Rachel. She found a wary respect in his eyes.

Kerick led Copernum's horse from the stall. The chancellor put on his cloak, adjusted his hood, and mounted up. He bid them farewell and departed into the rainy night.

Rachel finally relaxed as Copernum passed out of sight. If the choice were hers, she hoped never to see him again.

Galloran replaced his blindfold. The incessant patter of rainfall had receded into white noise during the meeting, but it gained renewed prominence in the silence. An unseen horse in one of the stalls stamped and whinnied.

"All clear," called a voice from above, startling Rachel. She looked up and saw Nedwin dangling from a rafter, the length of his body reducing the drop to less than eight feet. He let go and landed on the floor in a crouch.

"I didn't know you were up there," Rachel said.

"That was the idea," Nedwin replied, crossing to Galloran. "My task was to monitor our guests. I took up my position just after the meeting began."

"We never agreed to your entering the stable," Galloran said.

"I had to hear," Nedwin said. "I stayed quiet. You didn't want Copernum to see me. He never saw me."

"I didn't want you to see him," Galloran responded. "That could not have been easy."

Nedwin forced a smile. There was no warmth in it. Rachel could understand. Copernum had held Nedwin prisoner and tortured him for years. Copernum had also harmed Nedwin's family, stealing away his elder brother's title by defeating him in a battle of wits. "I'll tell you what was easy—the negotiation. Much too easy."

"Happy to install me as king so he can betray me later?" Galloran asked.

"Sounded that way," Kerick said. "After issuing all those pardons, you'll be surrounded by enemies. The majority of your ruling class will be spying for Felrook."

"Agreed," Galloran said. "Fortunately, I don't intend to wage this war with secrets. Nor do I intend to remain in Trensicourt for long. I need Trensicourt for manpower. My faith is in the prophecy. Once I am crowned, all my effort will go into mobilizing for war."

"To that end you need control of the kingdom," Nedwin said. "Quickly and without bloodshed."

"To leave evil men unpunished and in positions of power is a grievous cost," Galloran said heavily. "The injustice sickens me. Yet I see no alternative. Not given our time frame and our goals."

"Rotten apples stay spoiled," Nedwin said. "Copernum and his allies will hang themselves with future crimes."

"Let's hope those crimes aren't the end of us," Bartley added.

"The viscount has a point," Galloran said. "We can't be too careful over the coming weeks. Including tonight. Our location and numbers have been observed by the most dangerous man in the current government. A surprise attack is possible. Stormy or not, we should make haste to our next temporary residence."

Rachel sighed softly. It would be nice to stay here, warm and dry, at least for the night. But she supposed that if staying elsewhere might prevent them from being slaughtered in their sleep, she probably shouldn't complain.

CHAPTER 6

DURNA

The walled city of Durna was positioned more than two miles upslope from the coast of the Inland Sea. The many buildings near the fortified waterfront were connected to the city by a protected highway. The walls around the port rose thirty feet, the walls along the highway were perhaps half as high, and the city walls soared to more than sixty feet.

Jason was beginning to catch on that the major cities of Lyrian had all been constructed to withstand invasions. Maldor was clearly not the first threat these kingdoms had faced.

The battle-worn fortifications of Durna were gouged and scarred. Mismatched stonework showed where broken sections had been replaced. Construction was underway down by the port, restoring shattered battlements. Although the ancient walls loomed tall and thick, anchored to imposing towers, they hadn't done their job. The king of Durna had surrendered to Maldor. He and his family were currently prisoners of the emperor.

"The port gates are the only entrances," Jasher explained. "There is one on the west side and another on the east, both heavily guarded. The only access to the city proper is to follow the highway up from the port."

"There have to be hidden ways through or under those walls," Aram said, surveying the city. "Durna is too big. Nobles. Criminals. They would grow weary of taking the long route. They would demand private passages. The city has stood for too long."

Bat, one of the two drinlings who had accompanied them on horseback, folded his brawny arms. "You're probably right. But we don't know of any." After traveling with the group for less than a week, the drinlings had already lost their accents.

"And we can't steal a ship unless we access the port," added the other drinling, a solid man named Ux.

"Can't we just stroll in through a gate along with the crowd?" Jason asked.

"Possibly," Jasher said. "Security will be tighter here than what you have encountered in the past."

"A governor called Duke Ashby oversees Durna for Maldor," Drake explained. "He is competent and driven."

Ux peered at the city through a spyglass. "We've found security to be a serious obstacle. Of course the entrances are heavily monitored, but we've witnessed wandering patrols and random searches as well."

"We've been entering the city by water," Bat said. "One at a time. Swimming. We reach the docks from the sea, looping around the huge defensive breakwaters in the small hours of the night. A two-hour swim at a brisk pace. The harbor is well guarded."

Jason looked out at the harbor. From their current vantage in a grove of tall, slender trees, they had an elevated view of the west side of town. The water of the Inland Sea looked gray-green under the predawn glow from the overcast sky. The port walls did not end at the water. Rather they extended out into the sea, encircling the harbor, with only a relatively narrow gap to allow vessels access.

"Too hard of a swim for us?" Jason asked.

"I expect," Bat said. "Drinlings don't tire."

"What about a small boat?" Farfalee wondered.

"The harbor mouth is well illuminated," Ux said. "The risk is great even as a lone swimmer."

"Then we'll probably have to brave the gates," Jasher said. "Which poses some problems. The whole empire is on the lookout for Lord Jason. Corinne is too regal and lovely. And we seedfolk are almost as conspicuous as you drinlings."

Jason glanced at the drinlings. Their golden-brown coloring was just outside the normal spectrum of human skin tones. And the coppery tint of their irises looked a little too metallic.

"Which is why we enter Durna quietly and lie low," Ux said. "Our kind would be detained on sight."

"My amar is gone," Drake said. "I can cut my hair short and make sure my clothes cover the scar at the back of my neck. Farfalee can wear her hair long and just not roll it up over her seed."

"I suppose if I trim my hair shorter and don't roll it I could pass as human," Jasher said. He raked his fingers through his long tresses. "Let it barely touch my shoulders, subtly cover the amar without giving me away. I dislike the feel of it, but I've done it before."

"We'll need nondescript clothing," Farfalee mentioned.

"These robes don't blend?" Jason asked.

Aram began to wheeze and grunt. Veins bulged in his thick neck. He backed away into the grove, looking for some privacy as he shrank with the veiled dawn. A couple of the horses neighed at his approach.

Jasher looked around. "I feel too exposed here."

"We have operated mostly from the woods on this side of town," Bat said. "We'll see trouble coming long before they see us."

There were numerous groves on this wild part of the slope above the Inland Sea. Jason and the others had taken up position here in the night, after weaving between some of the farms and outlying settlements south of Durna.

Aram returned, adjusting a smaller set of robes, face damp with perspiration. "You could let me go in alone and try to ferret out a secret entrance. I have experience with this sort of thing. We have plenty of money for bribes."

Farfalee shook her head. "I think Jason had it right from the start." Jason tried to resist a proud grin as she continued. "We should flow into town with the morning crowd, in ones and twos. People come here to buy and trade. They come looking for work. They come for entertainment. The imperial guardsmen may be watching for Jason, but almost certainly none here have ever seen him. We dress as peasants. We look humble and hungry, and walk into the city with the rest of the unwashed masses."

"Bat and I could bring the swords," Ux offered. "Jason's and Corinne's. Even sheathed they would draw interest. They look too fine. Unsheathed they would immediately give you away. We'll swim them in."

"What about my armor?" Aram asked. "My sword?"

"Your sword would drag us straight to the bottom," Bat said.

"We could use it to anchor a ship," Ux grunted.

"I could pose as a wealthy merchant," Drake offered. "Well fed, well dressed, a debonair peddler of oversized weaponry."

Farfalee laughed derisively. "Why not portray a wealthy noble on a pilgrimage? We could supply you with riches and hire servants. Our weapons could be disguised in your armory."

"Don't give me ideas," Drake warned, eyes flashing with relish.

Jason couldn't shake the feeling that they were making this harder than it needed to be. "Do we have to take everything into the city?" he asked. "I mean, we're only going there to steal a ship and leave. What if we reunited on the water?"

Farfalee nodded pensively. "We would have to get hold of a smaller craft outside the city and rendezvous beyond the harbor mouth."

"There are many options," Bat said. "Finding a small craft would not be difficult."

"What if Farfalee, Corinne, and one of the drinlings met us on the water?" Jasher proposed. "They could bring Aram's gear, the torivorian swords, and the orantium. We shouldn't need the globes for our hijacking. Success will depend on slipping away quietly."

"I would prefer to help cover the hijacking with my bow," Farfalee said.

"That would be ideal," Jasher said. "It might not be wise. You and Corinne are too attractive. You'll stand out more than the rest of us going into the city. With a tireless drinling on the oars, a rendezvous at sea might be a reasonable solution."

"We will need to know how to meet," Farfalee said.

"I can still swim into the city," Ux offered. "Then I can swim out with the details. Bat could stay with you. Then the two of us can help you manage your boat."

Farfalee sighed. "My bow could be useful inside the city, but I admit that this alternative would reduce the overall risk."

"I'll stay close to Jason," Jasher promised. "Aram and Drake can make their way into the city separately."

"So no servants for me?" Drake verified. "Not even one? Maybe an older fellow? Or a kid?"

"Maybe next time," Jasher consoled. "For the present, we need

89

to locate some apparel."

"I'll go," Aram offered. "When I'm small, I'm the least conspicuous of us."

"I'll follow him," Drake said. "The rest of you lie low and try to stay out of trouble."

The following morning Jason trudged toward the western gate. He wore coarse, itchy trousers and a long shirt with laces over the chest. His dingy old boots had hard soles and were falling apart. Six copper drooma clinked in one pocket.

He followed a wagon and a group of people on foot. The wagon kicked up dust, which he did not try to avoid, since he knew that whatever clung to him would improve his disguise.

Aram had cautioned him to enter the city as part of a group. The crowd would pressure the guardsmen to hurry and be less thorough.

Jason did his best not to glance back at Jasher, who trailed him by a few hundred yards. Jasher was unarmed except for a knife. The seedman toted several pots and pans, as if he meant to sell them. His hair had been shortened to barely reach his shoulders, and he wore a flat twilled cap.

The port wall loomed ever closer. Uniformed guards patrolled the top, coming in and out of view among the battlements. The others on the road paid little heed to Jason.

At last the wagon slowed and then stopped in the shadow of the open gates. A bespectacled man in a raised booth watched the proceedings with a narrow gaze, quill in hand, parchment ready. Jason counted five soldiers on the ground.

The man in the wagon began shouting answers about his cargo to the man with the quill. A pair of guardsmen searched his wagon, looking underneath and examining the bales and barrels in the bed.

None of the people on foot were allowed to proceed without questioning. A line formed as the quantity of people seeking admittance outnumbered the guards. Jason felt nervous as he took his place in line. He struggled to keep his expression neutral. He avoided eye contact with the guards but tried not to deliberately look away from them either.

The wagon was waved through, freeing up a couple of the guards. The line began to move faster. A husky man with a thick mustache and stubbly jowls confronted Jason. "Name?"

"Lucas, son of Travis."

"State your business."

"I have to find Gulleg the barber. I have a bad tooth."

The guard grunted and squinted. "You're not familiar. Where are you from?"

"I'm up from Laga."

"Laga? Quite a trip."

Jason rubbed the side of his jaw. "A man back home tried to help but made it worse. I was told Gulleg is the best. I've been walking two days straight. Can't sleep with the pain."

"Duration of your stay?"

"I'm hoping Gulleg can see me today."

The guard harrumphed softly. "You were told right. Gulleg is good with teeth. Took care of my brother last year. Hope you brought money."

"Six drooma," Jason said, jangling his pocket proudly.

"Six?" the guard snickered. "Gulleg is no country barber. But he does have a soft spot for the downtrodden. He might find a way for you to sweat off the difference. You keep out of trouble. And keep off the streets. We don't tolerate vagrants."

The hefty guard moved away, his attention shifting to a lanky man with a handcart. Jason strolled past the gate, praying that he looked less conspicuous than he felt. The exchange had gone as planned, right down to him not having quite enough money.

Jason was not supposed to wait for Jasher. The seedman would follow as he chose. The next step was to find the Salt Sea Inn, a small establishment about ten buildings inland from the waterfront, on a road called Galley Street. The port of Durna alone had more structures and businesses than many of the towns Jason had seen in Lyrian.

The main road leading away from the gate was broad and busy. Up ahead a pair of mounted soldiers was squabbling with a man, insisting he move his wagon. The teamster kept maintaining that he needed to unload supplies.

Deciding he would rather steer clear of confrontations with soldiers involved, Jason turned down a side street. On one side of the lane a line had formed near a dilapidated cart, where a bony woman ladled chowder from a deep vat. The beige concoction looked thick and chunky. It smelled delicious.

Jason had copper in his pocket, and he was hungry, but his orders were to proceed directly to the inn. He continued down the street, noticing other carts on the sides selling goods or food, although none were as busy as the chowder cart.

Not one building in the port area stood taller than three stories, unless you counted the pair of bell towers near the water. The structures tended to be low, square, and solid—some residences, some businesses.

After winding around for some time, and asking directions twice, Jason found Galley Street. It was narrow, grimy, and crowded, and it featured lots of inns. The air smelled of salt water and burned food.

Not long after reaching Galley Street, Jason found a battered board hanging over a nondescript entrance. Weathered and cracked, the light-blue board held the words "Salt Sea Inn," hand painted in black by an amateur. The establishment looked narrower than many of the inns on the street, and among the least prosperous. The Salt Sea Inn had small, grimy windows, and the unremarkable door was six steps down from street level.

Jason descended the steps and entered. The common room reeked of fried fish, sweat, and wood smoke. Craggy men slumped at tables or at the bar, many of them alone. Jason saw no women, and no groups larger than three. He caught a few sidelong glances, surly looks that hinted he didn't belong.

Without a plan, Jason would have backed out onto the street and found another inn. But he was supposed to find the curly-haired barkeeper and ask for a room with a view of the coast. That was how Bat had explained Jason would connect with Nia and the other drinlings.

Behind the bar a man with curly brown hair was wiping a mug with a dirty rag. A tiny hoop pierced one ear, and tattoos crawled across his wiry forearms. Jason crossed to him and leaned against the bar, hoping he looked less out of place than he felt.

"What'll it be?" the barman asked.

"I need a room with a view of the coast," Jason said.

The barman smirked. "Nothing like that here, mate. Ashley can show you what we have. Ashley!"

"One moment," a female voice answered from the kitchen.

A man seated at the bar swiveled to face Jason. He had a droopy face with rough skin and three parallel scars on his jaw. Silver teeth glinted as he spoke. "What are you playing at, bumpkin?"

"Excuse me?" Jason said.

"Look at the manners on this one!" the man chuckled, brushing shaggy hair back from his brow. "You smell like dung. Run back to your farm, boy. This place is for men of the sea."

Jason noticed that the comments had drawn the attention of some of the other customers. They appeared to share the sentiment. At best they looked amused by the prospect of trouble. Several expressions seemed hostile. Should he try to ignore the insult? Should he stand up for himself? He didn't want to draw too much attention.

"I could use bodies in my rooms," the barman intervened.

The man at the bar waved away the comment. "I can leave his body wherever you like. Go on, hayseed, scurry out of here. Last chance."

"Morley, I can't have you running off paying—"

"I'll cover the cost of the room," Morley barked. "Unless you'd side with a stranger over a regular?"

Everyone in the room was watching intently. The curly-haired barman shrugged. "It's your money, Morley." The barkeeper locked eyes with Jason. "You had better go."

Jason was at a loss. He needed to connect with Nia. But if he started a fight, it could lead to lots of unwanted attention. Soldiers might get involved. Also, alone and unarmed he would probably end up dead.

"Is there a problem here?" asked a voice from behind.

Jason glanced back to find Jasher crossing the room. The seedman had already discarded his pots and pans. Jason felt relief at the sight of him, and also a bit embarrassed that he had messed up a simple task by seeming too out of place.

"What's it to you?" asked Morley.

"I sent my servant ahead to book a room," Jasher replied.

Jason took the cue and gave a shamefaced half bow toward Jasher.

Morley looked over at Jason and coughed out a harsh laugh.

"Fine servant you found! What are you, brothers? Cousins? You two had better shove off. Take your comedy elsewhere. You picked the wrong inn." Morley turned and hunched over the bar as if the discussion were finished. He picked up a bone off the platter before him and nibbled at the scant remaining meat.

Jasher approached the man calmly, his expression serious but not overtly threatening. Most other men in the room watched with interest, some hiding their attention better than others. Jasher stopped directly behind Morley. "Would you care to explain yourself?"

"To a farmhand?" The man spun and stabbed a dagger at Jasher. The seedman twisted, avoiding the thrust, and grabbed Morley's extended arm at the wrist. With his free hand Jasher seized Morley by his shaggy hair and flung him to the floor.

Still clutching his dagger, Morley glared up at Jasher.

"Stay down," Jasher warned. "Isn't there enough trouble in your life without seeking more?"

"Who do you think—" Morley began as he started to rise. He didn't get more out, because Jasher kicked him hard in the ankle, a quick sweeping motion that dumped Morley back onto the ground.

Jason managed not to flinch away from the sudden flurry of motion. He tried to watch the crowd in case somebody attacked Jasher from behind. He noticed a bottle on the bar that might serve as a better weapon than nothing if things escalated.

"Don't try to get up again, or you'll lose the option," Jasher threatened. "Crawl out of here. Don't provoke strangers. You never know who you're speaking with."

"You somebody important?" Morley mocked. "Growing some nice carrots this year?"

Jasher's expression remained stern but controlled. "You assume too much, friend. I know what you are. I know what this place is. In your line of work, have you never played a part? Have you never dressed or acted out of character?" Jasher looked around the room in disgust. "How raw are the amateurs in this town if the patrons of an establishment such as this assume everyone is as they appear? Are we your first visitors from beyond the region?"

The crowd seemed mildly embarrassed. The reaction made Jason relax a bit. They might manage to bluff their way out of this after all. Morley was temporarily at a loss for words. When he spoke, there was uncertainty in his tone. "We get word when talent comes in from abroad."

"Depends on the talent," Jasher scoffed. "My business was not with anyone in this room. This may astonish you, but in my line of work, depending on the stakes, I don't always want my business known. And now I have a roomful of attention. I had heard better things of Durna than this. I want your full name, Morley."

Morley put away his knife. Fear twinkled behind his eyes. "Don't be that way. I was just having a laugh. Maybe the disguise worked too well."

Jasher met eyes with many of the men in the room. "Is this space secure?"

He got a few nods and grunted affirmations.

Jasher turned back to Morley. "It better be. So help me, friend, if this sparks trouble, you'll answer to fiercer men than I."

Morley got to his feet. "These are good lads. You're in safe company."

Jasher gave a curt nod. "Then let's pretend we never spoke and that none of us have heard of the Order of the Noose."

At this last phrase Jason noticed many eyes widen. A majority of the men turned away. Morley set some drooma on the counter and hastily limped toward the door. Jasher posed like he was considering what to do next. Jason tried not to draw attention.

The bartender cleared his throat. "My apologies for your trouble, sir. You're welcome to a room here, on the house."

Jasher surveyed the area. Nobody met his gaze. "I'd prefer to pay," he finally said in a lowered voice. "I'm more at ease when others are indebted to me."

The barkeeper bobbed his head. "As you will. Ashley?"

A woman scurried around the counter, eager to please. She had reddish hair and a broad build, and wore a conciliatory smile. "Right this way, if you please."

Jason followed Jasher, keeping silent as he tried to play the role of humble servant. Ashley led them into a comfortable room, closing the door behind them. She mentioned a couple of amenities as she handed Jasher the key. He thanked her.

"Did you have to mention the Order?" she asked.

Jasher shrugged. "The circumstances required intimidation. I had to sound like somebody to be reckoned with. You'll notice I didn't directly claim membership."

"Well, you certainly got their attention," Ashley said.

"She knows what we're doing here?" Jason verified.

"Ashley and her husband are part of the resistance here in Durna," Jasher said. "They're harboring a third of our drinlings."

"Sorry about the cold reception," Ashley said. "The local smugglers have claimed the Salt Sea Inn as their own. The arrangement has advantages. Since most of the aristocrats smuggle goods to some degree, the smugglers keep the authorities from snooping around much. But the clientele can be unruly, and lately they've been more territorial than ever."

"So the Order of the Noose is a smuggling ring?" Jason checked.

"A secret order," Jasher said. "Most laymen have never heard the name. It is never mentioned casually. Even the boldest smugglers only refer to the Order with reverence."

Ashley folded her arms. "Now every smuggler in town will be wondering what business the Order has here."

"Better than them speculating about seedmen and drinlings," Jasher said. "The Order seldom, if ever, crosses the emperor. If word trickles up to the local soldiers, it shouldn't create much of a stir. Your patrons will be curious, but they won't look too hard. The Order has too deadly a reputation."

"Unless some of them decide you were bluffing," Ashley warned.

"We'll keep out of sight," Jasher said simply. "There will be nothing to investigate."

"Let's hope not," Ashley said. "Stay put for now. We'll move you to your actual quarters after the inn gets quiet." She exited the room. Jasher bolted the door.

"You were great back there," Jason said. "Thanks for bailing me out. I was making a mess of things."

"No harm done," Jasher said. "It's to your credit that you seem out of place among those men."

"Now we wait?"

Jasher gave a nod. "We hope for a long, uneventful day."

Jasher got his wish. It was the small hours of the night before a cloaked figure holding a candle jostled Jason awake. Wiping his eyes, Jason accepted a hand as the figure helped him to his feet.

The figure was more than half a head shorter than him. The hood flipped back, and Jason recognized Nia. Jasher stood behind her.

"I heard you were winning friends today," she told Jason with a smile. Nia looked older, well into her thirties. She was as fit as ever, but her features had noticeably leaned out and matured. Nia had looked to be in her early twenties when he'd last seen her. He supposed that with a life expectancy not much more than two years, such changes were inevitable.

"I have a way with smugglers," Jason replied.

"Me too," she said. "It's called hiding. Let's get you to safer quarters."

They moved out into the hall. The few undersized windows were tightly shuttered. Nia led them to some stairs, then down another hall. They stopped at a grimy window that overlooked a cramped, filthy courtyard with a single door. It looked like part of an alley that had been walled in by buildings.

Nia opened the window, climbed out, dangled, and dropped. Jason did likewise, followed by Jasher. Nia jerked her chin at the door. "Looks like a back door to one of the surrounding businesses. It's actually the front door to a collection of rooms with no opening out to the street. Just this entrance and a hatch up to the roof. A perfect spot to lie low."

Nia used a key to open the door. A pair of broad, heavily muscled drinlings stood guard just inside, swords ready. Taking a small oil lamp from a shelf, Nia led Jason and Jasher past the stolid guards, then up two flights of stairs and through a doorway to a windowless room.

While Nia closed the door, Jason and Jasher sat down on a cot. She flung her cloak over the back of a chair and sat as well.

"How are the others?" Jasher asked.

"Aram and Drake arrived safely," she confirmed. "They didn't pick any fights with locals."

"He started it," Jason complained.

"We know," Nia assured him. "The owners are rightfully chagrined. Their regular customers keep creating problems for those involved with their secret enterprises. A few of the smugglers suspect something is going on around here and are curious. They prod and pry when they can."

"Sounds like this won't be a safe haven much longer," Jasher said.

Nia shrugged. "They should probably stop housing rebels here for a season. Any real suspicion from the authorities could prove disastrous. Farfalee and Corinne will meet us on the water?"

"Along with Bat and Ux," Jasher said. "I saw no warship in port."

"The *Valiant* is scheduled to arrive in three days."

"We'll take it the first night?" Jasher verified.

"That's the plan."

"We want a specific ship?" Jason asked.

Nia nodded. "An interceptor. Maldor constructed a fleet of eighty to win the western coast and conquer Meridon. He only built three to cover the Inland Sea. And three were all he has needed. Big warships have never sailed these waters. The smaller vessels are no match for an interceptor."

"Where are the other two interceptors?" Jasher inquired.

"They reliably sail between Angial, Russock, and Durna. They mostly patrol the coasts, stopping unpredictably at the smaller towns. Occasionally they check the islands. Except for Windbreak, of course. No sane person would set foot there."

"Do you know how to sail a ship?" Jason asked.

Nia waved a casual hand. "I try not to fret about the minor details."

"You're kidding," Jason checked.

"A few of us have some nautical experience," Nia said. "Mostly we'll rely on Aram's instruction."

"We have the required manpower?" Jasher asked.

"Yes," Nia replied. "We can spare eight fighters to help us get out of the harbor and still retain enough drinlings to crew the ship, along with eighteen fighters down below to pull the six emergency sweeps."

"Resources?" Jasher pursued.

"We're all armed, with supplies to spare. Three clans contributed warriors and funds. This will be the biggest drinling offensive in many lifetimes."

"Have things been quiet here in town?" Jason wondered.

"No revolt in years. After the city fell to Maldor, the serious dissenters were weeded out. The smugglers and traders support a healthy black market, much of which is unofficially permitted. The guardsmen have grown overconfident, the leadership complacent."

Jasher clapped his hands together. "Good tidings at last. The next few days should be uncomplicated."

"We'll need to stay out of sight," Nia said. "Surprise is crucial. If our foes catch wind of our plot, it won't work. They have ready means to block the harbor mouth, and troops to spare."

Jason frowned. "I hope no smugglers draw attention to us."

"We'll keep our ears open," Nia said.

"I'll help," Jason assured her. "Your hearing may have started to go." He had started teasing Nia about her age after she had begun to flaunt looking older than him back at Mianamon.

Nia leaped from her chair and slugged Jason on the shoulder, a response she had learned from Rachel. Except Nia hit a lot harder. If they worked at it, drinlings could pack on pounds of muscle overnight. Apparently, she had kept up with her exercising. "You using a razor yet?"

Jason grinned. This felt more familiar. The Nia he remembered had been brash and playful. "I'm glad you can still tease. I was worried you'd gotten all serious in your old age."

"Nope. Just smarter, stronger, and more mature. You wouldn't understand."

Jason looked around the windowless room. "I'm glad we'll get to rest for a few days. I'm sick of sleeping on the ground."

"We'll have time to strategize," Jasher said with relief.

"We'll watch and listen," Nia added.

"And sleep?" Jason asked hopefully, stretching his arms.

Nia gave a nod. "Those of us who need it."

CHAPTER 7

CORONATION

Not only did everyone in Trensicourt turn out for the procession, but many from the surrounding countryside had flooded into the city as well. Peasants and nobles, grandparents and youngsters, tradesmen and merchants and farmers alike lined the streets, rooftops, and balconies of the parade route. Bells sang throughout the great city. Vendors hawked baked treats, sweet nuts, and handkerchiefs emblazoned with the royal crest of Trensicourt. Spectators hollered and cheered, waving arms and handkerchiefs and banners. Many laughed. Many wept.

Arrayed in splendid ceremonial armor, the rightful king of Trensicourt rode at the front of the procession on an enormous white charger, gleaming like a knight from a fairy tale. Flanked by a mounted honor guard, eyes uncovered, Galloran took his time, waving and pausing to greet individuals packed along the edges of the road. Flowers and garlands snowed down from the crowded rooftops and terraces.

Behind Galloran came a cavalcade of five hundred horsemen, riding in formation. Thousands of foot soldiers followed, bearing pikes, axes, or swords. After them marched troupes of musicians, filling the air with music, followed by an athletic host of drummers and dancers, leaping and tumbling through the streets. Jesters capered about, pulling pranks and feigning clumsy accidents with one another. Jugglers followed, and acrobats, and men who performed startling feats with fire. At last rolled a gilded coach, from which Dolan hurled handfuls of bronze drooma into the jubilant crowd. A large honor guard protected the burnished vehicle.

Leaning against the stone railing of a palace balcony, Rachel surveyed the scene. From the lofty vantage, the crowd noise shrank to a distant roar, and the members of the parade were reduced to tiny figures gradually advancing in tidy patterns. She wished she could be closer to the excitement.

Ferrin peered through a long telescope. He passed it to Rachel, allowing her to zoom in and observe details. She found Galloran leaning down from his horse to shake the hand of an elated boy in the crowd.

"Quite a turnout on short notice," Ferrin approved.

"I had less than a week to make the arrangements," Copernum sniffed. "But the prospect of Galloran returning provided all the motivation necessary to prod extra effort out of everyone involved and to draw a prodigious crowd. I have never beheld the populace more swollen with emotion."

"They sure love him," Rachel said, lowering the telescope.

"How could they resist?" Copernum replied. "A figure of legend has descended from the heavens to walk among them. Most know little of Galloran the man. They are infatuated with the idea of him. They have swapped tall tales about him. They consider him the lost treasure of our kingdom. It will be interesting to study how their attitudes evolve as he dwells among them."

"For most men that would pose a larger problem," Ferrin said. "The reality of Galloran does much justice to the tales. I've never met a truer man or seen a more capable fighter."

Copernum gave an amused sneer. "This from a displacer."

Ferrin grinned. "It must sting to host me."

Rachel rolled her eyes. Ferrin and Copernum had taken jabs at each other during the entire procession. Why were men so in love with bravado? Didn't they get how pathetic it seemed? She glanced over her shoulder at the chancellor's apartments. The opulent residence occupied a sizable portion of one of the tallest towers of the castle. She thought about how Jason had slept here one night, narrowly escaping an assassination attempt.

"Because you killed my cousin?" Copernum asked dryly. "You and I were adversaries back then. Ever since you joined the rebellion I have found you much more intriguing."

Ferrin folded his arms. "I would have expected that my siding with Galloran would further diminish me in your eyes."

"On the contrary," Copernum insisted. "Don't misinterpret my previous affiliation with the emperor. I courted his good opinion to benefit Trensicourt. My posturing with Felrook was political maneuvering on behalf of the kingdom I serve, nothing more. If Galloran can keep us equally safe with less demeaning methods, I will support him wholeheartedly."

"You want me to believe that you're glad I'm here?" Ferrin asked.

Copernum plucked a leaf from a vine and crumpled it in his palm. "I despise displacers as much as the next man. And I disliked you even before I learned what you were. I'm not appreciative that you murdered my relative."

"Lester challenged me to the duel," Ferrin reminded him. "I dispatched him in self-defense."

"And then I had you decapitated," Copernum said. "It suffices. Were the charges against you just? Perhaps not. Did I love my cousin? Not particularly. But your impudence toward him was an indirect insult to me. You received a sentence. It was carried out. Since you are a displacer, losing your head did not end your life. You wisely fled the city. Perhaps in the end I'll be relieved that you survived. You are a resourceful person, Ferrin, and our cause will need capable allies in the coming months."

"Galloran is entering the castle," Rachel reported.

"Alongside his closest companions," Copernum noted. "With a couple of exceptions."

"I'm not sure we're particularly close," Ferrin replied.

Copernum cocked his head slightly. "No need to take it personally. Galloran shrewdly omitted you from his retinue. Drinlings and seedfolk add to his mystique. But you? All of Trensicourt will be gossiping about his mismatched eyes. Having a displacer in his company would only fuel further speculation about his loyalties. There are plenty of guardsmen in this town who would recognize you."

"Why aren't you down there with Dolan?" Ferrin wondered.

Copernum pulled his mantle more snugly about his narrow shoulders. "I do not crave public attention. There are circumstances when such appearances are necessary. Otherwise, I prefer to exert influence quietly." Copernum turned to Rachel. "Why do you suppose Prince Galloran elected to keep you out of the procession?"

Rachel shrugged as if she didn't care. Galloran had told her she would be safer and more comfortable in the castle. It had bothered her a little to be left out, but this was his kingdom, and she figured he knew best.

"I expect he wants to keep you shrouded in mystery," Copernum answered. "Ostensibly for your protection. Mostly because you're too young. He doesn't feel you look the part—the abnormally gifted Edomic adept. Your wholesome appearance does not match the rumors currently circulating. To be honest, despite the whispers that had reached me, I had dismissed your worth myself until you put me on the floor."

Rachel combed her fingers along her temple, tucking some hair back. "Whatever his reasons, I'm happy to do what Galloran wants."

"Such flagrant loyalty," Copernum murmured. "Would that I had so devoted a servant."

"I trust him," Rachel said.

"Evidently," Copernum replied. His gaze strayed to Ferrin, then returned to Rachel. "Surely you realize that an adept of your talents needn't take orders from anyone. At this point in history you're invaluable, more precious than orantium. Utterly unique."

"I try to help out," Rachel said, the flattery making her self-conscious.

Copernum looked to Ferrin. "Is she truly so innocent?"

"She's not weak," Ferrin assured him. "Nor is she foolish. What are you playing at, Copernum?"

"Nothing," he said, holding up his long hands. "I just wonder if Rachel appreciates that entire kingdoms would rally around a gift like hers. Maldor would trade all but Felrook to have her, either to slay her or to train her."

"I think you're exaggerating," Rachel said, hoping the hotness in her cheeks was not visible as a blush.

"Which is why I label you innocent," Copernum replied with a small bow. "The prince has entered the castle. Today accomplished everything he had hoped. The two of you should go greet your friends and celebrate."

Ferrin inclined his head a fraction. "Thank you for your hospitality."

"At your service," Copernum replied. "I should like to become better acquainted with both of you."

Ferrin led Rachel away from the balcony and out of the luxurious residence. On the way down a stairway he leaned close to her. "What did you take from that?" he whispered.

"Be wary of Copernum," she replied softly.

"Could you feel him cuddling up to us like a snake?" Ferrin asked. "Like a constrictor maneuvering for a deadly hold before the squeezing begins."

"He tried to kill Jason," Rachel said. "He tried to kill you. He tortured Nedwin for years. He's only acting nice until he has another option."

"Exactly right. He suspects we might be valuable. Did you notice how he tried to plant doubts and build trust? During such conversations, I like to imagine flattering words as a noose being tied round my neck. He gently tried to make you feel he appreciated your worth more than Galloran does. He tried to portray himself as a wise confidant. Nothing too drastic. He settled for patiently nudging our minds toward certain conclusions."

"Don't worry, I'll never trust him."

Ferrin walked beside her in silence for a moment. "Do you trust me?"

"Not completely."

"Good."

Rachel didn't get to talk to Galloran on the day of his procession until the companions who had set out together from Mianamon gathered for a private evening meal in the royal chambers. After the parade Galloran had met with a variety of nobles, merchants, scholars, artists, and other influential members of society. Everyone seemed desperate for his attention, and he had patiently greeted the endless flood of well-wishers, giving each as much personal interaction as circumstances permitted.

Galloran had saved Rachel a seat immediately beside him. For the first time that day he put on his blindfold. "We can speak freely here," he said. "I won't chance spies reading your lips through my eyes."

"Did anyone ask about your eyes?" Nollin inquired.

"Not a soul," Galloran replied. "Everyone noticed. Nobody spoke of it. The lack of commentary suggests they assume I'm ashamed, which I probably should be."

"No reason to feel shame," Nedwin said. "You did what was necessary to stay in the fight."

"I'll address the matter after my coronation," Galloran said.

"The coronation will proceed on schedule?" Nollin asked.

"Day after tomorrow," Galloran replied. "Dolan has already announced my legitimacy. The grand duke will do the honors."

"This has been a long time coming," Nollin said. "How do you feel?"

"Like a stranger in my own home. Most of the people I once admired are gone. Many honorable men could once be found among the nobility of Trensicourt. Not so anymore. Those who remain are cautious and compromising at best, plotters and back-stabbers at worst. But the kingdom will be mine, and with it a substantial host of soldiers, and that is what we most need at present."

"Good food," Io commented.

Rachel had been so attentive to the conversation that she had neglected to start eating. The table was burdened with crispy fowl, peppery venison, delicate fillets of trout, pots of soup, baskets of bread, platters of fruit, and trays of vegetables. A feast fit for a king, which Rachel supposed made sense under the circumstances.

"I'll agree," Ferrin said, spreading soft white cheese on a dark hunk of bread. "The road has its charms, but meals like this are scarce. The pleasure of city food prepared by experts nearly excuses the exhausting politics."

"You had it easy today, displacer," Kerick grunted. "The sun was hot during the procession, and the progress slow."

"At least you benefited from better company," Ferrin countered.

"Am I that boring?" Rachel complained.

"Not you," Ferrin clarified.

Galloran leaned toward Rachel. "I have meant to ask how you enjoyed the companionship of the acting chancellor."

Rachel swallowed a bite of bread. "Ferrin compared him to a snake."

Ferrin bobbed his head. "Copernum was everything you expected, Galloran. He has a definite fixation on Rachel."

"Unsurprising," Galloran replied. "His master has shown uncommon interest in her. I don't want Rachel ever left alone with him. Or anyone, really. Trensicourt is infested with treacherous manipulators. The sooner we're off to war the better."

"Agreed," Io seconded heartily.

"It's fine with me," Rachel inserted. "I'd much rather avoid guys like Copernum." She at least wanted the appearance of having some say in the matter.

"Will the more prominent schemers let you mount a war?" Nollin asked.

"I spent the day investigating attitudes on the subject," Galloran said. "Some won't want to make it easy. If I intended to wait a month to start a campaign, it might not be possible. But riding the current tide of high emotion, I expect to succeed. My most cunning enemies will rejoice to find Trensicourt mobilizing for war. The cleverest among them will gladly hurry me out of town. They will find many opportunities in having me away on a doomed offensive."

"How do you intend to counter them?" Nedwin asked.

"I'll do what I can," Galloran replied. "Who knows how the war will progress? Who can say how long it will last? Many options close to us if Trensicourt falls. I'll leave a trusted steward in command, along with a reliable aide or two. Apart from that I'll have to lay aside my concerns about the politics of Trensicourt for a season. According to the prophecy, an assault on Felrook is the key to dethroning Maldor. Until that goal is achieved, all other matters are secondary."

Looking around the table, Rachel wondered who Galloran might leave behind. Hopefully, none of the group who had set out together from Mianamon. She had already said good-bye to too many friends.

"I will grant you one thing," Nollin said, wadding a napkin and tossing it aside. "You are not asking your allies to assume the greatest risk. Your present course will leave Trensicourt quite vulnerable."

"This offensive is our last hope," Galloran said. "I intend to pursue it with every resource I can muster. Sacrifices are inevitable."

After Rachel finished her meal, she noticed Tark sitting alone at a small table away from the others. She went to him. "How did you enjoy the parade?"

"Not much," he replied in his deep, raspy voice. "I would have been happier blowing a sousalax than trotting astride an overgrown pony. I disliked leaving you alone with Copernum and Ferrin, but it didn't seem my place to protest."

"Copernum wouldn't have done anything to me with Galloran around," Rachel said.

Tark lowered his voice. "Isn't just Copernum I worry about."

Rachel gave a small grin. "I'm not totally defenseless. I know a few tricks."

"I've seen you knock people flat with a word," Tark said. "And I saw you set the walking dead aflame. But I vowed to Lord Jason that I would protect you, and I mean to keep my oath. I did that duty poorly today."

"Today was unusual," Rachel said.

"Aye, and if I let unusual conditions stop me, I won't be any help until this whole affair is over. I'm happy to admit that I'm in way over my head. I never expected to get involved with the high matters of great men. But I made two promises to Lord Jason: to help Galloran fight his war, and to watch over you."

"You've done great so far," Rachel assured him. "The war is on schedule and I'm doing fine."

"Keep me near, if you can," Tark urged. "I want to be of service."

"I'm glad to know I can count on you," Rachel replied, a hand on his arm.

Tark sniffed uncomfortably and looked away. "Now, don't go relying on me too much. I'll give you my best, but don't forget to keep practicing that Edomic of yours."

"Deal."

The coronation featured even more pageantry than the procession into the city. Simply to stand at the back of the throne room for the ceremony cost no less than a hundred drooma.

Trensicourt had celebrated nonstop ever since the procession. For two days the streets had remained mobbed by revelers, regardless of the hour. Citizens thronged the plaza outside the castle to hear heralds recite the words spoken within.

Rachel sat in the throne room at the front of the elevated gallery. Tark was seated on one hand, Io on the other. Galloran had appointed the two men as her personal bodyguards for the duration of their stay at Trensicourt. Io looked handsome and dignified in his finery. Strange how much he had matured in half a year. Not just in appearance—his attitude had become more serious, although he remained very considerate. She tried not to think ahead to his hair going gray by winter.

While waiting for the ceremony to begin, Tark and Io kept stealing sidelong glances at her—as if she didn't already feel conspicuous enough! Yesterday Rachel had been fitted for a special outfit: a fine, dark robe with a veiled, broad-brimmed hat and black lace gloves. Nollin had come up with the idea. The goal was to make her appear mysterious, and the tailors had succeeded. The ensemble looked like an eccentric, stylish funeral outfit. Her attire attracted much attention, but at least the veil enabled her to avoid eye contact. When she turned her head toward the onlookers gazing her way, all eyes wandered elsewhere. Nobody wanted to get caught staring.

A hush fell over the room as a herald announced Galloran, complete with a dozen titles such as Protector of the Realm, High Commander of the Army, and Crown Prince of Trensicourt. Regal and tall, Galloran strode into the room, the train of his robe dragging behind like a cape designed for a giant. Three young attendants followed, holding the trailing ends of the purple garment.

Silence reigned as Galloran ascended the dais, shed his robe, and sat on a small, ornate chair before the Grand Duke of Edgemont, a husky man with a forked beard and costly attire. Dolan sat on the dais as well, as did Copernum and several other high lords of Trensicourt.

Rachel felt happy for Galloran. He looked very regal, and he had certainly earned this moment of glory.

Dolan arose and spoke to the assemblage. The speech struck Rachel as long-winded, as if he were trying to exhaust every possible way to express his joy at the return of the heir to the throne, all the while missing no opportunity to compliment the job he had done as regent in preserving the realm through the kingless years.

Next, Copernum stepped forward and spoke of his support for Galloran and his relief that the kingdom was whole again. Thankfully, his speech was shorter.

At last the Grand Duke of Edgemont issued a long ceremonial proclamation. Rachel was glad for the veil, because it allowed her to secretly yawn during the plodding recitation. Toward the end of the pronouncement a boy in a fancy doublet brought the crown to the Grand Duke of Edgemont on a silk pillow. Still reciting ceremonial words, the grand duke lifted the crown from the cushion, held it high, then deposited it on Galloran's head. A flourish of trumpets followed as Galloran accepted his royal scepter.

The Grand Duke of Edgemont retreated, and Galloran arose. The room erupted with cheers. Rachel hooted and hollered as loudly as anyone. The jubilation maintained a deafening volume for at least thirty seconds. Galloran raised both hands. As the applause subsided, Rachel could hear the sustained murmur of distant cheering from outside the castle. Word had traveled quickly.

"Fellow citizens of Trensicourt," Galloran began, raising his voice as best he could. A hush fell over the room. "I come to the throne more than a decade too late. Most of you are aware that I am no friend of the emperor, Maldor. I have spent the past years in active defiance of his ambition to dominate Lyrian. Some of those years were spent actively fighting him, some in the dungeons of Felrook, and the most recent years were spent gathering intelligence in preparation for a final stand against his bid for absolute power.

"The kingdoms taken by Maldor have fallen under the heavy yoke of his tyranny. His lust for dominion knows no bounds. As his power grows, he squeezes ever tighter, shrinking freedom and limiting opportunity. He rewards cowards and traitors willing to prosper by informing on friends and allies. He raises the cruel, the ruthless, and the treacherous to the highest offices. He limits the spread of knowledge to make his subjects ignorant and more docile. He will live for centuries. Left unchecked, his rule will usher in the darkest era in the long history of Lyrian. Civilization will continue to regress until most of the natural joy has been crushed from life. Those he rules will live in constant fear, mistrusting one another, unable to pursue excellence in any endeavor without risking his interference."

Galloran paused. The room was silent except for the low rustle of people shifting uncomfortably. Clearly, nobody had spoken this candidly about Maldor in Trensicourt for years.

"Contrary to what he would have us believe, the emperor has not yet captured the continent. Although he is well on his way, the kingdom of Kadara continues to tie up the majority of his armed forces along the eastern coast as they lay siege to the cities of Kadara, Highport, and Inkala. The drinlings remain free, as do the Amar Kabal in the Seven Vales. And though we may have made some unwise compromises, Trensicourt also remains a free kingdom."

Galloran paused again. Was he hoping for a reaction from the audience? Everyone was listening intently, but nobody cried out.

The freshly crowned king raised the fingertips of one hand to his temple. "There has been considerable speculation about my eyes. Yes, the spies of Maldor are watching as I gaze upon you. Maldor took my sight when I was captured. He offered to restore my vision by grafting in the eyes of displacers. The offer involved no pledges of fealty. I felt that I needed my sight to wage war against him, so I accepted his gift. This is why, when dealing in sensitive matters, I wear a blindfold. In combat I am happy to let Maldor watch me slay his servants."

This earned a ripple of laughter that spread through the room and expanded into applause.

"A long road has taken me home to Trensicourt. I have seen much, learned much. My daughter, Corinne, the current heir to my throne, is living for the present in exile, alive and well."

Enthusiastic cheers followed the announcement. Galloran waited for the furor to calm before continuing.

"I have been to the oracle of Mianamon. She has passed away, but she shared a final prophecy with me before she expired. She told me how Maldor can be defeated. There were many witnesses present. Starting tomorrow, Trensicourt will be aggressively at war with Felrook."

Rachel did not think the room could have become quieter. Everyone seemed to be holding their breath.

"We will not stand alone. The drinlings will stand beside us. And after long years of neutrality, the Amar Kabal will be entering the fight."

This announcement drew excited discussion rather than cheers. Galloran held up his hands.

"Naturally, I cannot share the specifics of our strategy. There will be other allies as well, including some who wield powers not seen in Lyrian for generations." Rachel caught Tark looking over at her. When he noticed her attention, he hurriedly glanced away.

"We must begin preparations for war within the hour," Galloran continued. "We will not wait to be besieged after Kadara falls. We will not bend our knees to Felrook and fade timidly into an age of darkness and oppression. Instead, we will move faster than our foes will believe possible. We will march out in force and seize the last real opportunity to fight back. This will be the final chance to stop Maldor from overrunning the continent, and I mean to take it." Emotion built to a climax in his voice. "The oracle has foreseen that we can triumph! I have fought the emperor for years from the shadows. Now, at last, we finally have the right allies and the right opportunity. The hour has arrived for me to lead us to victory in open battle!"

Here the crowd exploded with cheers. Rachel's heart swelled with his stirring words. His defiant enthusiasm was contagious.

"Too long has Trensicourt watched and waited. Ours is a proud heritage of victory in warfare. We are just as brave and capable as those who preceded us. Braver. More capable. Rested and ready. Other kingdoms have wondered what has kept us out of the fray, much as we have all wondered why the Amar Kabal have not emerged from their strongholds to confront the greatest threat our peace and prosperity has known. We were waiting for the right moment, as were they. That moment is upon us. If we continue to wait, the opportunity will pass us by. Instead, we will strike alongside the same allies who overthrew Maldor's master. The emperor will not steal our freedom. He will not control the lives of our wives, of our children, or of our unborn generations. We will not let him!"

Now the room thundered with approval. Rachel found herself wanting to rise to her feet. The power of his message touched her deeply, and most around her clearly felt likewise. There was determination and anger in the tumult. The nervous tension that had sustained the earlier silence was releasing. Rachel looked around. These people were hearing words that should have been spoken long ago. Words they might not have believed from anyone less than this storied figure, their exiled king, standing before them in glittering raiment, fortified with legendary prowess and cunning, his bold words spoken with certainty.

It took some time for Galloran's raised hands to quiet the clamor. "Some may wonder why I share my intentions so openly. I mean to lead you honestly, as my father did before me. When we charge into battle, I will be at the front. Also, there will be no way to hide our preparations for war. The endeavor will be massive, and no matter what precautions we adopt to conceal our intentions, word of our efforts will reach the emperor. So why hide? He would not have had time to counter the attack I intend if I had warned him last month. He has planned like a commander confident that no further trouble awaits him. The placement of his forces is sloppy and lopsided. We will capitalize on this mistake with blood and victory!"

Again the room went wild. Io and Tark were standing. Rachel felt herself being swept up in the excitement. The people believed, or at least wanted to believe.

"I will issue this warning once," Galloran continued. "Any sympathizer of Maldor has this day only to get out of my kingdom. Starting tomorrow, any individual employed by him will be guilty of treason and sentenced to death. This includes all the minor governors and lawmakers in the outlying towns within the boundaries my father ruled. This includes any man or woman wearing an imperial uniform. Imperial servants are the enemies of this kingdom, and I authorize the citizens of Trensicourt to execute the sentence I have prescribed. Throw off your imperial yokes. We have larger battles to fight."

Galloran waited again for the approval to subside.

"If any man would care to challenge my right to rule, or to call us to war, or to denounce the emperor, speak now and face me in combat." Galloran gazed solemnly over the multitude, one hand on the hilt of his sword. Nobody stirred.

"Let the celebrations of the previous days suffice. Now is the hour to make ready for war. Lords, call your vassals. Summon your knights. Ready your soldiers. Heralds, take my words to the far reaches of our kingdom and beyond. Call the men of Lyrian to arms. Now is the hour to prepare, for our host will march before the week is out. As your king, I am honored to serve alongside you in this monumental cause. The future generations of Trensicourt will look back on this day with reverence. We stand at one of the great turning points of history. We must not fail! We will not!"

Galloran turned and left the dais, leaving the room in a state of enthusiastic pandemonium. Years of uncertainty and oppression had combined with the elation of their king's return into a more fervent atmosphere than Rachel had expected. She realized that many of those present had been desperately hoping to hear words like Galloran had spoken. People around her who had seemed nervous minutes ago were clapping one another on the back, emboldened by the prospect of taking action behind a leader such as their new king. A minority in the crowd brooded, arms folded, expressions clouded, but even the most pensive onlookers tried to look positive as they were jostled by their neighbors.

Down on the dais Rachel noticed Copernum, eyes roving the assemblage from beneath his large, tricornered hat. He surveyed the scene calmly, as if gathering data. From across the wide space his sharp, calculating eyes found her, seeming to penetrate her veil. His small frown bent into a faint smile, and with a swirl of his cloak he exited the room.

CHAPTER 8

HIJACKERS

Nia burst into the small bedroom. Jason jerked his head up and squinted at her, tense from being startled awake.

"Are we under attack?" he blurted.

She was smiling. "No, it's good news! The *Valiant* has been spotted on the horizon."

"About time," Jason said, relaxing. The ship was three days behind schedule. Everyone had been getting really antsy. He blinked and wiped his eyes.

"Sorry to disturb you," Nia said. "I thought you'd want to know."

"I'm glad you told me." The room had no window, so he lacked outside light to help him gauge the time. "Is it morning?"

"Not quite daybreak," she said. "You can go back to sleep if you want. In fact, you probably should. Tonight is the night!" Nia exited, closing the door.

Jason sagged onto his side and closed his eyes, but he failed to sleep. Eventually he went and found some breakfast. There was a new energy among the drinlings. Concerns had been expressed that the *Valiant* might have been diverted because somebody had caught wind of the planned hijacking. Every day their strike force had remained in hiding had increased the chance for somebody to discover them. But now it looked like all would proceed as designed.

Jason stewed all morning and into the afternoon. He spent a lot of time on his feet—testing the weight of his new sword, aiming the crossbow Aram had given him, foraging for snacks, listening for news. Pacing. Fretting.

Tonight's endeavor would be like nothing he had ever done. Hijacking a ship in the middle of the night? This was a big town, surrounded by high walls. The ship would be guarded. There would certainly be fighting. If he and his friends messed up, they would all die.

Nobody expected much of him. According to what Jason knew of the plan, he was basically cargo. After the ship was secure, Drake and two drinling escorts would hustle him aboard. But so much could go wrong. What if they ran across a stray patrol on the way to the ship? He would have to help them fight their way clear. If an alarm was sounded before they boarded the ship, soldiers could come rushing to the waterfront, and he might end up in the thick of the battle.

Jason had practiced for months so that he could contribute in a fight. But since learning to use a sword, he had never confronted an opponent with his life on the line. That test might come tonight, meeting an enemy in combat, no blunted edges, no practice gear . . . no second chances. Skill would be involved, as would composure, as would luck. Either he or the opponent would survive. The prospect sent nervous thrills tingling through his body.

Jason knew he would not be fighting alone. Drake and others would probably be there to bail him out. But anything could happen. Worst-case scenarios could leave him alone in a sea of enemies. No matter how he tried to distract himself, he could not stop anticipating the possibilities.

Not long before sunset, somebody knocked on his door. Jason had his sword out, dueling imagined enemies. He hastily tossed it aside. "Come in."

Aram entered, still small, and glanced from Jason to the sword on his bed. "Restless?"

"Not too bad," Jason lied.

Aram smirked. "My room is directly below yours. I could hear you clomping around."

Jason was not one to blush, but the sudden warmth in his cheeks hinted that this might be an exception. He looked away from the undersized half giant. "I was just doing some exercises."

Aram plopped down on the edge of Jason's bed. "Truth be told, I'm a bit edgy myself."

"Yeah?"

"This is a major operation. With so many people involved, I can hardly believe we haven't given ourselves away already. These drinlings deserve a lot of credit. They have discipline."

"Think we can pull it off?"

Aram hesitated. "You know I used to work as a smuggler."

"Right."

"I've taken plenty of chances in my day. Risk was part of the job. But the risks were carefully measured. Thanks to my precautions, the chances of getting caught remained low. I stayed in situations where nine times out of ten, if I did get apprehended, I would be able to bargain my way out of serious trouble. Even among the officials appointed by Maldor, most consider smuggling necessary to some extent. The service fills a need. I was careful about where and when I operated. I was careful about who I worked with. Careful about what goods I moved. Careful about who I bribed."

Jason could see where Aram was headed. "And now we're rushing into something crazy?"

Aram shook his head. "Not necessarily. Not overly crazy. This could work. How do I put this?" He stared down at his clasped hands. "During my career, I occasionally came across opportunities for a really bold mission. A job that might produce a mountain of money overnight or really enhance my reputation. A big score—a chance for glory, riches, or both. These types of jobs almost always involved harming the interests of the emperor in one way or another. Or else they had the potential to draw his attention.

"I created workable plans for several of those missions. I devised strategies that made the projects feasible, kept the risk within reason. But the price of failure in those instances was much too high, so I played it safe. I never implemented those plans. Chasing the big score gets greedy men killed."

"But tonight . . . ," Jason prompted.

"Tonight we're going to hijack an interceptor. Among other duties, it will be my responsibility to captain the ship. I have the most experience at sea, so the job fell to me. I've drilled the drinlings on procedures. They mastered their knots and lashings with shocking ease! They're highly adaptable. Every man knows his role. But most have never sailed a ship like the *Valiant*. For good or ill, our success depends largely on me—whether I trained them right, whether I lead them effectively.

"I love the sea. I've captained before. I've dreamed of becoming shipmaster of an interceptor, Jason. There is no finer vessel afloat. The basic design came from the Kadarian warships, but Maldor perfected it. To captain the *Valiant* will be a thrilling privilege that I never expected to actually experience."

"But you're also nervous?" Jason guessed.

Aram shifted in his seat. "I'm discarding years of good judgment. Our actions tonight will publicly insult the emperor and all those in his service. Don't get me wrong. I've been in tight spots before. Things have gone poorly, and I've fought my way free. But I never sought out such situations. This hijacking will have every imperial agent on the Inland Sea after us. It will draw the personal attention of the emperor."

"Is the plan good?" Jason hoped.

"Superb. They won't be expecting anything this bold. They couldn't possibly anticipate the amount of manpower we've assembled. This hijacking is daring enough to fall completely outside of their expectations. The *Valiant* made port today. Most of the crew will be carousing and enjoying the inns tonight. Those standing guard in the middle of the night will be disgruntled and careless. What could happen to an interceptor moored in a port firmly under imperial control? These soldiers haven't seen real action for years. In combat situations surprise means a lot, and it should be entirely on our side."

"So you're more worried about afterward."

"I'm worried about everything. Too much could go wrong. And if things go wrong, they will go very wrong. If our surprise is somehow foiled, this could end disastrously. If our enemy takes more clever or effective action than we've anticipated, we could be massacred. And even if we get away, it is only the beginning. We'll be sailing to an island nobody has survived, with every soldier in the region after us. Not a favorable scenario."

"Wow," Jason said, feeling he now had a better grasp of why he should be freaking out.

"This is the sort of scheme you devise as an idle fantasy, and then lay aside."

"But we can't lay it aside."

"If we're determined to get to Windbreak Island, this is probably the only way. No better alternative exists. The prophecy claims we have to get there. Greedy or not, we're being forced to pursue the big score. It goes against my instincts, which makes me edgy."

"I'm pretty wired too," Jason admitted. "I think I get what you mean. I've spent most of my time in Lyrian trying to avoid danger. Tonight we're charging straight into it."

Aram rubbed the sides of his nose with both hands, partially hiding his face. "Truth be told? My instincts keep telling me to run. And listening to my instincts has kept me alive so far."

"You think we should run?"

"Not all of us. I was speaking about myself."

Jason felt shocked by the admission. "You don't really want to ditch us?"

Aram gave a weak smile. "I definitely *want* to run. I've never liked sitting still. I almost took action yesterday, before the *Valiant* had been sighted."

"You almost left?" Jason gasped. "Really?"

"I wouldn't bring it up if I meant to actually do it."

"Then why bring it up at all?"

"I thought it might mean something for you to know that the thought of you helped keep me here."

"Me?" Jason asked.

"I had to ask myself how committed I was to this cause. I had to confront whether I was willing to go all the way, to venture into dangers from which I had little chance of returning. I knew Jasher and Drake wouldn't give up. The mission would go forward without me, and I could picture my presence making little difference whether it succeeded or failed. But then I thought about you. I thought about a young man who didn't belong to this world, who had managed to make a difference without many of the skills I might have supposed were necessary. And I realized that if a stranger like you held true, a man of Lyrian like myself had no right to depart."

"Wow," Jason said. He could hardly believe his actions had mattered so much to a warrior like Aram. "So you're not leaving?"

"I'll hold true."

"Even though your instincts don't like it?"

"Even so." Aram stood up and crossed to the door. "I'll be growing soon. Antsy or not, you should try to sleep. We won't get underway until the stillest hour of the night."

"Thanks for talking with me," Jason said. "It helps to know I'm not the only person feeling anxious."

"We should all be anxious! Maybe it will keep us sharp. This is a grim endeavor. We'll need to be at our best tonight."

Jason wondered what his best would look like. He hoped he would measure up. "I'll give it everything I've got."

"I believe it," Aram replied. He glanced at the weapon on the bed. "Don't wear out your sword arm."

Jason slept restlessly, tossing and turning, waking up at intervals. When Drake came for him, Jason was awake, staring silently at the darkness. He rolled out of bed as soon as the door opened.

"Did you sleep?" Drake asked.

"Sort of," Jason replied. "I felt tense."

"Hiding away like this for most of a week would make anyone edgy. I'll be glad to get on the water. Been some time since I toured the Inland Sea."

Jason buckled on his sword and grabbed his crossbow. "Where are the others?"

"Some are already moving into position," Drake replied. "The idea is to reach the docks without looking like fifty people."

A male and female drinling awaited outside his room. Jason had not learned all the names, but these two were called Thag and Zoo. Both looked to be in their twenties. Both spoke English without much confidence, but seemed to banter cheerily with their comrades in their native tongue. Zoo was slender for a drinling, but had a sinewy toughness. Thag's hulking muscles were developed to the point where it seemed they would limit his movement.

Drake led Jason and the two drinlings down to the enclosed alleyway outside the secret rooms. Overhead, a rectangular section of black sky glittered with stars. The curly-haired barkeeper waited at the far end of the little courtyard beside a ladder that led up to a window. Jason climbed the ladder behind Drake and entered the inn. A few drinlings lingered in the common room.

"The other drinlings will follow behind us," Drake said. "Most have gone ahead. Come."

Shadowing Drake, Jason exited the front door and climbed the steps to the street. He kept his crossbow hidden under his cloak. Nobody had weapons visible. The street was silent.

"How late is it?" Jason whispered.

"Less than two hours until first light," Drake replied. "The moon has set. We're going directly to the *Valiant*."

They advanced along the side of the road at a brisk walk. The drinlings had their hoods up. A calm breeze blew against Jason's back.

"Wind from the southwest," Drake mentioned. "Close to ideal."

The road ended at the waterfront. The bulky shapes of sailing vessels loomed in the darkness, lit by stars and a dozen dockside lanterns. Other lamps shed light aboard a few of the ships. Fires danced along the top of the sea wall that stretched out into the harbor: torches and cressets. At the mouth of the harbor, where the two walls almost met, a pair of bonfires blazed, the flames reflecting off the dark water.

The largest ship by far was off to the right, a long vessel with three towering masts rigged with numerous sails. Four lanterns brightened the deck. Jason saw at least two soldiers patrolling.

Drake furrowed his brow. "We should have the ship by now."

He led them back a block, then along a cross street. They carefully approached the dock again. They came out closer to the *Valiant*, the name of the huge ship visible on the side. At the end of the next street over, a couple of inns remained brightly lit. Music could be heard from one of them.

Nia emerged from the shadows. "Come with me," she whispered.

"What's the problem?" Drake asked as she led them to a dark nook shielded by a low fence. They had a clear view of the *Valiant*.

"A patrol of six guards was roaming the docks," Nia said. "We had to wait until they moved beyond sight of the *Valiant*. We took them quietly."

"They'll be missed sooner or later," Drake warned. "Probably sooner."

"The plan is in motion." She nodded toward one of the lit inns. Aram came staggering out, wrapped in his huge leather cloak. He lumbered toward the *Valiant*. "More soldiers than we would prefer are still celebrating at the inns. They must sleep less than I do."

"This late, none of them should be terribly useful in combat," Drake murmured.

Jason watched Aram amble along the pier toward the *Valiant*. As he approached the ship, a soldier came to the top of the gangplank. "You there," the sentry called in a raised voice, "state your business."

Aram shouted his reply. "Some seamen at the Broken Barge were bragging about sailing aboard an interceptor. Never seen one up close." He started up the gangplank, swaying unsteadily.

"Now you've seen one," the soldier said. "I must ask you to come no closer."

Still walking, Aram waved a dismissive hand. "Don't spoil a beautiful night! I just want a peek."

"Turn around, sir. At once. This vessel is imperial property." Three other soldiers had joined the first one at the top of the gangplank.

Aram kept coming, taking his time as if the steepness of the gangplank were tiring him. "Don't be sour just because your mates are out having a good time. I wore your colors for a season, in service of the emperor. Never aboard a ship like this, mind you."

All four of the soldiers drew swords. "I'm in command here," a different soldier said, his voice stern. "If you wore our colors, you know our duty. You've been out too late, friend. You're not thinking right. Go on home. Don't make us remove you."

Aram was now three-quarters of the way up the gangplank. He stumbled and fell forward. After lying still for a moment, he rolled onto his side. "More comfortable than it looks," he said. "Maybe I'll take a breather."

"You will not," the lead soldier said, sounding exasperated. "Get on your feet and shove off. Last warning."

Aram let out a long moan. "I may have overdone it tonight, lads. Something I ate wants back out. I don't think it means to come quietly."

The lead soldier gestured for two of the others to approach Aram. They sheathed their swords and started down the gangway.

Aram began to sing, the words strained, halting, and some-what off-key. "Old Ingrim was a man of the sea, the sort you'd hope to know. He'd buy you a drink if you shot him a wink, then tell you—"

Retching sounds interrupted his tune.

The two soldiers had reached Aram, but they paused, look-ing at each other. They spoke to Aram too quietly to be heard. Crouching, each grabbed an arm, grunting as they helped the huge man stand. Once they had Aram on his feet, they gazed up at him, clearly impressed by his size. One of them kept a hand on the hilt of his sword. The other kept a hand on Aram, steadying him.

"Don't tell my wife about this," Aram blustered. "The woman is hard enough to stomach when I mind my manners. Don't send me home. I'd be safer in a nice cozy cell. Hear my advice, lads—if you're ever tempted by marriage, get a dog instead. You'll thank me."

Aram took little wobbly steps without going anywhere, as if struggling to maintain his balance. He hunched, leaning from one side to the other, a hand on each of the soldiers for support. Then he doubled over, making retching sounds again.

Figures began to appear on the opposite side of the *Valiant* from the gangplank. They stealthily advanced on the soldiers from behind.

"This is disgraceful," the lead soldier complained. "Walk him down to—"

His words were cut off as he was blindsided by attackers. The two soldiers at the top of the gangplank went down silently. Aram wrapped his powerful arms around one of the soldiers helping him, snapped his neck with a precise jerk, then swiftly did the same to the other man.

"Now," Nia breathed. She led Drake, Jason, and the other

drinlings out of hiding and toward the warship. One of the drin-lings extinguished the dockside lantern nearest the *Valiant*. The night air smelled of brine and wet wood. As Jason reached the pier, he found that unless he stepped softly, his feet boomed too loudly against the planks.

Aram had hoisted the two soldiers on the gangplank over his shoulders and now carried them up to the deck. Presumably the splash would be too loud if he simply tossed them in the water. Jason was impressed by Aram's performance. The distraction had fully occupied the soldiers while several drinlings had accessed the far side of the *Valiant* by rowboat and climbed up to the deck.

A drinling beside Jason carried Aram's heavy shirt of over-lapping metal rings, the armor clinking as he ran. Jason followed the drinling up the gangway.

"To your places," Aram commanded in a loud whisper. "Do every task we rehearsed." He shed his heavy cloak, accepted the armored shirt from the drinling, and put it on. Drinlings swarmed into position, some grabbing lines, some climbing the masts. Aram began striding about, giving specific instructions. Jason took up his position beside Nia near the top of the gangplank.

"Dousing the lantern was the main signal," Nia murmured. "Our fighters should be advancing along the walls." She held a bow with an arrow nocked and ready, eyes scanning the docks.

Jason stared at the impressive walls that stretched from dry land out into the water of the harbor. By the light of the distant cressets along the top, he could not yet see any activity. A sudden clash of steel rang from below the deck. Then he heard a strangled cry from beyond the ship, off to the right in the darkness.

Jason didn't know all the details of the plan. Jasher, Aram, Nia, and an older drinling named Heg had been the architects—dividing up the teams, issuing assignments, and deciding how they would signal one another. Jason knew that Jasher was leading a group to sabotage some of the other craft in the harbor. A couple of small assault teams were supposed to charge along the walls, slaying sentries in order to stop the watchmen from closing the harbor mouth. The majority of the drinlings were working to secure the *Valiant* and get underway.

Crossbow ready, Jason watched the port. Every second that they went undetected increased the chances of their escape. Drake gripped Jason by the elbow and nodded off to the left. Flames were spreading across the deck of a large two-masted ship and leaping up into the sails. A moment later no fewer than five other fires started on five other ships, each moored to a different pier.

"Lantern oil," Drake murmured. "No other ship in port could possibly outpace an interceptor. But three might be able to chase us to Windbreak Island in time to cause trouble. Jasher wanted to torch a couple others for good measure."

Scattered drinlings began to converge on the pier alongside the *Valiant*—the raiders returning from the neighboring ships. A bell began to clang from the mouth of the harbor. Other bells on the wall took up the call. The sentries had caught sight of the rapidly spreading fires.

Jason surveyed the dock, finger near the trigger of his crossbow. The incessant bells made him feel jumpy. No more operating in secrecy. Trouble was coming. The only question was how long it would take to arrive.

Drinlings raced up the gangplank, making it bow and bounce. Three drinlings paused on the pier beside the *Valiant* to spill a generous quantity of lantern oil. Torch in hand, Jasher came racing along the dock. He sprinted onto the pier, dropped the torch in the pool of lantern oil, and kept running as flames licked across the planks behind him.

"Cast off!" Aram bellowed. "Away we go!"

Jasher pounded up the gangplank and sprang aboard just as the *Valiant* drifted away from the pier. A moment later the gangplank dropped into the water. Ships burned on either side, a few of them already becoming infernos as the flames spread from sail to sail. Men poured out of the nearest inns. Several raced for the pier where the *Valiant* was departing. They were met with a volley of arrows from the near side of the warship. At least one man was hit. Several others dove for cover.

Aram personally dumped the four soldiers who had guarded the *Valiant* over the side, all the while shouting orders about their heading and the state of various sails. Jason could not decipher the specifics of the nautical jargon, but it all sounded very official.

Jason heard water sloshing. Peering over the side, he saw three huge oars helping to propel the *Valiant* toward the harbor mouth. He assumed there were three more on the opposite side.

"The sweeps don't accomplish much for a vessel this large," Drake commented. "But they offer a little hope if we get caught in a calm. And they can add a little speed in situations like these."

"Nobody rows like the drinlings," Jason said, remembering his voyage from Ebera to the Durnese River.

"We have some of the best oarsmen in Lyrian aboard," Drake agreed. "The harder they row, the stronger they get."

The big waterfront bell towers added their gonging clamor to the alarm. The *Valiant* was now away from the pier and heading for the gap between the breakwaters. The fire on the dock was dying out as men beat at it, but the burning ships were lighting up the night. On two of them the fire had climbed to the highest sails, which meant that flames were stretching eighty feet into the sky, throwing fierce highlights onto the billowing smoke.

"We're away," Drake said calmly. "They can't catch us from

the docks. Their only chance is to block the harbor mouth. They have a pair of enormous winches on each side of the opening that can raise heavy chains to close off the gap."

"Think our guys will stop them?" Jason asked.

Drake rubbed the back of his neck. "Our lives depend on it. Each drinling squad has a sledgehammer and a few flagons of lantern oil. They'll try to smash and burn the winches into inoperability. They shouldn't meet too much opposition. Nobody expected an attack tonight, least of all from inside the city. Their hardest chore might be to repel the reinforcements until we're through."

"Do they have an escape plan?" Jason queried.

"A risky one. Some of the drinlings used a skiff to board the *Valiant* while Aram distracted the guardsmen. Two drinlings were assigned to tie it to the stern with a long rope, so it will drag behind our ship. If the drinlings on the wall make it to the end of the breakwaters, and if we successfully slip through the gap, and if they're still alive, they can dive in and swim for the skiff. Once out to sea and away from immediate danger, we can welcome them aboard. Any stragglers who miss the skiff will have to swim into open water and try to get away unaided."

Jason peered anxiously ahead, trying to make out what was happening atop the sea walls. The hellish light of the blazing ships added to the illumination from the watch fires. Figures were running on the walls. The ship felt like it was advancing in slow motion. The breeze was weakening, and the oars could only do so much. Aram barked commands and occasionally climbed the rigging himself in the attempt to get the sails into the best possible position.

The bells continued to clang. Jason glimpsed fighting near the bonfire at the end of the left sea wall, silhouettes attacking one another. More combat became visible around the big bonfire on the opposite breakwater. A body fell from the wall. Jason hoped it was an enemy. After the fighting stopped, Jason could see fig-ures attacking the great wooden winches, firelight glinting off the metal heads of sledgehammers. The left winch burst into flames, followed by the right.

Aram hollered the loudest, his rumbling voice audible over the panicky bells and the cheering of the other drinlings. Jason wondered if the drinlings on the wall could hear the gratitude. He wished the ship would sail faster. It was like riding a turtle during a jailbreak.

Back on the dock the fires were spreading. All the ships burned fiercely. A flaming mast had collapsed onto a pier, setting it ablaze. A second ship had ignited another pier. Whirlwinds of sparks spun up into the night above great sheets of flame. As a whole, the wild conflagration was beginning to look apocalyptic. If control was not soon gained over the fires, the entire waterfront would be lost.

The *Valiant* cruised toward the dark gap, oars sloshing, sails not slack but not bulging. Many guardsmen could be seen rac-ing along the sea wall, best visible as they passed torches or cres-sets, sprinting toward the gap where the winches now blazed. The guardsmen moved faster than the ship, but they had more dis-tance to cover.

The wind rose enough to fan the flames on the dock and fill the sails. Masts creaking, the ship accelerated in response.

The gap drew nearer. Jason tried to will the wind to push harder. As the ship approached, he gauged that the opening between the sea walls was probably eight or nine times wider than the *Valiant*. Standing on the deck, Jason was still a good fifteen feet lower than the walls. The closer the ship drew to the sea walls, the harder it became to see the activity up top. Jason gazed ahead at the darkness of the open sea.

"We're through," Drake said as the front of the ship nosed into the gap. "Too late to raise a barricade now."

Relieved, Jason directed his attention to the unseen drinlings on the wall. He could hear blades clashing. Would any of them make it? He looked up at the breakwater as they sailed past, alternately glancing from one side to the other. The ship was nearly halfway through the gap before he saw three figures dive off the wall to the right. Moments later a pair dove from the wall on the left. Knowing there should have been five drinlings on each wall, Jason kept watching for other survivors.

"Down!" Drake shouted, tackling Jason to the deck.

For a moment the brusque action startled and bewildered him. Then arrows began thunking against the ship, a few at a time. A drinling plummeted at least thirty feet from the rigging, an arrow in his ribs. Jason grimaced as the body struck the deck with finality. Bearing shields, Thag and Zoo stood over Jason and Drake. As several drinling archers launched arrows of their own, Drake dragged Jason to a hatch and clambered down with him.

"I shouldn't have left you exposed like that," Drake apologized. "Very sloppy."

"I'm all right," he panted.

Drake shook his head. "We were target practice. They had a deadly angle on us. I was too fixated on making it out of the harbor. I should have taken us belowdecks from the start."

"Think any of the drinlings from the wall will make it?" Jason asked.

"Depends how far back the skiff is trailing. If it was me, I would have jumped earlier. Soon as the front of the ship reached the harbor mouth, we were free."

"They might have been stuck fighting," Jason said.

"They did us a brave service," Drake replied. "Without them I doubt we would have gotten away."

"All clear," Zoo called down from outside the hatch.

Jason and Drake returned to the deck and looked back at the sea wall of Durna. The bells rang more quietly. The winches still burned beside the watch fires. In the background, flames raged along the dock.

"Anybody make it to the skiff from the wall?" Drake asked.

Thag held up three fingers.

Drake nodded and led Jason to the front of the ship, where Nia stood with a shuttered lantern. The blackness of the Inland Sea stretched out before them, with only the stars to show where the water ended and the sky began. Jason felt unsteady, drained after the stress and excitement of their narrow escape. It had all been so frantic. People on both sides had lost their lives. He hardly knew how to handle the sudden, dark calm. He felt bad for the drinlings who had fallen, but thrilled that the daring hijacking had succeeded.

Nia opened the shutter twice for a few seconds each time, then twice quickly. A moment later four quick flashes answered from farther out to sea, just right of their current heading.

"See that?" Nia called.

"I saw!" Aram answered. He shouted steering instructions.

"Corinne and Farfalee?" Jason asked.

"Together with Bat and Ux," Nia replied. "Four flashes means they're all there." She grinned at Drake. "We pulled it off."

"Your people were spectacular," Drake said.

"We lost some on the wall, and Gaw was killed on our way through the harbor mouth. Any lost life is tragic, but our losses could have been worse. Should have been worse."

"They were as surprised as we had hoped," Drake said. "Several ships will be totally lost. It will take months to repair the piers. News of this hijacking will shake up more than this region. An interceptor is a serious prize, and we torched their waterfront as well. Many across

Lyrian will hear the tale. Word of this victory should help Galloran as he recruits for his revolt. Tonight the empire looks vulnerable."

Jason hadn't stopped to consider how the hijacking might bring hope to Maldor's enemies. Drake was right. Any bully looks less tough after somebody stands up to them. Jason tried not to dwell on the drinling who had fallen to the deck or the warriors who had died on the wall. Tonight was a big victory, a major step toward fulfilling the prophecy. Maybe they could actually pull it off!

"Maldor will demand vengeance," Nia said. "He'll want to make an example of us."

"We'll have his full attention going forward," Drake agreed. "It was the price we paid for transportation to the island. With imperial troops behind us, and the Maumet before us, I have a hard time imagining how the oracle saw any of us surviving to seek out Darian the Seer."

"Don't write us off yet," Jason said, feeling emboldened by their success. "We have a fast ship and lots of good fighters. We'll find a way to finish the mission."

"Such reckless optimism," Drake said dryly.

Jasher came up behind them. "We have another advantage. The emperor can't be certain where we're going. Even if he confirmed our identities, our destination would be difficult to guess. The Inland Sea is large. We will not be easy quarry."

"The oracle saw a way for us to survive," Jason added. "We just have to find it."

CHAPTER 9

A PROPOSAL

On a gray afternoon, Rachel roamed the woods, unsettled because everything felt much too familiar. The moss on the towering trees looked dark beneath the overcast sky. Rain drizzled down, just enough to dampen her. Up ahead a small decorative bridge spanned a little stream. She knew that on the far side her name was carved on a beige post, inside a heart.

Rachel approached the little bridge in bewilderment and traced her fingers over the engraved letters: *R-A-C-H-E-L*. This bridge was on the property her family owned. This forest was part of her backyard.

Glancing behind, Rachel observed ranks of thriving trees. What had she expected to see? She scowled pensively. Should she be here? How had she gotten here? Had she set out from her house to wander the woods and think? That felt wrong. But where else could she have come from? The memory almost came into focus, then dissipated.

She could not see her house up ahead, but Rachel knew it stood just beyond the top of the rise through the trees, along with three additional buildings that her parents frequently loaned to artists. At first they had made the spaces available to select friends. Then friends of friends. Eventually they had needed to make a reservation list. Painters, writers, sculptors. Occasionally musicians.

Why did the thought of home spark an urgent longing? Rachel wanted to run. Ignoring the silly impulse, she strolled up the hill, basking in the familiar sights and smells. She felt lucky to live in such a beautiful place.

The house had lights on in defiance of the gray day. Was it getting darker? Rain still sprinkled down. Rachel climbed the steps to the wide, rustic deck. She found the rear sliding door locked. She went around to the front door and found it locked as well. Shouldn't she have a key? She checked her pockets. Nope.

Walking away from the door, Rachel peered through a living room window. There were her parents, comfy in their favorite chairs, each with a book, steaming mugs nearby. The sight of them made her heart swell with relief and joy.

Rachel rapped on the window, but it made hardly any sound. She knocked harder, but it was like banging on a huge slab of stone rather than a fragile windowpane. "Dad!" she shouted. "Mom! I can't get in!" All they had to do was look up and see her at the window. They didn't.

Frustrated, Rachel hurried to the front door and knocked heavily. Again there was no sound. She tried the doorbell. Normally, she should have heard it chime even from outside. She heard nothing. What was going on?

She looked down at the fancy welcome mat, a gift from a visiting artist. THE WOODRUFFS, it read in flowery script. Clusters of costume jewels added sparkle in two corners. The artist had insisted that they actually use the mat. Rachel frowned. The mat seemed to taunt her by proclaiming that this was her home. If that was true, why couldn't she get in?

Rachel circled the house. She slapped random windows after checking to see if they were unlocked. None were. No matter how hard she pummeled the glass, she could produce no noise. She looped back to the window where she could see her parents calmly reading. Dad was sipping from his mug. Mom turned a page.

Rachel pounded the glass with both fists, to no avail. She waved her arms and shouted. She backed up, picked up a stone the size of her fist, and hurled it at the window. The stone bounced off, making no noise until it struck the ground. What had her parents done to the house? Made it soundproof and bulletproof?

Desperate, Rachel picked up another rock.

"Can I help you?" asked a female voice from behind.

Rachel whirled and saw Sharmaine, her favorite artist who had ever resided with them. When had she come back? Sharmaine had short pink hair and dark eyeliner. She wore a denim jacket covered with pins, beads, and ink doodles.

Sharmaine had grown up in Michigan. She painted pieces of wood and then wrote original haikus on them in fancy calligraphy. She had given Rachel a painted wooden segment that read:

> When Rachel pole vaults
> She soars like a swift pirate
> With a huge peg leg

The plank had a doodle of a pirate beside the haiku. It was one of Rachel's favorite treasures.

"Hi, Sharmaine," Rachel said. "I was trying to get their attention."

"Rock through the window would do it," Sharmaine replied curtly. She wasn't showing any recognition. If anything, she seemed wary.

Rachel glanced at the rock in her hand. "They couldn't hear me."

Sharmaine gave a cautious nod. "Let's try the front door."

Rachel almost protested, but decided against it. She followed Sharmaine to the front door. "You remember me, right?" Rachel checked.

"Sure," Sharmaine said vaguely. She knocked on the door. It made a sound! A normal knocking sound, just how it should.

A moment later her dad answered. "Hi, Sharmaine. Who's your friend?" He was looking at Rachel with blank courtesy.

She had seen her father show that expression to other people. But never her. He knew her. He loved her.

"It's me," Rachel said meekly.

"Have we met?" he asked, still with the neutral politeness appropriate for a new acquaintance.

"I'm your daughter," Rachel said, insulted that she had to spell it out.

Her dad looked to Sharmaine, who shrugged. "I found her outside your window holding a rock."

Dad returned his gaze patiently to Rachel. "Our only daughter died years ago," he explained. "Did you know her?"

Rachel suddenly realized that she had been away in Lyrian for a long time. It all came rushing back. She must look older or different. "It's me, Dad. I'm just older. I'm back." Tears welled in her eyes.

Her dad glanced at Sharmaine. The glance communicated that they clearly had a situation on their hands.

"I'm not crazy," Rachel blurted, wiping at her eyes. "Ask me anything; I can prove it."

"Where do you live?" he asked gently.

"Here," Rachel answered in a small voice. "I live here."

"Why don't you come inside and sit down?" her dad offered, as he would to a needy stranger.

Rachel turned to Sharmaine. "You remember me, right? You gave me the haiku? About the pole vaulting?"

Sharmaine held out a painted plank. "If you want a haiku, I can spare this one." Rachel accepted the wooden rectangle. Sharmaine looked at Rachel's dad. "You okay?"

"I've got this," he replied. "Thanks, Sharmaine."

Sharmaine turned away, and Rachel followed her dad inside. He escorted Rachel to the living room and offered her a seat on the sofa. Her mom was no longer present.

"Make yourself comfortable," her dad said. "I'll be back in a second."

Rachel took a seat, the painted plank in her hands. Turning it over, she saw little gravestones doodled at either side of a haiku.

> *Most loving parents*
> *Try to dodge conversations*
> *With their dead children*

The words struck Rachel like a physical blow. Fearful chills made her skin prickle. What was going on?

She stood up, surveying the familiar room. The correct pictures hung on the walls. The correct knickknacks rested on the mantel. The scent of herbal tea wafted up from half-empty mugs.

"Rachel?"

Startled, Rachel spun to face her mother, who had just entered the room. "Mom?"

Her mom cocked her head sympathetically. "No, dear, I'm not your mother."

Exasperated, Rachel pointed to a nearby picture of the

three of them. "Look at the picture, Mom. Does the girl in it look familiar?"

"She was our daughter," her mom sighed serenely. "You're not her, dear."

"I am her, Mom. What's the problem? Do I look that different? Ask me anything."

Rachel's mom looked her straight in the eye, her expression becoming stern. "You are not our daughter. Our little girl has vanished forever. It's time you confront the truth. Merrill and I have moved on. You should as well."

Rachel suddenly recognized that her mom's eyes were completely black. Thinking back, she seemed to recall that her dad's were black too, and Sharmaine's as well, although she had failed to notice at the time.

"You're not my mom," Rachel whispered.

The woman smiled. "That's right. Now you're getting it. Somebody here has been looking for you."

Maldor stepped around the corner into the living room. Rachel had never seen him, but she knew his identity as surely as she knew that she must be dreaming.

"I'll leave you two to talk things over," her dream mom said, stepping out of the room.

Rachel faced Maldor, glaring into his black eyes. "This is a dream."

"We need to talk."

Rachel stared at him. "It feels real. I feel awake. Is that really you?"

"As close as we can manage at present. Have a seat."

"I'll stay standing."

"No need for hostility. I'm here as a courtesy."

The statement made Rachel furious. "Get out of my house!

Get out of my mind! You weren't invited! You don't belong here!"

Maldor held up his hands soothingly. "Don't lose your temper. I'll leave soon. First, we must talk. Your friends are going to die, Rachel. All of them. Soon. Unless you save them. I just wanted to give you that chance."

Concern for her friends warred against her rage at the mental intrusion. After a moment, Rachel bridled her anger enough to respond rationally. "You're not here to help them. Or me. You're here to mess with my mind. How do I get rid of you?"

"Don't be so hasty," Maldor warned. "This illusion took considerable time and effort to establish. You should hear my proposal."

Rachel took a deep breath. What if she attacked him? What if she used Edomic to set the sofa on fire and hurl it at him?

"You can't hurt me here," Maldor said. "I can make this much less pleasant, if you wish."

"Don't read my thoughts," Rachel snapped.

"They're hard to miss," Maldor apologized. "After all, this is your mind."

"Doesn't feel like it."

"I imagine not. You have so little control. I could teach you to lock out incursions such as this."

Rachel frowned. "That's a class I might sign up for."

"Shall we talk?" Maldor said, sitting down. "Tark or Io could get badly hurt if this takes too long. The more quickly we converse, the safer they'll be."

"Fine. All right." Rachel sat down on the sofa. She had never felt so conscious in a dream before. So alert and lucid. It seemed no different from full consciousness.

"Where did Jason go?" Maldor inquired.

Rachel felt panic. She tried not to think about him.

"Windbreak Island? Interesting. That explains much. I don't see how he'll survive. What guidance did you receive at Mianamon?"

"Get out of here!" Rachel yelled.

Maldor snapped his fingers. The sofa folded up around her, trapping her in a cushioned embrace. She remained in a seated position, cocooned from her ankles to her mouth. She could only manage muffled protests. She tried to will the sofa to release her, but it refused to budge.

"Hmmm," Maldor mused. "Fascinating prophecy. I suppose there must be some minuscule chance for his survival. This is very useful information, by the way. Do you think your quests could possibly work? An attack on Felrook would be suicide for all involved. If I permit you to speak, will you be civil? Blink once for yes, twice for no."

Angry and frustrated, Rachel blinked once.

The cushions unfolded from her mouth. "We'll beat you."

Maldor laughed. "She glimpsed one way, Rachel. The oracle glimpsed a single unlikely chain of coincidences that could stop me amid countless ways to fail. She neglected to offer many specifics. Now that I know what you are trying to do, it will be that much easier to stop you. Thank you, Rachel, for this priceless intelligence."

Rachel squirmed. The sofa held her fast. She wanted to shout with frustration. Hot tears threatened.

"Don't blame yourself," Maldor urged. "I could have acquired this knowledge by a hundred different methods. Not that it matters. The oracle set you on a path that will require more than a miracle. It will require a prolonged series of miracles. Darian the Pyromancer is dead, Rachel. He has been dead for eons. Which Jason and his comrades will never learn, because they will perish

146

at Windbreak Island. I won't need to twitch a finger. The Maumet will see to their fate. And Galloran will undoubtedly die leading his foolhardy siege. There is no question."

Maldor leaned forward. He spoke softly. "That prophecy is one of the nicest gifts anyone has ever given me. It brings me considerable peace of mind. I had worried that it might be dangerous. According to the oracle, somewhere in the future awaits some remote possibility of me coming to harm. I'll be sure to defend against that implausible eventuality. Thanks to the prophetess, I now know where to focus my efforts."

Maldor snapped his fingers, as if concerned Rachel's attention might be straying. "Look at the situation with a practical eye. The prophecy will put all of my most capable enemies into extremely vulnerable positions years before I could have managed it on my own. I will win my war twenty years earlier than expected, all thanks to the dying words of a withered schemer."

Rachel had no response. She wanted to weep. She wanted to scream.

"You're concerned about your friends," Maldor said tenderly. "I'm here to make an offer. I've thought about you in the months since you escaped my servants at the Last Inn. With the passage of time, I've grown increasingly certain that I wish to train you."

"Never," Rachel gasped.

Maldor smiled. "Don't be so quick to deny me. At least hear the proposal, so you can understand who your refusal will be killing. Look at this through my eyes. Soon I will have subdued all of Lyrian. There will always be decisions to make, a vast empire to manage. Much of that will become tedium, and most of it can be handled by underlings. Once Lyrian is conquered, I can see myself regretting not having an adept like you to train. Edomic talent tends to be hereditary. So many gifted bloodlines have failed that you may represent my last opportunity to pass my knowledge forward to a worthy apprentice."

"I don't want it," Rachel said.

"No need to play games. No need for posturing. No need to act brave or defiant. We're alone here. You may not want to employ Edomic in all the same ways I use it, but you crave the knowledge. You've been working hard to attain greater knowledge ever since you discovered your talent. I can feel how you relish the power, how you exult in it. I can feel how you yearn to gain enough mastery to destroy me. I will install means to prevent you, but you're resourceful. In time you may find a way to thwart my precautions and overthrow me. You'll certainly have a better chance than any of your comrades."

Rachel closed her eyes. She tried to wall her thoughts away from him, to close her intellect to his scrutiny.

"We're in here together," Maldor chuckled. "It's too late to deny me admittance. Listen to my offer, and I will depart. I want you to come to me voluntarily. If you do, I will grant absolute, unconditional mercy to ten of your friends. Any you choose to name. Jason, Galloran, Corinne, even Ferrin. All are eligible. Not only will I spare them, but I will ensure that they live out their days in peace and comfort. If Jason so desires, I will even send him back to the Beyond. Perhaps he will have the good sense to stay put this time. Do not respond now. Mull it over, take a few days— weeks, even—without my presence to distract you. Think hard. You cannot imagine all you will learn, all you will achieve, all you will become. Most would offer me anything for this chance. I extend the opportunity to you freely, with generous promises attached. Respond by coming to me. Or by not coming to me. The choice is yours."

Maldor stood. The sofa unfurled back to its normal shape.

Maldor looked around. "You had a pleasant home. I can see the appeal. But your parents have moved on. So should you. Farewell, until we meet again."

Maldor walked out of the room.

Rachel's dream mom entered with a tray of cookies. Rachel eyed her numbly. Her dream mom set the tray in front of Rachel on the coffee table. "There we go. Peanut butter, your favorite."

"You're not my mom," Rachel said.

The black eyes betrayed no emotion. "Of course not. Have a cookie."

"I want to wake up."

Her dream mom was walking out of the room. "Then have a cookie."

Rachel was left alone. She selected a peanut butter cookie and held it up. The texture was as she remembered. It was still slightly warm from the oven. She sniffed it suspiciously. The cookie smelled delicious.

She took a bite. Just as the flavor started to hit her tongue, Rachel opened her eyes. She was in her room at Trensicourt, on her wide, soft bed. It had not felt like waking up. Not a bit. Her mind felt equally conscious as when she had sniffed the cookie. There had been no transition. Her eyes had been closed. Now they were open.

By the moonlight spilling through the window, Rachel could see a pair of lurkers beside her bed, like human shadows made three-dimensional. Reflecting none of the silvery glow, the figures were easily the darkest shade of black in the room, the kind of darkness found only in the most obscure reaches of space, beyond all starlight.

Her first impulse was to scream. But Tark and Io were in the next room. If she cried out, they would run in, attack the lurkers, and die. Clenching her teeth, she held the scream inside.

The lurkers were here. They had been here for some time, all during her dream, at least. As far as she understood, they would show no aggression unless provoked. She thought about her charm necklace, the one that helped keep lurkers out of her mind. It was packed away. Lurkers weren't supposed to be a threat in a city.

She stared at the motionless duo. Jason had told her that standing up to his lurker had helped. She should show no fear. Maybe she could learn something about them. Her hands were clenched into fists, her nails biting into her palms. She tried to calm herself and focus her thoughts.

Why did you invade my dreams? Rachel asked with her mind.

The lurkers remained perfectly still. *We are messengers,* the lurker on the right replied.

It was a relief to perceive a coherent response. It made them seem less alien. *I thought you never came into cities,* Rachel conveyed.

Very seldom, the lurker responded.

Maldor insisted, Rachel guessed.

We could not refuse.

Rachel furrowed her brow. *Was that really Maldor in my dream? Or just you?*

Him through us, the lurker replied. *We can reach one another.* Even without elaboration, she clearly understood that it referred to the other lurkers. They could keep in mental contact regardless of distance. *He was near one of us.*

Rachel remembered conversations with Jason and the charm woman. If she wanted to know where these creatures originated, who better to ask? *Are you like me? Are you Beyonders?*

We are Beyonders. We are not like you.

You're from a different Beyond. Maldor controls you?

Within limits, by treaty.

Why come to me in a dream? Why not communicate like this? Why show me my house and my parents? Why torture me?

We do not belong in these forms. A dream is more natural to us.

Dreams are more like the place you come from? Rachel guessed.

More than the rest of this. She could feel its disdain.

Are you trying to get away? Rachel asked. *Are you prisoners? Are you trying to escape and get home? Is he controlling you?*

The other lurker entered the conversation for the first time, the second mind recognizably different. *So many questions. Not your concern. Our assignment is complete.*

The two lurkers darted across the room and sprang from the window. It was a long drop, but Rachel knew it would be no problem for the torivors. She had seen a torivor leap from the wall of a high ravine and land lightly.

The sudden absence of the torivors was almost more unsettling than their presence. Lurkers had invaded her mind, her dreams. Maldor had just spoken to her. He had spied on her thoughts, her home, her secrets. He had learned the prophecy. And he had made her an offer.

Why hadn't she worn the charm necklace? Why had she assumed she didn't need it while at Trensicourt?

Another question loomed, more terrible than all the others. Rachel tried to ignore it, but the sickening concern was inescapable. She wished she could bury the thought, keep it secret, even from herself. Maldor had emphasized that only one path would lead to his destruction, while billions would lead to his triumph. After learning the prophecy, he would be more prepared than ever to stop them. Rachel shivered. What if, by leaving her mind open to him tonight, she had already ruined the possibility of anyone defeating him?

CHAPTER 10

AVENGER

I t's an interceptor," Aram said, lowering the spyglass and passing it to Jasher. Aram was short again, his voice pitched higher than at night. More than two days out from Durna, Jason, Nia, Jasher, and Aram huddled together at one side of the *Valiant*. Minutes before, a drinling high on the mainmast had spotted a ship on the eastern horizon.

"It's on a course to intercept us," Jasher said. "Of all the foul luck!"

"Don't scold luck," Aram said. "Word of the debacle in Durna must have traveled more swiftly than we imagined."

"Maybe from displacer to displacer," Jason guessed.

Aram grunted. "By displacer or eagle or gossiping fishwives, the word is out, and imperial vessels are checking the sea lanes away from Durna."

"There are only two other interceptors in the whole Inland Sea!" Nia complained. "What are the chances?"

"Does it matter?" Aram replied. "One has found us. How do we respond?"

"How we deal with the interceptor is most vital in the short term," Drake agreed, approaching the group alongside Farfalee.

"How they found us so quickly may matter more as time goes by."

"We razed their waterfront," Aram said. "They started looking hard. They found us."

"Too quickly," Drake said.

"Weren't you the one predicting disaster?" Nia asked Drake.

"Only because I hate being wrong," Drake replied. "Personally, I would much rather beat the odds and live. I expected travail, but not such early detection."

"I haven't let my eagles fly since the day before our rendezvous," Farfalee reminded everyone.

"Could our foes have anticipated our destination?" Jasher asked. "Doesn't seem likely. Sailors have avoided the sight of Windbreak Island for generations. Who could have leaked our intentions?"

"Impossible to guess," Drake said. "But whatever we do about our visible pursuers, we should be braced for more. Our enemies must have uncovered our plans. In situations like this, I'm slow to credit coincidence."

"What do you suggest?" Farfalee asked Aram.

"The wind is from the southeast. It will benefit both ships. Given our current positions, I expect we could evade the other interceptor and win a race to Windbreak Island. But the other ship will never lose sight of us. We'll be trapped between the abominable guardian and the oncoming interceptor."

"What if we engage them?" Jasher asked.

"You're familiar with our armaments," Aram said. He was referring to the miniature catapults—three on each side—poised to launch burning pitch. "The enemy ship will be similarly equipped. Most likely we would roast each other, which would serve the emperor fine."

Jason winced. The prospect of combat aboard flaming ships with no land in sight was not appealing.

"We don't just need to survive this," Drake muttered. "We need to make it through virtually unscathed, or the rest of our efforts will be hobbled."

"What about our orantium?" Jason asked.

"It's our biggest advantage," Farfalee agreed.

Jasher scowled in thought. "The problem becomes how to get close enough to deliver the explosives without taking fire ourselves."

"Would the catapults fling orantium farther than pitch?" Jason wondered.

Drake shook his head. "Probably not much farther."

"What if we moved a catapult to the bow and went straight at them?" Farfalee asked.

Aram shrugged. "Unconventional. Might catch them off guard. We might get off a few spheres before they could adjust. Once they adjusted, the maneuver would swiftly bring us into close range."

"Orantium impacting the deck of the other ship would cause damage," Jasher said. "But orantium against the hull near the waterline would sink them."

Aram chuckled. "That would require quite a shot."

"We want to hit them before they can hit us," Nia said. "And it would be best to strike the hull near the waterline. Would losing some dead weight help us sail faster?"

"Only a little," Aram said.

"We should run, but let them get close," Nia replied. "I have a plan."

Jason stood at the stern beside Farfalee, watching the interceptor gradually gaining on them, sails billowing in the breeze. The sun would set before long.

"They don't seem to suspect anything," Jason said. "They're trailing straight behind us."

"They assume we're incompetent sailors," Farfalee replied. "Getting directly between us and the breeze gives them a chance to steal wind from our sails and gain even more quickly. Aram is deliberately doing nothing to counter the tactic. And he doesn't have us rigged for maximum efficiency."

"How is Corinne?"

Farfalee shook her head sadly. "Green as ever. I had hoped that the larger vessel and calmer water would reduce her stomach problems. Not so."

Jason nodded. Journeying southward last year, Corinne had been seasick all the way from the Silver River to the Durnese River aboard a drinling longship. Not an hour after coming aboard the *Valiant*, she had fallen ill again. She was currently in a cabin belowdecks. When Jason had visited, she had been flat on the floor, perspiring and moaning, a bucket at her side. He hadn't stayed long.

Behind the *Valiant* and off to one side, a school of kitefish leaped from the water, more than a dozen in total. They looked like a cross between barracuda and manta rays, long bodies sporting wide, winglike fins. The kitefish sprang into the wind, triangular fins spread wide, gliding smoothly upward, then hanging suspended before plunging back into the water.

With nets and rods, several of the drinlings worked round the clock catching kitefish and other sea life. Drake had explained that because of the high salt content, only select species of fish could survive in the Inland Sea.

"Would kitefish attack people?" Jason asked. They looked large enough.

"They mostly prey on other fish and birds," Farfalee answered.

"You don't have anything like them in the ocean?"

"Not really."

"I wonder where they came from," Jason said. "If the Inland Sea is too salty for most fish, how did they get here in the first place?"

"Wizards," Farfalee answered. "Anciently, this sea was lifeless. Using Edomic, wizards engineered fish that could withstand the intense salinity. Several species of bioluminescent seaweed, as well. The introduction of fish to the Inland Sea allowed for settlements to develop. Without the tampering of ancient wizards, there would be little life or industry here today."

"It must have been hard for the wizards to create new life," Jason said. "Rachel told me that living things resist Edomic."

"Which is why very few wizards ever produced even simple life-forms. Only the most learned and powerful could engineer life, and only four or five ever managed to spawn what we would consider intelligent life."

"Can Maldor do it?" Jason wondered.

"If so, we have seen little evidence. His supporters are culled from preexisting races. It required some skill to evolve a botched race into the manglers, but it was adaptation, not true creation. Maldor is both powerful and talented, but probably not yet skilled enough to truly produce his own life-forms."

"You knew some of the great wizards of Lyrian," Jason said. "Like Eldrin."

"I was not close to Eldrin," Farfalee clarified. "But in my youth I spent some time in his presence. He was not a particularly kind man. He struck me as brilliant but abrupt, much more interested in his own plans and goals than in the people around him. All of his intelligent races have reason to dislike him. After all, at the same time he brought the Amar Kabal into being, he also designed our eventual extinction."

"He made it harder to have kids over time," Jason recalled.

Farfalee nodded. "We've grown less fertile. Only six children have been born to the Amar Kabal during the past thirty years. My son, Lodan, is one of them. I could hardly believe I was going to be a mother after lifetimes of trying. I may be one of the last. As a people we will endure only as long as our seeds stay healthy and keep getting planted. Drake is not the first of us to be reborn without a functional amar. Nor will he be the last."

"Could somebody use Edomic to fix the way Eldrin made you?"

She shook her head. "Such expertise no longer exists. Even the most capable wizard from ages past would probably fall short of the task. Only Eldrin could have given our race the chance to endure, and he opted to limit our population, much as Zokar did with his creations."

"I know your laws forbid it," Jason said, "but what if you studied Edomic? You know, learned to repair yourselves."

"Some among us have argued that we should study Edomic. My brother is one of them. Such thinking is foolishness. We were engineered to have little aptitude for Edomic. The most adept among us could never achieve enough power to justify the risk. Any of the Amar Kabal who tamper with Edomic risk fulfilling the prophecy that such activity will bring about our demise."

"Labeling me a fool behind my back?" Drake asked from behind.

Farfalee turned to face him. "I've issued no labels that I would hesitate to repeat in front of you. You are a fool to toy with Edomic and to advocate its use to other seedfolk. You could bring about the end of our race for the lofty aspiration of igniting small fires without tinder."

"I still normally need tinder," Drake explained. "But I can manage the feat without flint."

"Foolishness."

"You speak Edomic better than I do."

"That's different," Farfalee insisted. "I only speak to communicate. Never to command."

Drake waved a dismissive hand. "Don't worry, Failie. No
prophecy would have included me. I'm a disgrace and an outcast."

Farfalee shrugged. "Your words, not mine."

He folded his arms. "Very well, sister, how would you label me?"

She looked at him seriously for a moment. "You are certainly
an outcast. But so is my husband, and I have greater respect for no
man living. You have made some poor choices, Drake, but here
we stand. You keep correcting your course. Few men are as true
to themselves and their instincts. I would say that you are much
closer to being a hero than a disgrace."

Drake looked away. Jason could tell her words had touched
him. Regaining his composure, the seedman squinted at the slowly
gaining interceptor. "This should time out well."

"Our pursuers will be in position before nightfall," Farfalee said.

"Think we can sink it?" Jason asked.

"Aram likes the plan," Drake replied. "As does Heg. As do I.
Bat volunteered to do the honors."

The plan was simple. With night falling, and the interceptor directly behind them, the crew of the *Valiant* would lighten
the load slightly by throwing some nonessentials overboard. A
drinling would jump into the sea along with the junk. He would
bring a pair of orantium globes. The *Valiant* would hold a steady
course, which would hopefully lure the pursuing ship right past
the drinling in the water.

"Will we circle back for him?" Farfalee asked. She and Corinne
had spent more days with Bat than the rest of them.

"It has been a matter of debate," Drake said. "Seems heartless to leave him. But we'd have to go against the wind. It could cost a lot of time. Bat claims he can make it to shore on his own. I don't know. Tireless or not, we're far from land."

Farfalee nodded. "If you're right about the empire learning our plans, we can ill afford to lose time."

"Hence the debate," Drake said. "Heg and Nia insist we should leave the drinling behind. Aram seems to be leaning their way. Jasher and I would rather return for him."

Looking out at the water, Jason envisioned himself stranded at sea, alone, no boat or land in sight, gentle swells rising and falling around him. He could think of few predicaments more intimidating. Clearing his throat, he asked, "What are the chances he could make it?"

Drake shrugged. "He'll go over the side with plenty of debris to help him keep afloat. Not quite a raft, but enough to rest on. Unlike us, he can drink seawater. He would bring provisions. If he can keep his bearings and survive, Bat might reach land within a week or two."

"Or he might die miserably and alone," Farfalee added. "Without an imminent threat, it strikes me as disgraceful to abandon a hero who risks his life to save the rest of us."

"What does Bat want?" Jason wondered.

"He insists that we shouldn't return for him," Drake said. "Claims it will jeopardize the mission and belittle his sacrifice."

"Bat has to say that," Farfalee sighed. "Drinlings were created to sacrifice in battle. The concept might even be supported by their physiology at an instinctive level. They view death in combat as the glorious fulfillment of their destinies. Eldrin taught them that they are expendable, and they believe it. Unless blatantly mistreated, drinlings will readily suffer and die for the good of their allies."

Drake nodded. "The prospect of the rest of us placing the

mission at risk to come to his rescue is utterly foreign to him. The group does not bend for the individual."

"If that's how he's been trained to feel," Jason said, "wouldn't we be taking advantage of him?"

Farfalee huffed softly. "If the imperials have learned our destination, returning for Bat truly could endanger the mission. For the good of all Lyrian, our mission must succeed. By design or not, Bat sincerely would not want us to go back for him. And he truly does stand a chance of surviving on his own."

"My sister the pragmatist," Drake said. "Should I tell Nia and Heg that we're willing to abandon Bat?"

Farfalee gave a reluctant nod. "If they recommend it, and Bat is willing, our need is too great to defy them."

"I'll convey our consent." Drake walked away.

Farfalee turned to Jason. "How do you feel about that decision?"

"I don't know. It kind of feels wrong."

"It does. But is it necessary?"

Jason folded his arms and scrunched his brow. "Maybe. Probably. What an awful choice."

She stared at the pursuing ship. "I doubt either decision could feel right. We can risk Bat's life, or we can risk the mission. The oracle warned that Lyrian must be purchased with sacrifice. I fear Bat may be one of many to come."

"What if he fails?"

"We will be even less able to go back for him. If his failure reveals our intentions, we probably won't be able to succeed with a similar ploy. If his failure goes unnoticed, we'll have to try again, perhaps involving the skiff or one of the launches."

Jason turned and watched Drake speaking with Nia, Heg, and Bat. Nia and Heg looked satisfied, and Bat looked overjoyed. The bravery of his smile left Jason resisting tears.

"How could we possibly show Bat how much we appreciate him?" Jason asked.

"We succeed," Farfalee replied.

By the time the glowing streaks of sunset began to fade from the western clouds, Bat stood ready to jump. Several crates, barrels, and pallets had been collected to heave over the side with him. The little raft of planks he would use as a personal flotation device was larger than a paddleboard, and some impromptu carpentry had made it quite stable. He had food, gear for catching fish, and an improvised snorkel. And of course he had the two orantium spheres.

"Stay low," Jasher cautioned. "Keep wreckage between yourself and the ship. Use the breathing tube to stay submerged whenever possible."

"Don't worry," Bat said. "They won't see me. I'll get close enough not to miss. They'll drown without knowing what happened."

"We can't have everyone crowding the rear of the ship to watch," Aram said. "Certainly not until after Bat strikes. Dump your debris, then man your stations. Jason has been near the stern all day. He and Jasher will serve as lookouts. Until the explosion we can't display excessive interest."

"It's time," Farfalee said. "Swim safely, Bat. We are all indebted."

Bat grinned. "Don't thank me yet."

Heg drew near and whispered something to Bat, who nodded and whispered something back. The two men gripped forearms. Bat looked eager.

"Positions," Aram ordered, his voice deeper now that he had grown. Drinlings moved to both sides of the ship. Bat got ready, his floatation device in hand.

Jasher and Jason strolled to the rear of the ship.

Aram gave the command. Crates, barrels, pallets, and other

wooden fragments went over the side along with Bat. The ship was advancing at a good pace, thanks to the steady breeze, so it did not take long before Jason saw the debris trailing on the water. He tried not to stare at Bat's flotation device.

The interceptor was closer than ever, not more than fifteen ship lengths behind. It would overtake the flotsam before long.

Jasher raised the spyglass, directing it at the ship, not the debris. "We're being pursued by the *Avenger*," he reported. "I can finally make out the name. Have a look."

Jason accepted the spyglass. "Do we seem too interested?"

"We've been gazing at them all day. You in particular. They've almost caught us. It would seem more peculiar if we didn't watch."

Jason peered into the eyepiece. The light of the dying sunset barely let him read the name of the ship. "Hopefully, they won't avenge anything today."

"They think they have us," Jasher said. "They've gained on us throughout the day. Lightening our load made us look desperate. They're focused on us, not the debris. They're prepping for battle. Making sure the pitch is hot, the catapults ready. Archers are stringing bows. Boarding parties are assembling. The captain is waiting to see what maneuver we'll try."

Once he lowered the spyglass, Jason had trouble spotting the debris. "Bat is closer to them than to us."

"If only he can fight the currents enough to stay in their path," Jasher said. "He just has to get close."

"What if they catch him when they abandon ship?" Jason worried.

"It's an additional risk he's taking," Jasher said. "If the *Avenger* founders, it should sail well past Bat before anybody gets in the water. He can keep low and swim tirelessly. They'll have many more pressing matters to worry about. I like his chances of avoiding our enemies. Making it to land should prove the tougher test. Watch it unfold through the spyglass."

Jason did as he was told. He could see some activity on the deck. A man was climbing the rigging. He and Jasher watched in silence.

"Concentrate on the right side," Jasher advised.

"You see him?"

"I think so. He's close. Almost too close. Get ready for it."

The explosion centered just above the waterline at the right front side of the ship. The bright flash sent wooden fragments flying. The percussive boom roared a moment later. Smoke bloomed upward. Once the view cleared, Jason saw a cave-sized hole.

"Yes!" Jason exclaimed. "He got—"

He was interrupted by a second explosion just above the waterline on the right side of the *Avenger*. He was viewing the explosion in profile, so it was a bad angle from which to appreciate the damage, but judging from the position of the detonation, the hole would have to be similar to the first.

Raucous cheering broke out aboard the *Valiant*. All pretenses abandoned, just about everyone crowded the stern, whooping and jeering and clapping. Bat's name was chanted in unison.

It was impossible to see what exactly had happened to Bat, but the listing *Avenger* must have sailed well past him before it really started to wallow. Aram ordered a few drinlings back to their stations. As twilight deepened, everyone else stayed put to watch the *Avenger* sink.

CHAPTER 11

ADVICE

Fingering the strand of charms around her neck, Rachel strolled along a crunchy trail of white pebbles. Sparkling footpaths wound all about the courtyard, past blooming flower beds, clipped grass, colorful shrubs, and leafy creepers ascending trellised walls. Fluffy springtime blossoms made the trees pink and purple. The aroma of nectar enriched the air, to the evident delight of fat, humming bees.

"Mind if I intrude?" asked a friendly voice.

Rachel turned and found Ferrin approaching. Since the day before her disturbing dream, the displacer had been away with Nedwin, delivering messages for Galloran. Rachel glanced over at the gazebo, where Tark and Io sat together. They were always near enough to keep an eye on her, but they tended to keep their distance lately. In some ways she suspected her spooky new outfit worked too well, intimidating even her friends. Tark looked at her inquisitively, as if wondering whether she desired his intervention. She waved a hand to dismiss his concerns.

Ferrin caught the gesture. "Thank you for restraining your attack dogs."

Rachel smiled. "They've been extra vigilant ever since . . . Did you hear?"

"Lurkers broke into your room and entered your dreams."

She nodded, a hand on her necklace. "I should have kept wearing this."

Ferrin shrugged. "Had this attempt failed, Maldor would have found some other way to contact you. If he was willing to order torivors into a city, he really wanted that message to reach you."

"Or he really wanted to scour my brain. He learned about the prophecy."

"I was informed. How did Galloran react?"

Rachel wrung her hands. "He didn't want me to worry. He told me Maldor already knew that we planned to attack. He told me Maldor would have learned the prophecy one way or another. He told me the lurkers could just as easily have searched any of our minds."

"But that response doesn't satisfy you."

"What if I blew it?" Rachel asked softly. "What if I already ruined our chance to fulfill the prophecy? What if I got Jason and Corinne killed?"

Ferrin shook his head. "It wasn't your—"

"I could have worn the charms," Rachel said. "But I was tired of them. I was relieved to take a break from wearing them, since the city was supposed to be free from lurkers. If I had worn the charms, I could have delayed Maldor from learning the prophecy. What if that would have made all the difference? What if we've already lost our chance to succeed?"

Ferrin watched her, arms folded, expression serious.

"What?" she finally asked.

"Maldor is very good at what he does."

"Getting information?"

"That too. But I meant destroying confidence. Spreading fear and uncertainty. What offer did he make you?"

A line appeared between Rachel's eyebrows. "Galloran promised not to—"

"Nobody told me about an offer," Ferrin said. "I just know how the emperor operates."

Rachel glanced at Tark and Io in the gazebo. She didn't want anyone to overhear. She had only shared this with Galloran. "Maldor promised that if I went to train with him, he would let me save ten of my friends. Any ten I choose."

"Do you believe him?"

"Should I?"

Ferrin sighed deeply. "I worked with Maldor for a long time. Immunity for ten people is the most generous offer I have ever heard him make. He really wants you, which probably means he would fulfill his promise."

"You think?"

"Just make sure you grasp the ramifications. Do you suppose a man like Galloran would accept immunity? He turned down Harthenham. Most of the people you want to protect would refuse the protection."

"Would you accept it?" Rachel asked.

"Me? Full immunity? Better if we don't discuss it."

Rachel lowered her voice to her quietest whisper. "Maldor seems so confident he'll win. I'm not sure he's wrong."

Ferrin almost replied, then stopped and indicated a slightly curved stone bench. "Sit down." They sat together. A fuzzy bee circled Rachel before zipping away into some nearby shrubs. Ferrin leaned close to her. "Maldor will probably win."

"Comforting," Rachel muttered.

"I'm not trying to comfort you," Ferrin said gravely. "Not right now. I wish I could console you with soothing lies, but I think what you need at the moment is the truth. The oracle told us that Maldor will almost certainly emerge victorious. We have a minute chance of stopping him. Such a small chance that it almost certainly will not happen."

"I guess I knew that," Rachel whispered shakily.

"That truth could be tempting to forget amid the rousing speeches and busy preparations. Galloran knows how to inspire and mobilize those around him. But don't let his rhetoric confuse the reality of the situation. If our aim is to dethrone Maldor, we've been warned that we'll probably fail."

"Right."

"You might be correct about the danger of Maldor learning the prophecy this early. The untimely warning may have already obliterated our meager chances. Any number of other mishaps or decisions may also have destroyed our opportunity for victory. Our cause might already be unwinnable."

Rachel nodded, not trusting herself to speak.

"You have a gift," Ferrin said. "Maldor wants to develop that gift. You could gain more power and position than any of the rest of us could dream. You could be second to Maldor. You could surpass him. You could one day become empress."

"I don't want that," Rachel whispered.

"Keep in mind, the alternative is not anonymity. The alternative is almost certain death and failure."

Rachel laced her fingers and squeezed her hands into one big fist. "You think I should go to him?"

"I think you should confront the truth of the situation. I can tell you're struggling under the weight of worries that you don't want to face and desires that you don't care to admit. I've seen your passion for Edomic. You would love to learn its mysteries from a true master. Don't bury the truth. Confront it."

"How? By accepting his offer?"

Ferrin shook his head. "Not necessarily. You have a choice before you. Confront the truth by honestly assessing the alternatives. Acknowledge the price of your options."

Rachel gave him a suspicious stare. "Is this how you go through life? Are you trying to turn me into a displacer?"

"Maybe a little. What is the price of denying Maldor?"

Rachel took a shuddering breath. "I probably die. My friends probably die. And we probably die for nothing. We probably lose."

"And you miss the chance to live in comfort and power for a thousand years or more," Ferrin added. "You miss the chance to master Edomic."

"Right."

"What is the price of accepting the offer?"

Rachel sighed. "I learn Edomic and get to live a thousand years."

"No. That is the reward. The price is that your friends will probably end up miserable. There are no happy people at Harthenham. There is no peace for those who abandon their ideals. Regardless of the pact you make, most of your friends will probably die anyhow, because they'll reject whatever pardon Maldor offers."

"True," Rachel said.

"Another part of the price is that you will cease to be who you are. No matter how valiantly you resist, after you enter into an arrangement like this, Maldor will corrupt you. Even if you bide your time and eventually overthrow him, you will not be the person you are today. You will become a person who you would otherwise never want to be."

"And the reward for denying Maldor?"

"You stay true to your friends. You let them face this evil on their own terms. You stand against this evil on your own terms as well, without letting it own you. And you keep that minuscule shred of hope that we might succeed."

"You think we still might win?" Rachel checked.

Ferrin shrugged. "The only way to know is to keep trying. We can guess what may have spoiled our chances of winning, but we can never know whether victory is still possible unless we see it through to the end. That is what Galloran understands and why news of your visit from the lurkers has not altered his plans."

Rachel leaned over and hugged Ferrin tightly. "Thank you," she whispered.

He stiffened with surprise, then hugged her back. "No need to thank me."

"I've felt really . . . I just couldn't . . ."

"I understand."

She held him quietly for a long moment before pulling away. "That was the best conversation I've ever had. I was feeling really lost. I didn't think anyone could help me."

"I did nothing. The choice is yours to make. You just needed to honestly consider your options."

"Nobody else put it so plainly. Not even Galloran."

Ferrin smirked. "The others were trying to spare you from pain. The truth can be devastating. We spend much of our lives protecting ourselves from it and shielding others as well. We use lies to take the edge off life. We dream of a better tomorrow. We hide from our regrets and inadequacies. We try to exaggerate the good and downplay the bad. We even manage to hide from the inescapable reality that sooner or later we and everyone we love is going to die."

"Cheerful thought."

"Not cheery, but true. When a decision really matters, Rachel, we have to ignore our comforting illusions. We must set aside our wishes and give heed to reality. Nobody can accept the truth while hiding from it. When a decision matters, we have to stare at the truth unflinchingly. Only then can we find peace in our choices."

Rachel smiled. "Tough love."

"You can call it that."

Rachel nodded. "Without totally lying, Maldor was playing me. I'd like to believe that he would spare my friends, because I want them to be safe, but you're right, it wouldn't end up that way. They wouldn't quit fighting. They wouldn't accept the pardon."

"And you want to believe we might win, when we probably won't," Ferrin reminded her.

"How do you keep yourself going if you feel that way?"

"If Maldor ever finds me, he will do worse than kill me. Returning to him would be folly, even if I returned after crippling your rebellion. He will never forgive a betrayal such as I have committed. I must resist Maldor, because I am forever his enemy. I also stay true to this rebellion in part because Galloran has a portion of my neck and could kill me at will. Mostly I stay true out of friendship. I admire your integrity, and Galloran's, and Jason's. I would like to see you succeed. I could hide in the wilderness for the rest of my life, but that does not suit my nature. This cause represents my last hope of living well. Our chances are dreadful, but at least we have a chance. Knowing the probable futility of our efforts, I still accept this bleak path as my best available option."

Rachel offered no reply. They listened to the birds.

Ferrin nodded toward the well near the center of the courtyard. "Would you like a drink?"

"I'm all right. How was your mission?"

Ferrin leaned forward, rubbing his hands together. "As far as we could reach by horseback in the time allotted, people are flocking to the cause. Most do not seem to fully appreciate how hopeless this campaign will be. Nearly everyone is ready to bet on Galloran. He'll have the men he needs to mount his assault. And the supplies, which is equally vital."

"How soon?" Rachel asked.

"Galloran hoped to be underway by tomorrow. He won't get his wish. But it won't take many more days. We'll be marching off to war much more quickly than I would have predicted."

Rachel stared down at her hands. "I never imagined myself going to war."

"I always pitied the first army that would try to assail Felrook. I had begun to assume it would never happen. Now I'll be part of it."

"At least we won't be alone," Rachel said.

Ferrin smiled faintly. "I'll die in good company. Probably a better end than I deserve."

Rachel regarded Ferrin thoughtfully. "What do you know about lurkers?"

"Less than you, probably. I've never had one in my dreams or heard one with my mind."

"Where do they come from?"

"Not our world," Ferrin said. "Their origin is a perfectly guarded secret."

"They told me their world is like our dreams. They don't seem to like our reality."

Ferrin nodded, as if the information fit his understanding. "Zokar brought the torivors to our world and established dominance over them. He subjected them to his will. Maldor wears a black jewel, the Myrkstone, which is somehow connected to the torivors. How he controls them is a secret, but it exacts a toll. He has been seen vomiting blood after sending torivors on a mission. He never dispatches them lightly."

"What if we could free them? Would they rebel against Maldor?"

Ferrin chuckled. "You have quite an imagination. Hard to guess how the darklings would respond to freedom. Nobody knows enough about them. Maybe they would turn on Maldor. Maybe they would go on a wild rampage. Maybe they would leave our world."

"Where are they kept?"

"At Felrook. Nobody is certain exactly where. Nobody wants to find out. Torivors are trouble, Rachel. The worst kind of trouble. They can sense our thoughts. You should put them out of your mind."

"I didn't invite them," she reminded him.

"I know."

She fingered her charm necklace. "I don't plan to take this off anytime soon."

"Probably wise. Has Copernum visited you lately?"

"No. I haven't seen him in days."

"That is for the best. Under no circumstances should he be trusted." Ferrin stood. "What are your plans for the remainder of the day?"

"I was hoping to brood. Then maybe mope a little."

"You keeping up with your Edomic?"

"Yeah. Three hours this morning. I'll work more tonight."

Ferrin nodded, hands on his hips. "I've been trying to devise some practical applications for your abilities. I want to have some spheres crafted the same size as standard orantium globes. We should put a little stone inside to help the replicas match as best we can. I want to find out how effectively you can manipulate them. It could prove significant in battle."

"Good idea."

"And locks. I want to teach you how locks work. You keep

pushing around larger and larger objects. I think you should also experiment with some delicate finesse. Shouldn't require a lot of clout, just knowledge of where to push."

Rachel grinned. "That could be useful."

"I expect it might. Want to give it a try?"

"Sure."

Ferrin took her hand and helped her to her feet.

CHAPTER 12

WINDBREAK ISLAND

Jason stood outside the small cabin, bracing himself for the smell. The stench of vomit always made him want to puke, and losing his lunch was not likely to help Corinne feel any better. He had volunteered to deliver the news because he felt guilty about not visiting her very often. Maybe he should have found another way to show his concern. Straightening like a soldier, he knocked with two knuckles.

"Yes," came the reply. She was trying to sound normal but not quite succeeding.

"It's Jason. Can I come in?"

"Just a moment." He heard her scuffling around. "All right."

Jason opened the door and found Corinne sitting on the floor against the wall. One of the cracks between the planks had left a straight mark on her cheek, so he knew she had been lying down. Her hair looked stringy, her lips chapped. A glowing length of seaweed cast green light on her pallid features. The smell was less terrible than he had expected. Her puke bucket was empty.

"Not using the bunk?" he asked.

She shook her head, a careful motion. "The floor feels

best." Her lips quivered and she squeezed her eyes shut.

"Lie back down."

Nodding faintly, she spread out on the floor and pressed a damp cloth to her forehead. She seemed to be perspiring, though it might have been moisture from the rag. He watched her breathe.

"Can I get you anything?" Jason asked.

"Water. Barrel. Corner."

He went to the cask in the corner, lifted the lid, and dipped in a little tin cup. He set it beside her on the floor.

"Sorry," she said. "Hard to talk."

"Don't worry about it."

Propping herself up on an elbow, Corinne lifted the cup and took a tiny sip. She paused, as if assessing how it made her feel, then tried a bigger sip. She started coughing, leaned over the bucket, and retched.

Stomach churning, Jason turned away. There was no escaping the smell. As it hit him, the room suddenly seemed warmer and more cramped. He clenched his teeth.

"Sorry," Corinne apologized wretchedly.

"Don't worry about me," Jason replied valiantly. "I'm sorry you're so sick."

Corinne picked up a rag and wiped her mouth. "I can't suppress the nausea. I can't will it away. Everything I eat comes back up sooner or later. I feel a little better right after I throw up. It never lasts long."

"I have good news."

She perked up a little. "What?"

"We can finally see Windbreak Island."

She gave a tired smile. "Dry land?"

"Dry land. Of course, it means we'll have to deal with the Maumet."

"Anything to get off this boat," Corinne groaned. "Maumets, lurkers, you name it. Have we spotted any other ships?"

"Nothing yet. If the emperor has learned our destination, Aram is worried ships might hide on the far side of the island."

"Why does it have to be an island?" Corinne lamented. "The only way off is more sailing. If we defeat the Maumet, maybe I'll just stay there, live in the library."

"I know you like books," Jason said.

She nodded, then grimaced. Her hand cradled her abdomen. "I'm already feeling queasy. . . . It never stops."

"Rest," Jason said. "We'll get you to dry ground soon."

She closed her eyes tightly and gently lay on her side, head cradled on the crook of her elbow. "Thanks . . . news."

Jason exited the cabin and walked away, grateful to escape the smell of her puke. He wished he knew how to comfort her. Whenever he visited, it seemed like Corinne would rather be alone. She either wanted rest or she was lost in her suffering. When he tried to talk to her or console her, he ended up feeling like a nuisance. He couldn't blame her. He hated the sensation of nausea. She hadn't had much of a break from it in almost a week.

On deck Jason went to the bow and peered ahead at the island, gray with distance. Jasher stood there as well.

"How long?" Jason asked.

Jasher glanced up at the sails. "The wind is dwindling again, and the direction has been inconstant. Could take most of the day. Could take longer."

"Do we have a plan?" Jason wondered.

"Farfalee and Aram have something in mind. We're about to confer. You should join us."

"Sure."

"How is Corinne?"

"Miserable."

"The voyage has been relatively smooth," Jasher said. "She will never be a sailor."

"I think she's fine with that."

Jasher led Jason over to where Aram, Farfalee, Drake, Nia, and Heg stood in a loose huddle. Heg had taken to wearing a wool cap he had found belowdecks. He stood shorter than Jason, but with wider shoulders and much bigger hands. Gray stubble lined his jaw.

"Have you started without us?" Jasher asked.

"You're just in time," Aram said, nodding a welcome to Jason. "First order of business will be to circle the island. I do not expect to find enemy ships lurking on the far side, but we can't risk getting attacked by sea while fighting the Maumet on land."

"Agreed," Jasher said.

"Once we're anchored, I propose we send two launches to shore," Aram continued. "One will land; one will wait on the water. The crew of the first launch will engage the Maumet and find out what exactly we're dealing with. The second crew will include Jason, Jasher, and Farfalee. If we can delay or restrain the Maumet, they may opt to hurry to the library. If not, they can witness the threat we're facing."

"The people in the first launch will be bait?" Jason checked.

"In a sense," Aram said. "They'll fight to hold the Maumet at bay."

"Who goes in the first launch?" Jasher asked.

"I'll lead a team of drinlings," Aram replied.

"You're our captain!" Jasher said. "We can't afford to lose you."

"My sentiments exactly," Drake offered.

Aram shook his head. "When the sun is down, I have the best

armor, the longest reach, and the biggest sword. I promise not to throw my life away. I want to help protect the others and inspect our enemy up close."

"Aram is taking this captaincy too earnestly," Drake said. "His caution is fading. He's ready to go down with the ship."

"I have no plan to die on Windbreak Island," Aram said. "There is a time for caution and a time for action. This affair with the Maumet will require action. If we make it around the island before nightfall, we'll land in the evening. If not, we'll make landfall before dawn."

"You could watch us attack the monster from the other launch," Heg suggested to Aram. "You're among the chosen ones named in the prophecy. We can't risk losing you. You should study our skirmish and lead a second squad."

Jason thought about what Farfalee had said about the willingness of drinlings to sacrifice themselves. Bat had risked himself for the group, as had the drinlings on the wall at Durna. Was it right to keep taking advantage of that tendency by letting them volunteer for the most deadly assignments? Jason wondered whether he should volunteer to join the first group.

Aram shook his head. "I'm the best equipped for this confrontation. You brought good men and women with you, Heg. I respect you, and I respect them. I'll not sit by and watch their demise when I might help prevent it. If I'm named in the prophecy, all the more reason I should be involved."

"I'll join Aram's squad," Jasher said. "Why plan for failure? Perhaps we can dispatch the Maumet on the first try."

Jason looked from Jasher to Aram. He didn't want the drinlings to die, nor did he want his friends to take the risk instead. Were there other options? Maybe he could help directly! Why should he always sit on the sidelines? "I'll come too," he offered.

"Sorry, Jason," Farfalee said. "I'm sure you'd make a good showing, but you're the last person we can risk."

Jason didn't like how automatically she shot him down. "I'm sick of hiding behind other people. Aram made a good point. Maybe those of us named in the prophecy have a bigger responsibility to get involved in stuff like this."

"You'll get your chances," Jasher pledged. "But I agree with my wife that we can only endanger you when it becomes most necessary. You're not hiding behind anybody. We all have our duties. Everyone aboard this ship is risking everything. Don't worry. Aram and I will watch our step. None of us are in a rush to throw our lives away."

"I'll second that," Aram grunted.

Jason decided he had better back down. If everyone was against him on this, it would do no good to keep complaining. Although part of him felt embarrassed to have his offer denied, a more secret part was relieved to avoid the danger.

"Maybe one squad isn't enough," Nia speculated. "Should we attack the Maumet with a larger force? Try to overwhelm it?"

Farfalee shook her head. "If numbers were the only issue, others would have destroyed it long ago."

"So eight of us are supposed to succeed where an army would fail?" Drake verified.

"We'll examine what we're dealing with," Aram said. "We'll test the effectiveness of various weapons—blunt ones, sharp ones, projectiles. I'll bring orantium."

"I wonder if Corinne would loan me her sword," Jasher mused.

"I'll loan you mine," Jason said.

Jasher shook his head. "If you end up going ashore, you'll need it."

"There will probably be no chance for a second party to go

ashore," Farfalee said. "If a simple diversion would work, the library would have been breached ages ago. I agree that we should test ourselves against the Maumet, but if it appears unbeatable, the landing party should fall back."

"I'm in no rush to die again," Jasher assured her.

"The guardian can transform itself?" Heg checked.

"We believe it can change form," Aram recounted. "According to Ferrin, the Maumet can mimic the properties of any material it touches. We have to find out how that works in practice, search for weaknesses."

"Any idea how far the Maumet can stray from the island?" Drake asked.

"We know it can't leave the island," Farfalee replied. "Otherwise, it would have done so long ago. But we have no idea how far it can venture into the sea."

Aram rubbed his hands together briskly. "Only one way to find out. If we're done here, I need to check our heading."

"Very well," Farfalee agreed. "I hate to risk losing any of our number, but I fear risk will be an inevitable companion for the remainder of our journey."

"I'll join Jason and Farfalee in the second launch," Heg said. "I'll organize drinlings to fill the remaining needs of the two squads."

The meeting ended and everyone dispersed. Jason wandered to the front of the ship to watch the island. The salty breeze came generally from the east, sometimes gusting from the southeast and occasionally blowing from the northeast. At times the *Valiant* turned into the wind at an angle, sails positioned to keep slicing forward. For some stretches the wind pushed the ship from behind at a good pace. The drinlings adjusted the sails often, and the sweeps sloshed endlessly.

The prospect of fighting the Maumet kept Jason patient as he watched Windbreak Island draw imperceptibly closer. He knew they needed to get there ahead of their enemies. But part of him was in no hurry. What if the creature decimated Aram, Jasher, and the rest of their squad? Jason frowned. What if it came out into the water and destroyed the people in his own launch boat as well? His frown deepened. What if the Maumet attacked the ship? Jason was not eager for answers to those questions.

All they really knew about the Maumet was that it could transform into different substances and that it had been feared by the most powerful people in Lyrian since the days of Eldrin. From the current distance Windbreak Island looked innocent, but Jason knew that it might end up as his cemetery.

Hour by hour the island came into sharper focus. Eventually shorebirds squawked above the ship, some with dark plumage and red feet, others white with gray tail feathers. By evening Jason could discern beaches, trees, and jagged hills. He could also see the enormous domes of a colossal building curving above the treetops on the eastern side of the island, near the crest of a long slope. Jasher confirmed that the gargantuan edifice was the Celestine Library. Supposedly, the location of Darian the Pyromancer awaited inside.

As the light failed, a larger Aram guided the ship in a wide circle around the island. Windbreak Island was several miles long and at least a few miles across, with steep cliffs on the northwestern side and several long sandbars to the southwest. Everyone aboard kept watch, but they found no hidden enemy ships. They anchored the *Valiant* off the eastern side of the island, near a pristine beach of white sand. The moon made the beach ghostly, and glowed off the five domes visible up the slope from the coast. The two largest domes overshadowed the other three. As Jason considered the library by moonlight, Farfalee came to his side.

"Quite a sight," she said.

"Have you been there before?" Jason wondered.

"No. But I did work for years in the Great Document Hall at Elbureth. The Maumet has dwelled here since our race was young. The Abomination is very old."

"Old enough to be getting weaker?"

"Wouldn't that be fortunate? We will know much more tomorrow."

"I looked for it all day," Jason said. "I never saw anything."

"We were all keeping watch. The creature has not shown itself. But I expect it is aware of us."

"What kind of books are in the library?" Jason asked.

"Many have speculated," Farfalee said. "Certainly the collection contains the majority of the oldest surviving writings in Lyrian. Many will be written in Sulcrix, a phonetic shorthand version of Edomic. Even the characters would be unrecognizable to most. Some of the texts will be in our current common tongue."

"Can anyone read Sulcrix?"

She nodded. "I can. Drake can read a little Sulcrix. Jasher less. I am quite fluent in twelve languages, most of them scholarly, some of them dead. My most obvious role in this mission will be locating the information we seek here."

"Looks like a big library," Jason remarked.

"Vast," she agreed. "Zokar wanted to seal off the information from his enemies without harming the texts, so he imprisoned the Maumet here. Presumably, he planned to move the Maumet elsewhere after his foes were vanquished."

"But he lost, so the Maumet has guarded the place ever since."

Farfalee turned to Jason. "You should rest. Tomorrow will be eventful."

Jason nodded. "Guess I might as well try."

* * *

By the time Drake jostled Jason awake, the launches had already been lowered into the water. Sunrise was perhaps an hour away. They wanted to reach the shore with light in the sky, but before the sunrise would shrink Aram.

The others were finishing a breakfast of unsweetened oatmeal. Jason accepted a bowl of lukewarm mush and began hurriedly eating.

"Quiet this morning," Nia observed, staring at the island. "What if the Maumet doesn't show itself?"

"I don't want to stray far from the beach on this first foray," Aram said, adjusting his leather cloak over his heavy shirt of overlapping rings. "If the Maumet means to lie in wait out of sight, we'll have to devise a new strategy. We had best move out before the daylight renders me frail."

Jason gulped down the last of his oatmeal before descending a rope ladder to one of the launches. Eight people fit comfortably in each. Farfalee, Drake, Nia, and Heg were all in his boat. Three other drinlings joined them, two of them at the oars.

Aram and Jasher were in the other launch, along with six drinlings, including Ux. Zoo was the only female going ashore.

The launches moved away from the *Valiant* toward the white sand beach. The swells were noticeable, rocking the launches gently, but could not have competed with ocean waves. The modest breakers seldom rose above eighteen inches as they curled against the shore. The drinling rowers maneuvered the launches with little difficulty.

The launches were roughly a hundred yards from the beach when a dark figure strode out onto the sand. In form it looked just like a lurker—a smooth humanoid shape without a face. But the similarity ended there. Although not clumsy, the figure did not move with the shadowy stealth of a torivor. It rocked slightly as it walked forward, kicking up sand with each stride. Composed of reddish-brown wood, the creature was much larger than any torivor Jason had seen.

"Is that the Maumet?" Nia asked. "It doesn't look so tough."

The wooden figure stopped at the center of the beach and held perfectly still, arms at its sides, facing the launches. It made no sound.

"Stay back," Aram called from the other launch. "Watch closely."

"It isn't entering the water," Drake murmured. "That's a good sign."

"Don't draw conclusions yet," Farfalee cautioned, setting an arrow to the string of her bow.

Jason's launch wobbled on the swells, holding steady as Aram's launch powered toward the shore. The Maumet made no move as the launch neared the beach. The craft rasped onto the sand, and the people inside piled out, weapons held high as they splashed away from the shallows. One strapping drinling remained beside the launch, ready for a quick getaway.

Aram, Jasher, Ux, Zoo, and three other drinlings fanned out and approached the Maumet in a loose arc. Jasher drew the torivorian sword he had borrowed from Corinne. The wooden figure seemed inanimate, more like a driftwood scarecrow than a fearsome enemy. The stillness was unnerving, because they had all seen it moving. Raising a fist, Aram signaled for his squad to halt.

With the squad in a loose semicircle before the Maumet, Jason could see that it stood at least ten feet high, making Aram look like the tallest of a group of children. Farfalee pulled an arrow to her cheek. Jason gripped the gunwale.

Aram had brought a pair of orantium spheres. Hefting one of

them, he flung it at the stationary Maumet. His aim was good, but the wooden figure dodged the globe, and it landed on the sand without bursting. Farfalee released her arrow, which struck the wooden creature in the chest and remained there. Showing no discomfort from the arrow, the Maumet rushed Aram. Drinlings closed from either side to help their captain face the creature.

The Maumet was quick. A leg lashed out and struck Aram squarely in the chest, sending him tumbling across the sand, ring mail jangling, his sword still in hand. A drinling soldier whacked the Maumet in the hip with an ax before getting clubbed in the head by a wooden forearm. Batting away the sword of another drinling, the Maumet kicked the warrior in the side, the blow simultaneously folding him over and sending him flying.

Jasher, Ux, and Zoo had been on the far side of the semi-circle from Aram, and they rushed the Maumet from behind. Ux crunched his mace against the creature's thigh, noisily splitting the wood. Zoo dove low, attacking an ankle with a pair of hatchets. The Maumet spun and swung a vicious backhand. With a beautifully timed swing of his sword, Jasher hacked the wooden hand off at the wrist. The severed hand turned to dust in the air.

Shaking free from Zoo, the Maumet hobbled away. A new hand promptly formed, and the cracks and gouges on the leg closed.

"Did it lose a little size to replace the hand?" Farfalee said, peering through a spyglass. "When the hand was severed, I think that mass was lost."

"So it adjusted," Drake said. "Reformed the hand with material from elsewhere."

"Will we have to destroy it one hand at a time?" Jason asked.

"I hope not," Farfalee murmured. "It's quick and strong."

Another drinling charged the Maumet. The creature caught

his war hammer by the haft just below the head and punched him in the face with its free hand. Instantly the Maumet turned a glossy white. The fallen drinling scrambled to his feet, wiping his sleeve against his face. Clutching the captured war hammer, the Maumet backed away so that all the combatants were in front of it, then held still.

Aram had risen, as had the drinling who'd gotten clubbed on the head. The drinling who had received the kick in the side lay motionless on the white sand.

"Did it change to sand?" Drake asked.

"I don't think so," Farfalee said. "Right color, wrong texture."

"Tooth enamel," Jason realized.

"The Maumet hit Kay in the mouth right when it transformed," Drake said.

"Tooth enamel!" Farfalee cried, in case those on the beach had not realized.

Aram threw his other orantium sphere. The Maumet flung the war hammer. The two objects collided in midair. Though at least ten yards away, the brilliant explosion knocked down Aram and a drinling.

The Maumet charged at those still standing. The drinlings and Jasher fell back and spread out, those at the sides trying to curl around and get behind the attacker. Aram staggered back to his feet as well, racing toward the combat. An arrow from Farfalee glanced off the Maumet's shoulder, chipping it.

The enamel figure kicked Zoo aside and used two hands to snap Kay's neck. Mace ready, Ux came in low and bashed the Maumet in the shin, shattering the bottom of the leg. The foot and lower shin all turned to dust, leaving behind a jagged stump. The Maumet plunged the spiky stump into Ux, who gurgled and twitched.

Jasher leaped from behind, swinging the torivorian sword in a vicious two-handed stroke. The instant the blade hit the Maumet at the waist, the creature turned a gleaming metallic color. Jason had hoped to witness a crippling blow, but he realized in horror that the Maumet had become torivorian steel.

An ax-wielding drinling whacked the creature in the thigh with a resounding clang. The ax fell from his hands, the bit notched. An arrow from Farfalee pinged off the Maumet's head. A hatchet thrown by Zoo clinked against the chest. None of the blows had scratched the reflective surface.

The lower leg and foot grew back, reducing the Maumet's stature a small degree, and then the creature snatched the nearest drinling and tore him in half. The Maumet now moved more jerkily, metal body shrieking as if resisting the motion. But it wasn't dramatically slower than before.

"Fall back!" Aram cried.

Four drinlings were now down. Only Jasher, Zoo, Aram, and the drinling beside the boat remained standing. While Zoo and Aram ran for the boat, Jasher dashed away from the water and retrieved the undetonated orantium globe from the sand. The Maumet pursued Aram and Zoo. The drinling by the launch heaved the craft into the water. Aram and Zoo splashed into the shallows.

The Maumet stopped at the edge of the water. Jasher hit it from behind with the orantium sphere. The explosion flashed, but the Maumet was indifferent. It turned to chase Jasher. The seedman raced across the sand, parallel to the waterline. Joints screeching, the Maumet tried to keep pace, but even with much longer legs, it could not quite pump them fast enough. Jasher pulled ahead and cut across to the water, sprinting through the shallows, then diving forward and swimming.

Aram helped the burly drinling who had stayed with the

launch row over to Jasher, who climbed inside, sword in hand. The Maumet paced back and forth at the edge of the water, metal feet sinking deep into the damp white sand with each stride, joints squealing like tortured dolphins.

Jason finally relaxed a degree. Toward the end of the skirmish he had thought Jasher would die again for sure, and he'd worried about whether the Maumet would care about crushing an amar. On the white beach four drinlings lay where they had fallen.

Aram's launch rowed close to Jason's. Aram had a scratch on his cheek and a bleeding gash on his forehead. A huge welt disfigured the side of Zoo's face. One eye was swelling shut.

"Opinions?" Aram asked, swiping blood from his eyes.

"We're in trouble," Jason said numbly.

"Was it toying with you at first?" Drake asked.

"Looked that way," Jasher replied. "It could have turned to iron the first time we hit it with a weapon. Fight would have been over."

"Maybe at first it wanted to stay faster and more flexible," Farfalee guessed. "The wood was fairly resilient, and it moved more gracefully."

"I thought I had it," Jasher mourned. "I meant to cleave it at the waist. But the instant my blade touched it, the Maumet transformed. Quick as a blink."

"If it does that every time, what are we supposed to do?" Jason worried aloud. Once the Maumet had turned into steel, it had won the fight so quickly!

"The creature is strong," Aram said. "When it kicked me in the chest, it felt like a blow from a mallet. The impact was not square, and still it might have killed me without my armor and cloak."

"Drinlings can take punishment," Heg said. "You don't slay us with a blow to the abdomen. But it killed Ibe with a kick."

Jason looked at the beach. He tried not to stare at the bodies. Minutes earlier they had all been alive and well. Those hardy drinlings had stormed the beach, ready for a fight, but the Maumet had killed them so savagely, so easily. Had the others not run away, they would have died as well.

Farfalee gave Aram a white bandage. He held it against the gash in his forehead as he spoke. "We knew it would be bad. I had hopes at first, when Jasher severed the hand. I envisioned us chopping off limb after limb, shrinking the brute until nothing remained. But after Ux took its foot, the creature got serious. The torivorian blade may have surprised it the first time. But clearly, if it chooses, the Maumet can immediately become any substance we use to attack it. Now I understand why everyone keeps away from this island."

"Look," Zoo said.

On the beach the Maumet crouched over Ux, probing him. The shiny metallic creature turned to gold-tinged skin, then to red muscle, then to white bone, then to brown leather, then finally to the black iron of Ux's mace. Metal screaming, the Maumet stood upright.

"Solid iron," Nia griped. "How do you fight solid iron?"

Jason shook his head in silence. He had no answer.

"We're fortunate that any of us survived," Jasher said. "We lost good people. Only the safety of the water let some of us escape."

"The library must be at least a mile from the coast," Jason said.

"Unfortunately, the task ahead will be as difficult as we anticipated," Farfalee said. "We should return to the *Valiant* and confer."

Drake chuckled darkly. "I'm afraid the only topic will be choosing how we die."

CHAPTER 13

FINAL
PREPARATIONS

The long stable contained more than a hundred horses, all of them impressive specimens, mounts for the elite of Trensicourt. Rachel paced down the center aisle, glancing left and right, murmuring Edomic phrases to those that interested her most. Galloran had instructed her to pick any mount she wished, and she wanted one that would respond warmly to her instructions.

Tark stood at one end of the stable, Io at the other. Neither man had struck up a conversation with her today. Rachel wore her veiled outfit of black robes. She now had three similar ensembles, and always wore one of them when out in public. In at least one way, the costume worked too well. Each day Io and Tark seemed to regard her with greater awe.

Rachel paused beside a large, dappled mare. She had learned many commands at Mianamon, but she tried something simple with only the slightest effort of will behind the suggestion. The horse backed up as requested. She gave more instructions, and without resistance or hesitation the mare reared, bowed, stamped a right foot, then a left, and at last sniffed the sweet grass on her flat palm without eating. Rachel hardly had to push to get the messages across. The mare seemed eager to please.

Rachel stroked the horse and told her to eat. "You're my girl. You're bigger than I was planning, but you're the one I want. White with gray spots . . . how about Snowflake? I know you might have another name, but Snowflake can be your nickname."

"Nedwin is coming," Io announced.

"Good," Rachel replied down the aisle. "I think I just found my horse."

The tall redhead entered the stable and moved toward her with long strides. "You found a suitable mount?"

"Better than suitable," Rachel replied, pulling her veil aside to better see him.

Nedwin drew near and regarded the horse. "Looks like a respectable choice."

"And she's smart."

"Smart can lead to ornery."

"Not Snowflake. We have an understanding."

"The king wishes to speak with us," Nedwin said. "Ferrin has news."

Tugging her dark veil back in place, Rachel followed Nedwin out of the stable. The building had been cleared for her inspection, so idle stable hands watched as the foursome strode away.

"Is it good news?" Rachel asked as they entered the castle.

"Not sure," Nedwin replied. "Based on his demeanor, nothing terrible."

They passed many soldiers on their way up Galloran's tower. Partway up the winding stairwell, six guards stepped aside to allow Nedwin access to a hefty door bound with iron. Nedwin unlocked it with a key and led the others inside.

Galloran, Ferrin, Nollin, and Kerick awaited them. Galloran wore his blindfold.

"The enigmatic lady in black," Ferrin greeted with a wry smile.

Rachel pulled her veil aside. "Ha-ha."

"The title has caught on," Nollin said smugly.

"Title?" Rachel asked.

"Galloran's Dark Lady," Nollin supplied.

Rachel had never heard anyone call her that. But nearly everyone she encountered besides Tark and Io had taken to calling her "milady."

"That's a little embarrassing," Rachel said, taking off her hat.

"It's statecraft," Nollin insisted. "We all have roles to play to add legitimacy to the forthcoming campaign. King Galloran is the saintly hero restored to his throne. Nedwin is the fallen but faithful squire reinstated to a position of influence. Kerick and I are the noble lords of the Amar Kabal, here to pledge the support of our people to the cause. Io is the drinling prince whose presence implies the backing of yet another ancient nation."

"And I'm the dirty secret," Ferrin said.

Nollin raised a finger in objection. "If your identity as a displacer is ever called into question, you are the turncoat who has provided all the secrets of Maldor's defenses."

"What about Tark?" Ferrin inquired.

"The commoner elevated to a station of high responsibility," Nollin replied smoothly. "Evidence that King Galloran recognizes the vital contributions the common man will make in the upcoming turmoil."

"Nollin is no stranger to politics," Galloran said, suppressing a smile. "We are fortunate to have him laboring on our behalf. Copernum and the other connivers at court have hardly known what to make of him."

"We all serve where our talents are best suited," Nollin said humbly, clearly gratified by the praise.

"I have summoned all of you here because we are ready for war," Galloran announced. "Our host will depart at first light. But two of you must remain behind."

Nobody spoke.

Rachel glanced at the others. Nollin seemed a natural fit to stay at Trensicourt and play political games. But who else? She didn't want to end up separated from more of her friends.

"Trensicourt will be left vulnerable in our absence," Galloran said. "I worry about treachery from within and attacks from without. I will leave enough soldiers to man the wall and the castle, but little more. A skeleton crew, really. To an extent, Trensicourt will have to rely on the strength of her walls and the attention our offensive will demand. Those two elements should suffice if we can prevent the city from collapsing internally."

"Who is to remain?" Io asked.

"I wish I could bring all of you with me," Galloran said, "but necessity dictates otherwise. After much consideration I have decided to elevate Nedwin to Duke of Geer and name him regent in my absence, fully empowered to govern the affairs of the kingdom."

Nedwin paled beneath his freckles. "This is too great an honor, sire. Pray let me remain at your side."

"No honor is too great for my most faithful servant," Galloran said. "Your house was stripped of your earldom by Copernum. For that reason I have created a duchy in your name. As much as I detest losing my finest scout as I head into the field, I need a man on the throne who I can trust. Brin must come with me into battle. For laying a siege, his engineering skills may prove essential. Nicholas has the mind for the job but not the body.

He will serve as one of your counselors, and his contacts will be at your disposal. Tark lacks experience in affairs of state. Bartley has waffled in the past. And obviously the regent cannot be a seedman or a drinling or a displacer. It must be a man of our kingdom."

Nedwin looked stricken. "Of course I am yours to command, sire."

Rachel felt bad that Nedwin seemed so devastated. She would miss him—he had proven himself amazingly reliable. They were all safer with him around. But she had to admit it was probably a good pick. Nobody was more loyal to Galloran.

"The job will not be easy," Galloran affirmed. "By my mandate Copernum and several of his cronies were preparing to take the field with us. But they have fallen ill, victims of a debilitating fever."

"Subterfuge," Nollin grunted. "The coincidence is much too convenient."

"Copernum knows a variety of recipes to produce such symptoms," Nedwin added.

"Nevertheless, I cannot force sick men into battle," Galloran said. "Whatever the cause, the symptoms appear legitimate. We lack the time and the means to expose the charade. I will take the majority of their men, leaving only their household guard. But I need not stress how dangerous these vipers might be to the kingdom once my back is turned."

"I will protect the kingdom, sire," Nedwin said.

"I know your feelings toward Copernum," Galloran said. "They are completely warranted. Do not move against him unprovoked. But should you catch him conspiring, you will have full authority to administer judgment and punishment."

"As you wish, sire," Nedwin replied.

"I do not mean to leave you friendless," Galloran said. "Nollin, you are not mine to command. But given your expertise with statecraft, and given the relationships you have already cultivated here, would you consider remaining with Nedwin to help oversee the kingdom in my absence?"

"Your trust astonishes me," Nollin replied.

"I know the Amar Kabal to be loyal and true, and I have seen evidence that you are more devoted than most. Some of our ideologies have differed in the past, but I know you do not want to see Maldor lay claim to this kingdom."

Nollin placed his palms together in his lap. "In truth, my strengths might be better applied to this task than to the siege of Felrook. I will stay if you wish, but please allow me to retain the company and security of my sole countryman."

Galloran gave a nod. "Three to stay behind instead of two. I hope you will not have need of Kerick's sword, but I understand the request. And I agree. Nollin, I ask you to serve as a right hand to Nedwin. Watch out for his interests, help him to comprehend the maneuverings of his enemies, and take what action you must to protect the throne and the kingdom."

"I shall do as you say until your return, King Galloran, or until the campaign ends in ruin. After that I make no pledge."

"It pains me to miss fighting alongside my people," Kerick admitted. "Nevertheless, I will remain with Nollin and Nedwin. I vow to protect them both."

"I am relieved to have that settled," Galloran said. "Nedwin, you will be granted the powers of regent in a private ceremony this evening."

"As you wish, sire," Nedwin responded.

He was saying the right words, but Rachel could tell that Nedwin was disappointed about the assignment. She supposed

Galloran could tell as well, though he offered no indication. It was hard to blame Nedwin. Staying in Trensicourt surrounded by plotting enemies would be no fun at all.

"I have had eagles from the Amar Kabal and the drinlings," Galloran said. "Both stand ready to march on Felrook. We will coordinate our marches so that we arrive together."

"What of the other kingdoms?" Ferrin wondered.

"A major insurrection is planned in Meridon," Galloran said. "It will begin tomorrow and might bring us some fighting men in time, though the revolt will probably prove more valuable as a distraction. I suppose at this late stage I can reveal that Vernon rescued the syllable guardian Trivett from the Isle of Weir, and they will be involved with the uprising.

"Minor mischief has been planned in a few other kingdoms. To my surprise, a group of four hundred treefolk are currently marching to our aid. They should join us before we reach Felrook."

"The treefolk have never left the jungle," Nollin said in surprise.

"The treefolk have never had more reason to care for matters outside their borders," Galloran said. "Through Esmira in the past, and now through Ulani, they have been kept informed of the relevance of our plight. Even so, four hundred is only token support. They could make a much more significant difference if they dared."

Nollin nodded. "We're fortunate to have any of their aid. I had time to observe them. They may not be quite as effective outside their native jungles, but the treefolk are serious warriors."

"They have been strengthened by hardship," Nedwin said. "They were invaded and nearly wiped out by Zokar. And deep in the heart of the jungle they must contend with fearsome predators that most of us can scarcely imagine."

"My business is complete," Galloran said. "Ferrin has some news."

All eyes turned to the displacer.

"Jason has done an excellent job of keeping my ear away from delicate conversations. A prudent practice, given my background, although the precaution limits our knowledge of how their mission is progressing."

"We know they hijacked an interceptor at Durna," Nollin remarked. "The empire is astir over it."

"We know more than that," Ferrin said. "I overheard a conversation today. I believe my ear was packed away in Jason's cabin aboard the ship, less bundled than normally, and he forgot that I might overhear as he entered conversing with Drake."

"What's the news?" Rachel asked.

"Jason and the others have reached Windbreak Island. They have confronted the Maumet, losing a number of drinlings in the process. They found the guardian virtually invincible, but I take heart that some of them survived the encounter. They are currently developing strategies to engage it."

"How does the timing of their progress synchronize with our attack?" Nollin asked.

"We have to trust the oracle," Galloran said. "She informed us when to begin our assignments. We complied. How long their quest takes will depend on the hardships they face and how far they must travel to reach the abode of Darian the Seer."

"Unknowable variables," Nollin agreed.

Galloran stood. "We all have arrangements to make for tomorrow. I will counsel with Nedwin, Nollin, and Kerick tonight after Nedwin is officially appointed regent. Thank you all for your service."

Rachel replaced her wide-brimmed hat and arranged the

dark veil over her face. She left the room behind Nedwin and walked down the stairs. Was she really about to go to war? With real battles? How much would the others be counting on her? Galloran often talked like her Edomic skills would provide them with an important advantage. Even though she had built up her endurance, she could only make a limited number of people freeze up or flop to the ground at a time. There were only so many flaming tables she could throw before running out of juice.

As panic threatened to unbalance her, she told herself to take it one step at a time. War was coming. It would be ugly. But it wouldn't start today. There was no point in losing her grip yet. What could she do right now? What preparations did she have to make? Not many. She had chosen her horse. Her gear would be prepped by others. She supposed she should go practice her Edomic.

At the bottom of the stairs, the group dispersed in different directions. Rachel noticed Nedwin walking down a lonely corridor, head slightly bowed. He staggered a little before disappearing around a corner.

"I was glad to hear Lord Jason remains alive," Tark was telling Io. "Not surprised, mind you. It will take more than a Maumet to stop him, mark my words. There's more to him than greets the eye. He'll find a way to enter the Celestine Library or I've never touched a sousalax."

"Wait here for me," Rachel said.

"Here?" Io questioned.

"I'll be quick," Rachel promised. "I just remembered something I need to ask Nedwin in private."

Tark folded his arms. "Begging your pardon, milady, you shouldn't go wandering off without—"

"We're in the castle. I'll only be a moment." She was already hurrying after Nedwin. She reached the bend in the hall in time to see him proceeding up a stairwell. She didn't get much of a look, but he no longer appeared particularly despondent. Maybe she was jumping at shadows, imagining how she would feel if she learned she would have to govern an entire kingdom.

Still she followed him, just in case. At the top of the stairs she found a quiet hall. Nedwin sat on the floor, back to the wall, elbows on his knees, both hands in his unruly red hair.

"Are you all right?" she asked.

He glanced over at her. "I heard someone following me. I thought it was you. I just need some time. You should go make ready for tomorrow."

"I'm ready," Rachel said. "I don't mean to intrude."

He lowered his hands, placing both palms on one knee. "I appreciate the interest. You're kind."

Rachel assumed that was the closest she would get to an invitation. She walked toward him. "Are you worried about serving as regent?"

He exhaled sharply. She thought the gust was intended as a chuckle. "An honor I did not seek and which I do not desire. Did you know that I have almost no fears left in me?"

"You're definitely not afraid of heights."

"I don't fear fire or water or starvation. I'm not afraid to fight. I fear no man or beast. I fear no illness. No punishment. No torture. I'm not afraid to die, Rachel. Part of me would welcome the release."

"You shouldn't talk that way," Rachel said.

He ignored the comment. "I have troubling dreams. I dislike my dreams. Aside from the tricks my mind plays when I sleep, I only have two fears left. Would you like to know what they are?"

"Okay."

"I'm afraid for King Galloran. I want to keep him safe. And I'm afraid of disappointing King Galloran. This opportunity to serve as regent will separate me from him. I will not be able to protect him. And I will be in a position to fail him."

"I'm sure you'll do great."

"I'm glad one of us feels confident. Rachel, through dark years that I would prefer to forget, I clung to the idea of Galloran. Trensicourt was not worth all I suffered. Not even freedom from tyranny was worth it. But that man was worth all I endured and more. I failed him when he was captured. I only survived in the hope that Galloran would need me. And he does. But I won't be with him."

"I'll be with him," Rachel said. "I'll keep him safe."

His eyes snapped to hers. "Swear it."

Rachel swallowed dryly. Suddenly she had to confront how far she would go in order to fulfill her words. The thought of her protecting Galloran seemed almost silly. He was the best swordsman in Lyrian. But it obviously mattered to Nedwin. He actually seemed to think her protection could make a difference. She imagined a soldier attacking Galloran from behind. Would she allow that? "I promise, Nedwin. I promise to watch over him. I love him too. I'll die to protect him if necessary."

His posture relaxed a little. "That is good to hear. Yours is no small gift, and he will keep you close." Nedwin sighed. "We have come upon hard times if I am the man he selects as regent."

"He couldn't choose anyone more loyal," Rachel argued.

"But he could find many more polished, more schooled in politics. Less scarred. Less damaged. Sometimes I can feel my mind unraveling. Once I was something of a social creature. No longer. I prefer solitude. I'm a good scout. Great, even. I don't expect I'll make much of a regent."

"But you'll do it?"

"If I refuse, I'll have failed him already. I would give anything not to fail him."

"You'll have help from Nollin and Nicholas," Rachel reminded him.

"I'll be forced to lean on them," Nedwin agreed. "Much as they would lean on me out in the wilderness, where I belong."

"You'll be terrific," Rachel encouraged. "The fact that you care so much makes you the perfect person for the job. Much better than some overconfident politician."

"Let's hope for the sake of the realm that there is sense in your words. I'm relieved to know you'll be watching out for my king."

"We'll all be watching out for him. Nobody wants to see Galloran harmed. But I'll make a special effort. I'll try to do what you would do."

Nedwin closed his eyes. "Thank you, Rachel. The thought affords me a measure of comfort. Can I give you anything?" Pulling on the leather strands around his neck, Nedwin produced several vials from within his shirt. "I've collected unusual substances from the far corners of Lyrian—expensive extracts, rare and useful. Pain enhancers, poisons, healing ointments."

"You keep them," Rachel said. "Carrying poison would freak me out. We should rely on our strengths. Mine is Edomic."

Nedwin nodded, eyes remote. "Mine is stealth, I suppose. And commitment. I don't suppose I could be more committed."

"That might be exactly what this kingdom needs."

Nedwin stood. With him seated, she had almost forgotten how abnormally tall he was. "Enough wallowing. I'll escort you back to your bodyguards."

"I can find my way."

"Let me guide you. It's one of my strengths."

CHAPTER 14

THE MAUMET

As the *Valiant* gently swayed and creaked, Jason sat in his cabin studying the prophecy. While reading and pondering, he munched on a thick burrito improvised out of flatbread and fish meat. Sunlight streamed through the porthole. Since she had memorized the prophecy, Farfalee had written down all the words spoken by the oracle, so that he could examine them. Jason had been insistent, because he felt their current plan would get them all killed.

After much debate, their best strategy involved circling the island, leaving a number of landing parties offshore at different points. A pair of squads at the far end of the island from the library would go ashore first, not advancing too far inland. If the Maumet attacked them, they would detonate an orantium sphere. At the sound of the explosion, squads would move in from the north and south to further delay and distract the Maumet. Teams on the eastern side of the island would race to the library in order to get the information and escape before the Maumet returned and killed them all. Jason, Farfalee, Aram, Jasher, and Drake would be members of the eastern teams.

That plan outclassed the others mostly because it sought to dodge the Maumet rather than defeat it. It amounted to a high-stakes game of steal the bacon. But the strategy had many flaws.

Farfalee had warned that it might take hours, days, or even weeks to find the desired information, depending how effectively the enormous library was indexed. Any major delay in finding the location of Darian the Seer could result in a fatal confrontation with the Maumet. Furthermore, the plan assumed that the Maumet would react to multiple intrusions by storming around the island and battling all the trespassers. However, if the Maumet was smart and meant to guard the library, it might react to the invasion by falling back to the library and slaying all comers.

Jason felt certain that if the plan was implemented, they would fail to get the information, and they would all die. Quest over. War lost. Just because their current strategy was the best they had devised did not make it the right plan. They would be relying on stupidity from the Maumet and a whole lot of luck finding the information swiftly.

Rubbing his eyes, Jason tried to force his strained imagination to deliver better options. The oracle had seen a way they could succeed. The thought would not quit pestering him. Out of all the possible futures, there had to be one where they survived the Maumet. There had to be a strategy that would work. They simply hadn't found it yet.

Jason stared at the freshly drafted parchment. Farfalee had warned that prophecies seldom gave many specifics. They did not lead you step by step, strategy by strategy, to your desired end. But Jason didn't need a full explanation of how to handle every upcoming problem. He just needed a clue.

Most of the words were inapplicable. Much of the prophecy specified who should go where and when. Much of it dealt with

Galloran's attack of Felrook. He focused on the lines that seemed to have the most relevance.

The last abode of Darian the Seer can be learned at the Celestine Library within the Inland Sea. The line referenced this part of the quest, but lacked details pertaining to their current problem. Jason knew where he needed to go. The trouble was how to get there.

Several utterances toward the end contained some potentially useful statements. *The parallel quests must succeed. Many present will perish. You must stand united.* Maybe many of them had to die in order to get the info from the library. Maybe by working together and sacrificing heavily they could pull it off. That line of thinking supported the current plan.

The most mysterious and potentially useful predictions were among her final words. *A secret from the past can ransom the future.* That seemed to hint that the information they would get from the seer could help them win the war. But maybe it meant a secret from the past could teach them how to defeat the Maumet and access the library. Farfalee, Jasher, and Drake had all lived a long time. Maybe one of them had forgotten an important detail.

The servant will betray the master. That one was hard to pin down. It could refer to anyone. Was it possible that the Maumet would betray Zokar and allow them access to the library? Was there some way to appease the guardian and win it over? The prospect didn't seem likely, but Jason was ready to consider any option.

The pleasant paths have crumbled. Lyrian must be purchased with sacrifice. Those lines seemed to justify throwing lots of people at the Maumet from different directions and hoping a few survivors would escape with the information. But Jason still disliked that plan. He couldn't picture any survivors. Sacrifice might be essential to their success, but success would not automatically spring from reckless, wasteful sacrifices.

The last lines sounded more like clues than any other part. *Our hope is red, like the blood of heroes; black as the bowels of the earth; and white, like a flash of orantium.* The mention of blood seemed to once again emphasize sacrifice. Jason found the other two lines more intriguing.

The bowels of the earth could refer to caves. What if a secret cave granted access to the library? Perhaps a cave that started underwater or had an entrance hidden on the island? A secret tunnel that would let them sneak to their goal unnoticed?

Although he considered the possibility worth mentioning to the others, the idea failed to spark much excitement in him. If an entrance like that existed, it had stayed hidden for hundreds of years. It would be extremely hard to find. And the only reason to believe it might exist was a vague hunch. The line in the prophecy could easily refer to something else entirely. It might just mean a black object. Or the line might have nothing to do with this portion of the quest. Besides, just because they gained access to the library by a secret way didn't ensure the Maumet wouldn't catch them. The guardian had no visible eyes or ears. If it was like a lurker, the Maumet might notice their presence with more than the five normal senses. But a hidden passage would be much better than a wild game of capture the flag.

What was white like an orantium flash? That kind of intense bright white was only really available from an orantium flash. What else came close? Sunlight on snow? Maybe an angel? Jason doubted a choir of angels would swoop down and rescue them.

Could orantium itself be the key? If the Maumet was made of iron when impact occurred, the answer was no. Jasher had hit it with orantium to no effect. But what if the Maumet had been made of tooth enamel when the orantium had detonated? The explosion might have pulverized it. The tooth fairy would have been cleaning up bits and pieces for weeks.

Was there a way to ensure the Maumet would be made of a fragile substance when the orantium hit? Strategically, tooth enamel had been an odd choice. The Maumet had been hit by iron weapons before it touched the tooth. It could have turned to iron at the start. It seemed to have selected tooth enamel out of curiosity. The others speculated that it had only assimilated the torivorian steel once it felt seriously threatened.

Would the Maumet feel threatened at the start of any conflict from here on out? After the skirmish, it had experimented with different substances, becoming skin and leather and iron. If they could just hit the guardian with orantium when it was fragile, the problem might be solved.

Jason resisted crumpling the parchment. Was he dwelling too much on orantium because it was their best weapon? The prophecy seemed to suggest orantium would be important, but it had already served them well. And certainly it would be important as Galloran attacked Felrook.

The Maumet could transform instantly. What if they threw an explosive sphere, and the Maumet changed to crystal as the globe connected? It would be blasted into glitter. Might the Maumet arbitrarily change into crystal on contact? Or was it too smart? The Maumet had lived a long time. It knew how to survive.

What if they attacked it with crystal weapons? Or weapons made of a brittle substance? Then if at any point the Maumet transformed into the brittle material, they would bombard it with orantium. The others had considered a similar strategy. But it relied on the Maumet being stupid. The creature had shown a single hint of recklessness. The Maumet had become tooth enamel and had lost a foot as a result. Could banking on a similar mistake be their best hope? Was that realistic?

What would be the ideal material for the Maumet to become? Glass? Crystal? Jason chuckled. Orantium would be nice. It would blast itself into nothing. But there was no way to even bring the creature in contact with orantium. Once exposed to air or water, the mineral immediately exploded. After a globe broke, the mineral would detonate before contact.

Wait.

There was an exception.

For the first time in quite a while, Jason found himself unable to resist a smile.

Within two hours they were ready to implement the plan. Gripping a collapsible spyglass in both hands, Jason felt he might burst with nervous excitement.

The tensest moment so far had come when Thag had rowed the bucket of orantium goo away from the *Valiant*. A single orantium globe was submerged inside the bucket, and he had crushed the sphere with a gloved hand.

He hadn't blown up.

Now a team of three drinlings was aboard a launch, rowing toward shore. Sails angled to make use of the light breeze, the *Valiant* was sailing away to the east in order to put some distance between the ship and the possible explosion. If a little pebble of orantium could blow apart a mangler, and a piece the size of a racquetball could demolish a castle gate, how big would the bang be if this plan worked?

Among other concerns, Jason was seriously worried that if the trick succeeded, Thag and the other two drinlings going ashore might wish it hadn't. Although the landing party was supposed to try to row away before the fireworks began, the drinling squad was very likely on a kamikaze mission.

As the ship glided farther from the shore, Jason watched the mission unfold through his spyglass. Framed within the magnified circle, the Maumet appeared on the beach before the launch landed. It looked to be made of stone, but it was hard to be sure. It might have been gray wood.

The tall figure held still as the launch landed. After securing the launch in the shallows, two of the drinlings splashed forward and attacked the Maumet. Thag hung back with the bucket of goo containing the orantium pebble.

Dodging a blow from a long arm, one of the drinlings slammed the Maumet with a mace, but the creature immediately turned to iron, taking no damage. Body shrieking, the Maumet brutally dispatched the drinling. Thag and the other fighter retreated hastily to the launch, leaving the bucket on the beach near the water.

The idea was to make the bucket look accidentally abandoned. Selling the ploy had already cost one life and might cost two more. Thag and the other drinling rowed away from the beach at maximum speed.

The Maumet stalked up and down the beach near the water, iron joints squealing. Then it paced over to the fallen drinling. Crouching, the Maumet extended a hand and changed color.

"Bronze," Farfalee said, peering through her own telescope. "He touched the ring."

Each of the drinlings had worn a few trinkets of diverse materials in case they fell in combat, to hopefully get the Maumet in a mood to sample substances. Jason knew the transformation was a good sign.

"Now obsidian," Farfalee reported as the Maumet became a glossy black. "The pendant. And now brass, the buckle on his knife belt. It went for everything we planted. Now it's moving toward the bucket."

"We can see that much without lenses," Drake murmured.

Jason swiveled his attention to Thag and the other drinling. Was the other survivor called Fo? Or had that been Fo back on the beach? They continued to row hard and had already put a fair amount of distance between themselves and the shore. Jason aimed the spyglass back at the Maumet.

Standing upright, brass body partially reflecting the water and the white sand, the creature stood over the abandoned bucket. Crouching, the Maumet touched the side of the bucket and turned to brown wood.

Jason held his breath.

"It's reaching into the bucket," Farfalee announced.

Jason lowered his spyglass, worried about the flash. Thag and the other drinling fell flat in the launch. Jason crouched, barely peeking over the side of the ship. Would it happen?

"He's thinking about it," Aram narrated hopefully.

Jason covered his ears, watching through squinted eyes. Would it happen? Would it happen?

Flaring a brilliant white, the Maumet erupted violently—a large primary blast followed by an enormous secondary explosion. The tremendous detonation sent vast quantities of sand and seawater spewing skyward. The concussion wave heaved water and sand outward and made the ship lurch, knocking Jason onto his backside. Even with his ears covered, the thunderous roar was painfully loud.

Regaining his feet, squinting as a peppering of debris began to rain down, Jason marveled at the steam and smoke mushrooming up from the blast site. Seawater surged to fill the gaping void of the blackened crater. Most of the white sand beach was simply gone, along with a great deal of the vegetation behind it.

The plan had worked! The Maumet had taken the bait, temporarily becoming orantium until the immediate consequence followed.

Thag and the other drinling stood up in the launch, pumping their fists in the air. Raucous cheering broke out aboard the *Valiant*. Drake hugged Farfalee, lifting her off her feet and twirling her around. Drinlings pantomimed the explosion and pointed at the churning smoke above the devastated beach.

Jasher clapped Jason on the back. "You just saved us all."

Jason could barely understand the words, because his ears were still ringing. "We owe the drinlings who delivered the orantium."

"They deserve thanks and praise," Jasher agreed. "But the idea had to come first. You're quite the trickster."

"I'll second that," Aram exclaimed as heartily as his small frame would allow. "I'll take cleverness over strength every time!"

Farfalee embraced Jason tightly. "You marvelous, brilliant boy!"

He had never seen Farfalee so unreserved. Nor Drake smiling so broadly. Jason hugged her back, enjoying the triumph of the moment.

Others pressed to congratulate him. Everyone was jubilant. The crew seemed even happier than when they had escaped the harbor. Hats were thrown high, some of them landing in the sea.

Jason realized that the threat of the Maumet had been hanging over them more heavily than any other concern. From the outset they had all known that this obstacle would probably end their lives. But now they had destroyed it with relatively few casualties. One massive blast and the threat had been vaporized.

Whooping and shouting along with the others, Jason managed to lose himself in the moment. There might be plenty of hardship still ahead of them, but right now they had a worthy cause for celebration.

CHAPTER 15

LIBRARY

Once the celebration over the demise of the Maumet subsided, the next phase of planning began. All agreed that haste was a top priority. They needed to secure the information from the library before the opportunity vanished. Even if the imperial forces of the Inland Sea did not know their current position, the tower of smoke rising into the atmosphere would be visible for many miles around. A number of vessels were likely to notice.

Within an hour Aram had the *Valiant* anchored off the eastern coast of Windbreak Island, just south of the new crater. Two launches made for shore, eight passengers in each, including Jason, Farfalee, Jasher, Drake, Aram, Nia, Heg, and a very pale and weary Corinne.

After landing on a strip of beige sand, Corinne flopped onto the beach, facedown, arms spread wide, as if trying to embrace the ground. Breathing deeply, she held the pose for a long moment. Jason squatted beside her, and she raised her head to look at him. Particles of sand clung to her lips, nose, and chin. Her face was ashen, with dark smudges under her eyes. Even worn out and sick, she remained pretty.

"Does it feel good to be back on land?" he asked.

She nodded. "I'm better already. Not all the way back yet. Might take a little time. The warm sand feels divine. I almost feel like eating something on purpose."

"We'll have to be fast," Jason said.

"Don't you dare," Corinne scolded.

"Our enemies could catch up any minute," Jason explained.

"I know."

"Farfalee said the research might take days."

"I like her."

Jason saw that the others were ready to move out. A pair of drinlings had been assigned to guard Corinne. "I have to go."

"Take your time. I'll come find you when I feel better."

"Such a nice beach," Jason said, looking up and down the narrow stretch of sand. "It would be a shame to barf all over it."

Corinne threw a handful of sand at him. He could tell she was already feeling more like herself.

Jasher strode over to Corinne and laid the sheathed torivorian sword on the sand beside her. "This belongs with you."

"Thanks. You're welcome to take it."

The seedman shook his head. "I have my own sword. I want you properly armed."

Another group of drinlings was heading toward the beach in the skiff that had trailed the *Valiant* out of Durna. "What are they up to?" Jason asked.

"Foraging," Jasher said. "You know how much food the drinlings require. They thought it wise to fill the hold while they have the chance."

"I hope they find stuff we can eat too," Jason muttered.

"We'll be all right," Jasher replied. "The *Valiant* was well provisioned when we took it. The drinlings have left the best stores for us."

Jason followed Drake and Jasher off the beach and into the vegetation. There were thick shrubs, some with big, glossy leaves, and tall palm trees. Before visiting Mianamon, Jason might have labeled it a jungle, but the plant life was tame compared to the southern rain forest. The absence of suffocating humidity and carnivorous plants was appreciated.

Although this forest was not draped with vines or teeming with wildlife, the foliage did screen the library from view as Drake and Jasher paralleled a burbling rivulet up the slope. After Jason pushed through ferny limbs for his first clear view of the Celestine Library, he stopped and stared.

The massive structure was magnificent. The overall impression was of multiple blocky buildings and thick towers inventively piled together to form a single elaborate complex. Seven domes were now currently in view, some higher or larger than others, all decorated with elaborate scrollwork and gilded patterns. Their staggered arrangement suggested there might be a few lower domes on the far side as well. Many huge windows and skylights interrupted the exotic masonry. Elevated walkways connected some of the towers. Arches and colonnades abounded. The vast library possessed little symmetry, hugging the sloped terrain like packages artfully arranged on a stairway.

"It's amazing," Jason said as Farfalee emerged from the brush behind him. "These guys took their libraries seriously."

"Think of all the knowledge inside," Farfalee said. "The texts on Edomic alone make this the greatest treasure house in Lyrian."

"It has held up well," Jason noticed. Although the tremendous building seemed ancient, there was no apparent damage. No tumbled towers or cracked domes or even broken windows.

"This library was built to last by the best wizards and craftsmen of an enlightened age," Farfalee said. "The structure is fortified with

Edomic. Protective mandates are expertly woven into the thick stone walls, the foundation, the wood, the glass, the furnishings, even the surrounding earth. Otherwise, the library would lie in ruins by now."

"Some similar sites have been spoiled by intruders over the years," Aram added. "Here, the Maumet kept away treasure hunters and vandals."

Farfalee started toward the Celestine Library across a field of feathery brush broken up by crooked sheets of jagged stone. Shorebirds circled and squawked overhead. As Jason advanced through the brush, small hopping insects cleared out of the way. At first he thought they were grasshoppers, but closer inspection showed they had eight legs and a vaguely crablike shape.

A generous plaza preceded the main entrance to the library. None of the flagstones was broken. No weeds sprouted up through cracks. A stone balustrade enclosed the area, with empty stone planters spaced at intervals, and statuary in the corners. A huge, dry fountain dominated the plaza's center. No fewer than twenty cherubic statues frolicked in the basin and on the shelves descending from the parched spout. All the marble toddlers had chubby features and dimpled joints.

On the far side of the plaza, thirty stone steps swept up to a massive, arched entrance. Giants would feel small in front of the heavy doors.

Farfalee led the group across the plaza and up the steps. Their footfalls seemed too loud. Several of the drinlings looked around disconcertedly, with weapons drawn. Jason did not blame them. The exterior of the library seemed too lavish to be so lifeless.

Farfalee paused before a set of double doors more than three times her height.

"No knobs, handles, or keyholes," Aram observed. He spoke softly, as he might at the entrance to a church.

"Solid," Heg noted.

Farfalee nodded distractedly. "We would fail if we sought entry by force." She placed her fingertips on the door and spoke an Edomic phrase.

As always with Edomic, Jason sensed the meaning without being able to pinpoint the individual words. It was always tricky to translate Edomic into English. Farfalee had basically asked the doors to open for a seeker of illumination.

Quiet as a drop of water sliding down a window pane, the massive doors swung inward, slowly and evenly, revealing an expansive lobby. A polished marble floor extended before them, seamless and swirling with slightly metallic colors. Light streamed in from various windows and shone from luminous stones on the walls. The air felt still and old without smelling musty.

"You knew the password?" Jason asked.

"I did not command with Edomic," Farfalee clarified. "Simple words and phrases are used to trigger preset commands in buildings such as this. I used what was once considered the standard Edomic solicitation for entry to a storehouse of learning. I was worried that the doors might be sealed by Edomic commands or that powerful wards might shield the building. Had that been the case, entry might have been close to impossible for any besides Maldor himself. But no special defenses had been engaged. The doors probably would have responded to any number of polite Edomic requests for admittance."

"Will there be safeguards beyond the doors?" Aram wondered.

"Definitely," Farfalee said. "Be forewarned—do not attempt to force doors in a place such as this. Some rooms or wings may be protected by powerful and even deadly commands. If a door is locked, let me be the judge of whether we should attempt to pass. Also, do not browse the collection. A repository of this renown will contain many traps, including books designed to harm the patron who opens them."

"Why?" Jason asked.

"Much of the knowledge here could be dangerous. Those who created and managed the library feared the collection falling into unenlightened hands. Hence, safeguards were installed. I know most of the clues that mark harmful books. Speaking generally, don't remove any of the texts from the library. Not a single page. And don't touch any of the art, weapons, or treasure that you see. Nearly any item of that sort will be rigged to unleash catastrophe."

"There will be treasure?" Aram asked, his voice pained. "And weapons? And we can't touch them?"

"Certainly not any of the pieces on display," Farfalee emphasized. "Nothing hanging on the walls, decorating the tables, or featured in niches. If in doubt, ask me."

Heg whistled softly. "Should some of us wait here at the doors?"

Farfalee gave a nod. "That might be a wise position for anyone lacking a particular assignment. I recommend that Aram lead a party to the top of the highest dome to keep lookout. Unless I am mistaken, the vantage will be outfitted with an array of optical enhancers. I'll keep Jasher, Drake, Jason, and Nia with me, to assist in my research."

"All right," Aram said. "Three with me. The rest man the door."

Farfalee led Jason, Drake, Jasher, and Nia through the entryway and into the lobby. High above, one of the smaller domes capped the vast chamber, perhaps forty yards across. The murals on the walls looked freshly painted. The lower murals depicted underwater scenes with exotic fish swimming among sharks, squids, eels, and other aquatic predators. Higher murals featured wizards on land, harnessing the elements to attack cities, combat armies, and battle monsters. The paintings and carvings on the domed ceiling showed clouds at sunset, birds, and a variety of fanciful winged creatures.

"I thought the Repository of Learning was big," Jason said, head craned back. "It was just a tiny satellite branch."

"Only two other libraries in Lyrian ever rivaled this one," Farfalee said. "Before abandoning us, Eldrin demolished both of them, together with several lesser repositories and the former residences of many wizards. Only the Celestine Library has remained untouched."

"I suppose we can thank the Maumet for something," Jasher said.

"I consider the guardian much easier to thank now that it has scattered on the wind," Drake remarked.

Three large archways led out of the impressive lobby—one directly across from the entrance, one to the left, and one to the right. All the archways had strange characters engraved above them.

Farfalee walked purposefully toward the archway across from the entrance. "We should find the index records this way. Dare I hope that some of the guides have survived?"

"Guides?" Jason asked. "As in workers? Librarians?"

"Not living guides," Farfalee explained. "No loremasters or historians would have survived these secluded centuries. The guides principally assisted in cataloging these larger libraries. They were Edomic constructs, not living, but brimming with information."

"Like computers," Jason said.

Farfalee looked at him blankly.

"In the Beyond, our libraries have complicated machines with information about all the books."

"Your computers might serve a similar function," Farfalee said. "But the guides are not mechanical. Nor are they truly sentient. Some nearly possess the illusion of life thanks to complex Edomic workmanship. Certain wizards devoted their careers to such projects."

They passed beneath the archway into a short hall. Along either side, heavy doors alternated with arched recesses housing stately busts. Instead of ending, the hall became a downward stairway, not steep, but quite long. It took fifty steps to reach the landing. Farfalee ignored the doors there and descended another long flight. And another. Jason realized that, as immense as the library had appeared from outside, much more of it was concealed underground.

The stairs deposited them in a tubular room that looked like the inside of a long barrel. No sunlight reached this deep place, and the stones in the walls glowed dimly, leaving much of the room in shadow. A counter stretched from wall to wall, restricting access. Behind the counter, rows of tall shelves extended into the distance. The smell of leather and old paper saturated the air.

"Look at all those books!" Nia exclaimed.

"This is merely the index," Farfalee said. "If we can't find any guidestones, we'll search here by hand."

Jason gawked in despair at the endless shelves. How many of those thick tomes would they have to examine simply to find the right area to begin their search?

Drake stretched his arms over his head and grimaced. "I think this is where I wander off and go for a swim."

Farfalee glared at him.

"Let me rephrase," Drake tried. "My instincts warn that I had best hasten to the beach to help keep watch."

Placing both hands on the countertop, Farfalee kicked her legs sideways and vaulted it nimbly. "Don't lose heart," she said, scanning the rear of the counter. "A facility of this quality would ordinarily boast any number of— Here we are!"

Farfalee crouched behind the counter and came up with a wooden tray of hemispheric stones. After placing the tray on the counter, Farfalee selected a blue hemisphere with light green veins.

Cupping the stone in her hand, she spoke in conversational Edomic without commanding intent, and a bluish, translucent man appeared beside her. Wearing a breastplate and helm, a hefty sword at his waist, the spectral figure stood tall, with broad shoulders and brawny limbs.

He greeted Farfalee in Edomic. She asked a question. Something about what other languages he could speak. Jason found that as he attempted to focus on the individual words they spoke, his comprehension grew muddled. He understood better when he only paid casual attention.

"Did she have to pick the dashing soldier?" Jasher grumbled.

"My sister has an eerie sense for these things," Drake replied, suppressing a grin.

"I don't mind the choice," Nia chimed in, sizing up the ghostly soldier appreciatively.

Pausing from her conversation, Farfalee turned to the others. "This should dramatically accelerate the search. Meet Tibrus. He is one of more than a hundred guides at our disposal."

"Do the others look like him?" Nia wondered innocently.

"If so," Jasher mumbled to Drake, "I may join you for that swim."

Farfalee rolled her eyes. "If I have a knack for finding attractive males, as my husband perhaps you should find the implied compliment."

"Do they only speak Edomic?" Jason asked. He had missed the answer about languages.

"Our current common tongue was in use well before this library became inaccessible," Farfalee replied. "The scholars of my youth worked hard to obscure certain knowledge by expressing it in Edomic. But many guides are capable of conversing in other languages if I first issue Edomic instructions to unlock the ability."

"I'll take one of those," Drake said. "My Edomic is out of practice."

Farfalee arched an eyebrow. "Ironic, since you unlawfully employ the language to ignite your cooking fires."

"I prefer to concentrate on the useful words," Drake answered. "I hold few academic conversations with campfires."

"Have you asked Tibrus if he knows where we can learn about Darian?" Nia inquired.

"I did. Tibrus specializes in medicine, the arts, and the strategy of warfare. But he told me where we can find several guides with rich backgrounds in history."

Farfalee thanked Tibrus in Edomic and set down his stone. The instant her fingers lost contact with the hemisphere, the wispy soldier vanished. She ducked behind the counter and came back up holding a small iron strongbox with a keyhole in the front. After setting down the heavy box, she moved along the counter a few paces, crouched again, and produced the key.

"These are some of the more expert guides," Farfalee explained, unlocking the container. "Since the library is vacant, Tibrus was kind enough to tell me where to locate the key."

"These guides are better than the others?" Jason checked.

"History is by far the largest section of the collection," Farfalee explained. "Tibrus warned that the expert guides can be trickier to handle, which was my experience centuries ago in the Great Document Hall at Elboreth. The experts are designed to carefully match the seeker of knowledge to appropriate volumes. They will steer the unworthy away from the weightier texts."

"Then why use the experts?" Nia asked.

Farfalee took six stones from the strongbox and placed them

in a row on the counter. "If we knew the name of the book we desire, any guide would suffice. But I have no idea what tome will inform us about the most recent abode of Darian the Seer. So our best chance will be to solicit an expert who can suggest how to locate that information. We must impress them and win them over. Jasher, would you prefer Edomic or common?"

He winced a little. "I'm more comfortable with common."

"It won't help your credibility," Farfalee cautioned.

"Neither will poor speech," Jasher said.

"Very well," Farfalee conceded.

"Why don't you consult the experts one by one, Failie?" Drake asked.

"Partly due to time," Farfalee replied. "Partly because the experts have varied personalities. Some prefer men to women. If necessary, I will solicit all of them personally. For the present we should share the task." She tapped four of the stones in turn, muttering a phrase about common speech each time. "You may each select one and see what you can learn."

Jason picked a cloudy white stone with fiery orange flecks. It felt smooth, cool, and somewhat heavier than it looked.

Farfalee told them the word they should speak to activate the stone. Jason felt a little nervous, because Edomic commands had never worked for him like they had for Rachel. But in this instance he just needed to pronounce the word correctly, not pour his will into the command to demand compliance.

Trying to match her inflection, Jason repeated the summons Farfalee had shared, and the stone instantly hummed in his hand and grew perceptibly warmer. A bald man with a hook nose and thin eyebrows appeared, leaning on a cane, his skin and clothes a luminous white.

"Common tongue, is it?" he said, sounding a bit cranky.

"It's my native language," Jason explained defensively.

The old guy waved a dismissive hand. "What a sorry state of affairs. Native tongue, you say? The current common speech does not even originate from our world, lad. It comes from the Beyond."

"I know," Jason said. "So do I."

This surprised the old guy. "You hail from the Beyond? Then you know the country our common speech is named after."

"England."

"Correct." The ghostly figure suddenly seemed more friendly. "Do you know how English came to be our common tongue?"

"From the Beyonders who came here?"

"The Beyonders planted the first seeds. There were many factors involved. The primary culprits were wizards. The wizards of Lyrian have long been fascinated with Beyonders. Some wizards have even traveled to the Beyond. Since English was utterly foreign to this world, a number of powerful wizards began using it for secret communication, both in writing and in speech. As the trend grew, the study of English became second only to Edomic for many wizards. Consequently, even outside the society of wizards, many of the learned and wise adopted the practice.

"Of the two languages favored by the wise, English was easier to master. And so interest in it increased. English became synonymous with learning and power. Diverse cultures spoke their own languages, and English besides. In time, English provided a means to converse across cultural boundaries. Gradually, English became firmly established as the common tongue of Lyrian. As an increasing number of children learned it from the cradle, English also became the primary language of many cultures."

"You know a lot," Jason said.

"It is my calling," the old man answered pleasantly. "Under

most circumstances I would consider the use of English inelegant, but the opportunity to converse with a native speaker of a Beyondic tongue is indeed an honor. What brings you to these hallowed halls of learning?"

"A single question, really," Jason said. "I'm looking for the last home of Darian the Seer."

The old man burst into laughter. Not brief laughter. The mirthful condition persisted long enough to make Jason feel awkward. The old guide partly got himself under control, then started up again, wiping tears from his eyes.

"Why is that funny?" Jason asked.

"My apologies, my young Beyonder. For how long have you inhabited our world?"

"Several months, now. Less than a year."

"And already you've turned treasure seeker?"

"I'm not a treasure hunter," Jason said. "I need information."

The old man nodded. "Information that will lead you to Darian's fabled treasure."

"No. I need information from Darian."

"My boy, surely you are aware that Darian must have died ages ago."

This was not news to Jason. Not long after hearing the prophecy, Farfalee had explained that Darian should have died well before even she was born. "Are we sure he's dead?" Jason asked the guide. "Was it confirmed? Did anyone find a body?"

The old man made a disappointed face. "Are you one of those?"

"One of what?"

"I thought we had seen the last of them."

"The last of who?"

The guide considered Jason shrewdly. "How much do you know about the question you are asking?"

"Not a lot. But I was told by a trusted source that Darian has information for me."

The guide narrowed his eyes. "How trusted is the source?"

Jason glanced over at Farfalee, who was conversing with a short, plump woman. "Hey, Farfalee. How much can I tell him?"

"Ask a guide to keep a conversation private and it will," she replied. "Even so, do not divulge more than seems needful."

Jason turned back to the old guide. "Do you have a name?"

"Bactrus."

"I'm Jason. Bactrus, will you keep everything I tell you private?"

"Every patron has the right to privacy. I will protect that right, if you desire."

"I do. I was told to come here by an oracle."

Bactrus smiled patiently. "My boy, many profess the gift of prescience."

"This was the oracle of Mianamon. The head oracle. She died to get the prophecy she shared with us."

"Mianamon you say? A young sect of truth tellers, last I heard, but reputedly legitimate. Perhaps they have fallen into error in the intervening years. This library has sat dormant for centuries, you know."

"I know. I'm pretty sure the oracle was legit."

"Time will tell. What do you know of Darian? Have you other reasons for suspecting he survives?"

"Just the word of the oracle."

"Allow me to furnish some general background. Like most individuals possessing abnormal skill with Edomic, Darian lived an extended lifetime. More extended than most wizards, in fact, which implies significant power. Thousands of years ago, toward the end of his career, already growing frail with age, Darian left his comfortable home in the city of Darvis Kur."

"The Drowned City," Jason interjected.

"You know something of our history," Bactrus approved. "This was long before the incident with Pothan the Slow, but yes, I refer to the same Darvis Kur that now lies in the Sunken Lands. Darian left his comfortable home for a secret abode in the wilderness, where he planned to end his days."

"Secret abode?" Jason asked. "How secret?"

"Most secret," Bactrus emphasized. "The disappearance produced quite an uproar. You see, Darian was undisputedly the greatest seer Lyrian had known. Past, present, and future were open to him as to no other before or since. Fire aided his visions, earning him the secondary title of pyromancer. He had helped and guided the people of Lyrian for generations. He was old, but there were still years in him. In spite of that, he vanished abruptly and with little explanation, which spawned rumors for centuries."

"What rumors?" Jason asked.

"Darian had many servants and disciples. Some claimed he had seen a vision of the place where he was supposed to die and that he had become obsessed with spending the remaining years of his life there. Others asserted he had been hoarding treasure over the years and wanted to die entombed with his riches. Some rumors even purported that Darian had found the secret to everlasting life and meant to prophesy in hiding until the end of time. These were some of the earliest and best documented assertions. Over the years there has been no shortage of additional speculation."

"So he might be alive?"

The spectral guide chuckled. "It would be an unprecedented feat. No matter his ability, no matter how diligently he conserved his vigor, Darian should have perished millennia ago. But who is an old library guide to label anything impossible?"

"Did anyone ever find his last home?"

"You must understand, treasure hunters tried to uncover this secret for a thousand years before giving up. The last abode of Darian the Seer is the stuff of legend, a mirage that has been pursued by countless doomed expeditions. Respected oracles and seers have sought the final dwelling place of Darian, including several truth sayers he had personally trained, but their efforts yielded nothing. As with other such legends, the only claims of success over the years came from unreliable sources with little or no proof."

"Now I get why you laughed earlier," Jason said.

"I am glad you can empathize," Bactrus said. "The hunt for the last abode of Darian the Pyromancer was abandoned as folly centuries before this library became dormant. I found it humorous that our first visitor in many long years came chasing such a far-fetched legend."

Jason sighed. "The idea of finding the last home of Darian the Seer has become a joke."

"It was a joke fifteen hundred years ago," Bactrus said. "Now it has been so long that most have forgotten the idea was ever amusing."

Jason glanced over at Farfalee. "The seed people I'm with knew of Darian, but they didn't seem to know how absurd the quest for his home is considered."

"Not surprising," Bactrus said. "Compared to Darian, even the Amar Kabal are young. The quest you describe is a fool's errand. The search for his final dwelling place has been long forgotten. Nevertheless, the name of Darian will endure forever. He truly was the greatest seer of all time."

"Great enough that if he knew he could live forever, he might have moved away from Darvis Kur before the city flooded?"

Bactrus smiled. "An interesting observation."

"Everyone may have forgotten this was ever a joke, but the oracle I spoke with was the real deal. Her predictions brought me here from the Beyond. She couldn't see his home, but she seemed certain we could discover the location here. We don't need the location to find treasure. We need it to learn a secret that can save Lyrian. Can you help me?"

"You have a flair for the dramatic," Bactrus said. "And I have a soft spot for the enthusiastic pursuit of hopeless causes. Besides, my job is to serve as your guide. If this is the knowledge you seek, I shall do all in my power to aid you."

"Where do we start?" Jason asked. "We don't have much time."

Bactrus furrowed his brow. "How long do you have?"

"We're not sure," Jason said. "Do you know what's going on across Lyrian right now?"

"I know much of what is written here," Bactrus said. "But I have learned nothing from outside since our last visitors arrived. The Maumet sealed us off from the rest of the world."

"What happened to the people here?" Jason wondered.

"Most tried to flee the island. Far as we could tell, the Maumet took them all. Some tried to hide here. The Maumet has never entered the library. It has never tried. Eventually those hiding here either took their chances with the Maumet or starved."

Jason frowned. "What happened to the bodies? You know, the ones who starved?"

"Apart from the Edomic spells preserving the walls, artifacts, and books here, there are a few simple constructs that assist with shelving and trash collection. These constructs deposited the corpses in a storage room."

"Gross," Jason said.

Bactrus shrugged. "Less unpleasant than some alternatives."

"Well, a lot has happened since then. You know about Maldor?"

"The apprentice to Zokar."

"Zokar is dead. Eldrin destroyed all the major libraries except for this one. All the wizards are gone now, except for Maldor, who is setting himself up as emperor. His forces will follow us here anytime. If they find us here, they'll kill us."

"An acceptable reason for haste," the old guide allowed. "Let me briefly review what you can find here pertinent to your search. I have aided many with research on this topic, though as you might guess, I have had no serious inquiries in a great while. The texts you desire are ancient and almost uniformly amount to unconfirmed speculation. All I can offer are a thousand different unverified theories."

Jason rubbed his forehead. "The information has to be here."

"The correct answer may lie camouflaged among those many guesses. In your lifetime, without interference and with infinite funding, you could perhaps pursue forty or fifty of those leads. The search would take you all over the world."

Jason thought of Galloran attacking Felrook. "We only have one shot. Even going straight to the right destination might take too long. Maldor is about to crush us. Are you aware of all the possible sources we could check? Is there another guide who might know something you missed?

Bactrus bristled at the question. "I am the chief guide for ancient history. And the last abode of Darian the Seer is an area of personal expertise. Any of the other guides who wished to be of service would refer you to me. I personally know the contents of every scroll, map, and volume relevant to your inquiry. You will find no other pertinent text in this library, unless you can read ancient Petruscan."

Jason turned to Farfalee. She did not look like she was getting favorable news from her guide. "Hey, Farfalee. Do you know ancient Petruscan?"

She brightened. "Petruscan? Actually, yes. Petruscan is the most obscure language with which I am familiar."

CHAPTER 16

THE PETRUSCAN SCROLL

Did you catch that?" Jason asked, turning to Bactrus.

"I heard her," Bactrus said, bewildered. "That language is not just dead. The cemetery where it was buried has crumbled to dust. Many of our guides possess extensive linguistic expertise. None here knows Petruscan. There was no need. We had no Petruscan texts. Very few survived elsewhere. How does she know Petruscan?"

Jason looked to Farfalee. "He wants to know where you learned Petruscan. Why won't he just ask you?"

"The guide will only directly address the patron holding the stone," Farfalee said. "But he'll hear my response just fine. In my youth I worked as a researcher for Eldrin in the Great Document Hall at Elboreth. He had assembled a sizable team to comb through ancient writings in pursuit of Edomic references. The task required several of us to master dead languages. To my knowledge, the only Petruscan texts in existence resided in the Great Document Hall, and a small team of experts on-site were the only people keeping the language alive. I was one of two among the Amar Kabal who learned to read it."

"Who was the other?" Jasher asked.

"Kale, son of Hannock," Farfalee replied. "His seed perished in the war with Zokar. After the war, when Eldrin razed the city he had founded and obliterated the Great Document Hall, I never expected to encounter Petruscan again."

Bactrus gave Jason a significant stare. "How is it that this remarkable woman came to be in your company?"

"The oracle sent seven of us to find Darian the Seer."

Bactrus giggled excitedly. "This oracle told you the information was here and sent the seedwoman with you—probably the sole person in all of Lyrian who can read Petruscan."

"Right." Jason struggled to restrain his excitement. It certainly appeared to be more than coincidence. Maybe the oracle had a more detailed plan than any of them had realized!

"Allow me to relate a brief account," Bactrus said. "High in the Sturloch Mountains northwest of here, there once stood a minor storehouse of ancient texts, most in unreadable languages. The modest collection was cared for by a small but longstanding order of loremasters. As the forces of Zokar began to plunder villages in the region, the loremasters sent many of the texts here to the Celestine Library for safekeeping. Those writings continue to reside here on loan, since the loremasters have never come to collect them. Presumably both the order and the storehouse perished. Among the loaned texts are the only Petruscan works currently within these walls—relatively recent acquisitions."

"Ask him why he suspects that any of those texts might be relevant to our search," Farfalee said.

Jason asked the question.

"The name Darian is mentioned several times on one of the scrolls," Bactrus said. "Petruscan characters were not used for his name, so it is the only discernible word on the document."

"Why would Darian be mentioned in a Petruscan scroll?" Farfalee wondered. "The Petrusian society was extinct long before he was born. By the time Darian lived, Petruscan was already a dead language."

"You heard her?" Jason asked.

"Yes."

"What can you tell us?" Jason prompted.

"I found the anomaly intriguing," Bactrus said, "but without a Petruscan translator I had no means to investigate. Petrusians wrote on metal plates. At least those were the only writings that survived. The text in question is written on a scroll. These writings could have been transcribed from metal plates, perhaps by a relatively modern scribe who translated the name Darian into more familiar characters. The scroll might preserve an arcane Petruscan prophecy regarding Darian. Seers have been known to prophesy about one another."

"Or it could be a hoax," Drake pointed out.

"The scroll could certainly be fraudulent," Bactrus told Jason. "Swindlers have created many false trails to the last abode of Darian the Seer. In bygone days, certain adventurers would pay handsomely for clues to unearthing the fabled treasure."

Farfalee raised a finger. "The scroll could be neither prophecy nor fraudulence. Some clever soul might have translated a sensitive message into Petruscan in order to conceal it."

"Is that possible?" Jason asked Bactrus.

The old guide scrunched his face in thought. "Perhaps even probable."

"Can you guide us to the scroll?" Jason asked.

"It would be my privilege," Bactrus replied.

Jason looked around. Drake, Jasher, and Farfalee had already returned their stones to the counter. Nia had exchanged hers to reanimate Tibrus.

"Nia," Jason scolded lightly, "what's with the soldier? Didn't Tibrus already tell us he isn't big on history?"

"I know," Nia replied. "But he isn't too proud to use common speech. My other guide insulted me. It looks like you four have this search for Darian well in hand, so I thought I might do some other research."

Jason glanced from Nia to the strapping warrior. "I'm not sure it could ever work out between you two."

"You deserve someone more substantial," Drake added with a smirk.

"At least tangible," Jason said.

Nia gave an exasperated sigh. "I really need his expertise. It's only a coincidence that he's attractive."

"Are you serious?" Jasher asked.

"Absolutely," Nia responded.

"Very well," Farfalee said. "The rest of us will accompany Jason and Bactrus."

Jason wagged a playful finger at Nia. "We had better not catch you in the poetry section."

Drake turned away, a hand over his mouth. Jasher developed a sudden cough.

Nia put a hand on her hip and cocked her head. "Very mature, Jason. It's important research. You'll see."

"What research?" Jason pressed. "You could be more specific."

"You're right. I could. But maybe I don't think you deserve to know."

"No hint?" Jason asked. "Not even a category?"

"You'll find out later," Nia replied.

"Tragic romances," Drake deadpanned.

Everyone laughed besides Nia and the guides.

Even with a guide escorting them along the quickest route, it was a long hike to the scroll. The Celestine Library went on and on, room after room, level upon level. They passed numerous stairways and branching corridors. In some of the larger chambers, bookshelves towered like cliffs, accessible only by systems of ladders and platforms. Aside from endless texts, the group passed masterful paintings and murals, meticulous mosaics, exquisitely detailed sculptures, mounted weapons of the finest craftsmanship, and tempting displays of priceless jeweled artifacts. Since the library was abandoned, Jason supposed he would be justified in salvaging some of the costly relics. Without the warning from Farfalee about Edomic traps, he would have paused to fill his pockets on more than one occasion.

Bactrus walked beside Jason the entire way. Despite his holographic appearance and the fact that his footsteps made no sound, the guide moved around as if he were subject to the laws of gravity.

"We're in the middle of a desperate war," Jason mentioned to Bactrus as they mounted a broad stairway. "Are there any weapons here at the library that we could borrow for the cause?" He tried to act casual, even though he had spent some time deciding how best to phrase the question.

"Most of the weapons and armor you see on display are priceless pieces of our permanent collection," Bactrus replied. "We did not even lend our books out to the wisest of wizards, let alone any of the artifacts housed here. I am afraid the armaments must remain."

"That's what I expected," Jason said.

"You could always try the cloakroom," Bactrus mused. "Visitors left their weapons and armor there. The policy was mandatory. Anything remaining will never be claimed and does not belong to the library."

"Worth a look," Drake said. "Nearly anyone with the funding or initiative to come here would have been well equipped."

"Although they probably would have retrieved their gear when they tried to flee," Farfalee speculated. "Also, some who fled might have claimed the equipment of others. But still, I agree, worth a look."

"You might also inspect the antiquities shop," Bactrus said. "The inventory is not technically part of the collection, since it was for sale. The exorbitant prices were meant to raise funds. But with no shopkeeper present to manage the inventory, any remaining items could reasonably be considered abandoned and available."

"Thanks for the tips," Jason said.

"I like how this guide thinks," Drake confided to Jasher.

In a distant wing of the library, at the end of a hall several stories above ground level, Bactrus stopped before a hefty door. "This section is restricted access," the guide explained. "Loaned texts in extinct languages. Much of the material here came from the same repository as the scroll you seek. More than half the content cannot be deciphered by any of our guides." He indicated a round depression in the center of the door. "Place your stone into the recess."

Jason pressed his stone into the depression. It fit perfectly. The stone glowed momentarily, tumblers rattled, and the door swung smoothly open. Jason kept the stone in his hand.

The room beyond was not large, but contained many shelves and cubbies. The few books on display were primitively bound. Metal plates, clay tablets, and tightly wound scrolls were much more prevalent.

Bactrus led them to a bulky cabinet full of small, square drawers. He indicated a particular one. Pulling it open, Jason found that the long drawer contained a scroll.

Farfalee removed the scroll, unrolling it carefully. Nearly a yard long, the yellowed document contained row after row of tidy, unrecognizable characters. Farfalee started at the top, squinting at the words. Her lips bent into a smile.

"It purports to describe a route to the last abode of Darian the Seer," she announced. "According to this document, our road will take us . . . through the Fuming Waste and into the mountains beyond."

"Dangerous country," Jasher said.

"But not particularly distant," Drake noted.

"Could this be real?" Jason asked Bactrus.

The old guide bent over the scroll, scanning it intently. "The scroll was certainly not written by Petrusians. As we established previously, although Darian lived long ago, by his time the Petrusian society had vanished and the language was out of use. And according to what your comrade has shared, the scroll does not purport to be a prophecy."

"Could it be part of a scam?" Jason asked.

Bactrus lowered his eyebrows. "If the scroll is fraudulent, Petruscan is an odd choice of language, since it was comprehensible to only a handful of scholars. It would have required a discouraging amount of work for a buyer to translate the content."

Drake folded his arms. "A swindler might have decided that the odd choice of language would lend the scroll an air of authenticity. Furthermore, the period required to decipher the message could allow the crook additional time to disappear before the buyer found the information disappointing."

"Did you catch that?" Jason asked Bactrus.

"Plausible reasoning. Does anyone claim authorship?"

Farfalee skipped to the bottom of the manuscript. "The author is described at the beginning and the end as 'the Steering Hand.' Would you like to hear a rough translation of the introduction?"

"Please," Jasher said.

Farfalee cleared her throat. She read haltingly, as if intent on choosing the most accurate words. "'Courtesy of the Steering Hand, herein the worthy seeker of enlightenment will find instructions to reach the final dwelling place of Darian, son of Thebrun, the renowned seer of Darvis Kur and author of more than two thousand verified prophecies great and small.' The account goes on to reveal the general location of the last abode of Darian, and then gets very specific naming landmarks to use as guideposts along the way."

"What do you think?" Jason asked, studying Bactrus.

The guide lifted his empty hands in a noncommittal gesture. "Genuine or false, the message would probably read the same. Only by following the directions to the end could you know for certain."

"Do we have a better option?" Jason asked.

"Over the years, all of the other leads have been explored with no evident results. The most promising leads have been pursued countless times. Since arriving here, this particular scroll has never been read, and thus it has never been tested. And thanks to the foresight of your oracle, you arrived with the one person in Lyrian capable of reading it. If you want me to guess which source you should rely on, this would be my pick."

"Good enough for me," Jason said.

"Me too," Jasher agreed. "We need a path, we need it quick, and circumstances certainly point to this scroll."

Drake frowned. "If the scroll is false, our quest will fail."

"True," Jasher said. "Do you expect to find a better option?"

Drake slowly shook his head. "I agree that this seems to be what we're looking for."

"There is a warning toward the end," Farfalee said.

"Tell us," Drake said.

"'Seek not this sanctum in the name of vanity or avarice. Enter with no instruments of war or tainted intentions. Calamity awaits the undeserving. Only the . . . chosen . . . can survive.'" She looked up. "'Chosen' may not be the precise word. But it is close."

Jason realized that all of his companions were looking at him. The oracle had specifically stated that he needed to find the last abode of Darian the Seer. Apparently, that made him the chosen one, at least in their minds. The attention made him a little uncomfortable.

"Do any of the other texts lead to the Fuming Waste?" Jason asked.

"Several," Bactrus answered, "although the same could be said for nearly any location in Lyrian that you would care to name."

"We'll need detailed maps of the Fuming Waste," Jasher said.

"Can you help us?" Jason asked the guide.

"We should adjourn to the geography center," he replied. "You will find not only the most thorough assortment of maps ever assembled, but materials with which to copy the contents of the scroll."

"We can bring the scroll to the other area?" Jason checked.

Bactrus gave a nod. "The texts are not to leave the library, but within these walls they are meant to be studied and used."

"Lead the way," Jason said.

Once again Bactrus ushered them along a lengthy route. At first they backtracked past familiar sights, but soon they forked off through new rooms, stairways, and passages.

"Being a loremaster here would be good exercise," Jason remarked as they passed a glittering stained-glass window. "Are we getting close?"

"Just up ahead," Bactrus promised.

Jasher held up a hand, bringing them to a halt, a finger to his lips. Jason listened. A male voice was calling their names from a distance. There was an edge of panic to the tone.

Jasher cupped both hands around his mouth. "We're here!" he belted. "Western wall, four floors up, near the third largest dome."

Jason was impressed by Jasher's clear sense of their location.

"On my way!" the distant voice answered.

"Won't be good news," Drake murmured.

"Jasher," Farfalee said, "perhaps you should wait here for the messenger. We can run ahead and start copying the needful information."

"Yes," Jasher said. He looked to Jason.

Jason turned to Bactrus. "Can you tell Jasher how to find us?"

The old guide issued terse instructions; then Farfalee started running. Jason and Drake followed, and the old guide as well. Jason noticed that Bactrus sprinted as swiftly as any of them and showed no signs of tiring. After a few more twists and turns, followed by a flight of stairs, they entered a large space dedicated to maps and atlases. A huge relief map of Lyrian dominated the floor, with the rest of the room built around it. A skylight above added natural brightness, and a balcony around the top half of the room allowed patrons to access high shelves or to gaze down at the floor map from above.

Bactrus directed them to an oversized book of maps dedicated to the Fuming Waste. While Farfalee perused the maps, he led Jason and Drake to collect paper, ink, and pens.

"Will the ink work after all these years?" Jason asked.

"Yes, if the bottle has been sealed," the guide replied. "Edomic was used to protect and preserve nearly all of our resources."

Jasher and one of the drinlings who had accompanied Aram burst into the room. "We have a situation," Jasher said.

"What?" Drake asked.

"Six ships on the northeastern horizon, coming this way, including an interceptor."

"The wind is still from the east?" Drake asked.

"Yes," Jasher said. "Aram found an observation room atop the highest dome. The ships just came into view using telescopes. They are still hours away. Aram thinks if we hurry, we might have a chance to escape undetected."

"Wouldn't that be nice?" Drake asked. "Farfalee?"

"Depends how long it takes to copy the scroll and a map."

"Captain Aram has already run ahead to prepare the *Valiant*," the drinling said. "He knows you will follow as soon as you see fit."

"Anything you can do to help us hurry?" Jason asked Bactrus.

The old guide pursed his lips. "Possibly. Ask your friend if she ever held an office when she worked at the Great Document Hall."

"Farfalee?" Jason asked.

"I attained the office of lesser loremaster," she replied.

"Ask if she recalls her words," Bactrus instructed.

"Farfalee?"

She spoke several Edomic phrases. They referenced fidelity in preserving the rich history of Lyrian, honesty in dealing with those seeking knowledge, and courage in protecting the documents in her care.

"Those are the words," Bactrus told Jason. "The scroll is not a permanent part of our collection. I could release it into her custody as if she were the loremaster who came to return it to Cirum Elsador, the repository from whence it came."

"Really?" Jason exclaimed.

"I have that authority," Bactrus said. "And she is, after all, the only remaining person who can read it. Ask your friend to pledge to see the scroll either safely delivered to Cirum Elsador or else returned here."

"I promise," Farfalee said.

"Have her touch the scroll to the stone," Bactrus instructed.

They did so, and the stone briefly pulsed with light.

Bactrus regarded Jason somberly. "The scroll is now under her stewardship. You also need a map."

"Yes," Jason said.

"We have diverse maps for purchase," Bactrus said. "All part of a service once offered by the cartographers here. They are not so finely detailed as some available in the collection, and the selection is limited, but I am aware of five commercial maps that together should serve your needs. As with the antiquities shop, since there is no proprietor present, I can simply let you take them."

"This could make all the difference," Jasher said. "It will save hours."

"You could attempt to copy our maps by hand," Bactrus told Jason, "but it would require considerable skill to match the detail. The commercial maps will most likely serve better than any copies you might render."

Bactrus led them to a side of the room crowded with counters, cabinets, and drawers. With his help, they collected five rolled maps. Farfalee scanned them to be sure. "These will serve," she decided.

"Take care in the Fuming Waste," Bactrus warned Jason. "The landscape is constantly changing. The main features should be relatively constant, but nothing on the maps can be guaranteed."

"Right," Jasher said. "To the entrance."

"Can you lead us there double time?" Jason asked Bactrus.

"I do not tire," the guide responded.

As they ran, Drake spoke up. "I'd like to peek at that antiquities shop before we go."

"I wouldn't mind a look at the cloakroom," Jasher added.

"Every minute counts," Farfalee reminded them.

"We'll hurry," Drake promised.

"I can lend you the stone," Jason said.

"Much appreciated," Drake replied.

"I wish we had time to hide the stones," Farfalee said. "I don't want to make it easy for our enemies to use these resources."

"Maldor could probably learn a lot here," Jason realized.

"If we lose the war," Farfalee said, "this library will provide the means to significantly enhance his power."

"Is there any way to lock the library?" Jason asked.

"It would require an acting loremaster who knew the words," Bactrus said. "We guides have no such authority. The outer doors will open to any Edomic greeting."

"Hiding the stones isn't worth the effort," Jasher panted. "If we bring the scroll, I can think of no immediate benefit the library can offer our foes. Unless perhaps there are useful items in the antiquities shop."

"Very well," Farfalee said. "You two check the cloakroom and the shop. But don't lag! The time will be best spent escaping."

They ran the rest of the way to the entrance without conversation. By the time they reached the lobby, Jason was damp with sweat and breathing hard. Only the drinling and Bactrus showed no sign of fatigue.

Jason handed the stone to Jasher.

"Does Nia know we're leaving?" Farfalee suddenly asked.

"We already found her," the drinling said. "She and the others have gone ahead. We're the last people in the library."

"Come on," Farfalee urged, leading the way out the front door.

Glancing back, Jason saw Bactrus giving instructions to Jasher. "Thanks, Bactrus!" Jason called, but the guide remained focused on the seedman.

Outside, Jason saw that afternoon was progressing toward evening. He raced alongside Farfalee and the drinling through the greenery down to the beach, where they found Corinne and Nia waiting, along with Zoo and a single launch.

"How are you feeling?" Jason asked Corinne.

"Much better," she said. She was on her feet and had some of her color back. "And I might stay that way. Nia did me a favor. She brought me a remedy for seasickness."

Jason turned to Nia. "Really?"

"Tibrus is a medical expert," Nia explained smugly. "He showed me a picture of an herb called langerhop that was once cultivated here on the island to help visitors who found the crossing unpleasant. He said it's a potent remedy, working well even in chronic instances. I found a huge patch of it growing wild on the south side of the library. Corinne already sampled some, and we loaded a lot into the launch."

Corinne gave Nia a big hug. "If this works, I'll owe you forever!"

Jason felt more than a little jealous. If he had been a bit more considerate, he could have been Corinne's hero!

"We should get that launch ready," Farfalee said. "We need to leave the moment Jasher and Drake return."

The two drinlings turned the launch around. Jason, Nia, and Corinne wandered over to it. Jason watched the sea lapping against the shore with wimpier waves than ever.

Within a few minutes Jasher and Drake came bounding out of the vegetation and sprinted across the sand. They held three black shields shaped like extremely rounded triangles. Drake wore a round steel cap and a breastplate that matched the shield. A dark, velvety cloak billowed behind Jasher.

The two seedmen leaped into the launch. The drinlings shoved off and then manned the oars. Grinning, Drake held out one of the shields to Farfalee.

"Titan crab," she said, hefting it.

"I almost got killed by a titan crab," Jason mentioned.

"Lighter than steel," Jasher said. "And a good deal stronger."

"I'll admit," Farfalee said, "titan-crab shields were probably worth the wait."

"The cloakroom was empty except for junk," Drake said. "But the shop looked untouched. You would weep to know the valuables we left behind. The art alone!"

"We concentrated on useful items," Jasher said.

"How novel," Farfalee commented.

Jasher gave her a lopsided grin. "But that didn't stop me from thinking of you." He held out a jeweled necklace and a fancy silver bracelet.

Farfalee could not disguise her pleasure. "Oh, Jash! You scoundrel! You pillaged for me! That necklace is divine! It's useful—it must be worth a fortune!"

"And since I have no spouse," Drake said, "I thought of you girls." He handed Corinne and Nia matching rings set with huge blue gems.

"It's lovely," Corinne gushed, her eyes dancing.

Jason could not help but notice that everyone was scoring major points with her today except him.

Nia said nothing. She held up the ring, transfixed by the glinting facets. At last she let out a low whistle. "I never imagined owning something so fancy."

"Facing grim peril should have some rewards," Drake said, rapping his titan-crab breastplate with his knuckles. "The extra shield is for Lord Jason."

"Really?" Jason said, suddenly feeling much better.

"We don't want to make it too easy for them to kill you," Drake insisted cheerfully. "Windbreak Island has been good to us. We have our scroll, and our maps, and several rare and valuable items besides. Now all we have to do is get away."

They reached the ship and climbed to the deck. As a group of drinlings took care of the launch, the *Valiant* set sail. Aram approached, and Farfalee filled him in about the scroll and the maps. Jasher showed off the shields and gave Aram a curved knife with a jeweled hilt.

"How do we get away?" Jasher asked.

"We took the time to study their heading from the observation room," Aram said. "They're coming from the northeast, on a direct course for Windbreak Island. So we'll slip away to the southwest, using the same easterly wind, and keep the island between us until nightfall. They'll want to search the island thoroughly, so they'll surely stop there for the night. If the wind holds, by daybreak we should be out of sight even from the observation room."

"A cogent plan," Drake said with mock astonishment. "You really must have been a smuggler! I was convinced you had made it all up."

Aram smiled. "I think we set sail just in time. Whatever our enemies may have known about our intentions before, they'll have a difficult time finding us now."

As the group dispersed, Drake pulled Jason aside. The seedman produced an elegant necklace set with extravagant gemstones.

"Drake," Jason said, "you shouldn't have."

Ignoring the comment, the seedman looked pleased with himself. "I also swiped a beautiful necklace for Rachel, lest she feel forgotten."

Jason smiled, wondering if Drake realized what he had just implied. "You think we're going to make it."

"What?"

"You think we'll have a chance to give it to her."

Drake tried to muster a tough stare. "Now, don't start putting words in my mouth. We're probably as doomed as ever."

Jason tried not to grin. "I don't blame you. I'm feeling pretty good too. Things could have gone a lot worse on the island."

"Things went plenty bad. But yes, we bested the Maumet, we found the scroll, and we might even get away before our enemies catch our scent. Things could have gone worse. There's still plenty of hardship and uncertainty ahead. Only a fool would predict we'd survive this . . . but who knows?"

"You brought the necklace just in case."

"Exactly. One never knows." He jangled the necklace. "Just in case."

CHAPTER 17

MARCHING

A warm spring sun glared overhead as Rachel rode along a wide dirt road through pastoral country. The sounds and smells of men and horses surrounded her and stretched out behind. She was glad that her status as the Dark Lady allowed her to ride toward the front of the column. It turned out that thousands of soldiers on the move churned up a great deal of dust just about wherever they went. Her position near the front helped her avoid the worst of it, and the black veils that screened her face provided additional protection.

Of course, she was not truly at the front. Not in a vulnerable way. Scouts ranged far ahead in all directions, and a vanguard of mounted troops rode well beyond the main body of the army.

Galloran had anticipated trouble crossing the Telkron River. Any of the viable crossings would create a bottleneck where a relatively small amount of fighting men and manglers could stall the entire host. But there had not been any resistance. Not at the Telkron, not before, not after. The scouts continued to report no threatening enemy movements. So far the experience of marching to war had been rather dull.

Snowflake was as good a horse as Rachel had hoped—strong, tireless, and quick to obey. The mare moved more smoothly than any horse Rachel had ridden. Tark and Ferrin rode near her, but conversation was scarce. Io had been assigned as Galloran's assistant and bodyguard, the same role Dorsio had once filled.

Galloran spent a surprising amount of time among the troops. He rode up and down the column during the day and visited their campsites at night, never lingering anywhere long, just allowing the men to see him and receive a few encouraging words. Sometimes Rachel wondered when he slept. It could not have been more than a few hours each night.

Galloran never wore his blindfold anymore except in private meetings. He had explained that a host of their size could go nowhere in secret. Some of the men had taken to brandishing their weapons at Galloran and shaking their fists when he rode past. At first Rachel had found the display disrespectful, until she realized they were sending a message to Felrook through his eyes. Galloran would sometimes scowl at the rowdy taunts to encourage them. He trusted the officers to maintain discipline and keep the joke from getting out of hand.

Every night Rachel slept in a tent on a comfortable cot. Tark and Ferrin shared the space behind a divider. Sometimes in the night Rachel would worry about lurkers intruding. She never took off the charms that shielded her mind. At times, in the dark, she clung to her necklace like a lifeline.

Galloran had a large tent that was used for meetings. Whenever a discussion was in progress, twelve burly guards surrounded the tent, three on each side. Rachel was not usually included in the discussions, but one evening after supper Rachel, Ferrin, and Tark were summoned to the pavilion. Galloran, blindfolded, awaited them with Io at his side. Bread and cheese covered a table topped by a large map.

"Good evening," Galloran said. "I apologize that my time has been spread thin lately. Much of my day is occupied with eagle messages and scouting reports. I wanted to bring you up-to-date on our progress and get your reactions to the current state of our campaign. I want you all to understand our situation, and would be interested to hear your evaluations."

"Happy to serve," Ferrin said.

"We are currently experiencing far less resistance than I had expected," Galloran said. "The country before us is not being burned or plundered to starve us. Our host is not being harassed. Our enemies have not bothered to destroy bridges or take any action to slow us. What does this tell you?"

"That we're walking into a trap," Ferrin said. "We're going exactly where the emperor desires."

"If that is the case," Galloran said, "I would still expect some token effort to impede us, if for no other reason than to make his approval of our movements less obvious."

"Such token resistance would suggest he views us as a threat," Ferrin replied. "Maldor is in no hurry to show us any such respect. He does not want to burn crops that his subjects are otherwise sure to harvest after we are corpses. He does not want the trouble of rebuilding bridges. He has elected to belittle us with a seeming lack of attention. He is telling your soldiers that he views them as harmless. He is inviting them to march to their deaths, offering no small victories along the way."

From behind her veil, Rachel watched Ferrin, impressed. He certainly had a sharp mind for strategy.

"I'm afraid that I agree with your assessment," Galloran said. "Maldor knows the prophecy. He knows where we are going. He knows we mean to besiege Felrook. And he is inviting us to try."

Ferrin nodded. "Why seek to slow us when he knows we are

marching to the battlefield where he holds the greatest advantage? Felrook is ringed with mountains. There are only three good ways to reach it. The western pass, which lies east of Harthenham. The northwestern pass, which is the narrowest. And the eastern plain, where the mountains fail. No doubt the drinlings will enter by the eastern route."

"Correct," Galloran said. "The Amar Kabal will join us at the western pass. The northwestern way is closer to the Seven Vales, but there is no use in losing troops trying to take two passes."

"We must keep vigilant," Ferrin said. "Maldor might be trying to lull us into complacency. Just when we think he is giving us easy access to Felrook, he might hit us hard."

"We're braced for a big ambush," Galloran said. "Our scouts and spies are working hard. Yet we have found nothing."

"Then we will probably face our first major challenge at the western pass," Ferrin said. "The walls have been built high and strong. Without the gatecrashers I doubt whether our forces could get through. Even with large orantium spheres the cost will be dear. We will pay in blood."

Rachel squirmed at the thought. Sometimes she was grateful for the veil to help hide her reactions.

"Or if Maldor holds to his current strategy," Galloran said, "he might opt to offer small resistance at the pass."

"Trap us in the valley with him," Ferrin said. "If he had a host ready to come from the east, we would be in trouble. The war would be over. Is Kadara still besieged?"

"His armies in the east remain in place at present," Galloran said. "I'm still in contact by eagle with Kadara, Inkala, Highport, and the drinlings. If he summons his armies home, we'll have advance warning."

Ferrin nodded. "The emperor might be quietly mustering a

sufficient host to deal with us. He could draw from his occupying forces all over Lyrian. The troops we are not facing now might have been withdrawn to hammer us all together."

Galloran nodded. "After winning our way through the western pass, we need to leave sufficient men to hold it. That pass will be our only retreat if an army floods in from the east."

"He may not even need to retake the pass," Ferrin speculated. "What if he places a large enough army on the far side? Without the walls and the towers in his possession, he could still close the way."

"He could very realistically do just that," Galloran said. "We'd be caught between two armies."

Rachel was impressed by how casually they could discus scenarios that could lead to their destruction. Hopefully, anticipating the possibilities would help them prevent the disaster from striking.

"If he can spare the soldiers," Ferrin said, "the emperor might summon forces from Meridon. How goes the revolt there?"

"The uprising amounted to less than we had expected," Galloran said. "A few interceptors were stolen. A few others burned. Most of the rebels fell. Vernon and Trivett perished. We will see no troops from the endeavor. In the larger scheme of things, the insurrection was a mere irritation."

Ferrin folded his arms. "Maldor's strategy is sound. We cannot take Felrook. No fortress in Lyrian enjoys more advantageous geography. As you know, it sits atop a mount in the center of Lake Fellion. If we try to construct a fleet of ferries, Maldor has ample armaments to sink them before they get close. And there is only one way up the cliffs to the castle gate. The path can be destroyed if needed. If left intact, the path allows very limited access. We cannot crash gates that we cannot reach. And Felrook is extremely well provisioned. Maldor could last for years against a siege." Ferrin paused, thinking.

"Go on," Galloran encouraged.

"The protective lake prevents soldiers from sallying forth out of Felrook and taking the offensive. To compensate, Maldor erected three keeps on high ground around the lake. The three strongholds fortify one another and allow counterattacks in the case of a siege. Taking any of them would be an enormous challenge."

"And the ferry is protected by a wall," Galloran said. "It could function as a fortress as well."

Ferrin nodded grimly. "Maldor could very well trap us between a castle we cannot take and an overwhelming host we cannot fight. The valley is large. He could hide massive reserve forces. He could design any number of ambushes. In short, if I were commander, I would not lead us into that valley."

"Nor would I," Galloran agreed. "Not using my own reason. We do not have nearly the manpower to attack the emperor directly. We are apparently marching into a trap that should kill us all. My faith is in the oracle, and in the quest Lord Jason seeks to accomplish. There is a piece missing to this puzzle. When Jason finds it, we must be in position to take advantage."

Ferrin exhaled slowly. "Such faith."

Rachel worried that it might be too much faith. Should she speak up? It wasn't like she had any real experience with battle strategy.

"Do not forget that faith in what the oracle saw is all we have left," Galloran said. "On our own, no matter how well we fight or how cleverly we strategize, we simply lack the resources to win. Maldor is too strong. Our options are either to walk the path Esmira prescribed or to withdraw and mount a defensive stand that buys us perhaps ten years."

"Maldor knows we're coming," Ferrin said quietly. "He knows

what allies will join us. We know our battle strategy is unsound. We suspect he rejoices that we are marching into a trap. We are giving him the chance to eliminate his remaining opponents with a single stroke. What would have taken him years will be over in weeks. Yet it is the only chance to defeat him, so we are going forward."

"What say you, Rachel?" Galloran muttered. "Are we fools?"

"Maybe," Rachel said. "Our chances look really bad. The oracle warned us that we would probably lose. So we probably will. But if the prophecy is our only hope, I guess we have to try." She looked at Ferrin. "The only way to know will be to see it through to the end."

"I agree with Rachel," Ferrin said. "We will probably perish. But I can think of worse ways to go."

"A small chance beats no chance every time," Tark said. "No matter how small."

"We have some advantages," Io said. "Maldor may understand what it means to fight the Amar Kabal, but his soldiers do not. Not really. Not even the eldest of the displacers. It has been too long since the seedfolk last marched to war. There are no finer warriors in Lyrian. No army can confront them casually. And we drinlings do not fall easily. We have built up our numbers larger than our foes could anticipate."

"Even if we fail," Galloran acknowledged, "we will make a respectable showing. Knowing there is any hope for success, I would not meet my end another way. Many of those I lead may not properly comprehend how dire the upcoming battle will be. Some of those particulars cannot be confided to the common soldier. Leading these men to probable disaster is my burden, but I am willing to bear it."

"They know it will be grim," Ferrin said. "Some of their

expectations may be unrealistic, but you lead brave men. Cowards would not have come. The simplest among them know that we will be at a great disadvantage."

"I am glad to know the four of you stand with me," Galloran said. "We know by prophecy that only if we stand united can we triumph. Ferrin, the nearer we draw to Felrook, the more I will have to rely on your expertise."

"I am here to serve as needed," Ferrin pledged.

"We have confronted some grave realities tonight," Galloran said. "We must not close our eyes to the hardships ahead, nor should we defeat ourselves by deciding the cause will be lost. We will defy the odds. The path to victory exists. We will find it. That is all."

Ferrin and Tark returned with Rachel to her tent. Once inside, they sat down together. Rachel felt mildly stunned by the meeting. She had never had such a thorough explanation of why they would probably lose. What information could Jason possibly find to reverse such a doomed situation?

"I appreciated the conversation with Galloran," Ferrin said.

"It's good of him to keep us informed," Tark said. "We have no real claim on that information."

"Not just for including us in his plans," Ferrin clarified. "I had already worked out most of what we discussed through my own observations. I was relieved for the confirmation that we are not following a deluded man. Galloran is attacking Felrook with his eyes open, so to speak. He understands the peril. He realizes that our offensive defies common sense. He leads us there for the only acceptable reason—to fulfill the prophecy."

Rachel frowned. Their strategy made no sense to Galloran or Ferrin. Jason's quest didn't make much sense either. They were all ignoring their common sense because of the prophecy. Was that right?

"What if the oracle fooled us?" Rachel asked numbly. "I used to worry about the oracle being mistaken, but what if it was deliberate? What if she was working for Maldor? What if he corrupted her somehow? What if we're chasing a false hope? What if this is all just a big scheme to trick us into making the dumbest military choices imaginable?"

The tent became silent.

"You heard how vulnerable we'll be when we attack Felrook," Rachel said. "Safe in his castle, Maldor just has to sit back and watch his armies destroy us. What could Jason possibly learn that would change any of that? What secret can erase fortresses and armies? What secret could possibly give us an advantage?"

"If we knew," Tark said, "Lord Jason's quest would be unnecessary."

"Is it necessary?" Rachel asked. "Or is it like the hunt for the Word? The magic word that could kill Maldor, protected by trusted guardians for years. The magic word that didn't work and was just part of a plot to mess up his enemies! What if this is no different?"

Head down, Tark shifted uncomfortably. He would not make eye contact with her.

"The oracle of Mianamon held that office for a long time," Ferrin said. "She had no reason to love Maldor. Quite the opposite. I have heard no rumors of Maldor holding any sway at Mianamon. Why would the oracle give her life to mislead us?"

"What if Maldor made a deal?" Rachel worried. "He likes bargains. He likes manipulation. What if he promised never to invade the jungle if she helped him crush us? What if the oracle lied to us in order to protect her people? She could have looked into the future to verify whether Maldor would keep his promise! She could have made a deal and been certain that Maldor would deliver! What if she sent Jason off on a quest for a nonexistent secret from a dead seer and sent Galloran to lead the last defenders of Lyrian to destruction?"

Ferrin gazed steadily at Rachel. His expression hinted at the thoughts whirling behind his eyes. "You could be right."

"Or what if Maldor found a way to deliver a false prophecy to the oracle?" Rachel went on. "The torivors can get into our minds. I know that firsthand. What if they blurred her visions? She could have been sincere and still have misled us."

"Again you could be right," Ferrin conceded.

"Is it too late to turn back?" Rachel whispered.

"Not for us," Ferrin said. "Not for Galloran, either, if he believed this theory. But if this theory is true, we would lose all hope. Unless we can *prove* the oracle misled us, I'm not sure we could ever convince Galloran to turn back."

"Do you think I'm right?" Rachel asked.

Tark kept his eyes on the ground.

Ferrin shrugged. "There is no way to be certain. Your theory would explain our reckless offensive. It would explain seeking impossible information from a dead prophet. It certainly is the sort of deception Maldor would invent, using our hope against us, giving us reasons to keep trying that only make us fail faster. It fits. But I'm not sure we could ever prove it. And you very well might be wrong. It is all speculation."

"Let's face the facts," Rachel said. "Which seems more likely? That the oracle of Mianamon somehow misled us? Or that our suicidal battle plan will be saved by some inspiring words from a prophet who died thousands of years ago?"

Ferrin chuckled. "Remember when I advised you to embrace the truth when facing hard choices?"

"Yes," Rachel said.

"I'm afraid I created a monster."

"Because I'm wrong?"

"Because you've discovered a possibility that I missed. And I'm having trouble explaining it away."

"We should bring this to Galloran," Tark said nervously.

Ferrin rubbed his eyes. "Should we? This doubt has the potential to destroy his faith. I know mine is already faltering. Without proof, I don't believe our theory is certain enough to sway Galloran from his course. We might only undermine his confidence."

"How could we get proof?" Rachel asked.

"The oracle is dead," Ferrin said. "If she betrayed us, she would have taken that secret to her grave. If Maldor got to her, none of that communication would have been in writing. The emperor would have used torivors for something so sensitive. If the oracle was fooled, even she had no idea. In either scenario we would find no proof at Mianamon. Maldor keeps his deepest secrets to himself. Only he or the torivors could provide the evidence we would need."

"What if I went to him?" Rachel asked dully. "What if I accepted his offer to study with him? I could try to find out if this is all another trick."

"There will be no evidence to uncover," Ferrin said. "It's all in his mind."

"Maybe I could get him to slip up," Rachel said. "He can be very candid in private. Maybe he would think I had no way to warn anyone. Maybe he would gloat. Maybe I could somehow get inside his mind and find the truth. Maybe I could ask him questions and study his reactions. Or open myself to the torivors and search their thoughts. Maybe I could warn you guys in time. Maybe we could try to warn Jason."

"Such a feat would be next to impossible," Ferrin said. "Even if you were to succeed, I don't see how you could get to Maldor in time to make any difference. Once this army crosses into the valley, we'll have passed the point of no return."

"So do we alert Galloran?" Tark asked.

"He is a very intelligent man," Ferrin said. "Galloran may have already accepted that our tiny shred of hope might be based on bad information and therefore entirely unfounded. It might already be part of the measured risk that he is taking."

"Had you thought this through already?" Rachel asked.

"Not to this extent," Ferrin admitted. "And I am more skilled than most at sniffing out possible intrigues."

"This is not just a risk Galloran is taking," Tark said. "It is a risk all of Lyrian is taking along with him."

Ferrin sighed. "I suppose it is our duty to make sure he has weighed this possibility."

"I'll second that," Tark said.

"We might not be right," Rachel fretted.

Ferrin began to fidget by repeatedly disconnecting his index finger and reattaching it. "A plausible theory is only a plausible theory. Possible is not the same as true. Heeding this conjecture could divert us from what was actually a valid prophecy."

"But if we're right?" Rachel pressed.

Ferrin looked away. "Then this war was over long ago."

CHAPTER 18

SWORDS IN THE NIGHT

Nobody had come to wake Jason yet, but the commotion could not be ignored. Heavy footsteps outside his cabin combined with shouted exchanges on deck had him rolling out of bed and tugging on his boots. He recognized panic and dismay in some of the exclamations. Jason strapped on his sword, picked up his shield, and bolted from the room.

Outside his cabin Jason nearly collided with Corinne, who was still buckling her sword belt. "What is it?" she asked.

"Not sure," Jason answered.

Drake appeared beside them. He looked grim. "Good, you're up. We have an unwelcome visitor."

"Who?" Jason asked.

"Come see."

Corinne and Jason followed Drake up to the deck. The sails hung limp. The *Valiant* had been stuck in a calm since yesterday morning, with only the sweeps and the faint currents to nudge the ship along.

The upside was that the same calm would be hampering their pursuers. Three days ago they had made a clean escape from

Windbreak Island, and they had not sighted an enemy ship since.

Except right now everyone was crowded to the starboard side of the deck, staring out at the water. Jason moved into position for a look. Corinne stayed beside him. She had not vomited since leaving Windbreak Island.

The night was still, the water nearly flat. A bright moon diminished the stars around it and left a gleaming trail on the tame ripples of the dark sea. Backlit by the moon, a tenebrous personage walked on the water toward the ship, holding a pair of swords upright, the silvery blades glinting in the moonlight.

"Oh no," Jason whispered, his insides constricting as chills of terror tingled across his shoulders. Two swords meant it was here to duel somebody. What would they do? They needed Galloran for this.

"A lurker," Corinne gasped.

The black figure did not hurry. Each measured footfall caused almost imperceptible ripples on the water, as if the sea were nothing more than a wide, shallow puddle.

Unable to look away, Jason stared in terror. The lurker was here to kill someone, and there was nobody to stop it. Anyone who intervened would die as well. Who had it come to kill? He tried to deny the awful certainty, but he knew. It had come to kill the person who needed to reach Darian. It had come for him. He was going to die.

Jason turned to Drake. "What do we do?" he asked quietly.

"We can't outrun it," Drake replied. "Probably not even if we had wind. You've seen how they can move when they choose. Unless we attack it, a torivor bearing swords can only duel one of us. Our only option might be to play its game."

"I can feel its mind," Corinne said. "It isn't being clear about who it wants."

Jason fingered the charm necklace Rachel had given him. Was there a way out of this? "What if we all hit it at once?"

Drake shook his head. "Then we open the door for it to kill us all. We can't take that chance. Our errand is too crucial."

As the torivor drew near to the ship, most of the drinlings fell back. Jason, Corinne, and Drake retreated to the far side of the deck, losing their view of the ominous visitor.

"Did you know they could walk on water?" Jason asked.

"I did not," Drake replied. "Almost seems like cheating."

"The lurker that followed me seemed to avoid water," Jason remembered.

"It might have been trying to conceal the ability," Drake guessed. "Running water?"

"Yeah, streams," Jason said. "Think that makes a difference?"

Drake shrugged. "Perhaps. It's having no trouble here."

Jasher approached Corinne. "Can you discern who it wants?" he asked urgently.

She shook her head. "I'm trying. It keeps repeating that we're going to fail. I can't sense anything else."

"Most likely targets?" Jasher asked generally.

"Us," Drake replied. "Those of us who were sent by the oracle. If Maldor knows what he's doing, Farfalee, Corinne, Jason, and Aram would top the list."

Jasher gave a nod. "Farfalee already translated the instructions and marked up the maps, making her less essential. Aram is very important while we remain on the water. I don't want to say too much. Could it still be selecting a target? I don't want to risk influencing it."

"It has nearly reached the ship," warned a worried drinling.

"Do not engage!" Farfalee called. "We went over this back in Durna. A lurker bearing swords can only slay one of us, unless we attack it. One of us may have to pay the toll for the rest of us to proceed."

A chill ran up Jason's back. It was him. He would have to pay the toll. Could he be wrong? Maybe he was wrong.

"Failie," Drake said. "What about the worst-case scenario?"

Farfalee deferred to her husband. "Jasher?"

"We do what must be done," he said.

"What worst-case scenario?" Jason wondered.

"If it wants somebody, we can't lose," Drake replied.

"It's coming aboard," a nervous drinling announced, retreating aft. An instant later the torivor came over the side of the boat and landed nimbly on the deck.

"Steady," Aram grumbled. "Give it space. Don't offer it an excuse to retaliate."

Both swords held ready, the torivor turned in a slow circle. No moonlight reflected off its dark form. It was blacker than the sea, blacker than the space between the stars. It made no sound. The shadowy entity stopped turning and faced Jason.

Deep down, Jason had known it was here for him. From his first glimpse of the sinister figure striding upon the water, he had felt an instinctive certainty. His mouth was dry. He could feel his pulse in his hands and throat.

Jason had seen lurkers in action. He was dead. He wouldn't last a second. There was no place to hide, no way to defend himself.

What if he jumped overboard? It could walk on the water. It would follow him. It would stab him to death in the sea.

Despite the hollow doom in his chest, Jason tried to hold himself together. An irrational part of him wanted to run, to hide, to scream. Glancing at his friends, he saw their concern, and he tried to take strength from their presence.

He was dead! There was nothing he could do. He knew he had been playing a dangerous game. He had theoretically known it might end this way. But part of him had resolutely expected to survive.

That was not going to be the case. Staring at the impassive torivor, Jason knew his life was over. It was almost as if it had already happened. What was he supposed to do? He tried to imagine how Galloran would handle the situation. Galloran would kill the lurker. But what if Galloran knew he couldn't kill the lurker? He would face it with courage. Like a hero.

Jason straightened. Tears threatened, but he refused them. Since his death was unavoidable, he should try to face it with courage. The lurker might take his life, but it had no power over his dignity. He would try to die well. It would give him something to focus on. He wished he could stop his fingers from trembling.

What about the quest? There was not much to be done about that. This would have to be all right. He had no alternative. The others would have to go on without him, finish the mission. He had known at the start that he might lose his life. He had known that sacrifices were coming. Others had already died bravely. Why should he always be protected?

Hopefully, his death wouldn't spoil the quest. Maybe his role had been to figure out how to destroy the Maumet. He had wondered why the oracle had placed an emphasis on him. He might have already done his part. The others would collect the information from Darian. It could all happen without him.

Jason tried to slow his breathing. He didn't want to die! He tried to plan. He had practiced with his sword. Maybe if he gave it everything he had, he would survive for a few seconds. Or maybe he should just stand there and force the lurker to strike him down in cold blood. Why give it the satisfaction of pretending to fight?

"It knows you," Corinne said. "It's trying to reach you."

Jason gave a nod. The charm necklace would prevent mental contact. His psychic inability might also block communication.

"It shared dreams with you," Corinne murmured, rubbing her elbows as if she felt a chill.

"Lurky?" Jason asked. Was this the same lurker he had met shortly after his return to Lyrian?

The air remained still, the sea quiet.

Jason resolved that if the lurker insisted on a duel, he would try his best. Whether a lucky victory was possible or not, he would feel better if he went down swinging. Maybe it would help distract him from the pain of the fatal blow.

The torivor extended one of the swords, the blade pointed directly at Jason. The dark being turned the weapon upright and tossed it to him, the sword traveling at the perfect angle for Jason to catch the weapon by the hilt.

As Jason reached out his hand, Drake stepped in front of him and intercepted it.

The lurker rushed forward, forcing Drake to deflect a flurry of swings. The blades chimed musically, each ringing collision reverberating over the water. Drake circled to his right, and the lurker stayed with him, pressing the attack. The seedman barely parried blow after blow.

Jason watched in a daze. The weight of his impending death had settled so firmly in his heart and mind that he felt astonished by the interruption. Drake was trying to save him. Jason felt a wrenching mix of gratitude and horror. Could the seedman possibly win?

Jasher stole the sword from Jason's sheath and joined the fight, attacking the lurker from behind. With preternatural grace, the torivor engaged the two seedmen at once, not only protecting itself but still actively attacking. Blood sprayed from Jasher's arm. Before the droplets had landed on the deck, Drake received a quick stab in the thigh.

A drinling up on the mast hurled a knife at the torivor. Without disrupting its attacks on Drake and Jasher, the lurker swiped the knife with its sword, like a batter connecting for a homerun. After the clang of contact, the knife streaked through the air into the chest of the man who had thrown it. He tumbled from the mast to the deck, landing loosely.

A scratch on Jasher's cheek. A shallow slash across Drake's side. Both seedmen were scarcely stalling death. They doggedly resisted the inevitable with all of their skill, but they could not possibly win.

Corinne drew her sword, and Farfalee was immediately at her side to restrain her. "No," the seedwoman demanded.

"But maybe—" Corinne protested.

"No," Farfalee repeated with finality.

Galloran had drilled all of the best swordsmen on how to fight torivors, not necessarily because he thought they could learn to defeat them, but rather to elevate their overall skills. Jasher had received the expert training, as had Drake, Corinne, Ferrin, and Aram. Galloran had shown them patterns the torivors preferred and how to defend against them. Jason had watched some of the sessions. It had been intense. Jason suspected that as skilled and experienced as Jasher and Drake were, without that training, they would have already fallen.

The chiming swords moved in a frantic blur. With flawless precision the lurker continued to alternate blows, in front and behind, striking ruthlessly, leaving no openings. Jasher was stabbed in the eye. Drake lost his free hand just above the wrist. Both seedmen kept fighting.

Jason realized that when the seedmen died, he would still have to take up his sword and fight his duel. They shouldn't have intervened! He was more grateful for their sacrifices than he could have ever expressed, but now three of them would die instead of one!

"Get ready!" Drake yelled. "Don't miss this!"

Whipping his sword fiercely, Drake charged forward. The lurker stabbed him through the chest, the blade piercing his titan-crab breastplate as if it were cardboard. Dropping his sword, legs churning to keep his momentum, Drake wrapped both arms around the lurker, hoisting it off the ground. The legs flailed. A dark fist pounded Drake on the shoulder. For an instant the lurker hung in the air immobilized.

And Jasher stabbed it through the back.

The torivor vanished with a blinding flash.

Jasher pulled the tip of his sword out of Drake and caught him as he slumped forward. Farfalee darted to them and helped her husband lay her brother on the deck. Jason and Corinne drew near.

Drake coughed wetly. One shoulder was misshapen, buckled where bones had snapped. As he rested on his side, the hilt of the torivor's sword protruded from his chest, the sleek blade from his back. Blood drained from his many wounds.

"We need a tourniquet on that arm!" Farfalee instructed.

"Failie," Drake chided softly, "I've . . . done this before. I'm past . . . the reach of medicine." He coughed again. His eyes shifted to Jasher. "We got it."

"Yes," Jasher said. "That was the bravest act I've ever seen."

"Always wanted to . . . go out with style."

"Drake," Farfalee managed, her face rigid. "Drake, I . . ." Her fragile composure shattered into sobs.

"Don't," Drake said. "I know. I love you too." His eyes shifted back to Jasher. "You killed a torivor!" The statement was powered by a moist chuckle. "First Galloran . . . now two can claim it."

"Three of us," Jasher corrected. "You more than I."

Drake closed his eyes tightly and clenched his jaw. He was having trouble breathing.

Jason couldn't hold back any longer. He knelt beside his friend. The words came in a rush. "Thank you, Drake. You saved my life. I wish you hadn't. I'm so sorry."

Drake grabbed Jason's forearm with his remaining hand. The grip was strong. Jason tried to ignore the leaking injuries. "No, Jason. No apologies. You saved *me*." He coughed several times. "I was . . . already dead. No amar. Squandered it. I could have ended . . . alone . . . a failure. Hating myself. This is better. Much better . . . than I deserve."

Jason felt vaguely aware of Corinne's hand on the back of his neck. He could not restrain his tears.

Drake released Jason and became lost in a fit of coughing and gasping. Jason wanted to turn away. Drake would die any second. But he could not turn his back on his friend, just in case those eyes opened again.

They did. "Take it out," Drake murmured.

Jasher crouched, bracing one hand against Drake, and withdrew the torivor's sword, the blade scraping against the cracked breastplate as it came free. No gore clung to the sleek weapon. Jasher cast it aside.

Rolling flat onto his back, Drake shuddered. Then he inhaled deeply. He stared up at the night sky. "We're going to win," he said, his voice calmer, less strained. "This is nothing. Keep going. They can't stop us. Jason, give Rachel the necklace. Tell her . . . tell her I'm sorry. Tell her . . . I wanted . . . to show her . . . my little valley. Tell her I tried."

His voice was growing weak. Farfalee smoothed a hand over his brow. "Shhh," she whispered. "Be still, Drake. You can rest now. You did it. Rest. We'll take it from here."

"Failie," he whispered, his hand twitching toward the back of his neck with little jerks. "Where's my seed?" His head tipped sideways. The breath went out of him.

Farfalee went stiff, her expression impassive, damp eyes sparking in the moonlight. Jasher placed his hands on her shoulders to still her trembling. She looked over her shoulder. "You're hurt!"

Jason looked at Jasher. Blood seeped from one eye. His upper arm bled. Jason had been so focused on Drake that he had almost forgotten about the other injuries.

"Nothing fatal," Jasher said. "I'll survive. The eye is shallow. Barely reached me. I might not even lose it."

Heg took Jasher by the elbow. "Come," he said. "Let me see to your wounds."

Jasher nodded, releasing Farfalee. She stood straight, struggling to hide her grief. Corinne hugged Jason. He hugged her back. She felt too slender. She had lost weight while seasick. The effort to comfort him seemed distant and insufficient, but he appreciated the attempt. Despite her presence, despite everyone aboard the ship, Jason had never felt more alone. The profound sense of loss left him empty, but not numb. Drake was gone. He tried not to look at the body.

"Where is our wind?" Jasher cried as Heg led him belowdecks. "Aram, more wind!"

"I'll see what I can do," the half giant growled.

CHAPTER 19

THE WESTERN PASS

On a bright morning, as Rachel prepared to mount her horse, a soldier sheepishly approached her. His tentative attitude did not match his large stature or his sharp uniform. He held a small scroll. He looked a bit like a child who had been dared to venture alone into a graveyard.

"Pardon me, milady," he said. "A moment of your time?"

"What can I do for you?" she asked, trying to sound friendly.

"Nothing, milady. I have a message for you from the king."

Rachel noticed Tark and Ferrin watching the exchange from a short distance away. She held out a hand, and the soldier passed her the scroll. She broke the seal and read it. Her veil caused a little interference, but the message was brief. Galloran meant to come speak with her tonight.

"The king is welcome anytime," Rachel said, returning the scroll to the soldier.

With a little bow he backed away, then turned and walked off. Did he seem relieved? Rachel thought so.

As she mounted her mare, Rachel wondered how a conversation with Galloran would go. She had a lot of pent-up feelings.

Part of her looked forward to a visit from him; part of her dreaded it. Her fears about the validity of the prophecy remained unresolved.

Each day that the army advanced without trouble reminded Rachel of their danger. The emperor knew they were coming but did nothing to hinder them. And why should he? His enemies were handing him victory. Rachel would not have been shocked to find complimentary refreshments waiting along the roadside.

Ferrin had conferred with Galloran. The displacer had reported that it was hard to read whether the king had already taken the possibility of a false prophecy into consideration. In the end Galloran had firmly maintained that they could not turn back.

Ferrin and Tark had accepted the verdict. Rachel was not comfortable with the decision but felt she had to hide her dissatisfaction. She had already vented her concerns through Ferrin. Her misgivings had been considered, and Galloran had made his choice. The others had moved on. Who was she to keep complaining? Who was she to be more doubtful than a displacer? Who was she to question a king?

Rachel took her place near the front of the column. Tark and Ferrin followed a respectful distance behind. Over the past days Rachel had found her confidence in Galloran eroding. Since their last meeting he had spoken with her twice on the road—short, pleasant conversations. Superficial conversations. He had not mentioned his discussion with Ferrin, and neither had she. The topic had not seemed appropriate anywhere they might be overheard.

Galloran had not reached out to her mentally for days. Rachel had decided not to trouble him by using her private telepathic access. If he wanted to communicate, he could reach out any time he wanted. He had a private tent.

Now he had announced that he would be paying her a visit, but not until the evening. She was left to stew about her concerns. The more she thought about the potentially false prophecy, the more disappointed she became in Galloran for dismissing such a likely danger, and the less she wanted to think about him, let alone speak with him.

After a long day alone with her thoughts, Rachel felt a blend of terror and relief when Galloran appeared at her tent that night. Only Io accompanied him. Ferrin and Tark left the tent, and Io stood guard at the door.

With a low groan Galloran sat beside Rachel on her cot and put on his blindfold. "Ferrin is worried about you," he said without preamble.

"I'm all right," Rachel lied.

"I regret that I have been so occupied," Galloran said. "There is much to manage."

"I don't want to be an extra burden," Rachel assured him.

"Ferrin suspects that you continue to fret about the validity of the prophecy."

Rachel stared at his blindfold. Maybe her friends weren't as oblivious to her worries as she had assumed. She realized that she was pausing for too long. "Actually, yes. I'm still suspicious that Maldor could have used the oracle to direct us right where he wants us."

"I can see how this idea would trouble you," Galloran said. "The possibility would make you feel as though my misapprehension was leading us into a massacre. You would feel bound by duty to quietly accept my ruling, even though that very silence could be killing us all."

"Something like that. I don't want it to be true. It just really seems to fit."

Galloran nodded. "The absence of resistance has created a terrible suspense among my soldiers. I feel the tension as well. Let me share what comfort I can offer. I knew Esmira better than most, both personally and through my aunt, the Pythoness. You realize that I could see her mind when we conversed. I searched hard and found no trace of deception."

"That's comforting," Rachel said.

"I did not expect deception from her. Esmira had an impeccable reputation. But I was aware of the potentially devastating consequences that could arise from even the smallest untruth. We were in a predicament where any degree of wishful thinking could have led us down a futile and deadly path. During my interview and when she issued the prophecy, I scrutinized both her demeanor and her mind. I am satisfied that the prophecy is authentic."

"Could Maldor have deceived her?" Rachel asked. "Could he have used torivors to plant a false prophecy?"

"The Temple of Mianamon is heavily shielded against mental intrusion," Galloran explained. "And perhaps no place in Lyrian is better insulated than the chamber where she gave us the prophecy. I sensed no torivors in our vicinity at any time after I won the duel at the Last Inn. Furthermore, even had torivors been granted access to Esmira, they would not have been able to confuse an oracle of her quality."

Rachel sighed. The responses made sense. But she still couldn't relax. "If she was so powerful, couldn't the oracle have guarded her mind against you knowing she was lying?"

"Possibly," Galloran admitted, "though I don't believe she would have been so foolish as to trust a bargain with Maldor."

"What if he meant it?" Rachel persisted. "What if Maldor doesn't care about the jungle? What if he promised to leave it alone if she helped him? What if she looked into the future and saw that he would really do it? What if she saw that the rest of Lyrian was lost either way, but that deceiving us would at least save the children of Certius?"

"You have really thought this through," Galloran said.

"Is there a chance I'm right?"

Galloran paused before answering. "I suppose there is a chance."

"Doesn't it fit what Maldor would do? Doesn't it seem like what he did with the Word?"

"It does. I just don't believe Esmira would stoop to dealing with Maldor under any circumstances. And I don't believe the emperor would offer to spare the jungle. Not in sincerity. His objective is total domination. He is certainly in position to achieve it. He did not need her help to defeat us."

"He didn't need the Word, either," Rachel argued. "He just likes to experiment with better ways to control everybody. He likes finding easier ways to win. He likes getting his enemies to destroy themselves."

"I see how this must have been eating at you," Galloran said. "You describe a plausible scenario."

"I'm worried that he's controlling us," Rachel said. "What if he's using your faith in the prophecy against you?"

"It's possible," Galloran conceded. "But what if our faith is the only attribute that can save us? What if your fear of Maldor is making you imagine a conspiracy where none exists?"

"That's the problem," Rachel said. "I'm not sure I'm right. But a fake prophecy makes lots of sense. If I knew I was right, I'd make everyone listen. But I'm not sure. Not a hundred percent. I can't be sure. I have no proof. There probably wouldn't be any proof."

"If it is any consolation, I cannot be absolutely sure either," Galloran said. "We can seldom be utterly certain about any choice."

"I could live with having only a small chance of victory," Rachel said. "I could handle the fact that we would probably lose. If our decision were between a small chance and no chance, I agree, we take the small chance. But I'm having a hard time dealing with the possibility that our small chance of winning might be based on a lie."

"If the prophecy proved to be erroneous, do we have a better road to travel?"

"We could live longer," Rachel said. "Who knows what other options we might discover? If the prophecy is a lie, there might be some other way to beat Maldor that we haven't noticed. Some hidden vulnerability. There might not be just this one crazy path the oracle showed us. Like with the Word, the prophecy could be a distraction from better ways to reach our goal."

"I'm not sure what vulnerability that could be," Galloran said. "Many of us, including the wise among the Amar Kabal, have sought such a weakness for decades. Maldor just keeps getting stronger. In truth, I was concerned that the oracle would see no road to victory. But she did. And so I am trying to walk it."

Rachel did not respond. She had tried for days to imagine a possible vulnerability but had come up with nothing. This moment was no different.

"I could send you home," Galloran said, breaking the silence.

"What?"

"We're marching to Felrook with an army. We have Ferrin. Whatever perils await us, I'm sure we could smash the defenses protecting the portal to your world."

"But wouldn't that mess up the prophecy?" Rachel asked. "We have to stand united. That doesn't sound united."

"If you aren't committed to this course of action, we won't be united. In that case, I would rather see somebody survive. I never meant to force you to help us."

Rachel thought about it. Galloran was right. He could probably send her home. She hadn't considered the option. But what about Jason? What about everyone? Was she really willing to give up? Did she really think the prophecy was false? She had worried that Galloran had been deluded, but he had clearly thought this through at least as deeply as she had. Were her misgivings just a product of her nervousness?

"I feel lost," Rachel finally said.

"Doubts can be that way," Galloran said. "Once they take hold, they can seem very real."

"What if they *are* real?" Rachel fretted.

"If there were no chance they could be real, the doubts would hold no power."

"Don't you have doubts? What do you do? Ignore them? How do you deal with them?"

Galloran rubbed his mouth and chin. "When I have doubts about a decision, I search for a better alternative. In this situation I see none. The only alternatives are different versions of waiting to be conquered. My next step is to examine the reasons I have to believe. I am confident that Esmira was a true oracle. I am confident that she would not have dealt with Maldor. I did everything in my power to verify the truthfulness of her words and came away satisfied. If I find my reasons satisfactory, I cast aside my doubts and proceed. Show me proof that my doubts are real, and I would feel differently. Show me a better alternative, and I would reevaluate my position."

"That makes sense," Rachel said. "It's just so hard. Attacking Felrook seems so hopeless. I can't imagine what secret Jason could learn that would make a difference."

"That is where faith becomes necessary," Galloran said. "I can't envision what he will learn either. If I could, Jason's quest would be pointless. Faith isn't knowledge, Rachel. Faith is a tool. Faith keeps us going until we get the knowledge. Faith keeps us striving until we reach the consequences of our most important decisions."

"What if we have faith in something that's wrong?" Rachel asked.

"Then we're heading for disappointment. But even misplaced faith can help us gain knowledge. We try to be smart about where we put our faith. And we adjust as we learn more."

"You're convinced the prophecy is real," Rachel said.

"I'm convinced. If I thought it was false, I would turn this army around. I do not wish to hand Maldor an easy victory."

"So I just need to forget about my doubts?"

"That choice is yours to make. If you mean to press forward, you must overcome your concerns. For anything worth accomplishing, we can always find reasons to doubt, just as we can also find reasons to proceed. I have weighed my alternatives. In these circumstances—with my fate in the balance, with your fate in the balance, with the fate of the world in the balance—I have chosen to side with faith and hope over doubt and despair."

"We had faith in the Word," Rachel reminded him.

"And the Word did not perform as we expected. It was not the end of the journey, as we had hoped, but it was part of the journey, perhaps a necessary part. Though I spent long years in the dungeons of Felrook, I do not regret my faith in the Word. That faith helped me eventually learn the truth of the matter, and brought me to where I now stand."

"Okay," Rachel said.

"This army is marching to war," Galloran said. "You must decide how you will proceed. I hope you will have faith in the prophecy and faith in my judgment. Without your participation

I'm not sure we can win. But if you ask it of me, Rachel, I will send you home. I can always press onward hoping that your role has already been fulfilled."

Rachel didn't need time to consider a response. She respected and loved Galloran. She had promised Nedwin that she would protect him. She couldn't imagine ditching him. "I won't abandon you. I won't abandon Jason and everyone. This conversation has helped me. I think I can manage my worries now. I'm sorry if I've been a pain. I didn't want to see us tricked because I didn't fully explain myself. Your thinking makes sense to me. I wouldn't be able to live with myself if I went home now. We have to try."

Galloran patted her shoulder. "We're lucky to have you. You're a very intelligent young woman. Please come to me if you have other concerns or if you perceive other alternatives."

He stood, removed his blindfold, and exited the tent. Ferrin and Tark returned a moment later.

Ferrin looked a little shamefaced. "Sorry. I talked to Galloran behind your back. I could tell you were having a difficult time, and I thought he could help better than anyone. I hope I didn't make you too uncomfortable."

Rachel hugged the displacer. "Thanks, Ferrin. I needed that. Galloran helped me. I feel a lot better."

Ferrin gently pushed her away, his hands on her upper arms. "Are you sure? Or are you pretending to be satisfied?"

"I'm pretty sure," Rachel said. "There's no way to erase all doubt, but Galloran gave me enough reasons to trust the prophecy again."

"We're marching into a death trap," Ferrin clarified. "The prophecy never promised success. None of that has changed."

"I know," Rachel said. "We still have plenty of reasons to stress out."

"The period before a battle can be worse than the battle itself," Tark said. "It certainly taxes my nerves more."

"I agree," Ferrin said. "Best not to obsess about it. From all appearances we will not have to concern ourselves with battle, not until we reach the western pass. For now we merely need to survive long marches and cool nights. Shall I brew some mint tea?"

Rachel and Tark approved.

As more days went by, the army passed through a region of fertile farmland and prosperous villages. Most of the people hid as the army approached. A handful of volunteers joined them. Up ahead, the Graywall Mountains drew nearer. Rachel knew that Felrook awaited behind those mountains, but she remained at peace with the decision Galloran had helped her reach.

When the army neared the mouth of the western pass through the mountains, they found a force of four hundred awaiting them—a hundred covered in moss, a hundred clad in ivy, a hundred draped in vines, and a hundred bristling with black thorns. Four of the more skilled acolytes who Rachel remembered from Mianamon stood at the front of the company, wearing stately gray robes.

Rachel enjoyed catching up with the acolytes, even if they regarded her odd apparel with uncertainty and treated her with remote courtesy. Rachel hadn't been close to any of them, but they brought news that Ulani and the other women were well; not to mention they provided practical support for the upcoming battle.

Galloran had prepared his men to expect the help of the tree-folk, but Rachel could tell that many of the soldiers viewed their new allies with emotions ranging from suspicion to wonderment.

After meeting with the acolytes and some of the leaders among the treefolk, Galloran decided to employ the majority of the tree-folk as scouts at present.

The day after pausing near the mouth of the pass, the Amar Kabal joined them. Thousands in number, the seedfolk were all mounted, the women favoring longbows, the men carrying swords and spears. Their armor looked light and fancy compared to the protective gear worn by the army from Trensicourt, and their weapons were of much more elegant workmanship. The seedfolk brought with them hundreds of orantium spheres, including more than twenty of the larger gatecrashers.

Among the Amar Kabal, Rachel was pleased to discover several familiar faces. Andrus and Delissa were with them. Andrus told Rachel of how he had collected Delissa's amar after she'd been blown into a deep gulf while trying to pass through Howling Notch. Delissa appeared younger than before, bright-eyed and fresh-faced, and seemed eager to test her marksmanship in the upcoming conflict.

Lodan, the only son of Jasher and Farfalee, was also with the host. Rachel told him all she knew about his parents and his uncle Drake. He looked unchanged from the last time she'd seen him, even though he had died in the interim. Since it had been his First Death, Lodan had been reborn at the same age as when he had perished. Jasher had been reborn not long before him, so standing together they would have looked like brothers.

Only one member of the Conclave accompanied the host. Rachel had last seen Commander Naman when he'd lost a duel against Galloran in the Seven Vales. He still had a high forehead and wide lips, but he looked so young!

Rachel, Ferrin, and Tark were included in the meeting when the scouts reported the state of the western pass. Rachel noticed that Ferrin seemed uncomfortable. He normally seemed in control, no matter the circumstances, but today he was quiet and distracted. Was it a reaction to the presence of the seedmen?

"What do you mean the gates stand open?" Naman asked, pacing rather than sitting. He wore a cloak over his armor and carried a slender, intricately carved mace. Rachel watched him with interest, wondering how many of her doubts he would share.

"The wall is deserted," the chief scout said. "The pass is undefended."

"We found no guardsmen at either side of the pass," a second scout confirmed. "The defenses at the wall have been dismantled. The barracks lie empty. We sent men up the mountainsides and found nothing. We are searching for a force on the far side of the pass, but as of yet we have uncovered no sign of life. Plessit, the first village beyond the pass, stands abandoned."

"Very well," Naman said. "Thank you for your report." He turned to face Galloran, who sat blindfolded. "What do you make of this, King Galloran?"

"I do not like accepting such a blatant invitation," Galloran answered. "The empty pass is clearly bait for a colossal trap. Maldor is not even trying to conceal his intentions. He knows what prophecy we heard and has elected to taunt us. By shamelessly luring us to proceed, he is testing whether we will see this through."

"The sieges of Inkala, Kadara, and Highport have all been called off," Naman said. "The imperial armies are racing west at an unprecedented pace."

"I have heard the reports," Galloran said. "The emperor waited to recall them until he felt sure we were committed."

"Are we committed?" Naman asked. "The full might of

Maldor's armies will reach Felrook not many days after us. We can't hold the eastern gap against them—it is a wide plain without a wall."

Rachel tried to keep her expression neutral. Was it wrong that she was happy to see Naman testing Galloran? He was the perfect person to do it—not only was he one of the biggest skeptics in Lyrian, but he also knew a lot about battle strategy. She understood Galloran's faith in the prophecy, but she didn't want it to make him ignore common sense in his preparations. Naman would make sure that didn't happen.

"The drinling host should reach the eastern gap on the morrow," Galloran said. "Not that they could plug the gap any more realistically than we could. But the drinlings will be in position to fall upon Felrook with us."

Naman snorted. "Perhaps you should rephrase that—they will be in position to gaze across Lake Fellion alongside us."

"Perhaps," Galloran agreed.

"The emperor has not bothered to mask his strategy," Naman said. "Why not thwart him? Our march has served to break the sieges in Kadara. The cities can now resupply, and their forces can regroup. By withdrawing now, we accomplish much at little cost. We waste his movement of troops and extend the war in the east for years."

Rachel had also considered this possibility. She watched Galloran with interest.

"He has no need to hide his strategies," Galloran repeated. "He knows our only hope of beating him is to proceed and take Felrook. The prophecy demands that we march on Felrook, and it warns that Felrook must fall. If we turn back before reaching our goal, the prophecy will never be fulfilled. The war would be officially over. We would return home to await our demise."

"Instead, we will go like livestock to the slaughterhouse," Naman said. "Once we are through the pass, Maldor will take it back, no matter how many defenders we leave. We will be trapped, then killed, and then the war will really be over."

"Not if we take Felrook before Maldor's armies arrive from the east," Galloran said.

"How do you propose we do that?" Naman asked.

"First, we take the keeps," Galloran said. "As you know, three keeps surround Felrook. They are not protected by water. They allow Maldor to send out sorties against attacking troops. But if they fall, they would provide stout shelter for a besieging army."

"The gatecrashers?" Naman asked.

"The gatecrashers will give us a major advantage against the keeps," Galloran agreed. "Our displacer knows secret ways into two of the fortresses. We may be able to take a couple of them with guile."

Rachel glanced at Ferrin. He noticed her attention and gave an uneasy smile.

"So we take the three keeps and the walls protecting the ferry," Naman said. "Call it four keeps, since the ferry is essentially a fortress as well. What then? Those walls will not house our entire host. They will provide scant protection against the horde that will descend on us from the east."

"Once we hold the keeps, we begin to study the problem of Felrook," Galloran said. "We engineer a way to attack the stronghold."

"You mean we wait for the other part of the prophecy," Naman said. "We hope that your companions slay the Maumet, find a dead prophet, and gain some inscrutable secret that will save us."

"Essentially, yes," Galloran said.

"This is folly," Naman protested. "It is not too late to turn back."

"We have had news from Lord Jason," Galloran said. "Ferrin?"

Ferrin stood. "My ear is with Jason. He informed me this morning that they have destroyed the Maumet and escaped Windbreak Island." Expressions of relief and excitement greeted the news. After a moment Galloran held up his hands, allowing Ferrin to continue. "They have the location of Darian the Seer in their possession. They have been heavily pursued. A lurker fell upon them, which they killed." This announcement created another stir. Ferrin glanced briefly at Rachel. She wondered how they would have defeated a torivor without Galloran.

"Let him proceed," Naman said.

"They spent several days caught in a calm; then other torivors, glimpsed in the distance, led a small fleet to them and chased them about the Inland Sea. They are finally preparing to disembark and journey over land to the last abode of Darian the Seer. They chose to share this information because they decided that if the emperor knew their movements, we deserved an update as well. A displacer cannot leak secrets that are already known. They hoped we would find their progress encouraging." Ferrin sat.

"Indeed," Naman replied, "I am relieved to hear that the second part of the prophecy has not yet unraveled into failure. Defeating the Maumet was an unexpected success. Yet we are all in agreement that Maldor has learned the prophecy and is using it against us." Naman didn't look at Rachel, but she cringed a bit anyway. "With foreknowledge of our movements he has undoubtedly created a perfect trap. We will be caught between an unassailable fortress and the full might of his armies. What information could possibly alter this unwinnable scenario?"

Galloran stood. "Just because you or I cannot comprehend the secret that can save us does not mean it isn't real. We have good reason to believe such a secret exists. We must let that suffice."

"You ask much," Naman said.

"*I* do not ask it," Galloran said. "The oracle saw what she saw. The truth she beheld asks this of us. We can resist our duty with logic, we can find reasons to turn aside, but the prophecy will not be fulfilled because we almost obeyed. We must finish what we have started. It will not be easy. We have been warned that this endeavor will probably end in ruin. But we are here because it is our last chance."

"You speak true," Naman said. "It is why we came. Besides, if I protest, I may find myself prematurely in the ground again. We proceed on the morrow?"

"We do."

Naman frowned slightly, but nodded. Rachel could tell he seemed satisfied, which was an encouraging sign. "How many men do we leave to hold the wall?" he asked.

Galloran rubbed his palms together. "Holding the pass will not win the war. If we fail to take Felrook, we will all perish. If Maldor wants the pass, he will take it regardless of how we defend it."

"But it is a highly defensible position," Naman said. "We should make him pay to have it back."

"Probably sensible," Galloran consented. "We will examine the wall when we pass it tomorrow. It will most likely be attacked from both sides. Those who remain there will not escape. We will guard it with an appropriate contingent of volunteers."

They went into particulars about how the remainder of the march would be coordinated, including the missions of scouts throughout the valley, the integration of the Amar Kabal among the human troops, and how the orantium would be allocated. They outlined strategies for contending with manglers and giants. They discussed how the drinlings would be used in the upcoming fight.

As Galloran and Naman moved into discussions about supply wagons and the dispersion of resources, Rachel began to lose interest. She knew it was important to keep everybody fed, but she had nothing to contribute to the conversation.

She managed to catch Ferrin's eye. *Is everyone all right?* she mouthed. He didn't seem to understand, so she repeated the silent inquiry.

His face fell a little. Enough to tell her that something was wrong. *After,* he mouthed back.

Rachel could hardly sit still through the remainder of the meeting. Could one of her friends have been hurt? Killed? She tried unsuccessfully not to think about it. When the strategy session finally concluded, Rachel left with Tark and Ferrin.

"Why didn't you tell me about the message from Jason before the meeting?" Rachel asked Ferrin once they were outside and had a measure of privacy. She moved her veil aside in order to see him better.

"I was having a private discussion with Galloran when Jason confided in me," Ferrin apologized. "As soon as I relayed the message, Galloran asked me to keep it a secret so that he could use it as surprise leverage when dealing with Naman. It only meant withholding the information from you for a few hours."

"I guess I can't blame you if Galloran specifically asked," Rachel said grudgingly. She wanted to make sure everyone was all right. At the same time, she was afraid to ask. "It's a good sign, right? That they got past the Maumet?"

"An excellent sign," Ferrin agreed. "Many have tried to defeat the Maumet to no avail. If one impossible task has been accomplished, why not more?"

"Jason is all right?" Rachel asked, her voice quiet, her body tense.

"Well enough," Ferrin replied. "They are under heavy pursuit. I am not surprised that Maldor sent torivors. Once the Maumet fell, his concern over their side of the prophecy would have increased a hundredfold. The emperor will throw everything he can between Jason and his goal."

"Are the others well?" Rachel asked.

Ferrin paused. He had that sickly look again. "Several drinlings have fallen. And I'm afraid I have bad news. One of our original delegation gave his life to defeat a lurker. It's a miracle they stopped a torivor without Galloran. It had come to slay Jason."

"Lord Jason is all right," Tark confirmed.

Ferrin nodded, his eyes on Rachel.

She paled. "Not Drake," she whispered.

Ferrin gave a slight nod.

Rachel felt cold and sick inside. How was it possible that Drake had gone out of the world and she hadn't known? She returned a little nod. "Oh."

"I know you were close," Ferrin said. "Jason said he died very bravely."

"I'm sure," Rachel said, trying to wall herself off, trying not to react to the terrible news. She wanted to lash out with Edomic. She noticed a boulder the size of a couch, and suddenly she wanted to throw it higher and farther than she had ever thrown anything. She wanted to crush it to dust. She wanted to tear the tent where she had just met with Galloran to shreds. She wanted to set the world on fire. In that moment of hurt and sorrow, she almost felt she could do it.

Instead, Rachel drew the dark veil in front of her face. For once her outfit felt completely appropriate to her mood. "Maldor will not get away with that," she finally managed.

"He won't," Ferrin said, giving her a hug.

Rachel let him hug her. She didn't want the contact at the moment, but Ferrin couldn't know that. He was trying to help. When the embrace ended, Tark took her hand and patted it. She could see the hurt in his eyes.

Rachel backed away. "I need some time alone."

Ferrin nodded.

Rachel turned, walking away from camp. She wished somebody would attack her. She wished Maldor had left defenders in the pass. She wished Maldor himself would come after her. He had sent that torivor. She had a message for him.

Somebody caught her arm from behind. Rachel turned. It was Galloran, his blindfold off, his eyes sympathetic.

"You heard my thoughts," she realized.

"They were impossible to miss," Galloran said gently.

"I don't . . . ," she began, but couldn't continue.

You don't know what you're fighting for if the people you most love are going to die, Galloran conveyed mentally.

Yes, she replied. *And at the same time, I want to fight more than ever. I've never wanted to hurt somebody with Edomic before. I've hurt people in the heat of the moment, in self-defense, but I've never felt like I do now.*

Leash those desires, Galloran cautioned. *I understand how pain and grief can fuel rage. In this moment, riding this tide of emotion, you could wield Edomic as never before. But the effort would be wasted. You might harm yourself, and for what? To scorch a field? To lob a boulder toward the clouds? Store up the emotion. Save it for when you really need it. Don't weaken yourself before the true battle.*

His words brought her back. The urge to lash out diminished as her anger dissolved into heartache. She felt utterly helpless. "They killed Drake."

"We can't reverse what happened," Galloran said. "But we will make them pay."

CHAPTER 20

LANDFALL

I'm out of tricks," Aram said, lowering the spyglass. Eight ships were visible along the seaward horizon, sails bright in the moonlight, the steady glow of lanterns illuminating their decks. "And we're running out of water. There is no room left to maneuver. Taking the wind into account, I don't see an alternative to the docks."

Jason studied the ships converging from all directions. Not much had changed since he had sent the message to Ferrin a few hours ago. The enemy vessels had spread wide, driving the *Valiant* before them. As land drew nearer and escape options dwindled, the pursuing ships drew closer together, led by an interceptor called the *Intrepid*.

After the prolonged calm had finally subsided, the *Valiant* had sailed north. They wanted to stay away from Angial, the largest city north of the Inland Sea, because it had a garrison with hundreds of soldiers. They had been making for Jerzon, a fishing village well west of Angial, but with reasonably good access to the Fuming Waste. But before they could reach the village, lookouts had spotted a torivor on the water. It had not borne swords, but not long after the sighting, imperial ships had forced them to revise their plans.

Aram had led the imperial vessels on an epic chase. He had tried the same trick on the *Intrepid* that had sunk the *Avenger*, but the new interceptor had carefully avoided following directly in their wake. Apparently, word had gotten out.

Jason watched the drinlings prepping hot pitch for the little catapults. The *Valiant* would end her final voyage with a firefight. They did not intend to leave the interceptor seaworthy. Over the course of the chase they had lost the skiff and one of the launches, along with five drinlings and five orantium spheres. The drinlings in the launch had managed to hit one of the smaller ships with orantium before flaming pitch had set their open boat ablaze.

After days of desperate maneuvering, they were out of alternatives. They were now heading for the town of Gulba. Heg had apparently scouted the town a few months ago. He had assured them that the town should house no more than twenty soldiers, but it did boast a pair of sizable piers and a large livery stable. The idea had been to steer toward Gulba, but to watch for a chance to slip through to a more northerly town. The wind and their pursuers had not cooperated, so now their options were either disembarking at Gulba or staging a battle on the water against eight enemy ships.

"Imperial schooner at the docks," came a cry from above.

"What?" Aram called, racing to the other side of the deck. He peered toward land through his spyglass.

"We can expect extra soldiers in town," Jasher said. He wore a patch over his injured eye and a bandage on his arm.

Even without a spyglass Jason could make out the dark form of the docked ship ahead. They just couldn't catch a break! Now they would be sandwiched between strong forces.

"Eight of you should take the remaining launch and land away from the dock," Heg said. "Let the *Valiant* draw away attention.

We'll bombard the schooner, the dock, and the incoming ships with pitch."

"Might be our best choice under the circumstances," Farfalee said. "We'll leave behind an orantium sphere."

"Take it," Heg urged. "You need them both more than we will. I'll stay and lead the effort. We'll make sure the *Valiant* burns. We'll fight until you're away, then make our escape into the wild."

Considering the large number of enemy troops involved, Jason wondered how many of the drinlings would survive to escape. Once again, others would risk their lives to try to get him to Darian.

"Who will go ashore in the launch?" Aram asked.

"Jasher, Aram, Jason, Corinne, Nia, and I," Farfalee listed. "And two drinlings. Who do you suggest, Heg?"

"Del is our best remaining swordsman," Heg said. "And Zoo has shown great composure under pressure."

"We could probably squeeze ten into the launch," Jasher said. "We might need the extra swords to win through to the horses."

"Thag and Fet," Heg said. "Our hardiest fighters. Maces should serve as well as swords."

"We had best prepare the launch," Aram said. "The breeze is picking up. We'll reach the dock swiftly."

"Try to catch up with us," Farfalee urged Heg. "Find horses if you can. It will be a long ride to the far side of the Fuming Waste. We can use all of the protection we can get."

"If we win free, we'll follow you," Heg promised, "whether mounted or afoot."

Jasher approached Corinne, holding Drake's breastplate. "It cracked, but it will still serve. It's light and will offer better protection than leather."

"Thank you," she said as she strapped it on.

Jasher turned to Jason. "I'll carry one of our last orantium spheres. You carry the other. Don't hesitate to use it."

Jason accepted it gingerly. Orantium was a powerful weapon, but the prospect of an accidental detonation made him nervous.

Jason, Corinne, Jasher, and Farfalee all wore torivorian swords. Farfalee had offered hers to Aram, but the half giant had refused in favor of his own enormous blade. The ten companions climbed into the launch along with packs full of provisions. Thag and Aram manned the oars. The overloaded launch floated lower in the water than Jason liked.

As the launch diverged from the *Valiant*, Jason tried to pay equal attention to the coast and the enemy ships. The town of Gulba looked quiet, with only a few lit windows. It was neither a large town nor a tiny hamlet. The enemy ships were converging rapidly, chasing the *Valiant* into port like a pack uniting for the kill.

"Speed could save us," Jasher whispered, loud enough to be heard over the sloshing oars and Aram's jingling armor. "We nab horses and we get out of town."

As the *Valiant* approached the dock, the drinling crew began launching fiery pitch at the schooner and the piers. By the time the interceptor collided with the opposite side of the schooner's pier, flames were leaping from some of the dockside buildings and spreading across both piers. Fire climbed the schooner's sails and blossomed aboard the *Valiant* as well.

The launch landed on a muddy little beach near a modest inlet sheltering smaller vessels. Farfalee sprang out first, a pack on her back, an arrow set to her bowstring. Alarm bells rang. Voices hollered. Figures could be seen running to the flaming docks, as well as disembarking from the *Valiant*. The *Intrepid* led the charge as the imperial flotilla sailed for the piers, driven by the rising wind.

Jason slung a pack onto his back, picked up his titan-crab shield, and stepped out of the launch and onto firm mud. Jasher and Aram held their swords ready, so Jason drew his as well, the blade silver-white in the moonlight. Positioned at the right angle, the torivorian metal picked up orange highlights from the burning dock.

"Heg told me the way to the stable," Zoo said. "Stay close."

Jason was glad that somebody knew where they were going. From his current position he could see no evidence of horses or a stable. Away from the dock most of the buildings were lost in shadow. A few had soft firelight or luminous kelp glowing behind shuttered windows.

As the group trotted away from the launch, Jason questioned whether he should hold the orantium sphere ready instead of his shield. He decided that he could drop the shield and reach the sphere easily enough if needed. The sphere would not block arrows. Jason had practiced fighting with a shield at Mianamon but had spent more time with only a sword in his hand.

Zoo led them between buildings, keeping to the shadows wherever possible. Disorderly clusters of people ran toward the waterfront, some only half dressed, a few in uniforms. Most were too focused on the dockside fire to notice anything else, but as the group rounded a corner, a pair of uniformed men down the road paused, looking their way.

"Who goes there?" one of them asked, drawing a sword.

Farfalee answered with an arrow. As the other ran for cover, she dropped him as well.

Running lightly, Zoo led them down a side street. At the next corner Zoo halted, then peeked her head around slowly. "We found it," she whispered. "There's a guard outside with a crossbow."

Jason was impressed with how clearly Zoo was speaking English now. The drinlings learned so fast.

Farfalee pulled an arrow to her cheek, stepped around the corner, and released. She nocked and released a second shot in a swift motion, then readied a third.

They sped to the large stable, a long wooden building with a gently sloped roof. From inside they heard horses stamping and whinnying. One seemed to almost scream. Zoo collected the fallen guard's crossbow.

Thag and Aram yanked the big doors open. The stable contained sixteen stalls on each side. Three soldiers were working their way down the stalls, slaughtering the horses. They had started at the far end and only had a few stalls left.

The soldiers looked surprised as the doors opened. Thag and Aram closed swiftly. One soldier charged forward. The other two backed away, their dripping weapons raised defensively.

Aram sidestepped a swing and clubbed the attacker with the flat of his blade. The soldier rebounded off the side of a stall and flopped to the floor. Racing past Aram, Thag engaged the next soldier, landing a crushing blow with his mace. The final soldier went down with an arrow through him. Aram stomped a heavy boot on the chest of the man he had toppled. "Where can we find more horses?"

"Gone," the man chuckled bleakly. "We set loose the steeds in the corral. I yield, by the way, if that matters."

Jason glanced around the stable. Only three horses remained standing.

"Three mounts," Jasher spat. "We have three horses."

A shadowy figure slipped through the door at the far end of the barn. Farfalee drew an arrow to her cheek, but hesitated. Zoo loosed a quarrel from her captured crossbow.

The figure caught the quarrel in one hand and rushed forward with inhuman speed. The lurker plunged the quarrel into Zoo, then stood back calmly.

Jason stared warily at the torivor. It stood so near, unmoving. His thoughts turned to Drake, and he felt queasy. At least the lurker had no swords. Still, what were they supposed to do now?

Thag approached the lurker from behind, mace raised.

"No," Aram ordered. "We need you." Aram looked down at the man beneath his boot. "How many horses did you scatter?"

Suddenly unwilling to speak, the man glanced at the lurker. The dark figure raised both arms. The horses in the stalls began to whicker and stamp. One reared.

Corinne raced at the lurker. Farfalee and Jasher both moved to stop her, but they did not react in time. Corinne held the tip of her sword level with the dark figure's chest. "Enough!" she cried angrily. "You've done enough!"

The torivor lowered its arms and retreated before her, shuffling back as she stalked forward. The tip of her sword shifted left at the same time as the lurker attempted to dodge left, then back to the right an instant before it skipped to the right. She kept advancing. It kept retreating.

Jason held his breath and watched in horror. It was as if Corinne had stepped in front of a speeding train. Her destruction was inevitable. Sure, a torivorian blade could injure a torivor. But you had to hit it. Now that Corinne had attacked, she had opened the door for the lurker to retaliate. Jason couldn't get thoughts of Drake out of his head. The idea of Corinne sharing a similar fate was too much. If anything, Jason would have wanted to step in front of a lurker to protect her, not the other way around! He knew too well how even an unarmed torivor could wreak havoc against opponents.

Raising his sword, Jason strode forward. Maybe if he could slip past Corinne, he could distract the torivor enough for Corinne to make a move. Jasher's hand clamped down on his shoulder firm enough to restrain him. "Too late," Jasher murmured. "The way is too narrow. This is up to her now."

Jason could see that Jasher was right. If he tried to dodge past her, he'd probably just end up distracting her and getting them both killed. The chance to help her had passed. He didn't resist the seedman's grasp. The sword in his hand made him feel like a poser. Jason wished he could rewind time. Nobody should attack an unarmed lurker! Why hadn't somebody tackled her? Why hadn't he tackled her?

"Get out," Corinne said steadily. "Leave and do not return or I will slay you."

Corinne stopped advancing and began to move her sword into a variety of defensive positions. The lurker would twitch and she would adjust. Jason found himself flinching with each tiny movement. She swiped at it, missed, and stepped back into a defensive stance. Her blade kept moving as if dueling an imagined foe, blocking invisible blows, occasionally poking forward in halfhearted thrusts. The lurker crowded toward her, knees bent, arms extended, feinting with its head and hands. She seemed to anticipate every feint, moving with the featureless creature instead of reacting to it.

Corinne shuffled back and lowered her sword to her side. The torivor flashed toward her at the same moment as she lunged, thrusting her blade forward. The lurker stopped just shy of the sharp tip. The torivor slapped at the flat of her blade, but she twisted it so the black palm tore open against the edge, bleeding light.

Corinne shifted the tip of her blade left, then right, keeping it pointed directly at the lurker as it sidestepped. The dark figure jumped up and back, sailing almost high enough to reach the rafters. Then it fell flat to the floor and blurred toward her legs. Corinne stabbed downward, the blade piercing the floorboards as well as the torivor. It disappeared with a blinding burst of light.

There was silence in the stable for a moment. Corinne looked over her shoulder at her friends, her expression tired and relieved.

Jason did not realize he had been frozen in horrified shock until it began to melt away. He blinked. She had survived. No, not just survived. She had killed it.

"Well done," Farfalee said, making no effort to hide her disbelief.

"How many horses?" Aram repeated menacingly, leaning his weight onto the fallen soldier.

The man beneath his boot looked flabbergasted. "She just . . . How did she . . . ?"

"We kill lurkers all the time," Aram replied casually. He leaned more heavily on the man, his boot pressing down with rib-creaking force. "Last chance."

Jason stood beside Aram, glaring down at the trapped soldier. The man glanced his way. He kept his expression hard.

"We scattered twenty or so," the man huffed with difficulty. "Emptied the corral."

Aram reduced the pressure. "Which way did they run?"

"Inland," the man said. "You won't catch them. It's a wide wilderness. The darkling spooked them."

"What other horses remain in town?"

"None," the soldier replied. "They were all kept here. They made us get rid of our own horses as well. We just got the order. We were supposed to eliminate any means for you to escape by land."

"There have to be outlying farms with livestock," Aram said.

"Sure, here and there. Nothing close."

Jasher, Farfalee, and Nia had already led the three remaining horses from their stalls. Thag had run past Corinne to watch the far door. Fet guarded the near door. Del knelt beside Zoo, leaning in close and feeling her neck. "She's gone," the drinling said, rising to help saddle the horses.

Jason looked at Zoo lying motionless. She had been so alive just moments ago. Another casualty from a lurker. Another fallen friend. When would it end?

"There has to be some mount you spared," Aram insisted. "Do you have a commander?"

"Captain Finley and Morgan the mercenary are currently astride their mounts," the man said. "That's all. You're lucky to have three. We knew you were coming. We were making quick work of it."

"Jason, Corinne, and Farfalee will ride," Jasher said. "They have to get away. The rest of us can fan out, head into the wilderness on foot, try to find our own mounts and catch up."

"I don't like it," Farfalee said. "We'll be too vulnerable."

"We'll be at your heels," Nia said. "Drinlings can keep up with horses over long distances. We can't outpace a gallop, but we can run day and night without tiring, eating as we go."

Jason moved toward one of the horses. Corinne stood beside another, looking a little shell-shocked.

"Where is your commander?" Aram asked the soldier under his boot.

"What am I?" the man complained. "An oracle? I suppose he's managing the defense of the waterfront."

"The horses may not have strayed far," Farfalee said. "Once away from the lurker, they could have slowed. We should go after them together."

"Some of us could ride double," Jason suggested. "Especially if it's just until we find more horses."

Farfalee nodded eagerly. "What if Jason and Corinne shared a mount? Jasher could join me, and Aram could take the third, just until we see if we can catch up to some of the scattered horses. We could bring extra bridles."

"Those ships are bringing more troops than we can handle," Jasher said. "You should get away while you can."

"Those ships could also be used to—"

Jasher interrupted Farfalee by placing a finger on her lips. He nodded at the soldier on the floor. "We should wait before getting too specific."

Jason looked at the man on the ground. His wide eyes lacked focus. His face gleamed with sweat.

"Are we finished with him?" Farfalee asked.

"Anything else to tell us?" Aram questioned.

The man licked his lips, eyes anxious. "Can't believe that girl killed a darkling. That's a sight I never expected to see. Quick as a rock viper, that one."

Crouching, Aram clenched both arms in a snug hold around the soldier's head and neck. The soldier soon went boneless. "He'll stay that way for some time," Aram promised.

"The ships in pursuit could shuttle soldiers ahead of us," Farfalee continued. "Anyone watching the *Valiant* could tell we wanted to go north. If we escape from here, they might head us off. We need warriors who can help us fight our way through ambushes, and we need woodsmen who can help us avoid them."

"Fine," Jasher said, lighting a strand of luminescent seaweed. "It will be hard to track the horses in the dark, but not impossible. If it comes to it, you three ride ahead."

"We need to move," Aram said.

"Are you all right?" Jason asked as Corinne mounted up behind him.

"Better than the lurker," she replied.

"That was amazing."

"I could feel its mind," she said. "Just like Father taught me. The concentration was tiring, but it could hide nothing. Even at the start I knew it would raise its arms and scare the horses right before it did. With it tracking us, I knew we'd never get away. Since it had no weapons, I decided to take a chance."

"Incoming soldiers," Fet warned from his position by the door. "Four. Wait, four and a rider."

Having collected extra bridles, Jasher and Farfalee sat astride their horse.

"Go," Aram urged. "I'll claim the inbound horse."

Nia climbed onto the third horse. Jasher and Farfalee led the way to the far end of the stable. Aram, Fet, and Thag crouched into position at either side of the stable door. As he rode down the central aisle of the stable, Jason noticed that not all of the stalls had dead horses inside. Some had been empty. He idly wondered whether the soldiers had saved their own horses, sending them off into the night to be collected later.

As Jason reached the door at the far end of the stable, soldiers came through the door near Aram. "We have a problem!" the lead soldier cried, hustling into the stable, trailed closely by the other three. "Fugitives fleeing on horseback!"

Fixated on the fleeing horses and the bodies in the aisle, the new arrivals did not see the danger lurking at either side of the door. Aram, Fet, and Thag attacked from behind, dropping all four effortlessly. Just before Jason lost his view into the stable, he saw Aram heading out the door, presumably to find the man on horseback.

The gate to the large corral hung open. They trotted over to it. Del stayed with them on foot, sword in hand, eyes roving the night. Jasher leaned down, studying the ground beyond the gate with a glowing strand of seaweed in hand. Behind them, from a distance, Jason heard the clamor of weapons and the shouts of many voices. Dockside flames rose above the rooftops.

Thag and Fet came running from the stable. Del climbed up to ride double with Nia. Aram rode around the side of the stable, looking too large for his newly captured horse even though it was the biggest of the four.

"They messed up," Jason told Corinne. "They were trying to make sure we didn't have any horses, but they left just enough for us to keep moving. Nobody will be chasing us on horseback. Not from here."

She nodded. He noticed that her hands were trembling. It took him a moment to realize that the shock of her combat with the lurker must still be setting in. She had been so brave.

"You sure you're okay?" Jason checked.

"I'll be fine," she replied. Her voice didn't sound very convincing. "The swordplay wasn't too hard. The mental side of it was . . . very taxing."

"Thag and Fet," Jasher instructed, "follow us on foot. Hopefully, we'll find enough mounts for all of us." The seedman picked a direction, and they took off at a canter, forcing Jason to drop his conversation with Corinne. He enjoyed the wind in his face and the feel of Corinne's arms around him. A guilty part of him hoped it would be some time before they found more horses.

They did not encounter any of the scattered horses quickly. The noise of battle receded. Behind them the town was silhouetted against raging sheets of flame. Beyond the blaze, too many ships crowded the modest port, red highlights reflecting off sails. Jason felt bad for any innocents who would have to rebuild their homes or businesses.

Jasher repeatedly leaned down to check the ground. Three times he dismounted to study the tracks more closely. Once they doubled back a short distance, having lost the trail.

Eventually they found seven horses grazing together. Apparently, the terror of the torivor had left the horses, because they did not shy away as the group approached.

Aram claimed the largest, transferring his saddle. With some rearranging, they soon each had a mount. Jasher, Farfalee, and Del were prepared to ride bareback. And they had four extra horses for Thag and Fet to choose from.

They had not ridden their horses hard from the stable, since three were carrying double and one was carrying Aram. Plus, they had paused a few times, and there was no sign of pursuit, so they decided to wait for Thag and Fet to catch up. Before long they heard the drinlings approaching at a sprint. A moment later they heard a galloping horse.

"One horse?" Farfalee asked.

"I only hear one," Jasher confirmed.

"Could Thag or Fet have found one?" Del asked.

"I heard two runners," Jasher said.

"Heg or one of our crewmates?" Del wondered.

"Maybe," Jasher said.

"The soldier at the stable named one other mounted man besides the captain," Aram reminded them. "A mercenary."

Farfalee slid off her horse and set an arrow to her bowstring. Aram dismounted and drew his sword. The hoofbeats of the approaching horse slowed, then stopped. Thag and Fet ran into view. "A lone rider," Thag called. Then he pitched forward to the ground, a long arrow in his back.

"Take cover," Jasher warned, dropping from his horse, putting the animal between himself and the archer. Jason did likewise.

After Jason landed, his horse walked forward. He hadn't kept hold of the reins! Lunging, he grabbed them and held the horse still. Near him, crouching behind her horse, Corinne pulled out her sword. Aram and Farfalee took positions behind boulders.

Jason's horse sidestepped restively. He patted the animal and murmured soothing words. Shield held ready, he stayed low, peering under the neck, worried about getting hit by an arrow. He still couldn't see their enemy. Glancing over at Corinne, he drew his sword.

"I'll ride him down," Del volunteered.

"No," Aram said. "You'll be an easy target. You won't get near him."

Running low, Thag and Fet reached them. The arrow still jutted from Thag's back.

"Hold fire so we can speak?" a deep voice called from the shadows perhaps fifty yards away.

"Your arrow told us all we need to know," Farfalee replied.

"I am alone," the voice responded. "Truce for a moment?"

"He just wants to learn our numbers," Jasher whispered.

"I count nine," the deep voice said. "One injured. All with horses. Shall we speak?"

"He's stalling us," Jasher whispered more quietly.

"We have nothing to discuss," Farfalee answered. "We must hurry. Run away, leave your horse, and we'll not harass you."

"You have plenty of mounts without claiming mine," the deep voice replied bitterly. "I despise incompetence. They should have left all their men at the stables until every horse was dead. Instead, they ran to the dock to fight the fire and watch the incoming ship."

Fet and Del were creeping toward the unseen speaker. A sudden arrow took Fet through the throat. Del fell flat behind cover. Jason pressed a little closer to his horse.

"Now you have eight," the voice informed them. "Sure you won't talk? You can't ride away if I keep putting arrows in you. I have plenty. I seldom miss."

Jasher gave his wife a nod. "Very well," she said. "Truce." She took her arrow from the string, but kept it in her hand.

A tall man dressed as a conscriptor strolled out of the night, using a metal bar like a staff. He wore no helmet, and his head was shaved bald. The glow of the burning waterfront shone behind him. He held a large crossbow at his side. A bow and quiver were slung over one shoulder. His armor and gear jangled softly with every stride. With a pang of distress Jason recognized him.

"Groddic," Jasher said.

"I know most of your names as well," the big man replied. "Farfalee, Jasher, Corinne, Aram, Nia, Dead Guy, Injured Guy, the other drinling who got down just in time, and of course my old friend Jason."

Jason remembered Groddic from Felrook. The tall conscriptor had brought him to his holding cell after his audience with Maldor. Suddenly the horse seemed like pathetically insufficient cover. Jason tightened his grip on his sword. What kind of chance would he have against a soldier like Groddic? He was the leader of the conscriptors. He was the conscriptor who had defeated Galloran. Apparently, Maldor was very serious about stopping them.

"What do you have to say?" Farfalee challenged.

"First, I want to congratulate you," Groddic said.

"He wants to stall us," Jasher repeated.

Groddic glanced over his shoulder. "Your crew tried to hold us at the docks. They were promptly overwhelmed. Many men are coming for you, but they lack mounts. Getting rid of the local horses was how we should have stopped you. We didn't get the job done, so we won't stop you here. Not unless I kill all of you myself."

Jason found Groddic's nonchalance distressing. He was a lone man approaching a sizable group with several proven fighters, but not only did he act unconcerned, he almost seemed exasperated. Jason glanced over at Corinne. She watched solemnly.

"Please try it," Aram invited.

"You're a large man," Groddic complimented. "None of you are incompetent. We keep losing torivors. That alone speaks volumes. It would be an interesting contest. I brought in Galloran, you know, years ago. I'll bring you in as well."

"Still stalling," Jasher warned.

"Let's get him," Corinne whispered angrily.

Releasing his horse, Jason crossed to her and placed a hand on her arm to still her. He could feel her trembling.

"I joined the chase in Angial," Groddic said casually. "The *Intrepid* waited for me to board her. Might have been a mistake. We just missed you at Windbreak Island. Nice work there. I never thought we would see the end of that Maumet. If you hadn't—"

"What have you to say?" Farfalee demanded. "Stop prattling."

Groddic's expression hardened. "I don't have tempting offers. Any of you could have access to Harthenham. You could have close to anything at this point. But I know you won't quit. Jasher was right. I was stalling. I intend to slay the lot of you. I'm just picking my moment."

"I could put an arrow in your throat before you took a step," Farfalee said.

He gave an easy chuckle. "That would officially end our truce. I would like to see you try."

Quick as a blink, Farfalee pulled her bowstring back and let an arrow fly. It took Groddic through the throat. Thag and Del charged forward. Nia as well. Jason raced around Corinne's horse. He didn't want to wait for Groddic to come to him. He was tired of hiding behind others. Corinne charged alongside him.

Staggering, Groddic raised his crossbow and shot Thag in the center of his chest. The thickset drinling went down hard. Gurgling, Groddic blocked Del's sword—once, twice, three times—before Nia ran him through with her sword from his blind side and Farfalee pierced him with another arrow. Del stabbed Groddic as well.

Jason and Corinne stopped short. The fight had ended as they arrived. The tall conscriptor went down and did not move. Del hurried to Thag. Nia checked Fet.

Jason could hardly believe the speed of the fight. He stood frozen, eyes roving from Groddic to the fallen drinlings.

"We need to go," Jasher called. "His purpose was to harm us and slow us. Soldiers are coming. They will be on our trail. They will try to loop ahead of us. They will scavenge for horses."

"Fet is dead," Nia reported.

"Thag won't make it," Del said.

Jason could see Thag feebly waving for them to go. Jason's eyes became wet. They were losing so many good people! The stirrup creaked as he climbed onto his horse.

Farfalee mounted up. "We must away."

Nia stabbed the fallen conscriptor once more on the way to her horse. Jason wanted to add a stab or two of his own. That was the man who had blinded Galloran! He had just killed Thag and Fet! But there would be no point. It would restore nothing. Jason nudged his horse forward, following Jasher into the night.

CHAPTER 21

TREACHERY

Nedwin had to fight his way awake. His senses knew that something was amiss, but he was in the middle of agony such as he could only suffer while asleep. After he'd lost the ability to feel physical pain, the sensation had begun to find new life in his dreams. The trauma had started innocently—a bone broken in combat, the dull ache of a bad tooth, a tumble into a campfire. Over time the dreamed pain had come to feel increasingly authentic, and nightmares of torture and the attending anguish had grown more common. After the worst dreams he would wake up shivering and drenched in sweat.

Nedwin had always been a light sleeper. The condition had spared his life more than once. But as the excruciating nightmares grew more immersive, he found himself snapping awake at minor disturbances less often.

Tonight he was once again imprisoned in the dungeons of Felrook. Some nights he suffered at the hands of Copernum, other nights Damak, and other nights Maldor himself did the honors. Currently he was under the power of a tormentor called Grim. It was the only name Nedwin had ever heard him called. He was a small man, with dexterous hands. Nedwin suspected that if Grim had learned the violin, he would have become a virtuoso. Instead, Grim had studied torture.

On occasion, while he was in the midst of dire torment, the pain and despair would be interrupted as Nedwin realized he was dreaming. In the past he had found ways to use that recognition to claw his way to consciousness. Over time, as the nightmares became more intense, it was getting harder for Nedwin to deliberately rouse himself from the agony. But the task was always easier when aided by outside stimulation.

Nedwin wrenched himself onto his side and opened his eyes, gasping, feeling like a drowning man who had finally found land. He did not sleep in his decadent bed. The softness felt foreign and made it harder to wake. Instead, Nedwin slept on the floor beside the bed, wrapped in some of the covers.

His hearing had been sharpened by years of receiving nervesong, a pain enhancer responsible for many of his most mind-rending agonies. Even after losing one ear, Nedwin still heard much better than he had as a child. Occasionally he would experience auditory hallucinations, but they tended to be inexplicable angry voices, and he had learned to separate them from actual sensory input.

Right now he heard faint noises rising from the city below—weapons clashing, glass shattering, assorted screams and shouts. The bells were not yet ringing, but they would probably start soon. A riot? An attack?

He detected disturbing clues from within the castle—the splintering crack of a forced door, dogs avidly barking in the kennel, the jingle of armor, a shout that cut off abruptly. Then he heard a sudden scuffle down the stairs from his room.

So the violence was inside the city, inside the castle, and

already inside his quarters. Nedwin resisted a jolt of panic. He felt no fear for his life, but ample concern that his opportunity to fail Galloran had arrived. He had known in his gut, in his bones, that his position governing Trensicourt would come to this. He was too new to the politics involved, and too many schemers had stayed behind with feigned sicknesses.

The bells should be ringing. Had they been compromised? How had his opponents orchestrated this so quietly? Nollin had been working his growing network of contacts, and Nedwin had spent most of his time snooping privately, but neither had caught wind of this coup. Nedwin had expected treachery eventually, but smaller in scale and not so soon. He needed to start moving. He needed to learn the extent of the trouble and to see if there was any action he could take.

The two guards stationed outside his room were reliable men. He should warn them. They could leave with him. If they stayed to fight, they would die.

Nedwin rushed to the door on light feet, but paused as he heard the clamor of swordplay. Too late. Eli and Tomlin had already engaged the attackers. "Nedwin," a voice shouted, "treachery!"

Belting on his favored short sword and placing a pair of orantium globes in a satchel, Nedwin dashed to the balcony. He never stayed anywhere without scouting multiple escape routes. If he got away, there would be time to return and face his enemies on his own terms. Best to disappear while they had the advantage.

The night was cool, the moon bright. Nedwin took a moment to stare from his balcony. Outside the castle wall Nedwin glimpsed a trio of giants rampaging through a cluster of soldiers. The overmatched humans stood no chance. Elsewhere a pair of riderless horses galloped wildly along a side street. Down in a courtyard Nedwin observed a large group of men driving back a smaller group.

For a moment he could not move. The event he had expected and feared had arrived—a massive coup on his watch. The city had fallen, the castle was falling, and he was the last to know. It had taken murderers at the door of his bedchamber to rouse him.

Even without hard evidence leading up to this night, he had no right to be shocked. How had he missed the giants? He had been vigilant! Clearly, he had not been looking in the right places. The giants must have been smuggled into the city as dwarfs. But when? How? He had watched for dwarfs! He had watched for conspirators! He had intercepted messages! He had eavesdropped on conversations! He had not been complacent.

Never badger a badger. Never squirrel with a squirrel. Never swallow a swallow. When enduring torture, Nedwin used to play word games in his mind, finding interesting combinations. In times of strife, strange word patterns would surface. *If you can't bear the bare bear, bore through the boring boar.*

This was no time to get flustered. This was no time to analyze his mistakes. There would be plenty of time later to rationally sort through what had gone wrong. He did not need to comprehend any of it yet. He had to act first and think later, or he would end up dead and no use to anyone.

A rope dangled beside the balcony. Nedwin had left it there deliberately. He quickly used it to climb to the top of the tower. The steeply sloped roof was not built for walking, but Nedwin was in no danger of falling. He loosed the rope and tied it again elsewhere, then climbed down to a lower roof that could take him places.

Nedwin could have claimed the king's quarters, but he had opted for the third tallest tower instead. Among other features it afforded better rooftop access to the entire castle.

Above him he could hear men trying to force the door to his

room. It would take some time. The stout door was thick, and Nedwin had added three interior locks. Nedwin tugged on the rope. He wished he could take it with him to make his disappearance more mysterious, but he knew he had tied it well.

Where to now?

What allies might need him? Despite his high position, Nicholas had refused to relocate to the castle. A savvy decision, considering the present circumstances. Nedwin decided that he would go directly to Nicholas after escaping the castle. The forces behind this coup would not leave Nicholas untouched, no matter where he chose to live.

Nedwin started running along the rooftop, using a smooth, sliding pace and deliberately choosing where to place each step to minimize sound. He had to sacrifice a little bit of stealth for speed, but with all the commotion in and around the castle, he doubted anyone would notice his subtle creaks.

He should try to reach Nollin and Kerick in time to help them escape. Their quarters were reasonably accessible. They had shunned the towers in favor of proximity to the garden courtyard.

Nedwin worked his way along a narrow ledge, ducking to avoid a couple of windows, his toes hanging over the brink. He leaped, grabbed a jutting beam, and swung onto a new rooftop. If he fell, he would die. Same if he were caught. But ever since the dungeons, most danger had lost its edge.

He arrived at the garden courtyard, then jumped from the rooftop into a tall tree. Leaves and twigs slapped at him as his hands and feet found limbs to halt his fall. There were no continuous ledges around the courtyard walls, so Nedwin took three quick steps along a thick bough, sprang with his arms outstretched, and caught hold of a windowsill.

Pulling himself onto the narrow shelf, Nedwin found the

window latched, but he forced it easily. The room was not occupied, although the bed had been slept in. He listened at the door, then peered into the hall.

In the distance Nedwin heard stern voices demanding surrender. Otherwise it was quiet, so he dashed down the hall to the suite where Nollin and Kerick were staying. The outer door had been forced. Inside he found their three guards dead alongside four other corpses.

"Nollin?" Nedwin called in a loud whisper. "Kerick?"

An inner door opened. Kerick looked out, a crossbow in hand. One side of his face was swelling and darkening. "Nedwin?"

Nedwin hurried to Kerick. "They came for me as well. We have to clear out."

"You just missed the action," Kerick said, letting him through the door. The room beyond was in disarray. Four more attackers lay dead on the floor. Nollin leaned against the wall. He was injured, his side slashed, one forearm badly broken.

"Can you move?" Nedwin asked. "We must not linger."

"I don't know," Nollin replied, wincing as he stepped away from the wall.

"Try," Nedwin said. "If you can't keep up, we should take your seed. Come with me. I know this castle well."

"Lead on," Nollin said.

Kerick helped support Nollin. Nedwin found a loaded crossbow near one of the corpses in the outer room. Stepping back into the hall, he heard commotion off to the left, so he headed right.

After a few turns Nedwin led the seedmen into a conservatory full of musical instruments. "Some of the rooms and halls connect in surprising ways," Nedwin explained. "The castle also hides many subtler passages. Galloran knew many of them. Nobody knows them all. I doubt anyone alive knows more of them than me."

Moving aside a huge harp, Nedwin pulled back a heavy drapery to reveal a spiral stairway leading upward. "It would be generous to label this a secret passage, but none use it, and few know about it."

They walked up the winding stair to a narrow hall. Nedwin passed two doors, then entered the third, revealing a storeroom crammed with art: sculptures, small fountains, urns, rolled tapestries, fine carpets, gaudy candelabras, enameled shields, a child-sized suit of plate armor, and endless painted portraits—some of them covered, more exposed—piled in tall stacks or otherwise wedged wherever they would fit.

As Nedwin started weaving his way across the room, he heard the seedmen behind him bumping into obstacles. He had always possessed excellent eyesight, but after the dungeons and the nervesong, his night vision was nothing short of incredible. He was only unable to see in the complete absence of light.

Pausing, Nedwin removed a strand of seaweed from his satchel, squeezing it to life. The length of kelp began to shed a soft blue radiance. This was his favorite variety of luminous seaweed, because it traveled well. Treated properly, it would still give off light a year after harvest. Whenever possible he tried to keep a few on hand.

On the far side of the crowded storeroom, behind a bell taller than most men, Nedwin opened a camouflaged panel in the wall, and they ducked into a dark, webby passageway. "We should be safe now," Nedwin said. "At worst we might run into Copernum himself or one of his most trusted conspirators. The secrets of these private corridors are closely guarded."

"You believe Copernum is behind this?" Nollin asked, his voice strained. The sleeve of the arm pressed to his side was darkly stained.

"I have no proof yet," Nedwin said. "We will know for certain soon enough. Trensicourt is being claimed for the emperor. Many were involved, but I expect to find Copernum at the root of it."

Walking along the corridor, Nedwin shielded the seaweed with his hands, letting a feeble glow seep between his fingers. As they rounded corners and descended cramped stairways, Nedwin paused at some of his favorite listening spots. The noise of skirmishes was failing. The guardsmen were not putting up much resistance. Many of them could have been involved.

Nollin mostly made his discomfort known with his labored breathing, along with the occasional sharp intake of breath as some jolt of agony surprised him.

"Where are we going?" Kerick whispered.

"I know five ways that will take us beyond the castle walls," Nedwin said. "I believe I am the only man alive familiar with two of them. Tonight we will use my favorite. The corridor originates at the same level as the deepest reaches of the dungeon. There is a labyrinth of hidden tunnels down there. I have found the bones of some who lost their way. I will leave the two of you safe in a vault beneath a mausoleum, where the passage lets out. Then I will go to Nicholas."

"He will be under attack as well," Kerick said. "He made no secret of his allegiance to us and to Galloran."

"But he will get away," Nedwin said. "He was more ready for tonight than any of us. He will have others with him. We need allies."

"You mean to keep fighting?" Kerick asked.

"I mean to win," Nedwin replied.

After checking a pair of other hideouts, Nedwin found Nicholas in his hideaway behind a cheap theater where actors performed mediocre comedies day and night. The theater had been there since Nedwin was a boy. His noble family had not approved of the establishment, but Nedwin had snuck out several times in low-born attire to drop a copper drooma in the tin and sit through stale jokes, predictable melodrama, and bumbling pratfalls. The actors tended to overplay their roles, and sometimes flubbed their lines, but among the botched romances, foiled swindlers, and peasants disguised as royalty there were always laughs to be had and taunts to be shouted.

Tonight the theater, like the rest of Trensicourt, was silent. When the bulk of your military was away and giants roamed your streets, you extinguished your lights, shuttered your windows, locked your doors, and prayed to be ignored.

The bells had never cried out the emergency. The attack had started and finished in the deepest hours of night. Nedwin figured some people must have slept through the commotion and would awaken to find a new regime in place.

When Nedwin had given the secret knock at the grubby door behind the theater, Minna had answered, a sturdy young woman with shoulders like an oarsman. She was both niece and apprentice to Nicholas, and she seldom left his side. After Nedwin assured her that he was alone and had not been followed, Minna had checked up and down the alley and called to a lookout for approval before granting him admittance.

Dressed in wooly nightclothes, Nicholas lay in a hammock in the corner of a small room. Minna left Nedwin alone with her uncle.

"Forgive me if I do not rise," Nicholas said. "I seem to have misplaced my legs."

At home Nicholas moved around in an ingenious harness he had designed that dangled from suspended tracks. At court he was pushed about in a wheeled chair. "You must have left in great haste," Nedwin said.

"After Galloran reinstated me as a lord, I should have known that within a fortnight my home would be ransacked and I would be left impoverished."

"What do you know concerning the events of this night?" Nedwin asked.

"Fragments," Nicholas replied. "I know the giants attacked from within the city, at least forty of them. The brutes opened the gates for a modest host of imperial troops. The giants were not allowed inside the castle. Neither were imperial troops. Paranoid as ever, Copernum is carefully controlling access. I sent some men in search of information. Only Minna and my two most trusted bodyguards remain with me here. The rest of my household is at another hideout known only to me and mine."

"How many men do you know are loyal?" Nedwin asked.

"Besides you? There are sixteen in my household. Beyond them I have fewer than twenty reliable allies. I would trust none of the remaining nobility. Did any of your guards get away?"

"None," Nedwin said. "I would only have trusted those who died defending my room. I had no opportunity to aid them."

"Nollin?"

"The seedmen fought off the first wave of traitors sent to take them," Nedwin said. "I helped Nollin and Kerick flee through secret corridors. Nollin is grievously injured."

"I have a man who can attend him," Nicholas said.

"Any aid would be appreciated," Nedwin said. "What can we do to retaliate?"

Nicholas laughed heartily. "If we're lucky, we get out of Trensicourt until Galloran returns. If Galloran fails, we never come back."

"I won't abandon Trensicourt," Nedwin said.

"Why not?" Nicholas asked. "Galloran did. His goal was to march on Felrook. He is accomplishing it. He took hasty and insufficient measures to protect the kingdom. He knew he was leaving a vacuum behind. He knew that opportunists like Copernum would rush in to fill the void. He did not wish it to happen, but it was a risk he gladly accepted in order to mount his offensive."

"He left Trensicourt in my care," Nedwin asserted. "In our care."

"A seedman, a scout, and a cripple," Nicholas chuckled. "Two of us knew little about the current politics within the city, and the third knew enough to keep his distance. I didn't know how, or when, but tonight was inevitable. The takeover was perfectly planned, flawlessly executed. We did not stand a chance of opposing it. Galloran left with our fighters. Too many plotters held back too many of their men in a city with too few committed guardians."

"I will not go quietly," Nedwin said. "I am the regent. I am expected to protect Trensicourt. I mean to oppose these usurpers."

"You did nothing wrong," Nicholas said. "You committed no mistakes. You were made captain of a sinking ship, Nedwin. You need not go down with it."

"I have my duty. It is too late to rejoin Galloran. I will not have him return to find an enemy on his throne."

"This is no longer your duty," Nicholas advised. "You are no longer regent. You have been ousted. Escape with me into exile. If Galloran returns, we can work with him to reclaim the city."

"And if his armies need to retreat here after being bested at Felrook?"

"I have already dispatched an eagle to warn him," Nicholas said. "He will know not to seek refuge here."

"You are free to go," Nedwin said. "You should bring Nollin—heal him or plant him. You should bring your bodyguards and your family. But leave me what fighting men you can and whatever trusted contacts remain."

"I will lend what meager aid remains mine to share," Nicholas sighed. "Do not proceed with your eyes closed. This is not a fight we can win. It would be a shame for you to throw your life away."

"My life belongs to Galloran," Nedwin said. "He left me here, and here I will stay."

CHAPTER 22

FOUR KEEPS

Under the cover of night Rachel sat astride her mare at the front of a large force. Galloran waited beside her, eyes blindfolded, Io leading his stallion.

The fortress before her was called West Keep. Watch fires burned atop formidable walls packed with restless soldiers. The upcoming assault would not take the defenders by surprise.

Rachel had longed for this moment. Her outrage over Drake's death had not diminished—if anything it had increased, as her grief turned to anger and as that pent-up fury lacked an outlet. She knew that nothing would bring Drake back, but payback would start tonight, minutes from now.

She had a key role to play. She knew Galloran had alternate plans, in case she failed to fulfill her role, but she did not expect to fail. The part of her that might have been afraid seemed to have died along with Drake.

Conquering and occupying the keeps would provide them some protection from Maldor's approaching forces. Bad news had followed their march across the valley to Felrook. Some of the scouts who had turned south after the pass had not returned.

Those who made it back had reported a host more than ten thousand strong massed at the southern end of the valley. It was a large enough army to give them serious trouble, although probably insufficient to defeat them. Except for leaving scouts behind to watch them, Galloran had ignored the force. He had decided the enemy troops were there solely to take and hold the pass in order to cut off their retreat.

Before they reached Felrook, news arrived that the pass had fallen. A handful of the defenders left behind had escaped up the mountainside. The rest had perished.

Not long afterward, an eagle from Nicholas had told of a coup at Trensicourt. Nedwin had been ousted as regent, and the city was now in the hands of their enemies. Rachel tried not to dwell on how terrible Nedwin probably felt about that mess. At least it sounded like he had survived.

No resistance had awaited their forces on the plains surrounding Felrook. As with the rest of the march, all had remained quiet. The town beside the ferry was abandoned. But the three keeps and the wall protecting the ferry were filled beyond capacity.

A drinling ran up to Galloran, saluted, and detailed the readiness of his soldiers. He was a burly man in mismatched armor, his face smudged with dirt, and he spoke English too rapidly to be easily understood. Galloran acknowledged his report and issued a few instructions.

The drinlings had united with the rest of Galloran's army on schedule. Rachel had been happy to find Io's father, Ul, among them, leading the wild clan. His hair was now completely white, but he still appeared hearty and strong. According to Ul, the drinlings had met with virtually no opposition during their long, quick march across the continent.

Rachel grimly regarded the solid fortress. It was not the only keep that would come under attack tonight. Once Galloran had organized his forces, Ferrin had schooled the leaders about the keeps. West Keep, North Keep, and East Keep were all of similar design. The big wall around each provided the main line of defense. The tall, thick walls had a single entrance with two sets of gates. The space between the gates passed below trapdoors and arrow loops where defenders could abuse attackers from cover. Rachel could hardly imagine how much courage it would take to charge such strong defenses, armed only with a sword, ax, or bow.

Each keep contained a large yard, along with extensive stables and barracks for horses and soldiers. The commanders lived in the keeps themselves—large, sturdy buildings, but not particularly defensible. If attackers could breach the wall, the rest would be relatively straightforward.

Naman had referred to the defenses around the ferry as the fourth keep. For planning purposes, the name had evolved to South Keep. Although it had no formal keep and contained fewer buildings than the other fortresses around Felrook, the walls of the South Keep were higher.

Ferrin had investigated the secret ways he knew into two of the keeps. Most of the passages had been sealed, or, in one instance, placed under heavy guard with an abundance of traps. But one way into East Keep was apparently unknown, or else those in command thought it impossible that their enemies knew the secret. The displacer was currently leading a sneak attack on East Keep using that obscure entrance. Rachel wondered if that assault had started yet. She hadn't heard any distant tumult of battle.

Moonlight waxed and waned with the movement of tattered clouds. When the pale light was brightest, Felrook loomed ominously above the lake, perched atop sheer cliffs rising vertically out of the water. The soaring towers and walls made Rachel feel like a mouse with aspirations to topple a skyscraper. She tried to ignore Felrook for the moment. They had to deal with the keeps before they could turn their attention to Maldor's greatest stronghold.

"The archers are in position," a seedman reported to Galloran. "The troops are ready."

"Proceed," the blindfolded leader directed.

The Amar Kabal had the finest bows in Lyrian, and the truest archers to aim them. The archers had assembled as far from the keep as their assignment allowed. The men on the wall made distant targets, but they were conveniently illuminated by the watch fires.

Three consecutive volleys of arrows soared through the night. Despite the great distance, a shocking amount of the projectiles found targets. Guards fell, screaming. The archers dropped back out of range before the guards could return fire.

Galloran signaled to Rachel. She idly wondered if he had been peeking at the events through her eyes and mind.

On the wall of the keep the main watch fires burned in elevated kettles. Rachel began to utter commands, shoving the kettles over, showering nearby soldiers with fiery coals and significantly reducing the amount of light available to the defenders. Even considering the distance involved, the effort felt simple, almost too easy to be called a warm-up, but she still enjoyed a pleasant rush of accomplishment. The tumbling kettles created quite a stir atop the walls as soldiers jostled one another.

The first wave of invaders charged forward, cumbersome shields held high. Rank after rank flowed forward around Rachel, Galloran, and their detachment of guards. The past few days had been spent preparing for this attack, including the construction of huge shields based on a design by Brin the Gamester. The unwieldy shields would be useless in hand-to-hand combat but would provide attackers with considerable protection from projectiles as they stormed the walls.

Rachel's next task would require the most finesse. The quantity of power involved was not great, but she had to execute it just right. As Galloran had made clear, this was her most essential assignment of the evening.

A crystal sphere the size of a soccer ball rested on the ground twenty yards away from her horse. Rachel commanded the gatecrasher into the air, then held it steady. The globe seemed light. She had never felt more focused. Mumbling a word, Rachel sent the sphere streaking toward the gate, driving it onward with her will. It passed well over the heads of the attacking troops, quickly leaving the fastest of them behind. Upon impact the crystal casing shattered, the mineral inside flared a brilliant white, and a tremendous explosion blasted the gate into kindling.

Rachel had been braced for a large detonation, but the penetrating thunder still made her jump. Snowflake flinched sideways, hoofs stomping, and Rachel murmured comforting words in Edomic. Even at this distance she felt a wave of heat after the blast. The front gate had disappeared; the stonework around it was cracked and blackened. A great curtain of smoke unfurled into the night sky.

A pleasant thrill accompanied the successful mandate, merging with the natural satisfaction of having demolished the gate. One more to go. With a second command Rachel sent another gatecrasher into the gaping blackness beyond where the first gate had stood. The sphere ruptured against the inner gate, the flash momentarily brightening the gap between the walls, and suddenly the way was clear.

Elation surged through Rachel. She had opened the way for

Galloran's troops to invade the keep! If she stopped now, she would have more than proved her worth. Galloran had encouraged her to stop at this point if the effort seemed to be too much. But she had no intention of holding back.

Stones and arrows sleeted down from atop the wall as the attackers charged the gate. Trebuchets flung boulders, and ballistae hurled flurries of weighty iron darts. The heavier projectiles smashed through the upraised shields, opening trenches in the advancing mass of warriors. Some of the smaller projectiles slipped through gaps, dropping scattered invaders among the charging mob.

Driven by painful thoughts of Drake, Rachel dismounted and prepped her will for the heavy work. The potential commands boiled inside her. Maldor wanted to kill her friends? Not without consequences.

A storehouse in the town beside the ferry had contained an abundance of lantern oil. A wagon laden with some of that oil presently waited on the road leading to the gate of West Keep, casks and barrels strapped in place. The attackers raced toward the keep at either side of the road, but not directly on it.

Speaking a word, Rachel set the wagon ablaze, along with the cargo. It was a challenging command, but it almost felt easy. She hardly acknowledged the resulting pleasure. Clenching her fists, she spoke words to push the wagon forward. Exerting her will and chanting additional words, she increased the speed of the wagon while keeping it stable. Stones and arrows bombarded the fiery cart. Casks ruptured, making the flames heave and spread. Rachel kept the portable inferno racing in the proper direction. When the wagon reached the gateless entrance perhaps fifteen yards ahead of the attackers, she gave one last mighty shove, throwing everything she had into the command. The wagon left the ground. Shedding a blizzard of sparks, burning boards snapped apart, and a sprawling wave of flame washed into the yard ahead of the attacking troops.

The effort left Rachel on her knees, gasping, a sharp pain drilling into her side. Her throat was raw, and she felt blood trickling from one nostril. At the same time, pleasure like she had never known coursed through her body, deliciously enlivening every nerve. Buoyed both physically and emotionally, she staggered to her feet, glorying in the triumphant rush of ecstasy. She had never exerted her will so hard.

"Well done," Galloran said, his blindfold discarded. "You should rest."

Rachel shook her head. She had launched her boulder into the sky, but Drake was still dead, and she was still standing. She suddenly wanted to throw her will against the wall of the keep, to slam against it with a tsunami of rage that would crush it to rubble. The desire felt compulsive, instinctive. Right now—hurting, exulting— such a command almost felt within her reach. But she knew the exertion would kill her, as surely as it would kill everybody on and behind the wall. Her own soldiers were already streaming through the entrance. Besides, they would need the wall to help defend their army in the coming days. With an effort she turned her attention to her next planned task.

Assistants had set aside twenty regular orantium spheres for her use, in case she still had energy left after the wagon. They would have to suffice. She sent four of them raining down above the gateway to get rid of the defenders harassing the attackers below. Then she propelled a sphere to each of the three visible ballistae. Finally, she sent the remainder sailing far over the wall to land deep in the yard beyond, well ahead of the brawling invaders. The explosions boomed like a string of giant firecrackers.

After hurling the last barrage, Rachel stumbled backward and sat down hard, her head throbbing, her ears ringing, her fingers and toes going numb. She felt dizzy, and her throat burned, the pain peaking each time she swallowed.

"No more," Galloran ordered.

Rachel heard more orantium exploding beyond the walls. Many of the seedmen had orantium to use at their discretion. They were mostly planning on using the spheres to destroy manglers and to pulverize locked doors.

She fought back to her feet. Her assigned tasks were complete. She felt a little ragged, but she wanted to unleash one more blast. Something big. Gritting her teeth, Rachel focused on the tower on the right side of the wall, where defenders continued to send stones and arrows down on attackers. It would take quite a push to tear off the top of it. Feeling slightly lightheaded, she prepped her will.

Strong hands gripped her arms from behind, pulling her down to her knees. "No, Rachel," Galloran said in her ear. "Let go. You're spent. No more." Holding her close, he followed the urgings with Edomic words of peace and relaxation.

Suddenly Rachel could hardly kneel, let alone stand. Her head spun. She slumped onto her side. Galloran gently released her. She couldn't even raise her head. Why had she thought she could knock over the tower? She felt empty now, weak, over-stretched. After pushing the wagon, the simple effort of hurling the orantium spheres had taken her beyond her limit. But the mighty tower had seemed vulnerable. Had she considered trying to shove over the entire wall? For a moment it had seemed almost fragile. Maybe she had failed to seize the opportunity when she'd had it. Or maybe the euphoric rush after pushing the wagon had made her grossly miscalculate her capacity. Rachel tried to rise but failed. Galloran steadied her. At least she remained conscious.

Drake was still dead. She tried to muster rage but only managed to feel empty and sick. Maldor had tried to kill Jason. He had killed Drake. He wanted to kill all her friends. She felt miserable, but anger was currently out of reach. She wanted to cry, but tears wouldn't come.

From a great distance the rumbling of other orantium detonations could be heard. All the keeps were under attack. Brin had created launchers for the gatecrashers at the other sites. At East Keep, Ferrin was going to try to open the gates from within, although gatecrashers were on hand as the backup plan.

Galloran helped Rachel sit up. What was he doing? Didn't he have a battle to oversee? He kept a supportive arm around her shoulders.

"We'll win tonight," Rachel said, her teeth chattering.

Galloran studied her with concern. "Are you all right?"

She nodded feebly. "Just tired. We'll win?" Her throat felt really sore.

"I expect so," Galloran said. "You were magnificent, but you pushed yourself too hard."

"Maldor is sorry?"

Galloran brushed her damp hair out of her face. "We gave him something to think about. Thanks to you. And to the orantium. Otherwise, storming these keeps would have cost at least half our strength. A few good men can hold a strong wall against a horde. We should have paid dearly for these strongholds. They were heavily manned and well provisioned. Your contribution here at West Keep made our advantage even more overwhelming. Your Edomic spared hundreds of lives. Perhaps even thousands."

"Maldor should have left them abandoned," Rachel said. How many people had she killed tonight? The kettles, the orantium, the wagon . . .

"No," Galloran said. "He's too good of a strategist. He didn't want to fight us at the pass, because we might have turned back. He didn't want to engage us in the valley, because at present his forces would have been outnumbered by better warriors. But with these keeps he hoped to sap our strength before his armies arrive from the east. He would never have handed them to us. Had his men repelled us here, we could not have fled."

Rachel turned to face Galloran. She felt a little less woozy. "His men won't stop us tonight. Not if the other attacks are anything like this one."

"Agreed. I do not think Maldor understood the extent of our orantium stores. He knew we had some spheres in our possession. I believe the quantity of orantium has surprised him, as have the gatecrashers, which is why these assaults needed to be simultaneous. Maldor believed these keeps would be a serious obstacle. His defenders were not ready for their gates to disappear at the outset of the attack."

Rachel listened to the clamor of battle inside the fortress. "What now?"

"We wait for victory."

Not long before dawn Rachel ate breakfast inside the dining hall of West Keep. She felt halfway back to normal—her body remained weary, but her mind felt clear. Galloran ate with her. Ferrin sat beside her. Other leaders and friends joined them, including Naman, Ul, Io, Brin, Tark, Lodan, a drinling leader called Obb, and a seedman named Herral. Naman had commanded the attack on North Keep, Obb had supervised the conquest of South Keep, and Herral had overseen the taking of East Keep.

Before Rachel had reunited with Ferrin, she had already heard men singing his praises. Apparently, he had been quite a hero

at East Keep, leading hundreds of soldiers past the walls undetected. They had taken the wall and opened the gates, attacking
the defenders in the yard from above as the main force rushed
through unhindered.

Rachel glanced sideways at Ferrin as she crumbled her bis-
cuits and stirred them together with her eggs. "Tell me about your
night. I hear you saved the day."

"I can share what I didn't do," Ferrin said. "I didn't singlehandedly blow open the gates, ram a wagonload of fire through
the breach, then commence with a hailstorm of orantium. How's
your head?"

"Feeling better," Rachel said. "It was good to stretch myself.
Hopefully, I'll have more endurance next time. But I want details!
I keep hearing how well things went at East Keep."

"We entered belowground. I disposed of some guards silently.
We had practically filled the dungeon before we had to blow a
door to proceed. The blast announced our presence, but our foes
responded poorly. We killed some sentries and made it to the top
of the wall before anybody really understood what was happening. Some orantium followed by brawny drinlings went a long way
toward clearing the top of the wall. While seedfolk archers rained
arrows into the yard, we reached the mechanisms and opened the
gates."

"The displacer offers a humble account," Herral said. "He slew
at least twenty foes, including three displacers, and lost his head
leading the charge along the wall."

"I got it back," Ferrin clarified.

"He personally opened the gates," Herral went on. "Then he
led a team into the keep proper by another secret way. Without
using gatecrashers, we lost fewer than a hundred souls taking East
Keep, and we slew better than a thousand."

"The offensive could not have gone more smoothly," Naman announced. "Attacking fortifications like these keeps, we should have lost at least five soldiers for every enemy slain. Instead, the balance of casualties was well in our favor. We lost fewer than fifteen hundred fighters in total, including fewer than a hundred at East Keep and fewer than two hundred at West Keep, where we enjoyed the greatest advantages."

"It was an inspiring victory," Galloran agreed, his eyes closed. "It will also be our only victory unless we take Felrook soon. The keeps were meant to hinder us, but the fatal trap remains. We will be outnumbered more than twenty to one when Maldor's armies return from the east."

Rachel plucked little chunks from her roll, pinching it apart instead of eating it. Last night had been nightmarish, and that had been a victory! What would defeat look like? She wished they had more time to enjoy their success.

"I'll start walling off the gateless entrances this morning," Brin said. "We'll make our captured fortresses as secure as possible. And I'll get to work on how we might crack Felrook."

"We must all bend our thoughts toward raiding Felrook," Galloran said. "We have no time to starve them out. We cannot flee. We cannot resist the coming tide of enemies. We must take Felrook before they arrive or else perish."

Rachel had already been thinking long and hard about how they might penetrate Felrook. She had come up with no brilliant schemes. She would put more thought into it as Galloran asked, but she hoped they wouldn't be relying on her to supply the answer.

"Felrook has secret passages," Ferrin said, "but none that lead in or out. I know of no fortress more secure—no gate less available, no walls less reachable, no defenses more comprehensive. With only one way up the cliffs, we cannot throw numbers at the problem. There is no access for siege towers or ladders. Expert climbers would be hard-pressed to reach the base of the walls under ideal conditions. The best trebuchet ever designed could not fling a stone halfway up the cliffs."

Ul leaned over and spoke to Obb in Ji, the staccato drinling language.

"We have orantium," Obb said.

"Which could create opportunities," Ferrin allowed. "It will be hard to deliver explosives. Even if we destroy the gates, the path up the cliff is rigged to collapse. How do wingless men attack a fortified island in the sky?"

"The task appears impossible," Galloran said. "It will require all our strength and ingenuity. But there has to be a way to succeed. We know this by prophecy. We must invent a way to accomplish our aim. Not just our lives, but the lives of every man, woman, and child in Lyrian depend on it. Obsess about this problem. Encourage your best men to wrestle with it. And the least of your men. Stay open to strategies never attempted before."

Ferrin leaned close to Rachel so he could whisper. "Translation? Pray that Lord Jason succeeds in his quest. Try not to lose your sanity in the meanwhile."

CHAPTER 23

THE FUMING WASTE

Shortly after dawn, from the shoulder of a craggy hill streaked orange and white, Jason viewed his first panoramic vista of the Fuming Waste. Bands of red, orange, yellow, pink, and white gave striking color to the limestone landscape. Stunted vegetation subsisted in sparse patches—contorted trees, scraggly shrubs, and prickly cacti. Two geysers were erupting, one not far below, the other more distant. Both spewed sparkling towers of scalding water and steam into the air. Within a minute or two the nearer fountain shrank to a bubbling froth and then stopped. The distant geyser kept gushing for a good while. A third geyser started up in the middle distance, just before the far one began to decline.

"It's lovely," Corinne said from astride her gelding. "Look at the new one!"

As the soaring eruption continued to stretch higher, refracted sunlight laced the spray with prismatic ripples of color. Behind the radiant display, the farther geyser continued to diminish.

"Three geysers in a row?" Jason said. "I hope geysers are lucky."

Jasher grunted. "If so, we have come to the luckiest place in Lyrian."

"I cannot vouch for their value as omens," Farfalee said, "but the waters of the Fuming Waste are certainly unruly. We're only at the outskirts. As we draw nearer to the mountains we will find hot springs, painted rivers, sludge pits, cauldrons, sinkholes, steam vents, mineral terraces, mud volcanoes, and geyser cones. None of our maps will be perfect, for the geography here evolves much more rapidly than anywhere else in Lyrian. We will need to proceed with care. There are volatile areas where the ground becomes wafer thin above boiling lakes or where scant layers of sand disguise wells of searing mud."

"Sounds perfect for a picnic," Jason quipped. "Who brought the sandwiches?"

"I have ridden this hazardous region before," Jasher said, "though I never came so near to the heart of the Fuming Waste as this journey demands. Certain indicators can help protect us. Watch for steaming ground. Watch for webs of cracks. Feel for warm pockets. Listen for gurgling. Listen for the earth below popping or splitting. We'll ride single file." He pointed into the distance. "The Great Yellow Cone is our first landmark. From there we must proceed across the Polished Plain to the Stepping-Stones, past the Giant's Bathhouse, and finally into the Scalding Caverns."

"And Rachel has the good camera," Jason sighed. "Anything after the Scalding Caverns? Maybe the Flaming Hot Ocean of Misery?"

"The Narrow Way," Farfalee said. "And finally our destination."

Jason could see the first landmark poking above a distant ridgeline. The conical mount was shaped just like a volcano that a child would draw, its coloring the same yellow and white as a lemon meringue pie.

During the long ride north they had not been spied by their adversaries, though as he scouted, Jasher had occasionally glimpsed enemy riders from a distance. The seedman had led their group on a lengthy ride inland before veering northward. The strategy had added at least a day to the trek, but it made the task very difficult for any soldiers who sailed north in order to cut them off or pick up their trail.

Two of Farfalee's messenger eagles had returned to her after she had set them loose the night they had abandoned the *Valiant*. She did not dare let them fly for fear of revealing their location. Instead, she kept them tethered to Aram's saddle, feeding the large birds from the group's rations.

Jason flicked his reins and followed Jasher down the rugged hillside. The seedman weaved along the slope, inventing the trail as he went. Aram pointed out a black scorpion the size of a lobster. Jasher warned that the smaller, orange scorpions had a deadlier sting. Jason didn't crave an encounter with either variety.

They saw no new geysers for more than an hour, but by sunset Jason had counted eleven. They made camp in a cove of red rock. In addition to their regular rations, everyone but Jasher and Farfalee sampled part of the five-foot pit snake Del had killed. The cooked meat was chewy and almost sweet.

The next day the Great Yellow Cone grew gradually nearer. Jason had a hard time gauging its size. It was certainly nothing to rival the mountains on the horizon, but it was a good deal taller than the surrounding mesas, drawing the eye more than any other feature.

As the day wore on, they more frequently passed steaming vents. Some were jagged cracks no wider than a pencil, others yawning holes large enough to swallow a motor home. They also came across bubbling pools of muck—some red, some black, some white, most a silvery gray. The mud varied in thickness from viscous sludge to watery syrup. Some pools coughed up an occasional slow bubble; others simmered vigorously. Most of them reeked of sulfur.

Throughout the ride Jason missed Drake. He missed his teasing comments, his reliable advice, and even his cynical predictions. He missed the steady competence of his presence. They were less safe without him. More than once Jason had caught himself wondering when Drake would return from scouting, only to remember that his friend would never be back. From time to time he rode with his head bowed to hide the tears.

They stopped for the night near a black pool with a churning disturbance near the center. After making camp, Jason went to stare at the pool while twilight faded. The constant disruption heaved dark fluid eight feet into the air, like a small, permanent geyser. The central churning kept the rest of the surface rippling vigorously. Jasher called the murky pool a cauldron, which Jason considered an apt description

As more stars emerged in the darkening sky, Corinne joined Jason beside the pool. For a long moment she watched with him in silence. Eventually he noticed that her attention had shifted from the pool to him. "Are you all right?" she asked.

"I'm good," Jason said, uncertain how else to respond.

"You've seemed extra quiet lately."

"Have you heard? We're being hunted."

"I'm serious."

Jason turned his attention back to the pool. "I don't know. It's been harder since we lost Drake. And then we lost so many people at Gulba. I guess it's getting to me."

"I'm glad to hear that," Corinne said.

Jason looked at her sharply. "You're heartless."

"No," she apologized. "I mean, I'm glad because I feel the same way. I feel . . . drained, sad . . . you know."

"I know. It's rough. I guess we try to look on the bright side. We're getting close. Maybe some of us will actually make it."

"All the rest of us," she said.

"I hope so." He glanced her way. "You were amazing against that lurker. I couldn't believe it."

"Neither could I," Corinne said. "I was so scared. But I could feel its mind, and I knew I had a chance. I also knew it would lead soldiers to us. It might have made escape impossible. It had no weapon. I felt like I had to try."

"I honestly thought you were dead," Jason said. "That might have been it for me."

"Don't talk like that," Corinne scolded. "Of all of us, you need to hold true to the end."

Jason looked down at his hands. Why him? Why did it matter so much for him to find Darian's home? He wasn't the best fighter. If anything, he was the worst. But the oracle had named him first. As a result, Drake had died to save him. Guilt twisted deep inside.

Corinne put a hand on his. Her hand was not soft. She had calluses from practicing with her sword. He squeezed her hand. She squeezed back.

Maybe Darian was alive. Maybe Darian would only share secrets with Beyonders. Maybe there would be a riddle that only Jason could answer. Maybe only his fingerprint could open the secret vault.

"We'll make it," Jason said. He tried to mean it. He mostly did. It seemed like she needed him to say it. "We'll find the message from Darian."

"I believe that," Corinne said. "Don't lose hope."

"I won't." She was sitting close.

Corinne patted his hand and rose. "You shouldn't sit here all night."

"Just a little longer."

She walked away. Jason stared at the churning sludge, feeling alone. Drake had died specifically for him. A big part of Jason wished that he hadn't. But it couldn't be undone. So now the responsibility was on his shoulders to make that mean something.

The next morning, not long after they began riding, the Great Yellow Cone erupted. Water and steam jetted upward for the better part of two hours, infinite droplets glittering in the morning light. By the end the entire conical mount glistened wetly.

Soon after the Great Yellow Cone went dry, Nia spotted the third messenger eagle returning. Jasher and Aram instantly became alert. As the eagle circled down to Farfalee, Jasher pointed at a distant figure atop a pink ridge, little more than a speck to the naked eye.

Jason felt dread pooling in the pit of his stomach. That tiny figure in the distance could spell big trouble. Aram had worried from the start that their enemies might find a way to track them using the eagles. Jason looked to the small half giant.

Aram swiveled his spyglass to where Jasher was pointing. "He has a telescope of his own," Aram snapped. "He's waving. He's turning his horse."

"They must have caught the eagle," Jasher guessed. "They came north and used it to track us."

"How could they have caught it?" Farfalee asked. The eagle perched on her arm, eating from her hand. "Eina would not have gone to them willingly. Until I send it with a message, while I remain alive Eina would only come to me."

Jason thought she sounded a little defensive. Farfalee had to feel terrible that one of her eagles had given them away. After all, Aram had warned her.

"It would have taken some craft," Jasher said. "Does it matter how they managed it? The damage is done. We need to pick up the pace."

By sunset they were in the shadow of the Great Yellow Cone. Aram had grown, which made Jason feel a bit safer. Spyglass in hand, Jasher scrambled up the side of the geyser cone. The climb was hundreds of feet. Much of the light had faded before he reached the top.

"A big group, still riding hard," Jasher reported upon his return. "Could be as many as thirty riders."

"How far back?" Jason asked.

Jasher inhaled through his teeth. "If we hold still and they ride through the night, they might have us."

"Then we had best not keep still," Farfalee said.

"We'll need to take care," Jasher said. "The Polished Plain lies ahead of us. The ground is thin there. I have always heard that horses are too heavy to cross it, and the information on our most comprehensive map agrees."

"Should we think about finding a place to make a stand?" Jason asked. "Try to catch them off guard? Hit them with a rock-slide or something?"

"Thirty is too many," Aram said. "We only have two orantium spheres. We should first try to outrun them."

"How far to the plain?" Farfalee asked.

"We could be there before sunrise," Jasher replied.

"The horses are tired," Nia said.

"We won't ride them hard," Jasher replied. "We don't want to attempt the Polished Plain in the dark."

After their evening meal they continued riding. There were enough clouds to mute the moon most of the time, forcing Jasher to light a length of seaweed. The glow let them see enough to avoid falling down a hole, but it would also give their pursuers an easy target to follow.

The worry of enemies behind them kept Jason from feeling too tired. He listened to the strange exhalations of the alien landscape—the burbling of sludge pools, the sighs of steam vents, and the gusty splashing of geysers.

After they paused for a quick nap and some food, sunrise found them at the edge of a spectacular plain that stretched ahead for miles. Less than an inch of water flowed across the flat, stony expanse, giving the surface a glossy shine. Every color was represented in streaks and swirls, with an emphasis on white, yellow, orange, red, and turquoise. Bubbling springs abounded, the water spreading more than flowing. Steam leaked up from everywhere. Crouching at the edge of the damp plain and extending his hand, Jason found the water lukewarm.

"We lack a good vantage anywhere close," Jasher said. "It is hard to judge how far back our pursuers remain. If they rode hard, they will have gained on us. Afoot it could cost us all day to cross the plain. The question becomes whether we proceed with or without our mounts."

Jason looked back. He couldn't see any sign of enemy riders. But they might lope into view at any second.

"Can we go around?" Del asked.

Jasher showed the drinling the map. "The plain is long, and it curves around our destination. Going around is not feasible. It might not even be possible." Jasher folded the map, staring forward. "The entire plain is essentially a frail crust over superheated water. Even without the weight of our mounts we could crash through at any moment. It will be like treading on weak ice."

"It's a good time to be small," Aram said. "What if we lead the horses?"

"It's a risk," Jasher said. "Cracks can spread. If a horse breaks though, it could start an event that could take all of us with it."

"Then we walk," Farfalee said.

"Our enemies will have the same choice," Jasher cautioned. "If they stay mounted, and the ground holds, they will catch us."

"Do you think it will hold for horses?" Farfalee asked.

"No," Jasher said. "I'm worried whether it will hold for us. If we walk and they ride, I believe theirs will be the greater risk."

"Then we walk," she repeated. "We had best make ready."

Working quickly, they took as much of their gear and provisions as they could reasonably carry. Jason checked his saddlebags for any stuff he might have missed. Corinne tried to communicate with the horses to run off and thrive in the wild but didn't seem optimistic about her success. Del volunteered to lug Aram's armor. Nia took his enormous sword.

"It's heavy," Aram warned her.

"I'll be fine," Nia said. "If anything, the exertion will just make me stronger."

"Tread lightly," Jasher advised. "If the ground starts to give, fall flat. We'll walk single file, not too close together. I'll take the lead."

"I'll bring up the rear," Del offered.

Walking behind Farfalee and ahead of Corinne, Jason ventured out onto the Polished Plain. Water splashed gently with each step. Jason noticed that the temperature of the thin layer of water varied from tepid to boiling. He felt tense, aware that he might break through into scalding water at any second. From time to time he sensed the ground creaking beneath him.

Jasher did not lead them in a straight line. He explained that he was trying to guess the safest ground, based on the presence of springs, venting steam, and the water temperature. He kept well away from the smoldering pools, where the ground had already given way. They advanced in silence, listening for evidence of danger. Several times Jasher edged back carefully as the ground crackled underfoot.

Jasher tried to keep them in warm water rather than hot, but it was not always possible. Heat radiated from the water and the ground, leaving Jason with lots of empathy for steamed vegetables. A greasy sheen of sweat and vapor clung to him all morning.

By noon the pursuing riders came into view at the edge of the plain behind them. The intervening steam made the tiny forms shimmer. Thankfully, Jasher had overestimated their numbers. Unfortunately, they were still close to two dozen.

After milling about at the edge of the plain for several minutes, the riders opted to remain mounted and came cantering toward them. Looking back at the oncoming riders made their progress since dawn feel pathetic.

Jason resisted the urge to run. At this point it wouldn't do any good. He couldn't outrace a horse.

"We have no cover," Aram pointed out. "If they reach us, they'll ride us down."

"Fan out," Jasher said. "Jason, keep your orantium handy. Try to throw it in front of a tight group of riders. Maybe we can help the ground to give. Farfalee, Nia, ready your bows."

They spread out, facing their enemies. Jasher held his torivorian sword in one hand and his orantium globe in the other. Jason did likewise. The moisture in the air made the globe feel slippery.

The horses were charging hard. There were so many! At least the orantium gave Jason some hope of defending himself and his friends. He realized that he would have to throw his globe as far as he could or else he would risk sending his entire group into the boiling lake. He would have to time it just right to take out the maximum number of riders.

Before long the pursuers had come half the distance from the edge of the plain. Water sprayed up as hoofs drummed across the steaming ground. The high sun made small shadows beneath them.

Jason's mouth was dry. How was he supposed to stand against a bunch of charging horsemen? Farfalee might drop a few riders with her bow. He supposed he would have to try to dodge and slash with his sword as best he could. Hoofs and weaponry would be coming at him all at once. How would he avoid so many threats? Would any of them manage to stand against such a brutal onslaught? This could be the end. Behind the riders, beyond the plain, Jason saw a geyser erupting.

And then suddenly three of the lead riders disappeared, dropping out of view without warning, flaky fragments of stone flipping up as water splashed high. Other riders sought to slow or swerve, but within seconds a huge section of ground had collapsed, leaving fewer than ten riders on the surface of the plain.

For a long moment the broken area was a steamy stew of horse heads and flailing arms, but the tumult grew still before long. Dismounting, the remaining pursuers abandoned their horses and proceeded on foot, giving the newly created pool a wide berth.

Jason glanced over at Corinne. She looked relieved and a little horrified. Her eyes met his.

"That got my heart rate up," Jason confessed.

She sheathed her sword. "I kept thinking, 'Of course they won't fall; of course this will be the one time twenty horses gallop across this fragile plain without making a single crack.'"

Aram watched through the spyglass, grinning like a child at the circus. "Eight remain."

"I can finish eight with my bow once they come within range," Farfalee said. "They lack cover, and I have plenty of arrows. The rest of you go on ahead."

"You shouldn't stay back alone," Jasher said. "What if you lose your seed?"

"I'll stay with her," Nia offered. "I have a bow as well."

Jasher nodded. "Wait until they are well within range or they will fall back out of reach. We'll await you at the far side of the plain. Our departure should lure them forward faster."

After wiping the lens of the spyglass on his sleeve, Aram took another look. "None are heavily armored. For Farfalee, filling them with arrows will be like a holiday exhibition."

"I might hit one too," Nia pointed out.

"Anything is possible," Aram replied.

Nia swatted him, brandishing his sword. "Don't forget who totes this while the sun is out!"

"I meant no insult," Aram said. "I've just never seen anyone shoot like Farfalee."

Jasher led all of them but Farfalee and Nia single file. Jason kept peering over his shoulder, watching for the soldiers to come within range. They all stopped when Farfalee and Nia started shooting. The exhibition did not take long.

Farfalee and Nia caught up to the others by late afternoon.

"I hit two," Nia reported. "I also missed twice, but one of my hits was fatal."

"I stand corrected about your marksmanship," Aram said. Raising his voice, he called ahead to Jasher. "Any chance of picking up the pace? This Polished Plain is one of the few places where little Aram has a definite advantage."

"We'll make it by sundown," Jasher promised.

They crept onward. The lack of sleep from the night before was catching up with Jason. The pace was not quick, but it was relentless, and the constant danger of the ground giving way kept him tense. They ate while walking. At one point Jasher's foot broke the surface, but he managed to skip backward before the crust shattered beneath him. In the end Jasher barely managed to keep his promise. Aram grew large perhaps ten minutes after leaving the Polished Plain behind.

The next day they reached landmarks more quickly. They sighted the Stepping-Stones—seven staggered columns of rock that increased in height—early in the day, and then left them behind by the afternoon.

The Giant's Bathhouse was a naturally terraced mesa with overflowing pools at various levels. The spilling water left behind colorful mineral deposits—elaborate draperies that gave the mesa the appearance of a huge cake dripping with frosting. Rolling clouds of steam billowed from a gaping cave at the base of the fanciful formation.

They halted for the night not far beyond the Giant's Bathhouse. Jasher informed them that in the morning it would only take a few hours to reach the Scalding Caverns. Once through the caverns they would follow the Narrow Way to the last abode of Darian the Seer.

"Do you think this will really be the right place?" Jason asked Corinne as they prepared to bed down. "Do you think we'll find Darian?"

"I expect so," she replied. "I can't imagine there was other information at the library that the oracle would have wanted us to follow. Having Farfalee along to read that Petruscan scroll had to be by design."

"I hope so," Jason said. "If we're wrong, I guess there isn't much we can do about it. The instructions make it sound like I should enter alone."

"Alone and unarmed," Jasher clarified. "The prophecy named you as the person who needed to collect the information from Darian. The rest of us are here to get you to your destination."

Jason nodded, trying not to display the heaviness he felt inside.

"We might be willing to guard the door while you're in there," Nia said.

"Think he'll speak English?" Jason wondered.

"He lived before English became prevalent," Farfalee said. "But if he's still around, who knows? If the prophecy sent you here, there must be some way for the two of you to communicate."

"Think we'll make it there tomorrow?" Jason asked.

"Depends on how long this Narrow Way will be," Farfalee said. "It is on none of the maps, and the instructions were unclear about the distance. The way should end at a waterfall. The entrance is under and behind the cascade."

The conversation died. Jason nestled into his blanket, and he could feel himself slipping toward sleep when Jasher sat up abruptly. Snapping back to full consciousness, Jason listened intently. After a moment he heard footfalls. It sounded like a single runner.

Farfalee and Nia nocked arrows. Jason grabbed his sword. Jasher had not risked a fire, but the moon was bright tonight.

The runner kept coming, feet pounding steadily. The oncoming stranger did not seem to be making any efforts at stealth. A few moments later Heg jogged into view.

"Heg?" Nia asked in disbelief.

The drinling stopped and waved. "You weren't easy to follow." He was only slightly out of breath.

"We were worried all of you had died," Jasher said. "The scenario looked bleak."

"Most of us did," Heg said. "I escaped into the water, swam to safety. I don't think anyone else made it. Certainly not those who stayed on dry land."

"How'd you find us?" Jason asked, amazed.

"I came north," Heg said. "I knew the general direction, some of the main landmarks. My best clues came from the horsemen on your trail. I followed them. Looked like their mission ended back on that watery plain. Unless I'm mistaken, some of them got to check how polished the plain appears from the underside. I knew I was getting close, because the soldiers with arrows in them were recently slain. This evening I followed your tracks from the edge of the plain."

"Well met," Del said, gripping forearms with his leader.

"I'm relieved to find you in such good health," Heg said. "It seemed the entire population of the Inland Sea had been mobilized to hunt you."

"We stayed well away from the coast," Jasher said. "Those horsemen back there were our first real problem."

"A wise strategy," Heg approved. "The coasts are definitely swarming. What became of the others with you?"

"We lost Zoo, Thag, and Fet while fleeing Gulba," Farfalee said. "Zoo fell to a torivor. Thag and Fet were claimed by Groddic."

"Groddic?" Heg exclaimed. "The chief of the conscriptors?"

"He paid with his life," Nia said.

"And what of the torivor?" Heg wondered. "The one that kept helping them find us?"

"Corinne killed it," Jason said.

"It had no swords," she added humbly. "I could feel its mind, anticipate its movements."

"Impressive," Heg said. He clapped his hands together. "I am relieved to have found you. I did not mean to interrupt your slumber. I doubt that I arrived in time to be of much service against our enemies. Over the past few days I have seen no evidence of further pursuit. For now we appear to have passed beyond their reach. But I will be more than curious to witness how this ends."

"We're glad to have you with us," Farfalee said. "Come share some of our food."

Jason fell asleep before Heg finished his meal.

CHAPTER 24

AMBUSH

Nedwin sat on a rooftop watching the sunrise, the morning air cool against his skin. Ever since the coup, regardless of the hour, the city had been markedly quieter. Nobody wanted to be noticed.

Including him.

Nedwin was positioned so that no onlookers could see him from the street below, nor from any of the neighboring rooftops, unless they were directly to his east. The sun peeked over the horizon, throwing long shadows among the forest of spires, domes, belfries, cupolas, gables, turrets, and chimneys.

A satchel containing five orantium globes sat at his side. A separate stash of twelve was hidden inside the castle. Most of the remaining globes had been delivered by a seedman messenger not long after Galloran was crowned. The king of Trensicourt had left behind all the orantium he could spare. Nedwin had detonated none so far.

Nicholas had gone. The legless lord had several hideaways prepared in the country outside the city. He had left Nedwin with some men, some contacts, a few letters of introduction, and the keys to some secret hideouts and storerooms.

Nollin had gone. Even after treatment it was not certain whether the seedman would survive. The wound to his side had been deep. He would remain with Nicholas until he either died or healed.

Kerick had remained. Nedwin now had a network of almost thirty men who he trusted. Most of them would be involved with the operation today in one capacity or another.

As Nedwin had expected, Copernum had orchestrated the insurrection. He had established himself as regent and claimed Trensicourt on behalf of the emperor. He had also announced the annihilation of Galloran and his army. Nedwin sensed that many doubted the lie, but nobody challenged the new regent vocally. Copernum had welcomed imperial soldiers into the city to help keep the peace during the transitional period. And he had stayed safely behind the castle walls.

The people of Trensicourt were unhappy, some were even angry, but the most capable of them had marched off to war. Intimidating patrols of soldiers and giants prowled the streets. The few open dissenters vanished promptly. Despite the atmosphere of oppression and uncertainty, people were returning to their daily business, conducting most of it indoors.

The majority of the soldiers and all the giants were barred access to the castle. Copernum was being very careful about who entered. Dolan, the grand duke, and certain predictable nobles were among the inner circle granted admittance, along with their personal guards and retainers.

Keeping the giants outside the castle had created an opportunity. Thanks to Aram and Jason, Nedwin knew what happened to giants once the sun came up, as it was doing now: They shrank.

Finding the lair where the giants hid during the day had been no small undertaking. In the days since the coup, most of his effort had focused on that one mystery. In the end the key had been following the food wagons.

He currently sat on the roof of a warehouse used to supply rations for the occupying force within the city. He and others had followed a number of giants during their nightly patrols. Not long before sunrise, the giants had all returned to the five main garrisons around the city.

At first Nedwin had guessed that the giants remained hidden at the various garrisons during the day, but he kept coming up against dead ends as he tried to discover where, specifically, they were housed. Then he had considered the morning food deliveries. The wagons went into the garrisons, remained unseen while food was unloaded, and then came out not long after dawn. All the wagons returned directly to a central warehouse. And that was where the tiny giants were unloaded. Nedwin had witnessed the process with his own eyes. The giants spent the day under one roof, sleeping and feasting, then returned to the garrisons with another food delivery before sunset.

Even in their small form, the giants ate a lot. It made sense to hide them where food was abundant and to limit the number of people who knew their secret by keeping the giants grouped at a central location. The logistics of maintaining five different covert holding areas at five separate garrisons would have been more complicated.

Of course, now that the secret was known, keeping the giants in a single location also made it easier to eliminate them. Or so Nedwin hoped.

He felt that the giants currently posed the single greatest threat to Trensicourt. There were more than eighty of the brutes, higher than the early estimates. That many giants backing the imperial guards every night was enough to make even the bravest revolutionary consider keeping his head down.

The imperial desire for secrecy increased the chance for success. There were not many human guards at the warehouse, and they kept out of sight. Most of them also helped drive the wagons. From what Nedwin could tell, no more than ten guards shared the secret, all of them senior conscriptors. The warehouse had only two entrances—a wide set of loading doors for the wagons, and a smaller door that led out the back. The guards protected the doors from the inside, probably to avoid drawing attention to the building.

The large warehouse had high, dirty windows. Reaching them had proven impractical—dangling upside down from the eaves would have left him much too exposed. So for reconnaissance purposes Nedwin had quietly cut holes in the roof.

As the sun elevated above the horizon, Nedwin reflected that this would be the first major blow against the usurpers who had staged the coup. To lose their giants would prove that their occupation was not as secure as it seemed. It would give others who wanted the empire out of Trensicourt reason to hope and reason to take action.

Losing eighty giants would also be a strong blow against Maldor. Of all the races of Zokar, giants were by far the rarest. They had aided Maldor in the past, giving him an undeniable advantage wherever they went. Nedwin felt eager to contribute to their extinction.

Although this would be his first military strike, Nedwin had already performed some minor mischief. Three days ago, toward the end of his search for the giants, Nedwin had accessed a garrison kitchen. For a moment he had been alone with three simmering kettles of stew. He carried multiple types of poison in the vials around his neck. He could have probably killed a fifth of the occupying soldiers.

But poison was a cowardly weapon, and the soldiers were tools, not masterminds. With access to a private bowl being delivered to Copernum, Nedwin would not have hesitated to make it lethal. A different set of rules applied to targeting a specific enemy. Poisoning a large group of soldiers was not only dishonorable, but it could lead to serious repercussions for the people of Trensicourt. Such unfair tactics would lead to unfair retaliation.

So instead Nedwin had seasoned the soup with a substance that would leave all who ingested it violently ill for at least a week. The feverish retching would be blamed on bad meat rather than shameful tactics. Although the enduring consequences would be minimal, over the short term the miserable symptoms would harm morale and reduce the number of guardsmen on patrol.

How would Copernum and his fellow conspirators respond to the death of the giants? They certainly would not want it known that their massive warriors had been wiped out in a single ambush. They would probably pretend to have sent them away. Nedwin suspected that only the most gullible soldiers and citizens would believe it.

Finally, Nedwin heard the first wagon clatter into the warehouse. He stole a couple of quick peeks as the second and third wagons rolled inside. It was a few minutes until the fourth arrived, and another short wait for the fifth and final shipment of miniature giants.

After the loading doors were closed and locked, Nedwin kept waiting. There was no need to rush the attack. He wanted them to have time to feel secure and relaxed. Let them eat. Let them unwind. Most of the giants would bed down, and the guards would settle in for another dull, routine day. Except for spoiled meat in the stew a few days ago, the city had been quiet ever since the night Copernum seized power. There was no reason for anyone to expect that pattern to break today, especially in this covert dormitory.

The sun climbed higher, reeling in the long shadows. Nedwin stretched. Too much inaction had left him feeling a little knotted. He rolled his neck, twisted his waist, extended his arms, and flexed his fingers.

He crept into position. There was no reason to hurry. Total silence was the goal, and he achieved it.

Late last night, while the giants were on patrol and the warehouse was still, Nedwin had constructed a hatch in the roof. Then he had erected a little tent over it. The tent would prevent sunlight from spilling through when the hatch opened. Even if he were spotted immediately, the plan should still work. But it would work better if he caught them completely unaware.

Easing the hatch open, Nedwin climbed down into the rafters. He knew that he might be seen at any moment. Movement tended to draw the eye, and there were many bodies below him. Most of them were slumbering dwarfs, but some were on their backs. All it took was one set of eyes.

He balanced up high in a shadowed corner crisscrossed with struts and beams. He watched those below him as best he could, motionless until he felt sure no gazes were directed his way. Inch by inch he reached the roost he wanted without anyone raising an alarm.

Below him four sentries clustered near the big doors by the wagons. Another pair of guards manned the smaller back door. Three-quarters of the dwarfs were asleep or at least trying. The others mostly conversed. A red-faced pair arm-wrestled across a square table. One dwarf whittled. Another munched on an apple. One read.

Nedwin held an orantium globe in each hand. The first throw was the trickiest. He wanted the globe to disable all four guards while damaging the loading doors enough for attackers to open them. It was a long throw. The pair by the back door was nearer.

After counting down in his head, Nedwin flung a globe toward the loading doors, pivoted, and hurled the other at the guards by the back door. Because the second globe traveled farther, they both exploded simultaneously. The blasts echoed loudly in the large, enclosed space. Nedwin noticed the undersized giants jerking and jumping with surprise.

The next two globes were for the little guys. They had kindly bedded down close to one another, so two spheres would go a long way toward ridding Trensicourt of giants. He threw the globes, watching as they curved downward. He covered his ears against the resounding explosions.

Obscured by smoke, Kerick led a group of fighting men through the back door. Gorson, the best man Nicholas had left behind, led more fighters through the damaged loading doors.

The dwarfs never stood a chance. They were not dressed for battle. Most had no weapons handy. Some tried to fight. Others scattered, trying to hide. Most appeared frightened and confused.

Nedwin held the fifth orantium sphere ready but had no occasion to use it. The uneven battle ended swiftly. Two of his allies had been injured, one killed. Kerick had been the most efficient, slaying at least ten foes. Nedwin wondered if any one man had ever cut down so many giants over such a brief period.

On their way out, the men splashed lantern oil around the room and started fires. That was the signal for Nedwin to return to the roof. His men would split up and disappear along prearranged routes. A few would stay near enough to watch for any emerging stragglers.

Nedwin would slip away quietly as well, using the rooftops as his roads. He needed to get away clean. He had other tasks to perform.

CHAPTER 25

DECISION

Beneath a bright sun Rachel walked along the top of the East Keep's wall, gazing out at Felrook, the ultimate immovable object, firmly anchored atop the highest prominence in the valley. Even if the imposing castle had not enjoyed such an elevated foundation, its soaring walls and lofty towers would have dwarfed the lesser fortresses around Lake Fellion.

So far Maldor's central stronghold had proven as unassailable as the loudest skeptics had feared. Since it rested on a massive pillar of solid stone in the midst of a deep lake, nobody had come close to finding a reasonable way to attack it.

And the armies from the east were closing in.

The military leaders were doing all they could to prepare. East Keep was in excellent shape. Ferrin had helped them capture the fortress virtually undamaged. The gates were intact, the catapults and ballistae still functioned, and the interior buildings had not been burned or bombarded.

Brin had kept men busy with heavy projects. At the other keeps, teams had walled off the smashed gates. Strategic trenches had been dug around the keeps and the town beside the ferry.

Traps had been set along likely approaches the enemy might use. Men fletched arrows and collected stones to hurl from the walls.

After making sure the keeps were fully manned, Galloran had sent forces to upgrade some of the ruins on the north side of the valley that held high ground. He had arranged his forces to defend against the inevitable onslaught from the east and the possible simultaneous attack from the soldiers who currently held the passes.

Rachel could not help noticing that the preparations mostly centered on withstanding the oncoming armies, not on conquering Felrook. Not that she blamed anyone. She didn't have any better ideas. They had sent scouts to probe for weaknesses. Those who made it back had nothing favorable to report.

The military leaders were preparing for the part of the campaign they could understand—how to go down fighting when the approaching armies arrived. None of them had a clue how to even bother Felrook. Every day that went by, it seemed less likely that a last-minute message from Jason could somehow turn things around.

Staring at the implacable bulk of the elevated stronghold, Rachel could not help but wallow in all her old doubts. She had striven to disregard her concerns about the prophecy. She had tried to ignore that their mission appeared increasingly impossible. She had attempted to borrow faith from others, to lean on their judgment in spite of all the evidence to the contrary. And here they were, without a workable strategy, waiting to die.

How long was she supposed to keep hoping? Until the enemy armies came into view? Until her friends had fallen? Until she was dead?

There was nothing else left to accomplish. There were no soldiers to muster, no roads to walk, no preliminary challenges to distract from the final goal. They had reached the end of the road, and victory remained as impossible as it had seemed from afar.

Rachel bowed her head. What if the rest of this depended on her? What if the point had been to get her to Felrook with an army ready to take advantage of the opening she would provide? She was the one person with an invitation into the stronghold. What if she accepted the offer, then found a way to create an opening for Galloran and the others?

Or was she just scared? Did she want to hide inside Felrook to avoid being killed by the oncoming armies? Did she want to call "time-out" and try to save herself and her friends before the war really started?

If she secured immunity for her friends, some might not take it. But some might, once the armies arrived and the cause was lost.

Rachel gazed at Felrook, trying to picture Maldor inside, trying to envision the lurkers. What good was she doing out here? At least if she went inside, she would be taking action. Out here she would sit still, use Edomic to protect her friends when the enemy forces arrived, and then die.

Or else Jason would suddenly reveal some hidden path to victory. Maybe some secret weakness to Felrook? Was that really possible? Was it realistic? And if it happened, might she not still be in a better position to take advantage of the weakness if she were already inside of Felrook?

Her Edomic had gotten strong. The fall of West Keep had offered proof. And she hadn't even reached her limit. Not really. She hadn't lost consciousness like with the zombies. But if she sat still, doing nothing, the help she might otherwise offer would be wasted.

Nobody would ever ask her to accept Maldor's offer in order to spy on him and try to harm Felrook from the inside. Galloran was far too protective of her. If she meant to get involved in that way, she would have to take action on her own.

How could she get to Felrook? She would have to steal a boat or something. Nobody would let her leave East Keep unescorted. And what did she know about handling a boat? She would never get close to Felrook on her own. If Maldor really wanted her, he would have to come and get her.

Rachel slipped off the protective charm necklace. Was she really doing this? There were only a few days left. If she wanted time to accomplish anything after her arrival, it was now or never.

She closed her eyes and projected her thoughts, pushing all her mental energy toward Felrook. *Maldor? Anyone?* She sensed no reply. *I'm not sure if anyone can hear me. I'll accept your offer to come train with you, but you'll have to get me there. I have no way to access your fortress. I'm at the keep east of you. Help me get to you, and I'll come.*

Rachel opened her eyes. Felrook looked the same. She had exerted her will intensely, but she sensed no reply. She slipped the necklace back around her neck. Should she try again from the edge of the lake? Maybe she was too far from the fortress? Was it possible that she had been heard, even though she perceived no response?

Ferrin surprised Rachel, addressing her from behind. "If we could tear down those walls with excessive staring, Maldor would already be homeless."

Rachel could not avoid jumping a little at the sound of his voice. Turning, she tried to smile, hoping she looked less rattled than she felt. How long had he been there? Had he seen her replace the charm necklace? "It's so big."

"I didn't mean to startle you."

"I was getting myself all wound up. I keep trying to see

something that all the others have missed. If they can get me close enough, I could at least throw our remaining orantium at it."

"We would be asking a few gnats to devour a bull," Ferrin said. "We could do some superficial damage with the remaining orantium. We could destroy the gates, but they would collapse the access path, leaving the castle entrance unreachable except by mountaineers. We could shatter some battlements. But to what end? Few enemy lives would be lost, and broken walls can be mended. Better that we use the orantium to defend ourselves. Our foes should pay to claim our lives."

"Do you think it will come to that?" Rachel asked. "A desperate last stand?"

"None of us want that to be the case," Ferrin replied. "Although we came here aware that we would probably fail, some naive portion of us stubbornly yearns for victory. But we have reached the hour when only a miracle could save us. I was sent to fetch you. Galloran wishes to confer."

"With me?" Rachel wondered.

"With those of us who set out from Mianamon together."

"Is there news?"

Ferrin nodded. "None of it good, so far as I understand."

Rachel drew her veil in front of her face. "Who died?"

Ferrin took her hand, his voice softening. "Nobody, as far as we know. We're simply running out of time. Come."

The displacer led her down from the wall, across the busy yard, and into the keep. Rachel had grown accustomed to stares wherever she went. She had learned that if she didn't want attention, she shouldn't dress like a mysterious mourner and show off her magical powers in front of thousands of witnesses. She and Ferrin climbed stairs to the upper hall. Six guards stood at attention outside the heavy doors—two humans, two drinlings, and two seedmen.

Inside they found Galloran, Io, and Tark. Only five companions were left who had set out from Mianamon together. They seemed a tiny group inside the long, airy hall. A fire roared in a huge hearth. The thick stone walls made the keep permanently chilly. The heavy doors thumped closed.

Galloran was not currently wearing his blindfold, but he held it in his hand. He rose and greeted them, offered them seats, then put it on.

"We have had little time to converse in private since marching to war," Galloran began. "Because the end is upon us, I want your counsel without the pressure of unfamiliar ears. Let me lay out our predicament as I understand it, and then please feel free to speak openly."

"Okay," Rachel said. The others nodded.

"Our scouts have been watching the east. The armies of Maldor will arrive in less than three days, their numbers virtually uncountable. If something does not change, no matter what tactics we employ, they will swarm in and massacre us all. We might not even get the opportunity to make them test our best defenses. If they so desired, they could wipe out our unsheltered forces, then lay siege to the keeps. Why storm the walls when they have all the time they desire to starve us out? Of course, if Maldor wishes to crush us faster, the bloodier option remains open."

"Can we run?" Ferrin asked. "Have you considered alternatives to the passes?"

"There are some lesser ways through the mountains," Galloran said. "No doubt you are familiar with some of them—minor trails, no true roads. We could flee into the western wilderness and let our foes hunt us. Some of our best woodsmen might win free, but the majority of our forces would perish in disorganized mayhem."

"Wouldn't that mess up the prophecy?" Rachel asked. "If we ran?"

"It could," Galloran said. "Destroying Felrook was our mission. Whether we fight the oncoming armies or flee them, without an assault of Felrook it seems we would be abandoning the prophecy. Ferrin, have you any idea how near Jason might be to his destination?"

"He keeps the ear well muffled," Ferrin said. "Voices are indecipherable. Anything I hear is faint. I know they were on horseback for several days. Certain sounds of their travel were unmistakable. But now they are on foot. What the change means, I cannot say."

"It could mean they're close," Rachel said.

"It could mean they ran into trouble and had to leave their horses behind," Ferrin said. "I do believe they remain alive and free."

"I wish we could signal our need to them," Galloran said. "Our lack of combat on the way here brought us to Felrook faster than anyone could have reasonably estimated. I'm not sure they could possibly guess our current state of urgency."

"Any progress on cracking Felrook?" Ferrin asked.

"None," Galloran said. "From the outset it appeared to be a problem without a solution. That remains unchanged. We appear to be utterly without recourse."

"Should we try anyway?" Rachel urged. "I mean, if we can't run, and we can't stand and fight, we might as well go down attacking Felrook. It would be the closest thing to what the prophecy wanted. Who knows? If they think we can't win, maybe they won't collapse the path up to the gate. It would be a hassle to rebuild. We have orantium. We have tough fighters. Maybe some of us could get inside. Maybe some warrior could make it all the way to Maldor."

"It would be a futile act of desperation," Galloran said. "But I would prefer it to doomed inaction or to the carnage that would attend a frantic retreat."

"When would we launch such an offensive?" Ferrin asked.

"We should give Jason every possible minute to provide a better alternative," Galloran said. "If we mean to attack Felrook with blind faith, I say we wait until the day before the eastern armies reach us. We will either breach the walls quickly or not at all."

Ferrin rubbed his eyes. "None of these alternatives inspire any hope in me. They are all madness."

"I heartily agree," Galloran said. "Rachel, we could still mount an attack on the gateway to the Beyond and send you home."

Rachel sighed. "It probably wouldn't get me home. Not really. The flow of time between our worlds is messed up. The oracle gave me a certain day that would get me close to my own time. I've been keeping track. That day is still more than four years away."

"Would you rather die than risk ending up in the wrong time period?" Galloran asked frankly.

"I don't know," Rachel said. "I mainly wanted to go home to be with my parents. I'm not sure if I'd want to live at any other time in my world. There are tons of time periods that would be nightmarish for a girl like me who grew up in modern America. Could we use that option as a last resort? If all else fails, maybe we can all fall back to the gateway and escape to my world."

"We would have to plan for it before the last moment," Ferrin said. "Maldor will not want us near his gateway once he has enough soldiers here to impede us. We would have to go there before the eastern armies arrive."

"It might be something to—" Galloran stopped, cocking his head. He pulled off his blindfold. "I sense lurkers." After they had reached Felrook, he had stopped wearing the charm Drake had given him to shield his mind. Galloran had decided that he would rather be aware of the lurkers than try to hide from them. "Closer than usual. More than one, closing swiftly." He rose to his feet, looking around. "They seem to be—"

Upper windows on both sides of the hall shattered, and wraith-like figures bearing swords dropped into the room. Two dashed to block access to the large door at the end of the hall. The other three loosely surrounded the small meeting. All five lurkers held a pair of swords.

Rachel felt a horrible chill. What was going on? Had she done this? Why so many lurkers? Why all the swords?

"This is unprecedented," Ferrin said, rising and drawing his torivorian sword.

"One for each of us?" Tark growled.

"No," Galloran said, his blade ringing as he unsheathed it. "I sense their intent. They want Rachel. They will do anything to take her from us. Three will oppose me at once if necessary."

"Not if I have a say," Io declared. Holding up an empty hand, he marched toward a torivor. The dark being tossed him a blade.

"No!" Rachel shrieked. "Don't fight them!" This wasn't what she had wanted. She had pictured some agent of Maldor helping her sneak away from East Keep alone in the night.

Heedless of her words, Io rushed forward. The lurker resisted him with casual grace. The blades chimed five times before Io was stabbed, and once more before the torivor cut him down definitively.

Rachel whimpered. She couldn't breathe. Her mind felt frozen. Her guts twisted in dreadful knots.

The torivors moved with liquid grace, unhurried but deliberate. The two at the doors came forward. Joined by one of the others, they formed a perfect triangle around Galloran, all facing him, all holding their pairs of swords vertically. Another lurker was nearing Ferrin, while the one who had vanquished Io came toward Rachel.

Tark edged over to stand in front of Rachel, his knife ready. As he leaned forward she laid a staying hand on his solid shoulder. No matter how horrified and ashamed she felt, she could not let this go on any longer or all her friends were going to die.

"No, Tark," Rachel managed, relieved that her voice held steady. "Wait."

None of the lurkers had tossed their swords to begin their duels. Rachel pulled off her charm necklace. *Why so many of you?* she asked the nearest lurker.

You desire passage to Felrook. Five were sent. Five came.

Don't do this, Rachel conveyed earnestly. *Don't harm them.*

Only you can prevent more bloodshed, the lurker informed her. *We will fight if opposed. Have your guardians stand down.*

Rachel looked to Galloran. Every part of her wanted to conceal that she had summoned these lurkers. Had he heard her exchange with them? Would he let her go without an explanation? She could not afford to wait. If she hesitated, her friends would die.

No, Galloran warned her sharply. *Don't succumb. This is extortion. He wants you. This incursion means Maldor is feeling desperate. Jason must be close to his goal.*

Her thoughts felt nakedly obvious. How much did he know? *I called them*, Rachel conveyed. *I asked for Maldor to bring me to him.* Could she explain that she meant to betray the emperor? Would the lurkers overhear? Were they overhearing now?

Rachel, Galloran communicated, the word full of despair. The emotion behind it made her feel lost. The king looked defeated.

I wanted to help, Rachel tried. *We seemed to be at a dead end*.

"It's really quiet," Ferrin said. He was edging away from the lurker facing him. "Are we in the midst of a silent negotiation? I take it they want Rachel?"

"She is willing to go," Galloran pronounced. "You don't need to do this, Rachel. We'll stand with you."

"Don't kid yourself, Rachel," Ferrin said. "He'll ruin you. Don't go because of us. Don't worry about me." He charged his lurker.

"No!" Rachel cried.

The lurker only defended itself with one weapon. Blades blurred and chimed. Ferrin's attack was so intense that for the first couple of moments they almost looked evenly matched. Then Ferrin was dodging away, entirely on the defensive. Then the lurker chopped him in half at the waist.

Ferrin kept swinging, forcing the lurker to crouch and continue defending itself. Ferrin's legs slid the lower half of his body toward the upper half. Within another few swings, the lurker decapitated Ferrin. The headless torso kept fighting. Pressing the attack, the lurker hacked off Ferrin's sword arm.

"*Stop!*" Rachel screamed with her mouth and mind. "*Stop and I'll come! Don't hurt him! Don't kill them or I stay!*"

Still holding two swords, the torivor backed away from Ferrin.

"No, Rachel," Ferrin said, pulling his head back into place. "Take it back." He reached for his arm.

"I'll come," Rachel repeated in a small voice, her gaze shifting to the nearest lurker. It was the only way to protect Galloran and the others. "Leave them alone and I'll come."

The torivor that had slain Io stepped forward. Tark moved to block it. "I vowed to protect you."

"I made my choice, Tark," Rachel said, her voice hard. "This is over. Protect Galloran. Serve him well."

The lurker stepped around Tark and hefted Rachel effortlessly over its shoulder. It radiated cold. She tried not to let her hands touch it.

Be strong, Galloran thought to her with the fierce urgency of a final message. *Do not let him own you.*

The lurkers scattered, heading for the high windows. Rachel's lurker leaped and then climbed the wall like a spider. Her weight seemed to cause it no trouble. *I'll do my best,* Rachel answered. *I'm sorry. I didn't know they would come like this. Win!*

The lurker carried Rachel out the window and down the wall, and crossed the yard at inhuman speed. Startled faces blurred by. Her lurker jumped halfway up a staircase, then onto a roof, and then sprang to the outer wall, nimbly climbing what remained. Once beyond the wall the lurker went from feeling like her own private roller coaster to her own personal race car. Wind gushed over her as they sped to the lake. She felt only mildly surprised when the water failed to slow them.

CHAPTER 26

THE NARROW WAY

It was well into the afternoon before superheated water spewed from the mouth of the Scalding Caverns. At first Jason heard a wet hissing, followed by a sloshing that reminded him of Jugard's cave by the sea. Then foamy water began to drool from the irregular gap along the juncture where the rocky slope straightened into a cliff. The flow of sizzling slaver increased, first gushing, then raging, gusting out in a sideways geyser.

After maybe ten minutes the steamy torrent began to slacken, calming until white froth ceased to bubble from the dark opening. As more minutes passed, the hissing and gurgling diminished until the cave became still. All that remained of the impressive eruption was the moisture glistening on the stony slope, the wetness rather narrow at the cave mouth, then widening until the slope ended at the shore of a sizable lake.

"We're going in there?" Nia asked incredulously.

"Now is the safest moment," Farfalee said. "The instructions specified that the best time to enter is immediately following an eruption."

They had awaited the event for hours. Farfalee and Jasher had already explained that they had to move through the Scalding Caverns quickly. The directions detailed every twist and turn of their route and emphasized that there were several points along the way where additional eruptions could occur. The timing of when scalding water would flood the caverns was inconstant, so the suggested strategy was to make no wrong turns and keep a brisk pace.

The entrance to the caverns was tucked up against an intimidating wall of cliffs that impeded access to the rugged mountains beyond. If they made it through to the far side of the caverns, they would supposedly exit into a tall, narrow ravine that would lead them to Darian.

They had awaited the eruption off to the side of the opening, so it did not take them long to reach the cave mouth. Jasher led the way, followed by his wife. Del and Heg brought up the rear. Jasher carried glowing seaweed, as did Nia, Jason, and Heg.

The beginning of the cave was steep, snug, and relatively straight. Beads of moisture clung to the warm walls, and the heavy reek of sulfur made Jason wrinkle his nose. As they progressed down the long, winding slope, Jason noticed that, unlike in other caves he had entered, the air was getting warmer the farther they went.

They shuffled forward as hurriedly as the moist slope would permit. In many places Jason had to duck or turn sideways. Where possible he braced his hands against the damp walls to keep from sliding. He could not shake the thought that if the cave erupted anytime soon, they would end up like ants exploring a fire hose.

After what seemed like an endless descent, the cave leveled out a little. Unfortunately, the way forward became more cramped. Before long they were crawling on hands and knees, the walls close on either side. Eventually the confining passage opened into a low room with a few branching tunnels, all of them smaller than Jason would have preferred.

After a moment of hasty deliberation, Jasher and Farfalee fell flat and slithered into the smallest opening. Jason ended up behind Corinne, watching the soles of her shoes as he scooted forward. He tried not to picture people getting stuck ahead and behind him, trapping him there until the next boiling eruption washed through. He tried not to speculate whether the heat or the lack of air would kill him first.

Jason hated when the low passage twisted. More than once, contorting his body to scoot around a corner left him panicked that he would get stuck. He felt tempted to shed his gear and leave it behind, but knew he would want it once he reached the far side. He kept worming forward, the muggy air smelling so richly of minerals that he could almost taste the grit between his teeth.

After some time they were able to crawl on hands and knees again; then at last they could walk. The way sloped down some more, twisting enough to leave Jason completely disoriented. The cave remained confining, and they often had to advance by turning sideways. If Aram had been big, Jason doubted whether he would have managed to squeeze through some of the tighter spaces.

The air kept getting hotter. It felt like hiking through an earthy sauna. They passed a misshapen cavity that steadily vented scorching steam. The way dipped lower. From down a steeply branching tunnel Jason could hear water hissing and churning. Everyone else seemed to notice the splashing as well, and by silent agreement they started advancing faster.

After a few more twists, turns, and branching corridors, the odor of sulfur became so oppressive that Jason started to gag. The air grew steamier. Even when he clamped a hand over his mouth, the pungent vapor coated his throat with silty flavors.

Abruptly the way opened into a tremendous cavern. A ledge wrapped around one side of the room. The wide chamber had no floor. Instead, down below, a thick, dark pool churned ominously, belching fat bubbles and noxious fumes.

"A true cavern at last," Heg remarked. "I was beginning to question whether these puny tunnels should be renamed the Scalding Rabbit Holes."

"This chamber is evidence that we're moving in the right direction," Farfalee called back. "Stay with us."

Jason inched out onto the ledge after Corinne. The blistering air stung his eyes, and steam fogged his vision. He tried to breathe through the material of his sleeve to help strain the smothering fumes. The narrow ledge was slick with oily dampness, which made every step risky. He edged forward cautiously, sliding his feet rather than lifting them. To fall would mean certain death.

At the far side of the ledge Jason followed Corinne into a crack in the wall. Bracing against the sides of the fissure, he had to chimney up for twenty feet before reaching where the tunnel continued.

Once the hellish cavern was behind them, they increased their pace again. Jason was relieved to find the air growing a bit fresher. "I can breathe a little," he said.

"What a treat," Corinne replied without turning.

"If the air had gotten any thicker, it would have become solid."

That earned a chuckle.

Their path was trending up more than down now, and they had a little more space to maneuver. From up ahead they heard loud gurgling and sloshing. Jasher started to jog, and the others matched his pace. Drenched in greasy sweat, Jason panted shallowly. His head started to pound.

They reached an intersection where the corridor forked. The sound of heaving water noisily emanated from the left passage. Jasher headed right.

From behind, the sloshing increased to a blustery roar.

"Faster!" Del called.

Their pace increased to a sprint. The cave was growing narrow, so Jason jostled against the sides as he ran, scraping his shoulders. He pulled against the knobby walls where possible to keep his momentum. The muscles in his legs burned, and a sharp pain corkscrewed into his side. The watery roar behind him increased in ferocity. A moist, sweltering gale swept over him. He expected a searing tide to overcome him at any moment.

The tight cave broadened into a roomy cavern. Leg muscles protesting, Jason dashed across the cavern, a couple of paces behind Corinne. He followed her up a slope at the far side of the room and into another cramped tunnel. A jagged stone protuberance slashed the outside of his upper arm as he blundered against it. He hardly felt the pain. Behind him he heard water hissing and surging.

"Duck," Corinne called back to him.

He relayed the message back to Aram and crouched low. Soon he was hurriedly crawling, his knees and elbows suffering because of his haste. His heart hammered rapidly. He felt like a participant in a nightmare marathon designed to drive claustrophobics insane.

"We might be clear," Heg called from behind. "The cavern behind us had many offshoots. I think it absorbed the eruption."

The way sloped more dramatically upward. The air kept feeling less suffocating. They no longer tried to crawl at a sprint, but they continued to hurry. After falling flat to wriggle through a low gap, they could stand again.

Steam vents and threatening gurgles became less frequent. The air cooled and freshened. Jason felt less edgy. The steepness tired his legs, but the evidence that they were on their way out of the subterranean maze boosted his spirits.

At last, drenched and panting, caked with grime, they emerged from an aperture near the bottom of a deep chasm. Vertical walls of rock loomed at either hand, leading to an unreachable strip of sky high above. Water flowed from wall to wall along the floor of the gorge, before slurping underground twenty feet below the gap they had exited.

"The river helps feed the caverns," Farfalee noted. "This is the Narrow Way. We must proceed until we reach the falls."

"Where's the trail?" Nia asked.

"The river is the trail," Jasher replied. "We walk upstream."

Fortunately, the river was not raging. The current was steady, but it slowed where the gorge widened. At some points islands or ledges poked out of the water. Most of the time they slogged upriver with the water level somewhere between their knees and waists.

Unlike in the Scalding Caverns, this water was cool. Almost too cool, though not unbearable. Jasher tried to choose the easiest route, avoiding deep pools and leading them onto ledges and islands wherever possible. On one long island they paused to eat and refresh themselves.

Corinne looked skyward. "Stars are coming out. Why is Aram still small?"

"Could be that the deep gorge is creating a premature twilight," Farfalee said.

"Aye," Aram confirmed. "The way my condition works, standing in a shadowy canyon does not count as sundown. I won't change until the sun drops below the horizon we would see from up top. I've developed a sense for it over the years. Feels like it will be another couple of hours yet."

After the break they plodded onward. In some places they had to wade up to their chests or even swim a little. The gorge grew gloomier with every passing minute. Jason was glad for his seaweed.

While they forced their way forward against a waist-deep current, Jason noticed Corinne shivering. She hugged her elbows close, and her neck was pebbled with gooseflesh.

"Corinne is freezing," Jason announced.

"I'll be fine," she replied hastily, unable to prevent her teeth from chattering. "The evening is warm."

"Water saps heat faster than air," Aram said. "I'm feeling it too."

"We'll pause to recover on the little island up ahead," Farfalee said. She held up a hand. "Wait a moment. Stop and listen." Everyone came to a halt.

"The falls," Nia said.

Jason heard them too. "We've got to be close."

Upon reaching the island, they could find no materials for a fire, but Jasher produced a dry blanket for Corinne to use after she had wrung out her clothes. Nia tirelessly rubbed Corinne's arms, shoulders, back, and legs to help warm her.

Heg stood on the far side of the island beside Farfalee, gazing toward the unseen falls. "Do you suppose we'll reach the falls tonight?" Heg asked.

"I expect so," Farfalee said. "I think we should press on until we get there. The sooner we learn what the seer has to offer, the sooner Galloran can benefit from the information."

"Aram, when will you grow?" Heg called.

"Not much longer."

In a single quick movement Heg drew his dagger and stabbed Farfalee in the chest. Cupping his hand against the back of her neck, he caught her seed as it came free. As her body collapsed, Heg held the bloodstained dagger point to her amar.

"No!" Jasher cried, face contorting with shock and rage as he drew his sword.

Jason had been removing some dried meat from his pack. He remained in a crouch, petrified with astonishment.

"Everyone keep still!" Heg demanded. "It would be tragic to see such a long and illustrious life obliterated."

Jasher restrained himself and gestured for the others to stand down. "What is the meaning of this?"

"We needed to have this conversation at some point before reaching the falls. Now seemed the opportune moment."

"You're not Heg," Del accused. "You can't be. What's going on?"

"Correct," Heg said with a smile. "I have been known by many names. Heg is the most recent. The drinling fought valiantly, by the way, but perished back at Gulba alongside his brethren." Heg's face suddenly transformed, and with it his voice. It was suddenly the face of Groddic. "In recent years I have most frequently been known as Groddic."

Jason could hardly believe his eyes. He stood upright, his hand near his sword. He glanced at the others, trying to gauge how they wanted to deal with this.

"The Wanderer," Jasher growled. "You're Zokar's shape-shifter!"

"I have been known by those names as well," the Wanderer admitted. "None who associate those names with me ever live to tell the tale."

"Groddic was the Wanderer all along?" Aram asked.

"Maldor was the only man alive to know my true identity," the Wanderer said. "We became partners long ago. Out of necessity I get no credit, but I was instrumental in his rise to power. He brings me in to fix his messiest problems. Like this one."

"We killed you," Nia said weakly.

The Wanderer shook his head. "Hard to slay a shape-shifter. I can heal my wounds too quickly, rearrange my insides. I pretended to succumb to my injuries back at Gulba. The decision could have gone either way. I knew I could probably take you. I stayed down because you had horses. Had I revealed myself, some of you might have escaped and spoiled my secret. I suspected a better opportunity would come. And here we are."

"You captured the eagle," Corinne accused, her teeth no longer chattering.

The Wanderer grinned. "I became a jungle condor, a bird much larger than any eagle. I can reshape myself into any living thing I have touched. I have lived a long time, sampled many lifeforms. Including Heg."

Jason thought about his orantium sphere. He couldn't throw it while the Wanderer held Farfalee's seed. He pulled out his sword. Whatever happened, he needed to be ready.

"Why are we talking?" Jasher asked. "Have you an offer?"

"That depends what the amar of your wife is worth," the Wanderer said casually. Keeping the knifepoint near the seed, he examined it speculatively. "I have never disposed of a sitting member of the Conclave."

"If you harm her amar, you will face the eternal wrath of my people," Jasher threatened.

"I have destroyed more than twenty amars," the Wanderer bragged. "There can be no vengeance against secret deeds."

"I cannot guess what terms you could possibly offer," Jasher said.

"Her seed is the only concession I can grant," the Wanderer said. "All Farfalee knew before she was cut off from her senses was that Heg stabbed her. She does not know it was the Wanderer. She did not know that Heg had any connection to Groddic. If you volunteer your amar to me, Jasher, I swear to safely plant her seed."

"What about the others?" Jasher asked.

"The others know my identity. They must die. But your wife could live. If you fight me, she dies along with the rest of you. Make your choice."

Jason held his breath, wondering which way Jasher would lean.

"I don't trust you to keep your word," Jasher said.

"I can alter my face at will," the Wanderer said. "My only lasting identity is my honor. I am not lying. Knowing as little as your wife does, what does it cost me to spare her? I will keep her seed safe until this war is over, and then she will be planted. Who knows? She might emerge as the last of your people."

"How do you propose to claim my amar?" Jasher asked.

"I won't let you near me," the Wanderer said. "Let Del execute you and toss me your seed."

"I would give all my lives for her," Jasher said. "But to do so now would be folly."

The seedman flung a knife and rushed forward, his torivorian blade held high. The Wanderer dodged the thrown dagger and plunged his blade into the seed. Jason felt as if the blade had entered his own body. Casting the seed aside, the Wanderer barely had time to draw Heg's sword before Jasher reached him.

The blades clashed furiously. Del and Nia followed Jasher, but hung back. The narrowness of the island made it hard for more than one attacker to engage the Wanderer unless they did so from the water.

Jason held his orantium globe ready, but there was no way to harm the Wanderer with Jasher in the way. He could hardly believe the Wanderer had stabbed the seed. That simple act had permanently extinguished lifetimes of existence. Another of his friends had fallen.

The Wanderer tried to stab Jasher with his dagger and lost his hand in the attempt. The severed hand dissolved into ashen dust. Jasher pressed a graceful attack, but the Wanderer defended himself with alarming skill. With a shake of his damaged arm, a new hand replaced the lost one.

"Watch the combat for an opening," Aram whispered to Jason. "Groddic stands between us and the waterfall, but while we keep him busy, you could make a run for it. Only one of us needs to survive."

"He can turn into anything he wants," Jason said. "He'd catch me before I went far, whether or not he had to interrupt the fight. We have to beat him."

"Are you about to grow?" Corinne asked Aram.

"Another minute or two," Aram replied, stripping off his clothes. "I should get my armor ready."

Jasher stabbed the Wanderer through the chest, the blade sinking deep, but had to lunge back to avoid a counterstroke. The fight went on. The Wanderer appeared indifferent to the injury.

"We have to cut him to pieces!" Jasher yelled. "No other wound will harm him."

"Many have tried," the Wanderer boasted with a laugh. "I've lost minor portions of myself over the years. More than enough remains to punish the lot of you."

Del and Nia had splashed into the river to get behind the Wanderer, but the shape-shifter fell back to the tip of the island, preventing them from attacking on dry ground. To further complicate matters, the Wanderer sprouted a heavy tail with a bony bulge at the end and used it to threaten the drinlings. Nia hit the bony knob with her sword, and the weapon flew from her hands.

"He has eyes in the back of his head!" Del exclaimed. "Literally!"

"I'm just getting started," the Wanderer laughed.

With a muffled groan Aram started to grow.

The Wanderer's tongue shot out from his mouth and coiled around Jasher's neck. Jasher slashed through it, and the severed portion disintegrated, but the seedman was late blocking the next thrust, and the Wanderer impaled him.

Dropping to his knees, Jasher cut off the Wanderer's legs at the thighs. The Wanderer thumped to the ground and lunged into the river. He did not surface. Del and Nia looked around intently, swords poised.

Still transfixed by the sword, eyes full of pain and frustration, Jasher looked back at Jason. "The amar can be resilient. We can't know the extent of the damage. Plant her immediately. I . . . I still have—"

His sentence was interrupted when his amar dislodged, bouncing off the island and into the water. Jasher slumped lifelessly.

Upstream from everyone, the Wanderer arose from the river. Heg's clothes were gone. His head looked like Groddic, but he was notably shorter. A flexible black shell covered his body like armor. He held no weapon.

Corinne leaped into the water and grabbed Jasher's amar before it could float away. His transformation complete, Aram dashed along the island toward the Wanderer, his enormous sword in hand, his armor jingling.

Rushing upstream, Del reached the Wanderer first. The drinling hacked at his chest, but the black armor withstood the blow.

Clamping an arm against his side, the Wanderer trapped the blade; then spikes sprouted on his free fist, and he killed Del with a punch to the head. The Wanderer kept the captured sword.

Nia fell back, sloshing noisily. "That shell is tough!" she warned everyone.

"Titan crab," the Wanderer said bemusedly. "I often reinforce my bones with the remarkable substance. The shell of the titan crab is the most durable biological material I have encountered. I'll use excessive quantities of it inside of me to disguise my mass when I wish to appear smaller."

"Are you doing that now?" Aram thundered. He waited at the end of the island. "You're looking tinier."

"Jasher robbed me of some mass," the Wanderer agreed. "And it cost me some size to armor myself like this. Come test your sword against me, half man."

"I think I'll keep the high ground," Aram replied.

"I'm between you and your destination," the Wanderer replied. "I am in no hurry. Much like Heg, I require no sleep."

Nia fell back to behind Aram and climbed onto the island. She retrieved Jasher's torivorian sword.

"We have time as well," Aram said. "I'll not be baited."

The Wanderer laughed. "Three of you have already perished. I could slay the rest of you a thousand ways." He dropped beneath the water.

"To me," Aram said.

Swords ready, Jason and Corinne dashed forward to stand beside Nia and the half giant. "I have orantium," Jason said.

"Don't use it too close to us," Aram said. "Jasher had a globe too. Might be worth retrieving." He crouched and slid Farfalee's torivorian sword from its sheath. "When the shape-shifter surfaces, fall back and let me deal with him. I won't let him win."

Kneeling and scrabbling, Corinne searched for Jasher's sphere. Jason scanned the surface of the river.

The Wanderer burst from the water and landed at the other end of the island. For a moment he had gill-slits at his neck, but they were abruptly covered by the glossy black carapace. He still held Del's sword.

Jason flung the orantium sphere low, at his feet. The Wanderer dove forward and caught it in an enlarged, softened hand. Rising to his knees, his hand returning to its normal size, the Wanderer threw the globe back at them.

Dropping his swords, Aram flung Corinne and Jason into the river. Nia dove forward, smothering the globe with her body as it struck the rocky ground.

Jason missed seeing the explosion. He heard it from under the water. When he surfaced, Nia was gone, and Aram lay at the edge of the island, one leg in the river, the side of his face blackened and caked with blood. The Wanderer charged him.

Jason heaved himself from the water. If the Wanderer killed Aram while the half giant was down, they were all dead. Jason got to his feet and gripped his sword as the Wanderer approached at full speed, eyes enraged. Jason had never felt more intimidated, but he stood his ground.

The Wanderer's sword swept toward him. Leaning forward, Jason met the blade with a strong blow from his own. Despite the Wanderer's sprint and the strength of his swing, he came to a skidding halt as his sword was knocked back by the impact. For a moment the Wanderer was unprotected. Advancing, Jason issued a quick counterstroke, narrowly missing but forcing the Wanderer to retreat a pace.

Their swords began to clash fiercely. Jason was mildly surprised to not be immediately cut down. He was mostly on the defensive, slowly giving ground, but he managed to sneak in a few attack strokes. Without the torivorian sword, Jason doubted he could have resisted the heavy blows or swung quickly enough to match the Wanderer's speed. Each slash he survived increased his confidence.

The combat felt different from how he had expected. There was no time to feel nervous. He knew he was fighting for his life, and to protect Aram and Corinne, but all he could focus on was blocking the next blow and watching for chances to attack. There was no time to plan or to give conscious thought to form or footwork. There was barely time to react, and occasionally a narrow opening to strike.

As the fight progressed, Jason felt less and less like he was holding his own. His wrists and elbows began to ache. The Wanderer was so quick and used moves and feints Jason had never encountered. Jason improvised defensive blows and dodged as best he could, but he began to feel sloppy, like he had lost his balance and was about to fall.

Then Corinne attacked Groddic from behind. The shelled warrior turned to confront her, allowing Jason a moment to recover. Her blade kept him busy.

Jason saw the Wanderer staring at him with a large pair of golden eyes on the back of his head. For the moment his rear was unguarded. And clearly Corinne needed help. Jason lunged forward as a tail sprouted from the center of the Wanderer's back. Just before the tip of Jason's sword could reach the Wanderer, the heavy bulge at the end of the tail slammed into Jason's shoulder like a mace, sending him splashing into the river.

Jason surfaced in time to see the Wanderer thump Corinne with his tail while he had her occupied with his sword. She tumbled into the water as well. Teeth bared, the Wanderer wheeled on Aram.

Crawling forward shakily, Aram grabbed Farfalee's torivorian sword, as well as the torivorian sword Nia had dropped. With one side of his leather cloak charred and tattered, the half giant rose unsteadily to meet the attack.

The Wanderer lunged and stabbed at Aram's chest. Raising both swords high, the half giant made no attempt to block the thrust. Instead, he pivoted, so the Wanderer's sword struck his coat of rings at an angle. The tip scraped across the armor, failing to penetrate.

Aram brought the torivorian swords down viciously, severing both of the Wanderer's arms at the shoulders, slicing neatly through the chitinous casing. As the Wanderer struggled to recover, Aram paced forward, torivorian blades hacking in rapid sweeps. Chunks of the Wanderer flew free, turning to dust when parted from his central bulk.

Shrinking as he sprouted new arms, the Wanderer tried a punch and lost the new appendage. The other limb broadened into a defensive rectangle of titan-crab shell, but Aram cleaved it in half. As the Wanderer spun to flee, a brutal horizontal slash bisected him at the waist. The bottom half of the Wanderer crumbled, and Aram savagely attacked what remained. A few more swings, and there was nothing left to cut.

The half giant sank to his knees, breathing hard, as Jason and Corinne returned to the island. Jason's shoulder ached, but he hardly felt the pain through his enormous relief.

"Want to know one of the many things I learned from Drake?" Aram asked without facing them. "With enough force behind them, torivorian blades can tear through the shells of titan crabs. The Wanderer appeared surprised. He had formed a thick shell, and was reinforcing it wherever the blades landed."

"Are you all right?" Corinne asked.

Aram glanced down at himself. "I'll live. I lunged away and got low while Nia shielded me from the worst of the blast. You two bought me enough time to recover. Thanks."

"I shouldn't have thrown it," Jason said, his insides writhing.

"You did the right thing," Aram assured him. "There was no way to anticipate what happened. You aimed low. You did it right. We had to try orantium. The shape-shifter was starting to look unbeatable. He caught the sphere, and Nia paid a price to protect us. That fight could have gone either way, Jason. We got lucky at the end. You two were magnificent. You crossed swords with the Wanderer and will live to tell the tale. I tried to act more stunned than I really was, and the Wanderer took the bait. He expected to finish me quickly. And I suspect he was overconfident about his shell armor. I would wager he has killed many an opponent while they fruitlessly strike at him."

"Are you all right?" Jason asked Corinne.

"I was using Drake's breastplate," she said. "The tail struck me there. How about your shoulder?"

Jason shrugged it, rolled it, and rubbed it. "Sore, but I don't think he broke anything. It might turn an interesting color."

"We got off easy," Aram grunted. "Others paid the price."

"Farfalee," Jason remembered. "Jasher thought she might have a chance if we plant her quickly."

Corinne went and gingerly collected the seed from where the Wanderer had tossed it aside. She held it in her palm while Jason and Aram investigated it. The casing was split on one side. There was no telling how deep the knifepoint had penetrated.

"I'm no expert at growing seedfolk," Aram announced, "but this island seems to be little more than a rock pile. All of the ledges and other islands have been similar. I have seen nothing growing down here. There is no soil, and infrequent sunlight."

"You're right," Jason said. "It won't do her any good to bury her seed under barren rocks."

"Back by the lake," Corinne said. "On the other side of the caverns there were some fertile areas by the lakeside. At least as fertile as the Fuming Waste gets."

"I won't fit through those caves until after dawn," Aram said.

"I can do it," Corinne offered. "I was paying attention to the way."

"I was trying to do the same," Aram said. "There were some puzzling junctions. You don't want to get lost in there."

"There could be fertile ground up ahead," Jason said.

"Possible," Aram allowed, "though not likely based on what I've seen."

Corinne had crouched to rifle through Jasher's pack. "Here is his orantium," she said, holding up the last of their spheres. Setting the globe aside, she kept searching. "I know Farfalee translated the directions. They must be in here somewhere. Here we go." She produced the pages of notes. "Thankfully, he kept them dry."

"I should double-check what I need to do," Jason said.

Holding a glowing strand of seaweed close, Corinne scanned the writing. "I see nothing they failed to tell us. The entrance is under the waterfall. You should enter alone and unarmed. If you are unworthy, you won't survive. There are no further details."

"I hope I'm worthy," Jason said.

"I've been watching all of this closely," Aram said. "That oracle knew her business. If I harbored any doubts before, they have flown. We would not have made it this far without each person she selected. Drake stopped the duel with the torivor. Corinne got rid of the spying lurker. Jason figured out how to defeat the Maumet. Farfalee translated the scroll. And the Wanderer required a team effort. Jasher weakened it. Nia shielded us. That same oracle who chose our team wanted you here, Jason. She would not have sent you to perish as an unworthy trespasser. I don't expect this seer has ever had a more worthy visitor."

The reasoning brought Jason comfort.

"I should go," Corinne said. "I want to get Farfalee and Jasher in the ground."

"It will be dangerous," Aram said. "You won't be able to start immediately after an eruption."

"I would face the same peril whenever I return," Corinne said.

"Let me study the instructions," Aram said. "I paid close attention, and I have a reliable sense of direction. Give me a moment to memorize what I need. Then you bring these pages with you and wait for us on the far side."

"Are you sure you can make it though without them?" Corinne asked.

"I could probably retrace our route even without studying the instructions," Aram claimed. "As we came through, I looked back often. Give me a moment."

The half giant sat staring at the writing, one finger sliding across the words, his lips moving occasionally. At times he would close his eyes, move his lips, and then check himself. Finally, he handed the pages back to Corinne. "Keep out of sight on the other side."

"I'll be careful," Corinne promised. She gave Jason a hug. "You be careful too."

"We'll see you soon," Jason said.

CHAPTER 27

SECRETS FROM THE PAST

By the time Jason and Aram reached the waterfall, the crescent moon peeked down into the chasm, rendering their seaweed temporarily unnecessary. The silver ribbon of water plummeted from a ledge half the height of the gorge, churning in a misty basin at the bottom.

"The water is dropping a long distance," Aram said, gazing upward. "The volume may not look impressive, but it is hitting with enough force to pin a man to the riverbed and keep him there until long after he drowns."

"I'll watch for barrels of air," Jason said.

Aram smirked. "I would approach from the side. If you end up pressed to the ground, claw your way under the falls." He tied a length of seaweed around Jason's wrist.

"I guess I should leave my sword," Jason said. He handed it to Aram. "I'll bring the shield."

"I'll stand guard until you return," Aram promised.

Jason was wet and shivering from hiking up the river. He stared at the falls, psyching himself up for the swim. He considered those who had lost their lives to get him here. Heg and the other drinlings. Drake. Jasher, temporarily. Farfalee, maybe forever. Nia. He had to push away the memories. If he dwelled on them now, he would be unable to go forward. "The secret behind those falls had better be useful," he muttered.

"Amen," Aram agreed.

Jason plunged into the cold pool. He approached the falls from the right, staying close to the wall of the cliff. The closer he came to the base of the waterfall, the more he felt currents tugging at him.

After waving at Aram, Jason held his breath and dove down, grateful for the radiance of the seaweed around his wrist, although at first all he saw was a shimmering screen of illuminated bubbles. The force of the falling water helped him sink quickly. He kicked and stroked hard, trying to get behind the falls. The turbulence actually helped him, drawing him downward and inward.

Sure enough, at the bottom of the basin, below and behind the falls, he found a large gap in the wall. Swimming inside, he passed along a short tunnel before surfacing in a placid pool inside a cavern. Jason breaststroked to where he could walk, then waded out of the water, shivering in the cool air.

Before him Jason saw a bronze door, incongruous against the natural stone of the cavern wall. He stared at it with relief. At least *something* was hidden behind the waterfall. People had died to get him here. Many other people were counting on him.

He wondered what Rachel was doing at the moment. Had Galloran raised his army? Were they on the move against Felrook? Living on the run, Jason and his companions hadn't had the opportunity to get much news. Rachel could be anywhere. He hoped her team was having an easier time than his group had endured. Maybe whatever the door concealed would keep her from suffering too much. After crossing to it, Jason found the door unlocked, and entered.

"Hello?" he called, feeling like an intruder. The word echoed down a long corridor. Beyond the doorway the walls were stone blocks, the floor slate tiles. "Anybody here?"

Leaving the door ajar, Jason crept forward. Eventually the hall turned. Ahead he could see a quivering red radiance. "Hello?"

Again the only answer was his voice returning from the emptiness. At the end of the corridor, Jason reached a circular room with a domed ceiling. Four bronze torches lit the space, held in sconces a few feet out of reach, the flames red as blood. He could not see or smell any smoke. The deep redness of the flames seemed unnatural.

Perfectly round holes of three distinct sizes riddled the wall opposite the entrance to the room. A tiny, neat picture was painted above each hole. Three bronze bins in front of the perforated wall contained spherical white stones, each decorated with a small picture. The stones in one bin were the size of marbles, the next held spheres the size of golf balls, and the last contained stones more comparable to baseballs. The stone spheres seemed to match the three sizes of holes in the wall.

Apart from the holes, engravings textured the wall: runes and glyphs and symbols that Jason had no chance of comprehending. To his surprise, among the foreign shapes and squiggles, he found one concise message in English, the familiar letters etched neatly.

Do not proceed uninvited. Leave behind all weapons. Deliver a single ball to a single hole. Choose wrong and perish.

Jason scrutinized the rest of the wall to make sure he had missed no other legible messages. After finding nothing recognizable, he returned to the section of the wall peppered with holes. There appeared to be equal quantities of small, medium, and large perforations—hundreds in total.

He began studying the little paintings above the holes. The details were so minute that the brush must have been no larger than a whisker. The images seemed totally random: Animals, plants, buildings, symbols, articles of clothing, tools, faces, food, flags, and a variety of other objects were depicted.

How could he know which ball to put in which hole? It had to be a complex lock, like the door at the Repository of Learning. Did the little paintings on the balls match the images on the holes? Could it be that straightforward?

Jason scooped out two handfuls of medium-sized balls and began sifting through them, looking for an image that matched an image on the wall. The little icons on the balls seemed just as diverse as the images on the wall, but he was having trouble finding anything that matched.

He decided to focus on one ball. He chose one decorated with the tusked head of a golden elephant. He liked the image because it was so distinct. Walking along the wall with the ball, he looked for a matching image above a hole. His eyes darted from hole to hole, glancing at everything but with emphasis on the medium ones. His eyes stopped on an image above one of the large holes.

He did not pause because the image was an elephant.

He halted because the image was the face of his father.

Unable to make sense of what he was seeing, Jason stared in stunned befuddlement. He drew close, squinting. The picture was not quite as perfect as a photograph, but it seemed as unmistakable. The resemblance was uncanny, like a really good caricature. But how could that picture be *here*? His father had never been to Lyrian. And this place was supposed to be really old.

Could there have been a man in Lyrian who looked like his

father? Could the artist have imagined a face that happened to look a lot like his father? Could it just be a coincidence?

Darian was supposed to be a seer. The oracle had made it sound like Jason was destined to come here. This couldn't be coincidence. The face was too spot on. This hole mattered.

Unsure exactly what he was looking for, Jason went to the bin of large balls and started sorting through them one by one. Would he find his father's face again? Perhaps it would be an image somehow connected with his father. Like what? His car? His dental office? A toothbrush?

After going through all the large balls, Jason had found no obvious candidate. He supposed a smaller ball could be placed in a large hole, so he moved down to the medium spheres. He stopped sorting through them when he found his mother's face.

The image gave him chills. It was just as accurate as the picture of his father. This was no coincidence.

Jason looked around. Was he really still in Lyrian? This almost felt like an elaborate practical joke. He half expected friends to jump out and yell, "Surprise!" But no friends appeared. There were no hidden cameras either. Just torches and a gloomy old room. Gazing at the image of his mother, Jason thought about all that had happened to bring him to this place. It was no joke. No accident. He was supposed to be here.

Confident that he had found the correct match, Jason placed the medium ball into the hole under his father's picture, then backed away. He could hear the ball rolling, followed by some clicks, and suddenly the floor of the room began to gradually descend.

Jason considered retreating to the hallway, but he opted instead to stay put. As the floor sank deeper, a passageway was revealed. When the floor rumbled to a halt, he could see down a long corridor lined with red torches. Apparently, he had made a decent choice.

The long corridor ended at a large square room with multiple circular tunnels in three of the walls. Four sconces held four more burning torches. Mystifying engravings decorated the fourth wall. Among them Jason found a brief message in English.

Proceed along the passage of your choice.

All the round tunnels were the same size—small enough that he would have to crawl. To reach some of the tunnels he would have to climb using the openings to lower tunnels. Tiny paintings wreathed the mouth of each tunnel.

Jason started studying the images, wondering if he would encounter another familiar face. To the side of one of the higher tunnels on the opposite wall from the entrance, Jason found a familiar logo—the profile of a white batter silhouetted against a blue and red background, a white ball coming his way. It was the logo for Major League Baseball!

That had to be for him, right? Baseball didn't exist in Lyrian, and Jason loved both watching and playing the sport.

Just to be sure, he investigated the pictures around all the other tunnels. None of them resonated like the baseball logo. That had to be it.

Jason climbed back up to the baseball tunnel and started crawling down it. He had not gone far when a heavy gate clanged into place behind him, sealing off his retreat. Without his seaweed Jason would have been left in darkness.

The round tunnel curved, climbed, descended, and turned. His elbows and knees throbbed, still tender from crawling too rapidly in some of the tighter sections of the Scalding Caverns, but his only choice was to press onward.

At length, without ever forking, the tunnel emptied into the largest room yet. Against the walls eight brazen dragon heads were spaced around the room, each bigger than a pickup truck. In the center of the room three bronze bins held stone balls. Holes of three sizes pocked the floor around the bins. Elsewhere on the floor were engraved messages. Jason skimmed the spidery runes until he located the message in English.

Drop one ball down one hole.

"I could have probably figured that out on my own," Jason said to nobody, his voice echoing gently.

Again pictures adorned the balls, and the holes in the floor had accompanying images as well. It took some time, but Jason eventually found a small ball with a tiny portrait of his sister, and a large hole beside the smiling face of his brother.

After dropping the ball down the hole, Jason heard it rolling, then rattling, followed by multiple noisy crunches. Hinges squealing, one of the dragon heads yawned open, revealing another corridor.

Jason trotted down the corridor until it delivered him to a vast hall. Torches hung high against the walls, leaving the middle of the chamber heavily shadowed. Containers of every description crowded the entire length of the floor, some resting on tables or platforms, others unsupported. The collection included trunks, chests, crates, baskets, coffers, cabinets, caskets, coffins, sarcophagi, barrels, kegs, strongboxes, jewelry boxes, and covered vessels. Exemplifying unlimited styles and sizes, the diverse containers were fashioned out of combinations of iron, bronze, copper, tin, stone, wood, ceramics, gold, silver, crystal, jade, ivory, enamel, and wicker. Wide varieties of craftsmanship were represented, from the ornate and the elaborate to the plain and even the shoddy.

At the far end of the room, illuminated by extra torches, rose a dais surmounted by a majestic throne. Plinths supported identical female statues at either side of the dais, and a broad altar rested upon a lower platform at the front.

This had to be the destination! He had made it! He could hardly believe his eyes.

"Hello?" Jason called, interrupting the silence of the cluttered hall. "Darian? Anybody?"

Lonely echoes formed the only response.

Weaving among the numberless containers, Jason made his way across the long chamber. As he neared the dais, he realized that what he had mistaken for an altar was actually a crystal-and-gold casket with a body inside. The casket rested atop a granite slab with abundant writing on the side. Among many unrecognizable glyphs Jason found the words "Darian the Seer."

Jason jogged to the casket. Inside rested an old man, small, shriveled, a few wisps of white hair on his spotted head. He wore scarlet robes embroidered with golden designs. Matching slippers covered his bony feet. His eyelids were closed and sunken. His lips were sewn shut. There was a yellowish cast to his wrinkled skin. He had clearly been embalmed.

Shivering, Jason gazed at the cadaver. This was an eerie place to encounter a dead body on display. How long had it been here? People had warned him that Darian should be dead. Still, he could hardly believe that this long, hard road had led him to a corpse. Why had the oracle sent him here?

Just in case, Jason tapped on the glass. "Hello? Are you kidding me? Hello?"

The cadaver did not stir.

Jason looked around in disgust. A gaping, blackened fire pit was set into the stone dais between the throne and the casket. From his slightly elevated position, he surveyed the enormous hall. The disorderly profusion of strange containers made the room look like a flea market or some overgrown garage sale.

He was meant to be here. The oracle had insisted. The faces of his family proved it. He had reached the end of the path. He had found Darian the Seer. Well, sort of. The old guy was fairly well preserved, but no more alive than a mounted deer head.

What was the point? Had his friends suffered and died for nothing? Had Galloran marched off to fight a hopeless battle?

Jason scrutinized the body. The face looked peaceful. Jason studied the faint white eyebrows, the curve of the slightly hooked nose, the little knob of the chin.

Backing away from the casket, Jason looked around the room high and low. Cupping his hands around his mouth, he shouted, "Hello? Anyone? I need some help!"

His plea went unanswered.

There had to be more to this. He roamed the dais and found engravings on the back of the large throne. He hunted eagerly for an English message among the nonsense and found it toward the bottom.

Open a single container. You will either find a prophecy, or you will die. Do not disturb more than one.

A flood of relief temporarily overwhelmed Jason. The seer had died, but he had left prophecies behind. Maybe this wasn't a dead end after all.

Returning to stand beside the casket, Jason stared out at the sea of containers. Which would the old seer have expected him to pick? Jason scowled. Would there be an obvious clue? A familiar face? What if he selected the wrong one?

Leaving the dais, Jason roamed among the receptacles. At first he felt most drawn to the big wooden chests bound in iron, partly because they looked like pirates might have hidden treasure inside. But there were numerous chests of that description. He scoured some for clues but found nothing. He decided he should look for something more unique, a container that related to his life in some way. He found a porcelain vessel shaped like a titan crab. The top of it obviously could be lifted off. But the titan crab had been a negative experience, so he kept looking.

Maybe he should pick the fanciest box he could find; then he could keep it. Something with jewels. Would Darian have foreseen he might choose that way? He examined a delicate ivory coffer inset with enamel and crusted with sapphires. It would be worth a fortune. But did it reflect anything about him? What box would Darian most expect him to select?

Paying close attention, unsure what exactly he hoped to see, Jason wandered aimlessly. He looked for words in English, or references to his world, or people he knew, and generally tried to stay open to any item that might call to him. He meandered for a long time. Many objects looked unique or valuable, but he could find nothing that he considered more personally suited to him than the rest.

Maybe he had already passed the container he should have chosen. Maybe he should have gone with his first instinct. Which had been the first container he had wanted to open? A big chest back near the dais. But wouldn't most people choose something near the dais? After reading the instructions, the first containers they encountered would be those by the dais. Maybe he should go to the far side of the room. Or maybe he should go back to the crab. Or the priceless ivory box. No, if he had been meant to choose those, he would have already done it, right?

Staring at the ground, Jason strolled away from the dais until he approached the far end of the room. Closing his eyes, he turned in a circle with his finger extended, came to a stop, and peeked. He was pointing at an elaborate container the size of a lunch box, carved out of glossy golden wood. It was an impressive piece of workmanship, but the embossed images were all vines and flowers. It looked sort of girly.

Jason sat down on the floor. Maybe he was going about this all wrong. If Darian was such a great seer, shouldn't the message be waiting in whatever box Jason opened? If the task was to guess what container Darian would have picked for him, the cause was hopeless. There were just too many possibilities. Who knew what criteria the seer would have used? But if Darian could really see the future, it shouldn't matter which box Jason picked. Whatever he chose would have to be the right one.

Standing up, Jason looked around. A golden coffer inlaid with tear-shaped jewels and lustrous pearls caught his eye. Resisting the urge to second-guess his decision, he walked over and opened it. The coffer did not explode. No poisonous gas leaked out. Inside he found a scroll.

Sitting and crossing his legs, Jason unrolled the scroll and found a message in English addressed to him. Relief flooded through him, and he began to read.

My Esteemed Lord Jason,

Although we have never met, I feel as if I know you. I have watched you extensively from afar. Should you ever read these words, you will have obtained them at great cost. You will certainly have reason to grieve, and you probably feel distraught and alone. Know that I appreciate what you and your comrades have suffered in order to receive my counsel. On behalf of Lyrian, I thank you.

Tears blurred Jason's vision. He wiped them away. Strange how appreciation in a note from some dead guy could matter, but it did. He felt a little less alone.

Please pardon my grasp of your language. I apologize in advance if anything I express seems unclear. I have not yet had occasion to communicate in English during my lifetime, nor do I expect to enjoy the opportunity before I expire. I learned your language exclusively by gazing into my flames. My only firsthand practice has involved the composition of messages to potential readers fluent in the future common tongue of Lyrian.

You possess a curious nature. The vital words I must share are few, so allow me the luxury of explaining my mission. Toward the end of my life, I learned to see the past and the future in exquisite detail. Through my visions I recognized that I was the truest seer Lyrian would ever know, and I beheld that without my aid Lyrian would fall into darkness.

I left my home and absconded to a remote setting where I could better control who would access my prophecies, a place that would endure until after my last prophecy held any relevance. You have found that secret lair. I tried to ensure that you would reach my final resting place through assignments given in other prophecies. One of those requests sparked the creation of the Petruscan scroll that led you here.

Although I enjoy vivid visions of the future, I cannot always be certain which of the branching paths the future will take. I see a multitude of possibilities with tremendous clarity, many of them conflicting. There are numerous possible futures where you never read these words. If you are reading these words, many other prophecies I authored have become irrelevant. I have done my best to guard Lyrian as far into the future as I could foresee. Only the coming years will reveal the degree of my success.

More than five thousand prophecies reside in this room.

At best fewer than fifteen hundred will actually be read. At worst just more than seventy will be shared. Beyond the five thousand prophecies the room also houses more than a hundred thousand lethal traps, most involving poisons of one sort or another. The vast majority will never claim a life.

I have done what was necessary to protect my messages. I have foreseen many who will seek to undo my work, and I have ensured that if they find their way here, they will perish.

You recognized clues to reach this chamber. A variety of choices lead to this room. Many more alternatives lead to certain death. I spent a great deal of effort ensuring that the choices of those I wanted here would bring them safely to this hall, while also ascertaining that the choices of my enemies would prove fatal.

I did not use clues on any of the receptacles that hold my messages in an effort to thwart cunning enemies who might use such a hint to intercept a prophecy meant for another. I trusted my visions to get my scrolls into the intended hands.

You were meant to find this message, Jason. In truth, of all the prophecies available here, yours is one of the most precious. If you read these words, it is because Lyrian teeters at the brink of unending darkness.

Should Maldor succeed, I am unable to view a time when Lyrian recovers. And I can see well beyond your day. Before the end of his reign Maldor will raise up others like him, and their dynasty of tyranny will endure for centuries beyond counting. Perhaps the only blacker end I have perceived for Lyrian involves the plague of Ebera sweeping the continent, an eventuality which has been prevented for the present if you have obtained these words.

I know you have fretted over why you were chosen to obtain this prophecy. Allow me to help alleviate that distress. It might be of comfort to know that some of the greatest figures throughout history have failed to recognize their own worth. In short, only with your involvement was there a chance for any who opposed Maldor to succeed.

Jason reread the words. Could they be true?

I can see that you will doubt my words. You want reasons. You want to understand. I will cite a few examples. If you are reading this message, you helped make key choices that saved your mission. You took action at pivotal moments that rescued your mission as well. But perhaps more than anything, your influence was required to assemble a team of dissenters with a chance for success. You were like a conscriptor working against Maldor. Without you the quest for the Word would not have been revived, and Rachel would have only associated briefly with Galloran. Nedwin would have never located his master. Tark would have never joined the cause. Nor Drake. Nor Aram. Nor Ferrin.

From across time I searched far and wide for a champion to rescue Lyrian. I had to search beyond our boundaries. Of any I could lure here, only you made victory possible. Both your direct actions and your indirect influence were necessary to give the free people of Lyrian a chance to avoid the tyranny of Maldor. Do not doubt your worthiness. Without you, in every scenario I examined, victory stayed entirely out of reach.

It remains to be seen whether all the rebels you united will play their parts as well as you have played yours. As you read this, victory remains possible, although by no means certain.

You came here for knowledge. The information I have for you will not assure victory. But it will make victory possible.

I helped steer the prophecies that brought you here. The oracle Esmira lacked the talent to upset Maldor's aspirations. I mean no insult to her gift. Even to me the problem appeared nigh insurmountable, and in the end our combined efforts might fail. For the good of Lyrian I reached out to Esmira from across the ages and helped guide her visions. We communed most clearly at the end of her life. I could not show her all she needed to know, but I was able to convey enough to point Galloran in the proper direction and to direct you here to discover the rest.

There are occasions when knowledge proves more powerful than physical might. Maldor commands with Edomic more potently than I, and his armies vastly outnumber the host Galloran has assembled. But one secret from the past can give Galloran the advantage he needs. The secret is ancient even in my time. I learned it by looking back, not forward. The message you must share with Galloran is that the mount where Felrook now rests was once known by another name. In ages past it was called Mount Allowat.

Jason paused. The name seemed vaguely familiar, but he could not place where he had heard it.

This knowledge may baffle you at present, but Galloran will surely grasp the relevance. Let us hope for the sake of Lyrian that it will help him achieve victory.

I have a second message for you to relay. It pertains to

your past, and my future. Again it is not a clue that you will decipher, but it may be of service to another. The message is for Rachel. It may save lives and spare you some grief. Tell her that Orruck already taught her all she needs to know. The former apprentice of Maldor meant to turn her into a weapon, and he shared a certain command he had crafted back when he aspired to overthrow Zokar. The command might serve her well in an hour of need.

These two messages are what you came to learn. Do not bother with the eagles. If the ear of the displacer does not suffice, the cause is already lost.

I have a final prophetic suggestion for you, Jason. This last message will only become relevant if you succeed and thwart Maldor. Lyrian will face many future dangers. You and Rachel came here from the Beyond. At the appointed time, for the good of Lyrian, one of you must return home, and one must stay. If you both stay, or if you both go, Lyrian will eventually fall.

That concludes the information I have to share. Never return here, Jason. There are no additional messages for you. Come again and you will die. To exit, press the round red jewel near the top of my throne.

Should Maldor fall, if your daughter ever has need of me, you may inform her that a prophecy awaits. Now speak to the ear and rejoin your friends.

From ages ago I bid you a fond farewell and wish you a bright future.

Your humble servant,
Darian

Jason could hardly see through his tears. He felt relieved to know how he had contributed, but he also felt torn about Drake, who he had personally involved and who had died as a consequence. Would others he had involved die as well? Had others died already? He felt relieved to have information to share with his friends, even though he didn't understand how it would help. And he wasn't sure how he felt about staying forever in Lyrian. If he was going to have a daughter here, he had to be the one to stay, right? Or was the daughter just one of the many possible futures?

After getting his emotions under control, Jason looked around the lifeless room, half surprised to find himself still alone. He had not felt lonely while reading. He had almost felt as if Darian were here with him. Technically, he was, Jason realized, gazing across the room at the casket.

Jason dug into his pack. He pulled out a little case bundled in rags. Pulling apart the rags, he opened the case and withdrew an ear wrapped in linen. Jason unwrapped the ear and held it to his lips.

"Ferrin," he said loudly, spreading the scroll in front of him so he could use it as a reference, "if you are asleep, wake up. If you're busy, stop to listen. Ferrin, I have the prophecy. It came straight from Darian, just like the oracle promised. We'll send the eagles as well, but you should bring it straight to Galloran. Please be true. Please don't betray us. Most of us died to get here. Corinne, Aram, and I are the only ones left. Farfalee might have lost her seed. We had to kill Groddic, who turned out to be the Wanderer.

"I'm rambling. Let me give you the message. I'm not totally sure what it means, but the mountain that Felrook is on was once called Mount Allowat. Darian thought that would be important. Also, he had a message for Rachel. Orruck already taught her what she needs to know. I guess it has to do with one of the Edomic commands he shared with her. It was something he invented to harm Zokar. That's all I was told. I hope it makes sense to you guys. I'll repeat the message again in a few minutes. I hope the battle is going well."

There was no way for Jason to confirm whether Ferrin had heard, but he intended to repeat and repeat and repeat to be sure. The ear felt warm and was not bleeding, so he knew the connection remained intact and Ferrin was alive. According to Darian, all their hopes now rested with the displacer.

CHAPTER 28

THE LAST WIZARD

Rachel waited for hours in the room where the torivor had left her. The lurker had delivered her through the window after scaling a high wall. She had been braced for a swift introduction to Maldor, but instead she had been admitted to Felrook without any formal greeting.

The room was comfortable, with a generous bed, rich carpets, an impressive desk, multiple chairs, a wardrobe, a bookshelf, and a table in the corner complete with a covered tray of food. There was a separate room for bathing, and beyond that a water closet. But the locked door was solid iron, and the window had no ledge. No matter how comfortable, the room was a prison.

After nightfall Rachel had used Edomic to light some of the candles and lamps around the room. She ate all of the food on the table and was especially grateful for the fresh fruit. Opening her window, she looked out at the night. The view felt like she was gazing from a mountaintop, easily the highest point in the valley. Cool air swished into her room. She was in no mood to sleep.

Io was dead. The pain and guilt of it stewed deep inside. Not only had she probably made a massive mistake by accepting the invitation to train with Maldor, but she had gotten Io killed in the process. She had not known Maldor would send armed lurkers. And she hadn't known Io would leap immediately to her defense against unbeatable foes. But even so, his death had been a direct result of her choice.

Rachel tried to shift the awful blame from herself to Maldor. The emperor had made her choice necessary in the first place. Without him none of this would be happening. He had sent the lurkers while she was with others instead of when she was alone. After what had happened to Drake, Rachel could not have imagined how she could hate Maldor any more, but somehow she was finding a way.

When the iron door opened, Rachel started, almost dropping her glass as she filled it with water from a pitcher. She had heard no footsteps to announce the visitor. Steadying herself, she took a sip and set the glass down.

A tall, spare man with close-set eyes and a narrow face waited in the doorway. He wore black robes overtopped by a gray mantle. Several guards stood behind him. "Good, you're awake. His Excellency will see you now."

"Is that an invitation or an order?" Rachel asked.

The man gave a faint shrug. "An invitation first."

Mustering her will, Rachel wanted to order the officious man onto the floor. She could do it. Then she could give the guards distracting commands and race past them. But race where? She would be wiser to form a plan before she revealed all she could do with Edomic.

"Fine," Rachel said, putting on her hat. She had held it tightly while riding the torivor. Now she arranged the veil to hide her face.

"Come with me," the man invited.

"Who are you?" Rachel asked as she stepped out into the hall.

"A servant of little import," the stranger replied. "An administrator of sorts. I am called Damak."

"I know your name," Rachel said. "You questioned Jason. You're Copernum's grandfather."

"I serve Maldor according to my talents," Damak replied. "Perhaps one day I will serve you as well. But not today."

He led her down some steps, through guarded doors, along a hall, through another set of guarded doors, and around a couple of corners. Then they reached an iron door at the end of a hall. Damak used a key to open it.

"I have the girl," he announced.

"Send her in," a voice replied. Rachel recognized the voice from her dream, although it sounded a bit more ragged. "Alone. Wait without."

"As you wish," Damak replied. He motioned Rachel through the door, then closed it behind her.

Sumptuously furnished, the spacious apartment was gloomy. All the curtains were drawn. Scattered candles provided pockets of light. Her veil further darkened everything, but she kept it in place. A figure stirred in a cushioned chair across the room. Blankets covered the slumped form.

"Come closer," Maldor beckoned. "Let me have a look at you."

Rachel stepped toward the speaker.

"Close enough," he said as she drew near his chair. "Turn around."

She obeyed, rotating once.

"I approve of your apparel," Maldor said. "Image matters more than many appreciate. I will have similar outfits tailored. Remove the veil."

Rachel took off the entire hat, setting it on a dark-red sofa.

Maldor leaned forward into the candlelight. She gasped. His features were the same as in her dream, but he looked ill. His skin was pale with a clammy sheen, his hair greasy, his face deeply lined, his eyes bloodshot, one more than the other. Pink drool leaked from one side of his mouth. Half of his face sagged limply, as if paralyzed.

"You find me alarming," Maldor said. Not all of his mouth moved when he spoke.

"You look sick."

"I suppose I must. Thank you for coming, Rachel."

"It seemed to be my only choice," she replied.

Maldor coughed several times into his fist. He held up a finger to indicate he would respond in a moment. After the fit ended, he dabbed his lips with a handkerchief. It came away bloody. He cleared his throat. "It was your only reasonable choice. You could have elected to die with your friends."

"Your lurkers killed one of my friends," Rachel accused.

"How unfortunate," Maldor said without conviction. "You asked for safe passage to Felrook. Your message was received by my torivors and relayed to me. I assessed the situation and dispatched an appropriate escort. It required no small effort, but I knew that there might be some who would intervene, regardless of what you desired. Please, sit down."

Rachel sat on the sofa beside her hat. Had she done that voluntarily, or had there been a suggestion buried in his request?

"Normally, I would not let anyone see me in this state," Maldor said. "As I mentioned a moment ago, image is important. But you are not just anyone. We must have an honest relationship. I want you as my pupil, Rachel. I want you as my apprentice, perhaps even one day as my friend. I want to witness the heights to which you will rise. I chose to let you see me like this so that you could behold the price I was willing to pay to bring you here."

"You're not sick," Rachel realized. "Sending the lurkers did this to you."

"Correct," Maldor said, one hand straying to the dark jewel in the pendant around his neck. "I am already recovering. I was in much worse condition scant hours ago. I summoned you as soon as I felt I could hold a conversation. All of this will heal." He gestured at his face. "The numbness is temporary. I almost over-reached. I do not intend to send out five torivors bearing swords ever again. You understand why I did it?"

"To make sure nobody stopped me from coming?"

"Exactly. To ensure you reached me. This conflict is over. I do not need to slay you or Galloran or Ferrin to win this war. The war ended the day Galloran marched his army through the pass. But with my armies poised to descend, I had to get you out of that keep before the opportunity vanished. You almost waited too long to make your choice. I do not relish injuring myself. I do not delight in straining my relationship with the torivors. I do not enjoy freeing five of my finest servants from their obligations with only one of them having claimed a life."

"They're all free?" Rachel asked.

"All five. That is the price for sending them out with swords. And they needed swords. Had they been unarmed, Galloran might have cut down all of them. Had they failed in their mission, it would be one thing. I can accept losing a torivor if it is defeated. But I commanded them to stand down if you agreed to come here. I harmed my health and lost five of my elite to bring you to me. And I would have done more."

"Why do you care so much?" Rachel asked. "You can't possibly trust me."

"Indeed?" he chuckled. "Trust has never been my habit. I have seen too many great wizards fall because they trusted apprentices."

"Then why do you want me? As a slave?"

Maldor chuckled again. It grew into a cough. "I need no more servants. I have plenty. All of Lyrian. I will install safeguards much more reliable than trust. You will be my apprentice. I only ask that you learn from me."

"What if I don't want to learn from you?"

He smiled with the side of his lips that worked. "I realize that you do not wish to become like me. But I know you want to learn more about Edomic. You do recall that I visited your mind. I am the last wizard in Lyrian, Rachel. None remain who can teach you the secrets of our order. You cannot begin to imagine the possibilities."

"If I work hard, maybe someday I can cough up blood too."

"I understand your hostility. I am not a pleasant adversary. Unfortunately, when you came to this world, you became involved with the losing cause."

"We haven't lost yet," Rachel said.

Maldor chortled. "Of course not. The prophecy! I had almost forgotten. Surely you realize that the prophecy allowed me to plan the perfect trap. I knew where my enemies were going, and I strategized accordingly. The prophecy only hastened their demise."

"We haven't lost yet," Rachel repeated.

"They have. Not all of them are dead yet, but they have lost. You haven't. You earned one last chance. Rachel, at this point hope becomes salt in the wound. You would be wiser to let go. I dispatched my finest servant to stop Jason and his friends. There will be no quarter given. They will all be killed. The tactic lacks subtlety, but at this juncture it is the prudent course. This servant never fails, Rachel. He is the same individual who brought me Galloran. In all probability Jason and those who accompanied him are already dead."

"But you're not sure," Rachel said.

"Not yet. I will be soon. Obviously, Galloran and the others will perish at my leisure."

"Don't I get to spare ten of them?" Rachel asked.

Maldor paused. "That was the initial agreement. I never canceled the bargain. Very well. Prepare a list, and I will honor it to the best of my abilities. You understand that the blame for any of your comrades who are already dead because you took so long cannot be placed on me."

"I'll blame you as much as I want," Rachel said. "You killed Drake."

He held up a finger. "I meant to kill Jason. Drake died because he intervened."

"You disgust me."

"Do not test me, Rachel," Maldor warned. "I find your raw Edomic talent intriguing. Partly through my doing, it has become a scarce commodity. But you are far from essential. I have been lenient today because I am aware that this transition will be difficult for you. You need to remember that the apprentice does not disparage the master."

Fuming silently, Rachel held her tongue. If she seemed too defiant, it might be even more obvious that she had come here hoping to open Felrook to an attack.

"I'm glad to see you have some restraint," Maldor said. "A little is better than none."

"How will this work?" Rachel asked.

"Our arrangement? Do not fret about that until after your friends fall. I assume you came here still hoping to aid Galloran in some way. Foolish, but predictable given your history."

Rachel frowned. Had he read her mind? Or was it really so obvious? "Why would you be here alone with me if you thought that?"

Maldor smirked lopsidedly. "You ask as if you could possibly pose a threat to me while I am conscious. Are you really that arrogant? Or perhaps just ignorant?"

Rachel felt her cheeks growing hot.

"Rachel, I don't worry about the threat you pose today. I don't worry about the threat you will pose next year. You have talent, but you are barely a sapling. One day, after decades of training, if you reach your full potential, you could pose a threat, which is why safeguards will be installed at the outset. If you were a threat to me now, I would have little right to take you as an apprentice."

Rachel nodded woodenly. Was he really so superior? Or was he trying to con her? Maybe he underestimated her. She couldn't wait years to challenge him. Galloran had less than three days. Would she get another chance like this? One on one, with Maldor weakened from sending out torivors? Here he sat, leering crookedly and coughing like a weak old man. If she meant to take action against him, this could be her best and only chance.

Maldor wiped his lips. "You really are a stranger here in this world. You do not appreciate who I am. Perhaps that is for the best. Insulting to a degree, but also strangely refreshing. As our relationship progresses, I will share with you some of my abilities, to establish primacy. You should not have to serve as my apprentice while doubting my prowess."

Rachel looked around the room. Her attention focused on a sheathed dagger resting on an end table. They were alone, Maldor seemed totally off his guard, and she would probably never find him in a weaker state. Speaking a command, Rachel unsheathed the blade; then, pouring all her fear and frustration into the directive, she drove it toward the form bundled on the chair.

Maldor mumbled words, and the dagger curved away from him, stopping with the point less than an inch from Rachel's throat. How had he done that? She had pushed hard enough to send that knife through Maldor and the chair behind him, yet it had completely slipped from her mental grasp. Motionless, she stared at it, sweat beading on her brow. Speaking in silence, Rachel tried to grab the knife with her mind, but it felt more slippery than a living thing.

"It will take more than that," Maldor said, letting the dagger fall. "However inept, that was unwise."

Angry and embarrassed, Rachel ordered his chair ablaze, throwing everything she had into the effort. Flames would erupt all around him. Both chair and occupant would swiftly be reduced to cinders. Maldor muttered a brief phrase, canceling her command. The gathering heat dispersed, and Rachel fell to the floor, her body shuddering uncontrollably. As the seizure subsided, Rachel was left with a queasy stomach and a blinding pain behind her eyes. She knew that Maldor had not directly afflicted her with any of the symptoms. They were the consequences of her failed Edomic mandate.

"Fire is more easily quenched than summoned," Maldor instructed. "You leave yourself extremely vulnerable if you try to call fire in the presence of another wizard. Would you care to attempt another attack? You are looking unwell, Rachel. As much as my misery would enjoy the company, perhaps you should yield."

Rachel fought to her feet. Her head was pounding. Her good judgment warned that he was clearly her superior. To attack again would only give him another opportunity to harm her. But she could not surrender. Her friends were counting on her to be strong.

In Edomic she suggested that Maldor fall to the floor. He

flinched forward and then tensed for a moment, lips trembling, bloodshot eyes furious. After an instant he relaxed and began growling suggestions of his own. Rachel found herself picking up the fallen dagger and holding the tip to her throat. He kept talking. Rachel tried to resist his suggestions, but the words were making her hazy. She found herself sitting down on the sofa and pricking both of her thighs with the dagger and then plunging it into a cushion beside her. None of the actions had been her decision. Nobody at Mianamon had ever been able to make her feel this helpless. She was little more than a puppet. Maldor stopped talking, and she sagged back against the sofa, breathing hard, dizzy. Her skull felt fragmented. Her ears ached deep inside.

"How dare you seek to control a will such as mine?" Maldor spat, real anger coloring his tone for the first time. "Attempt it again, and I will open your throat for such insolence."

Rachel heard him as if from far away. It was almost impossible to focus on anything but the pain flashing through her skull and raking the backs of her eyes. Dimly she grasped that Maldor was so outraged because her suggestion had momentarily worked. For one tiny instant, a period no longer than the space between heartbeats, he had almost obeyed. Only with real effort had he resisted. And he had not liked that at all.

"I can see that you are in no condition for further conversation," Maldor continued. "Allow me to briefly explain the terms of your apprenticeship. Whether to test me or to flaunt your inability, you have shown yourself capable of treason. As insurance against further treachery, I will give you the eye and the ear of trusted displacers and bind a key word to you that will enable me to destroy you at my leisure. I believe you are familiar with the concept. By coming here you have already accepted this apprenticeship and the attending safeguards.

"At present you require rest. I want you healthy in time to watch my armies crush the pitiful allies you brought into my valley. I may deem that the pain incidental to your failed assassination is punishment enough. Or I may decide otherwise. Either way I will have my servants prepare a concoction that will hasten your recovery. For now you have my permission to sleep."

Maldor uttered a brief Edomic suggestion, and consciousness fled.

CHAPTER 29

DESTINY

Staring from the window of his room at East Keep, Tark contemplated the virtues of a singlehanded assault against Felrook. Beneath a sickle moon, pale highlights gleamed on the black stone of the fortress, making it appear only half-substantial in the darkness, a ghostly blend of light and shadow.

Tark gripped the windowsill. His hands were large and strong for his stature. He felt the edges of the masonry digging into his calloused fingers. How would he mount his solitary assault? Paddle across the lake, cloaked in darkness? Quietly scale the cliffs and then the wall? Or would it be more honest to charge up the path in broad daylight? After all, the point was to die.

He bowed his head, reliving Rachel's abduction in his mind. Lord Jason had charged him to protect her. Io had fallen defending her. Even the displacer had risked his life. But at a word from the girl Tark had stood aside and let the lurker bear her away. *She* had protected *him*! It was supposed to be the other way around!

Shame curdled in his gut. It was a disturbingly familiar sensation. He didn't deserve a clean death. He could have had one many times. Plenty had been offered. He might have had a good death if he had gone off the waterfall with his companions. He would have earned a noble death if he had continued to fight Maldor rather than accept an invitation to Harthenham. It would have been a worthwhile death to go back for Lord Jason at Harthenham. And it would have been a gallant death to perish defending Rachel as his lord had requested.

Tark had found reasons for running away every time. The waterfall had seemed pointless, as had his private war against Maldor. Dying alone at Harthenham had struck him as a more fitting end for a craven. But Jason had come. After Harthenham, Tark had needed to protect Jasher's seed. And then earlier today Rachel had ordered him to stand down. He would have had no chance of stopping the lurkers. Giving his life would have made no difference. Tark supposed that every coward had his reasons.

Back at Mianamon the oracle had assured him that he would have a role to play before this war was over. She had told him he would know when the time came. Well, the time had come, and he had let the opportunity pass him by. Maldor had claimed Rachel, and there was nothing he could do to change it, except perhaps to surrender his life in a hopeless attack.

Tark scowled. Would a hopeless assault against Felrook be a penitent act of courage or a wasteful display of self-pity? He would not be attacking. Not really. He would be abandoning his duty yet again. His duty to Galloran. Maldor's armies were coming. Jason had not only charged Tark to protect Rachel—he had also directed him to serve the king. Rachel had charged him with the same mission. If he had no hope of rescuing Rachel, he would be a better servant if he stayed and died beside Galloran.

A knock at his door startled Tark from his brooding. Who

would be calling at this hour of the night? He heard no commotion outside the keep, no evidence of a sneak attack. Curious, Tark went to the door and opened it.

Ferrin stood there, looking dazed. "I thought you might be awake."

"What is it?" Tark wondered.

Ferrin gave half a smile and tapped the spot on the side of his head where his ear was missing. "I have news. I was on my way to Galloran, but I thought you might want to hear as well."

"News of Lord Jason?"

"He did it," Ferrin said simply. "He learned the prophecy. I had myself convinced that there was no way some words could repair this debacle, but Galloran was right. The information is everything that we were promised. It could enable us to destroy Felrook."

"What did Lord Jason learn?" Tark exclaimed.

Ferrin shook his head. "Galloran has earned the right to know first. But you deserve to be there."

Tark's mind whirled as he followed Ferrin toward Galloran's quarters. What could the information be? It must refer to a secret way into Felrook. If they could sneak their forces into the castle discreetly, the battle might be quick and decisive. They might rescue Rachel! When Maldor's armies arrived, they would find their leader dead or captured, with Galloran safely behind unassailable walls. Jason had learned of a secret entrance. What else could it be? What else would leave Ferrin proclaiming a possible victory?

Two seedmen, two drinlings, and two men of Trensicourt guarded the doors to Galloran's quarters.

"I have urgent tidings for the king," Ferrin said with certainty.

The lead guard turned and knocked. Lodan answered, having replaced Io as Galloran's assistant and bodyguard.

"Rouse the king," Ferrin said. "We bear urgent tidings."

"The king has not yet slept," Lodan said. "He seems to have lost the knack. But he excels at pacing and at consulting maps. Come inside."

"Not for a moment," Ferrin replied. "Have the king put on his blindfold. My presence at this hour could provide hints."

"As you will." Lodan stepped away. A moment later he returned. "All right."

Tark followed Ferrin through the open door. Lodan closed it, then followed Tark. Galloran faced them from across the room, still fully clothed, standing beside a table buried in maps. He had his blindfold in place.

"You are toying with my hopes," Galloran said.

"Not toying," Ferrin replied. "He did it. Jason told me the prophecy."

"Will it help us?"

"It is a precious secret. We should limit those who hear it. If the secret becomes known, Maldor could counter us."

"Yet you brought it to me," Galloran said. "Thank you for your integrity. Who is with you? I heard another enter. Tark?"

"Yes, Your Majesty," Tark said. "I could wait outside."

"Nonsense. But not a word leaves this room. For now we keep it between the four of us. Let me be the judge of who else should know."

"Two messages," Ferrin said. "One is for you. It is the key to fixing all of this. Apparently, the other message could help Rachel. The message for you is that Felrook is built atop Mount Allowat."

Galloran froze. Then he raised a hand to his lips, covering an irresistible smile. "The mountain where orantium was mined anciently."

Ferrin nodded. "The mining was abandoned because they

encountered a vein too large to extract. They sealed off the mine and kept the location a secret."

"And millennia later," Galloran murmured, "Maldor unwittingly built his fortress on top of it. Esmira saw true. Indeed, our hope is white, like a flash of orantium."

"They must have sealed the mine with the lake," Ferrin said. "Who knows what other precautions they took. Accessing the vein could be difficult."

"We have tomorrow and the next day," Galloran said. "The day after that, Maldor's armies arrive. If we time this right . . ."

". . . the war could end with a single blow," Ferrin finished. "I should get to Lake Fellion at once. I can leave my nose above the water and search for the entrance to the lost mine."

"Agreed," Galloran said. "What of the message for Rachel?"

"Evidently, she learned what she needs to know from Orruck," Ferrin said. "He taught her some words that could prove useful, a command he had developed to overthrow Zokar."

"Orruck only taught her two commands," Galloran said. "If Darian thinks they might be useful, we need to get her a message."

"Telepathy?" Ferrin asked.

Galloran rubbed his chin. "She is inside the castle. If I were out on the water, I might be close enough to reach her. She needs to know that she must flee Felrook."

"You can't tell her how we mean to destroy the fortress," Ferrin said.

"No," Galloran agreed. "If Maldor somehow extracted that information from her, he might thwart us. We can warn her to escape, and give her a time frame. And we must tell her that the commands she learned from Orruck should prove useful. The rest will be up to her."

"I should get to the lake," Ferrin said.

"Right away," Galloran agreed. "Bring seaweed. The glow will be visible, but you will need the light. Send out several boats, all with seaweed. It should confuse them. They will probably fire upon you."

"I'm not terribly worried about that," Ferrin said. "I should go."

Tark grabbed Ferrin's arm. "I can help. I was a diver. And a miner."

"Right. Come on."

Ferrin started to pull away, but Tark held him. "After we find the mine, somebody will have to start the explosion."

"Yes," Ferrin said. "It will not be the sort of task a man could possibly survive."

Tark nodded, tears of relief shimmering in his eyes. "Since we set out from Mianamon, I've wondered why I was included. I don't mean to sound pompous or selfish, but I can't help suspecting . . . I think this might be my destiny."

CHAPTER 30

JUSTICE

The castle was finally silent. Nedwin had waited long into the night, prowling the hidden passageways, listening to feet walking, armor jangling, clothes rustling, fire crackling, doors closing, locks clicking, liquid pouring, utensils clinking, lips smacking, and furniture creaking. He had caught fragments of hushed conversation and heard muffled giggles. He had listened to a woman humming an infant to sleep. But eventually the fires had burned low and stopped snapping, the quietest discussions had ceased, and people had quit haunting the corridors.

There would be guards posted at certain doors, and many sentries out walking the walls, but the halls of the castle were as deserted as they would ever get. Soft snores and skittering mice were the loudest exceptions to the silence. In another hour the kitchens would revive as bakers got an early start on fresh bread, but until then the castle belonged to whoever could furtively claim it.

The target he had chosen for tonight was not a matter of vengeance. After weighing his options for days, Nedwin had concluded that his decision to pay Copernum a visit was not driven by personal prejudice. It was an important step toward reclaiming Trensicourt. It was a matter of justice.

Galloran had treated Copernum with leniency. And how had Copernum repaid the undeserved mercy? With treason. He had stolen the kingdom while his king was away. He had murdered good men in the night. He had openly claimed Trensicourt for the emperor.

Copernum had not even tried to conceal his crime. By announcing it publicly, in essence he had confessed to high treason. The punishment for treason was execution.

Despite his many unsavory characteristics, Copernum was an excellent strategist. While he survived, Trensicourt would be much more difficult to reclaim. The usurpers already lacked their giants. Without Copernum's leadership, the false government would be significantly more vulnerable.

It would not be easy to reach him. Copernum had abandoned his former rooms and claimed the royal residence as his own. Nedwin knew of no secret ways into the royal tower. If Galloran were familiar with any, he had kept the knowledge to himself. In the interest of making the tower secure, it was possible that no such passages existed.

But long ago Nedwin had noticed a single vulnerability. A certain balcony was theoretically accessible from a particular window across the way. Nedwin had never been able to avoid noticing such things. Taking advantage of the vulnerability would require skill, and a little luck. Nedwin felt sure he could do it.

There was another option, much less subtle. Nedwin knew where to find the stash of twelve orantium globes. With liberal use of the spheres he could probably blast his way through doors and guards quickly enough to reach Copernum. But Nedwin knew that if he entered with orantium, he would never escape. The commotion would rouse too many guards.

Nedwin wanted to survive. There would be many other targets besides the giants and Copernum. The deceitful chancellor had started a dishonorable war, a sneaky war, the kind of war without banners or trumpets, a quiet war waged in the darkest hours of the night, and Nedwin was uniquely suited to this form of combat.

Galloran would not want him to throw his life away. How could Nedwin keep serving the king and his causes if he let the guards cut him down? The other men still loyal to Galloran needed his leadership and expertise. He would enter quietly, claim Copernum, and escape to fight another day.

The castle remained still. The hour to act had come.

Nedwin passed into an empty room through a hidden panel. He wore moccasins and quiet black clothes. Stealth was his armor. He wore a short sword nearly broad enough to pass as a cleaver. The heavy blade would serve well for tonight's errand.

Listening carefully, Nedwin hurried down a hall and then climbed a winding stair. He reached the desired door, a monstrosity of wood and iron. With slender tools he coaxed the lock. The resultant click boomed like a gong to his ears. He held still, senses straining. The sleeper within breathed evenly.

After putting the tools away, Nedwin produced a handkerchief. Among the vials around his neck he found the desired solution, and he dampened the cloth. He eased the door open and strode to the bed. A stocky man in his fifties lay on his side. He had bushy eyebrows and black hair poking from his ear.

Nedwin firmly placed the handkerchief over the sleeper's nose and mouth. The man gasped, shuddered, and fell still, his breathing slower than before. His eyelids had squeezed but never opened. He would not wake until late in the afternoon.

After pocketing the handkerchief, Nedwin shut and locked the door. Pulling a rope and grapnel from his pack, he crossed to the window. Using tools belonging to Nicholas, Nedwin had fashioned the grapnel himself for this very purpose, sizing it to grasp the desired balustrade. His life would depend on it.

Setting the grapnel aside for a moment, Nedwin checked his three crossbows—two small, one large—all excellent weapons designed and crafted by Nicholas and his niece. He knew from experience that the small bows would fling their quarrels with astonishing velocity for their size. The larger bow could be fired twice, as it held a pair of quarrels. All three bows were loaded and ready. He strapped them into handy positions on his body. If a shot was not fatal, the substance on the tips of the quarrels would leave a man unconscious in seconds.

Opening the window, Nedwin gazed at the balcony of the royal tower, above him and separated by a wide gap of empty space. Too high to reach from the ground, the balcony was only available from this solitary window. Leaning out, Nedwin could see the kennels.

He took a deep, steadying breath. He would have to be quick. He had no room for error. There was no guard on the balcony, but at least two awaited inside. The balcony was three floors below Copernum. If he failed to dispatch the guards silently, the endeavor would fail. If the guards reached the balcony before him, he was a dead man.

This maneuver was risky. It was by far the greatest risk he would take tonight, the price he had to pay for access to a very cautious man. Hefting a crossbow, Nedwin aimed at the kennels and fired. Out and down the quarrel flew, finally thumping against wood.

As he desired, the dogs started barking. Grapnel in hand,

Nedwin climbed onto the windowsill. The barking dogs might offer some cover for the upcoming clamor. Nedwin threw the grapnel and leaped from the ledge before knowing whether it would catch.

As Nedwin fell through the darkness, the grapnel pulled the rope higher, using up the slack. He took solace that the throw had felt true. Somewhere above him the grapnel clanged against the balcony. Even masked by the barking dogs, the noise of the grapnel seemed to rival an orantium blast. The rope jerked taut as the metal claw took hold of the balustrade.

Instead of free-falling, Nedwin was now swinging toward the tower. The balcony projected far enough that he had some upswing before reaching the wall. Nedwin extended his legs to absorb the impact. It felt like he had jumped off a roof but had landed well. As he swung back away from the wall, he was already climbing.

The grappling hook had a good grip. He had kept hold of the rope. He had not fallen and splattered against the paving stones of the courtyard more than fifty feet below. Now it was a race.

Hand over hand he ascended—long smooth pulls. For his height he was not a heavy man, and his gangly arms had more strength in them than some might expect. Few men could climb a rope faster. But would he reach the top fast enough?

Nedwin heard the door to the balcony open. He could not panic. He was almost there. Hurried footsteps approached the end of the balcony. The guard had clearly seen the grapnel and was rushing to investigate. He had not called out a warning. Nedwin had five more feet to go. From the sound of the footsteps, the guard would reach the grappling hook just before Nedwin reached the top. If the guard kicked the grapnel, Nedwin would die. If the guard looked over the edge, he might have a chance.

When the guard looked over the edge, Nedwin reached up, grasped him by the collar, and yanked with everything he had. The unprepared guardsman came over the railing and plunged headfirst to the courtyard. He did not cry out, but he landed loudly. The dogs barked with renewed vigor.

With a small crossbow ready, Nedwin climbed over the balustrade. The door stood open. He heard another man coming. The instant the guard appeared, he received a quarrel in his heart from ten feet away. Nedwin closed the distance and covered the man's mouth as he slumped into oblivion.

His next crossbow ready, Nedwin entered the room. No other guards presented themselves. He knew the layout and quickly confirmed that no other soldiers were stationed on this floor of the apartment. He listened. There would be guards outside the main door to this room. There would probably be a guard or two immediately outside of Copernum's bedroom door. In spite of this, Nedwin heard nobody responding.

He had to hurry. If anyone tried to check in with the guards he had eliminated, his cover would be blown. He raced to the fireplace, where embers glowed at the hearts of charred logs.

The chimney extended down to other levels, but layers of iron bars had been inserted below this point to forbid access. The last time Nedwin had checked, no bars prevented upward access from here. This floor was part of the royal residence.

Ducking into the warm fireplace, Nedwin climbed. Copernum had once sent an assassin to kill Jason. The assassin had accessed his room through the fireplace. Nedwin could not help smiling as he reached the royal bedchamber.

Copernum was asleep. Nedwin could hear him breathing. Listening intently, he detected nobody else in the room. Avoiding embers, Nedwin crept silently from the enormous fireplace.

Alarms would sound when the dead guard was discovered in the courtyard. The yowling dogs could summon alert eyes to the scene at any moment. A million other factors could lead to the discovery of his intrusion. He did not have much time.

On light feet, by the faint glow from the fireplace, Nedwin crossed to the bed. His hair mussed, Copernum slept with his mouth open. His neck looked scrawny. A strong blow from the short sword might cut all the way through.

Copernum had personally tortured Nedwin throughout the final years of his incarceration. The chancellor had experimented with nervesong much more than any of the other torturers, lifting Nedwin to excruciating plateaus of agony. Nedwin frequently relived those experiences in his nightmares. Last night, in fact, Copernum had supervised the festivities.

Nedwin had dreamed of giving Copernum a dose of nervesong. He carried some in one of the vials around his neck. He had fantasized about letting his tormentor sample the anguish he had administered so liberally.

But tonight was not about vengeance. Tonight was about justice. Any extra time he took might get him caught. Nedwin did not belong to himself. He belonged to Galloran.

Nedwin did not need Copernum to know who was dealing the death blow. Nedwin did not need to see the recognition and terror in his eyes. It was enough to anonymously bring the traitor to justice. One swift stroke. A more merciful death than Copernum deserved. But it would suffice.

Nedwin drew the sword. It rasped faintly while escaping from the sheath. Copernum mumbled and shifted slightly. Nedwin raised the weapon high and brought it down hard.

The sharp blade sliced through the scrawny neck. Nedwin did not pause to relish the success. It was simply a mission accomplished. He moved away from the bed, back toward the fireplace. But then he paused.

The sword was sharp and heavy. Almost a cleaver. And Copernum had a skinny neck. But the neck had bones and muscle and tendons. The blade had cut through too cleanly. And why had there been no blood?

When Nedwin turned back, the body was leaning over the far side of the bed. There was still no blood. The severed head remained on the pillow, glaring at him. It was not an expression that had frozen on the face at the moment of the execution. The traitor was clearly still alive.

Copernum was a displacer! No wonder the head had separated so neatly! The knowledge stunned Nedwin. The secret had been kept perfectly. Yet there was the proof, a decapitated head that clearly remained alert.

Raising his short sword again, Nedwin charged the bed. The headless body turned, lunged, and plunged a sword into him. Nedwin staggered back, falling to the floor. Copernum must have kept the sword by his bedside. There was no mistaking that the wound was fatal. It didn't hurt, but he was going to die.

The body reclaimed the head, and Copernum came to stand over him, his eyes narrow. "That was very foolish, Nedwin." He rubbed his neck. "You could have injured me. Fortunately, I have a few secrets. It will take a better man than you to claim my life. Revenge is an ugly business, Nedwin, as you are aptly demonstrating."

"Justice," Nedwin managed. At any moment he would pass out. He clung to his awareness.

"Justice, you say? Yes, you learned much about the emperor's justice at my hands. I would love to give you another taste of justice. Or why just a taste, when we could have a feast? We used to have such times, the two of us."

Hands trembling, Nedwin produced a vial from around his neck. He swiftly uncapped it, raised it to his lips, and upended it, swallowing the contents.

"No need to poison yourself," Copernum chuckled. "You have escaped me. Your wound is plainly lethal. This time death will have to be justice enough. It would have been more entertaining to take you alive, but I can still make an example of you."

Nedwin tried to reply, but his voice would not cooperate. There was still no pain, but his vision was dimming, and he could hardly breathe. Copernum continued to talk, the words unintelligible, like a low conversation heard through a thick door. An irrelevant conversation, Nedwin realized. He had failed. He closed his eyes. No! What if he got up? What if he found the strength to pull the sword from his body? What if he used it to strike down the traitor? Maybe Copernum would finally stop talking. The man had always talked too much, especially during torture.

Nedwin tried to sit up. He could not even raise his head! He tried to swallow, but his throat was not working. He could not open his eyes. He seemed disconnected from his body. Where was he? Oh, yes. The royal bedchamber. He had failed. He was dying. So this was what it felt like. He wondered what would come next. While Copernum droned on, he painlessly slipped away.

CHAPTER 31

A PRUDENT PRECAUTION

Tark trudged toward his tent, a steaming bowl of stew cradled in one arm. No longer stationed inside East Keep, he now slept near the shore of Lake Fellion with Ferrin and several others who had worked around the clock to learn the secrets of the lost mine hidden below the water.

After entering his makeshift home, Tark sat and blew across the surface of his stew. He dipped his spoon and tried a tentative sip. It would not do for him to burn his tongue and ruin the taste of his final supper. With the armies of Maldor poised to arrive sometime tomorrow, the cook had included extra meat, vegetables, and seasonings.

Most men who understood anything about the coming battle believed that tonight would be their last. They had no idea that tomorrow morning Galloran would initiate a massive retreat. If Tark succeeded in his task, most of the host Galloran had assembled should survive.

Tark sipped the salty broth. Whether he succeeded or failed in the mine tomorrow, he would not see another sunset. He had paused to ponder that thought on the way to his tent, gazing westward, appreciating the red highlights on the distant clouds as seldom before.

The exploration of the lake had succeeded. They knew where the mine was located. Ferrin had scouted it and given extensive details on where to find the sealed portion of the tunnels. All that remained was for Tark to follow the instructions, unseal the closed section, and cause an explosion like Lyrian had never known.

His third bite of stew contained some meat and onion and required some chewing. He had tasted better stew, but not often. As his farewell supper it would suffice. How was he supposed to make up for all the meals he would never eat during a single sitting? The idea was ludicrous. It was enough to enjoy a simple stew while contemplating his upcoming assignment and all it would mean to so many.

He heard the conversation begin in the tent beside him without heeding the words. It was not common to overhear conversations in Ferrin's tent. Unless engaged in a scouting mission or a strategy session, the displacer kept to himself these days.

"I want an explanation" were the first words from Ferrin that made Tark start paying attention.

"Think it through," answered a voice. Was that Naman? "Everything hinges on this operation. Must I elaborate? We simply cannot afford the risk."

"You could afford the risk up until tonight?" Ferrin replied with incredulous contempt.

"Keep it down," Naman replied in a softer tone. "There is no need to cause a scene."

Tark set his stew aside and walked out of his tent. Less than ten paces away, six seedmen clad in light armor stood in front of Ferrin's tent. The seedmen did not seek to stop Tark as he crossed and entered.

Naman and Ferrin both looked over at the intrusion. Naman seemed mildly bothered, and Ferrin looked disgruntled. An additional pair of seedmen guards flanked Naman.

"What's going on?" Tark asked.

"Nothing you need fret over," Naman said. "We're just addressing some security concerns. You have a big day looming. Get some rest, Tark."

"Security concerns?" Tark asked, his eyes on Ferrin.

Ferrin met the stare with a neutral expression. "Now that I've supplied the location of the mines and scouted them, I'm being arrested."

"No need to make it sound so dramatic," Naman said uncomfortably. "It's just that you know exactly how to stop our secret offensive tomorrow. The high command of the Amar Kabal will sleep better knowing you are free from any temptation of honoring old loyalties."

"Your soldiers have kept a close watch on me throughout this process," Ferrin said. "Isn't that insulting enough? If I meant to defect, I could have done it long before now."

"But not with such vital information," Naman replied. "Invaluable information that could turn the tide of the war. Information that could earn you forgiveness from any past indiscretions. You have submitted to other measures to ensure your loyalty. We will release you after events play out tomorrow."

Ferrin shook his head. "I submitted to my friends. I submitted to Galloran. If he wants me with him tonight, I would oblige. But I do not sense his involvement in this."

"Galloran is trying to contact the girl again," Naman said. "He has much on his mind. The logistics we will face tomorrow are intricate. It will be impossible to sufficiently prepare for all contingencies. There is no need to bring him into this."

Ferrin reddened slightly. "There is considerable need. I did not betray my people for you. I did it for a select few, including Galloran. Keep away from me, Naman. Despite appearances, I remain a displacer. We have a long history with you seedfolk. I will not be made the prisoner of my enemies."

Naman's countenance darkened. "If you openly admit that you view us as enemies, the need to take you into custody is increased, not diminished. I had hoped to keep this civil. Tark, you may want to step outside."

His expression unreadable, Ferrin looked to Tark.

"Is this really necessary?" Tark asked. "Ferrin has proven loyal. He could stay with me."

"I appreciate the sentiment," Naman said. "I know you have spent months as comrades, and you are right to show some loyalty. Ferrin has served all of us well. We mean him no harm. He will be comfortable. He will be released tomorrow as a friend of the Amar Kabal, the first displacer to receive such an honor. We are simply ensuring that he can be released as a hero."

Ferrin fixed Naman with a level gaze. "If you arrest me this evening, do not ever call me a friend. It would be a greater insult than I could bear."

"As you wish," Naman replied stiffly. "Will you come quietly, or must we drag you from here piece by piece?"

Ferrin looked to Tark. "Make sure Galloran hears of this." He turned his eyes back to Naman. "Or is Tark to be detained as well?"

"Tark's allegiance is not in question," Naman replied. "He is welcome to convey whatever information he likes to Galloran. I will stand by this decision before any authority in the land. It is a just and prudent precaution."

"Take me with him," Tark offered. "If Ferrin is to be held under guard, hold me alongside him."

"No," Ferrin said. "I would rather that news of my arrest reach Galloran. I'll go quietly, Naman, though under protest."

"Your protest is noted," Naman said. He nodded to the two soldiers in the room, who moved forward, seized the displacer, and ushered him from the tent.

Tark followed. The seedmen outside formed up around Ferrin, marching him away.

"Make no mistake," Tark heard Ferrin say, "the Amar Kabal have not made a friend tonight."

Tark stood outside the tent in the fading twilight. It would do no good to seek out Galloran immediately. The king was on the water, and would be for the better part of an hour.

Returning to his tent, Tark found his soup still reasonably warm. The musician had never trusted Ferrin, but he disliked the decision to arrest him. Keep watch on him? Sure. But seizing him like this seemed a certain way to provoke him. Tark would definitely share the news with Galloran. Now that the seedmen had made their move, he hoped the Amar Kabal would keep the displacer under very close guard. Something about Ferrin's brooding calm throughout the confrontation had left Tark feeling uncomfortable.

CHAPTER 32

TELEPATHY

Someone was calling to her. It was not the first attempt. He sounded far away. It was hard to focus on the words. The meaning escaped her. She would respond later. Right now she was too tired.

The petitioner persisted. Not loudly, but earnestly. The plea for her attention blended with her disjointed dreams, gaining and losing prominence. The voice was familiar. Some instinct insisted that she concentrate.

Rachel, are you there? I know you can sense me. Rachel, you must heed me! Rachel, can you respond? Wake up, Rachel! Wake up!

Rachel opened her eyes. It was Galloran, his mind calling to hers. Her room was dark. She was in bed. She sat up. She felt disoriented. Her mouth was dry and tasted horrible. She was at Felrook! She had tried to attack Maldor and failed! The vicious headache she had expected was almost nonexistent.

Rachel. Respond to me, Rachel! I have vital news! Rachel?

The fervent words tickled at the edge of her awareness, faint as the last bounce of an echo.

Galloran? she replied, putting some effort behind it.

Rachel! I have sought to reach you for two days.

Two days? Where are you?

On the lake. I could perceive your mind, but you were not lucid.

She was already feeling much more alert. *I'm so sorry about how I left! I thought I might be able to help from inside Felrook. I had no idea it could be dangerous for you guys.*

I understand what you were attempting, Galloran replied. *We were almost out of options. You were doing your best. Io was an unfortunate tragedy. You must not blame yourself. He chose to attack. Wartime decisions inevitably lead to casualties.*

I tried to attack Maldor, Rachel confessed. *He was sick from sending the lurkers, and I hoped to surprise him. I never stood a chance. I tried my best and overexerted myself. I've been unconscious. Two days?*

Yes. We have little time. Jason shared the prophecy with us.

Really?

The eastern armies are on schedule. They should arrive by midday tomorrow. Rachel, you must flee Felrook before then. You must get well away. If not you will die with . . . minions.

What? I missed part of that! The communication was growing even less distinct. She got out of bed, her legs wobbly. Her mouth tasted disgusting. She padded to the window and opened it, gazing out at the calm evening. The last of the light was fading in the west.

You must escape Felrook by tomorrow morning, Galloran repeated. *Otherwise you will die beside Maldor and his minions. We have found a way to stop him. I cannot be more specific than that.*

I'm not sure I can escape.

Darian the Seer had a message specifically for you. I think it is meant to help you survive. He wanted you to know that Orruck taught you—

The voice in her head was gone. Rachel leaned out the window and exerted her will. *What? Galloran? I lost you again! What about Orruck?*

The words returned to her mind so faintly that she bowed her head, eyes closed, not daring to breathe. *Orruck taught you what you need to know. One of the commands Orruck imparted was developed by him to harm Zokar. The seer felt . . . useful.*

Orruck taught me to call lightning, Rachel replied, unsure whether he could hear her. *A massive burst of lightning. I've never tried it. And he taught me words to turn stone into glass. Do you think I need lightning?*

Rachel?

I'm here! Do you think I need lightning?

The voice in her mind grew stronger. *Lightning or the other command. Lightning is volatile. Plan an escape. Take any risk necessary. You must be gone by midday. Your life depends on it. Figure out how Orruck's commands might prove useful. Otherwise you die tomorrow. Come to me if you can. I will be in the western hills. I cannot sustain this communication. I apologize.*

She could feel the strain behind his words. *I heard. I'll do my best. Good luck.*

Be brave. You can do this. I am counting on you to escape.

Is Jason all right?

He lives. The words were so weak, she wondered if she might have imagined them. *Escape. I'll watch for you.*

The distant communication had evidently taxed Galloran to his limits. He would need his strength for whatever was happening tomorrow. *I got the message. Go rest. Thank you.*

Rachel backed away from the window. She lit candles and lamps with Edomic. Her gentle headache felt like the result of sleeping too long rather than the punishing backlash of failed

Edomic commands. The effort of will to ignite the candles did not seem to enhance the pain. Neither had the conversation with Galloran.

She stopped to wonder whether Maldor could have overheard the exchange. With mental communication she usually sensed only messages targeted at her. But Galloran sometimes picked up thoughts she didn't mean to send.

If Maldor had sensed their conversation, there was nothing she could do about it now. If he had that ability, or if the lurkers had used their abilities on his behalf, she would just have to hope that nobody was paying attention.

There were two pitchers on the table. One gave off a strong odor. The scent triggered memories. She had wakened several times to sip that pungent solution. Her recollection of those moments was hazy—her head and shoulders propped up by pillows, a cup offered by a gnarled hand, a taste like nutty egg yolks accented by a distinctly metallic tang. Sometimes the drink had been warm, other times room temperature. Unable to resist her weariness, she had always sunk right back to sleep.

How heavily had they drugged her? The agony she had begun to experience after challenging Maldor lingered only as a vague discomfort. But she had lost two days! She had intended to find some way to help Galloran from inside Felrook before the enemy armies arrived. Instead, she had spent the time in a stupor.

She could not rest any longer. The other pitcher smelled like water. She poured some into her cupped palm and splashed the liquid against her face. Then she filled a glass. Walking to the window, she swished around a mouthful and spat it out. Then Rachel gargled another two mouthfuls. The gargling reduced the hideous taste in her mouth. The foulness went beyond the nasty flavor of oversleeping. Some of the vileness had to be a consequence of the medicine.

Slowly sipping water, Rachel tried to decide what she should do. According to Galloran, she did not need to fret about winning the war from inside Felrook. Jason had come through. He had delivered the prophecy, and Galloran had learned some secret that would let him destroy the fortress. She just needed to worry about getting out.

But how could she do that? Maldor had proven much more powerful than her. Using all her strength while he was weakened, she hadn't managed to scratch him. Maybe she could slip out of the fortress with a series of Edomic suggestions. Working with Ferrin, she had learned how to pick locks. Was it possible that she could make it all the way out of Felrook by picking locks and nudging minds?

The prospect seemed unlikely. She would have to get past too many guards. She could distract a few temporarily with Edomic, but eventually they would catch on, and an alarm would be raised. Besides, what would prevent Maldor from sending a torivor to retrieve her?

Rachel rubbed her face with both hands. Despite her many worries, Jason had done his part. How did he keep succeeding against all odds? What would he do if he were trapped here? She had to think like him. She had to find a way.

Galloran now had the information he needed. It was terrific, surprising news, except that it meant coming here had been totally unnecessary. She should have had more faith in Jason and his mission. If she had just held on a couple days more before caving in to her fears . . .

Then again, Jason had received a specific message for her. Darian had provided a clue. Was it meant to reach her here?

Could she still be within the boundaries of the prophecy? Or had that clue been meant to find her under other circumstances? Had she already blown it?

There was no rewriting history. She had made her decision with the information she'd had at the time. She had to accept her situation. Her focus needed to be on what she would do now.

If she discounted the clue from Jason, she would be adrift without a compass. She had to trust that the message pertained to her current situation. The secret of her escape must involve what Orruck had taught her. The former apprentice of Zokar had forced her to demonstrate her ability to push objects with Edomic. He had also taught her a command involving lightning and a command that could turn stone to glass.

Rachel had never attempted the lightning command. The phrasing would not allow the directive to be issued on a small scale. Galloran had warned that electric commands tended to be unstable. In ancient times, even the strongest wizards had generally avoided them.

But could that instability work to her advantage? Might Maldor struggle to counteract lightning? Or would he undermine the command as he had with fire, forcing Rachel to deal with the consequences of a failed mandate?

The electric command called for huge opposing charges that would produce the equivalent of a serious lightning strike. Such a powerful command could have been created to attack a mighty wizard. But the concept of commanding lightning had seemed familiar to Galloran, which implied that a lightning spell was not particularly unusual. Supposedly, Orruck had developed one of those commands to harm Zokar. If he had developed the command on his own, wouldn't it be unfamiliar? Or could he have authored a specific type of lightning command?

Galloran had never mentioned seeing a command turn stone to glass. But Rachel had never discussed that command much with him. She had successfully uttered the command numerous times. It had never seemed remarkably challenging or mysterious.

Could turning stone to glass be the command Orruck had developed? How could it have harmed Zokar? How could it harm Maldor?

Maldor was not made of stone. But Felrook was a different matter. Could Zokar have had a similar fortress? Turning the walls of Felrook to glass would certainly make the stronghold more vulnerable. Of course, to accomplish the feat a wizard would either need infinitely more power than Rachel possessed, or else a very long time to transform the fortress segment by segment.

How else might Maldor be vulnerable?

Rachel wished she understood more about the relationship between Maldor and the torivors. Controlling them took a heavy toll on him, which meant that they probably weren't willing servants.

What did she know about them? The lurkers were not native to Lyrian. They had been summoned from another world. The Myrkstone that Maldor wore was somehow involved with dominating them. Could she turn that to glass? Could she destroy it?

Was she foolish to imagine that the lurkers might help her if given the chance? When she had communicated with them, they had never felt evil. Alien, yes, but not hateful. If anything, they had seemed indifferent. They fulfilled their orders, but they did not seem to personally care about their assignments.

Folding her arms on the windowsill, Rachel rested her chin. How essential was she to all of this? Maybe she had already done her part by smashing the gate at West Keep. Did it matter if she escaped? At least if she died, it would mean Galloran had succeeded. That was better than total failure, right? Of course, living to enjoy the victory would be nice too.

Could Galloran really have found a way to win? The notion seemed impossible, but he was no fool, and Rachel had sensed no uncertainty behind his words.

The lock to her room rattled, and the door opened. Turning away from the window, Rachel beheld an old crone in a drab, hooded robe. A huge mole bulged near the corner of her eye. She appeared mildly surprised to find Rachel on her feet. A pair of uniformed guards stood behind her. "You woke early," the woman said, her voice tremulous with age. "How do you feel?"

Wanting to appear worse off than she felt, Rachel rubbed one temple. "Sore and dizzy. I wanted fresh air."

"You should lie down," the woman encouraged. She waved the guards back, and they shut the door.

Clutching her side and taking small steps, Rachel crossed to the bed. "I remember your hands," Rachel said truthfully. The knuckles were red and swollen, the nails dark and sharp like claws. "You've been tending me."

"I have," the woman replied. "You have rested fitfully. If you need more of the potion, I can provide it."

"I think I've slept long enough," Rachel said, sitting gingerly on the edge of the bed.

The woman tottered close and rested a palm against Rachel's forehead. Then the crone felt her cheeks, and her neck, and ran her fingertips from the back of her head down her spine. "More potion does not appear necessary. You have mostly recovered. It would be better for you to rest on your own."

"What is your name?" Rachel asked.

"Zuza," the woman replied with a small nod.

Can you hear me, Zuza? Rachel asked forcefully.

The woman hesitated. *I hear you, child.*

I thought Maldor got rid of everyone with Edomic talent.

He spares a few of us as he sees fit. My ability is small. I make myself useful.

You're a healer?

Yes.

"Maldor wants to train me," Rachel whispered.

"I am aware," Zuza replied.

Where does he keep the torivors? Rachel wondered. She studied the old woman for a response, her eyes and mind straining.

What do you care about torivors?

Rachel could sense no answer peripheral to the reply. She pushed to uncover hidden thoughts. *I need to speak with them.*

The old woman made a sound that was half laugh, half croak. *You would do well to keep away.*

Do you love Maldor? Rachel questioned.

I love that he no longer tortures me, Zuza answered. *I love that he lets me live. I help him recover when he is overspent.*

Rachel nodded. *I must speak with the torivors. I have my reasons.*

Zuza gave a derisive snort. *You must still be addled by the potion. You should lie down.*

Where are they kept? Rachel repeated.

Can you not feel them, child? Their power is muted by their prison, but not entirely contained.

Rachel searched with her mind. Zuza was right! As Rachel concentrated, she could vaguely sense them near, but it was hard to get a sense of direction. *Are they all around us?*

The woman shook her head. *You need much more experience before attempting to consort with the darklings. Put them far from your thoughts. If you continue to please him, Maldor will doubtless introduce you to them in time.*

Rachel closed her eyes, actively trying to identify where she felt the lurkers. Below her. Not directly below. She pointed a finger. Opening her eyes, she saw that she was pointing downward, away from the window.

Zuza looked where Rachel was pointing. *More or less.*

Not far down, Rachel conveyed. *Not down in the dungeons. Not too far from here.*

Maldor likes to keep his pets close, Zuza explained. *You are also near his quarters. You are better off near him than in the dungeons, you have my word on that.* "You should get back in bed."

"I've slept long enough."

"Maybe you should consume more potion, sleep through another day. The additional respite may not be necessary, but it might do you some good. Tomorrow will not be pleasant out there." Zuza inclined her head toward the window.

How tight is his hold on the torivors? Rachel asked.

Tight enough, Zuza responded.

I need your robes, Rachel conveyed.

No, Zuza told her firmly. *Do not make me call the guards.*

Rachel sighed and lowered her head. "Maybe I'll have some of your potion after all."

"Very prudent, my dear," Zuza approved. She tottered over to the pitcher and poured the pungent fluid into a cup.

Rachel scooted back into bed. As Zuza shuffled toward her, Rachel issued an Edomic suggestion for the old woman to drink, pushing as hard as she dared. Zuza raised the cup to her lips and began swallowing. Rachel repeated the suggestion every few seconds. The old woman's eyes grew wide with panic, but she kept drinking, thin streams of fluid running down the sides of her chin.

Rachel rolled out of bed and took the nearly empty cup from Zuza, and she forcefully suggested that she sleep. The old woman sagged so suddenly that Rachel dropped the cup and nearly dropped Zuza as well. With an effort Rachel scooped the woman up and dumped her on the bed.

Rachel stripped off the woman's robes and arranged the covers so that Zuza could not be seen, reducing her to a vaguely humanoid lump. Rachel stashed her own clothes behind the bed and dressed in the hooded robes. She pulled the cowl as far forward as it would go, tucked her hands back into the sleeves, and tried to mimic Zuza's hunched stance.

With Edomic words on her lips, Rachel rapped on the door. The lock clicked and the door opened. Rachel did not dare look the guards in the eyes. Instead, she shuffled from the room, head bowed, eyes on their boots.

"Back to sleep again?" one of the guards inquired, poking his head into the room.

Rachel nodded and gave an indistinct grunt.

"Off to your quarters, then," another guard said, prodding Rachel.

"Why did you cover her head?" a third guard asked, stepping into the room.

Rachel shrugged with attempted nonchalance. There had been three guards, not two, waiting in the hall. The one who had entered the room was about to discover Zuza beneath the covers. One of the remaining guards held the keys. In Edomic, Rachel suggested that the guard hand her the keys, and then followed that up by suggesting the guards enter the room. She motioned through the doorway for emphasis.

The guard passed her the keys, and both strode through the doorway as if the idea had been their own. They paused after a few steps, but it was too late. Rachel hauled the heavy door shut.

Banging and yelling ensued. The protests were audible, but

the iron door muffled the worst of the noise. Anyone happening by would hear the faint commotion, but thankfully the protests were not carrying very far. The noise was less than ideal. She knew a command to induce sleep, but it only worked well if the subject was unaware and unoccupied. And she doubted whether she could have held control of all three guards for long enough to coax them into drinking the sleeping potion.

Rachel tried to calm herself. For the moment she was free. The moment would not last. How best could she use this opportunity? She could not imagine successfully using Edomic to bluff her way all the way out of Felrook. There would be too many guarded checkpoints. With Galloran's army outside, the whole fortress would be on high alert. But the lurkers were not far.

Lowering her head, Rachel reached out with her mind for the torivors. All she could sense was a direction, not the halls she needed to travel to get there. She began making her best guesses. She walked down a hall, turned a corner, and then quickstepped down another. She was up too high. More and more the torivors seemed directly beneath her. She needed stairs.

She passed a pair of soldiers who paid her no mind. Apparently, mysterious cowled figures were not an uncommon sight.

Eventually Rachel had to backtrack. A locked wooden door blocked the new way she wanted to go. She knelt and peered at the keyhole, then spoke a quiet Edomic command. She willed a twisting movement from the moving parts inside the lock. It had worked on 90 percent of the locks Ferrin had provided. It worked on this one.

The door clicked open, revealing a short hall. Behind an unlocked door she found a stairwell. Upon reaching the bottom of the stairs, she felt much nearer to the torivors. They were still lower than her, and off to the side. Her path toward them led her around a corner and into the view of two armed guards flanking an iron door. They wore the armor of conscriptors, and they clutched poleaxes. Swords and daggers hung ready at their waists.

Rachel knew that if she turned around, she would attract more attention than if she proceeded. Beyond the iron door the hall continued and then rounded a corner. If she walked past the guards and around the corner, she could regroup and figure out how to deal with them.

"Who goes there?" one of the conscriptors inquired before Rachel reached them.

Keeping her face down, Rachel stopped walking and shook her head, hinting that they shouldn't question her identity. She waited in silence.

"We have to ask your business down here," the other conscriptor apologized, obviously concerned about who he might be addressing.

Maybe she could fake her way through this. Rachel did not try to disguise her voice, but she made it cold. "Maldor should have warned you I was coming. I am here to inspect the torivors."

"Inspect the torivors?" the first conscriptor exclaimed. "Who are you?"

"That is none of your affair," Rachel replied harshly.

"I'm afraid it is," the other guard said, starting to sound rankled.

Switching to Edomic, Rachel suggested they flop to the ground. Both complied, their dropped weapons clattering. Rachel suggested that they keep still; then with a command and an effort of will she levitated both poleaxes and held the blades to their throats.

The combination of suggestions and commands left her feeling taxed, but she tried not to show it. She stood with her head bowed and her hands behind her back. The men were no longer pinned by her will, but the weapons at their throats seemed sufficient to keep them still. "Will you open the door, or do you mean to delay me further?"

"We don't have the key," the first conscriptor said, no defiance in his tone. "Only the emperor comes here, and never often."

"I know," Rachel lied, showing the keys she had taken from the guard upstairs, perfectly aware that none of them would open this door. "I am asking whether you intend to keep wasting my time."

"If Maldor sent you," the second guard responded, "and if you have the key, you are welcome to enter."

With a word and a gesture, Rachel sent the poleaxes sliding down the stone floor of the hall. "Stay on the ground until I am gone, worms. See that I am not disturbed."

The guards remained motionless on the floor. Rachel stepped past them and scraped a random key against the keyhole. She uttered a quiet command and felt the workings of the lock stir, but not enough to grant her access.

Despite her increasing heart rate, Rachel tried to stay calm. The mechanisms of some of the trickier locks at East Keep had to be turned left first, and then right. While she continued to rattle the key against the keyhole, Rachel uttered a pair of commands, first twisting the innards of the lock one way, then coaxing other moving parts in the opposite direction.

The lock disengaged, and Rachel opened the door. Deciding that it would be most convincing to offer no additional comment, Rachel stepped through and closed the door. She was left in total darkness.

For a panicky moment she envisioned lurkers all around her. No, they were in the vicinity, but she still could not sense them clearly. Some barrier still intervened.

Starting at the doorway, Rachel felt her way along the wall

to a corner three paces from the door. Following the next wall, after several small paces, she discovered a step down. She was on a landing at the top of a stairway. The stairs descended directly toward where she sensed the torivors.

Feeling higher along the wall, Rachel found a sconce holding a torch. She lit the torch with a word and removed it from the sconce. The trembling flame revealed a long stairway, probably forty steps. Unsure how long she had before the guards she had bluffed would initiate an angry pursuit, Rachel rushed down the stairs.

At the bottom of the stairs, a short hall ended at a large mirror. Closer inspection revealed that the mirror was a polished metal door perforated by a grid of tiny holes. Eight pegs resided in the centermost holes of the top row. It was a lock like the ones Jason had described at the Repository of Learning and at the lorevault of Trensicourt. She had no idea how Edomic might help her open it. Inserting the pegs by trial and error would take weeks or months or years. Maybe longer.

Rachel could perceive the torivors behind the door. *Can you sense me?* she wondered, projecting the thought with all of the energy she could muster. *I need to speak with you. Can you answer?*

Although she could discern their collective presence, she recognized no individual thoughts. She was on her own opening the door. If she failed, this entire excursion would be for nothing. More likely than not, the day would dawn with her chained in the dungeon.

Rachel studied the door. It looked as though it had been fashioned from the same metal as the torivorian swords. The door itself was not going anywhere. But the door was anchored into the stone of the wall.

As soon as her thoughts turned to the message from Darian, Rachel knew what to do. Summoning her inner strength, she spoke a command to turn all the stone around the perimeter of the door to glass. She felt the directive succeed. The stone took on a glossy sheen and gained a hint of smoky translucence.

Raising her voice and extending one hand, Rachel mentally rammed the door with everything she had. For an instant the door shuddered. Tiny fractures zigzagged across the surrounding glass. Dropping to one knee, Rachel kept up the pressure. The effort made her teeth ache down to the roots. Responding to a final surge of willpower, the door exploded inward, tearing free as its glass moorings shattered in a shower of shards.

Rachel dropped forward to her hands and knees, her torch clacking against the floor and rolling in a semicircle. She felt the cool stone beneath her palms. She could taste blood in her mouth. Her headache was returning. Her teeth ached and tingled. Her tongue felt numb. But her mind remained clear. She retrieved the torch and stood.

The room beyond the empty doorway was black. Her torchlight did not penetrate the darkness.

She could feel the lurkers beyond the threshold, their presence no longer muted or indistinct. There were dozens.

I need to speak to a representative, Rachel conveyed.

You, a torivor replied with recognition. *We are seldom visited.*

I may not have much time, Rachel emphasized. *I need to understand your relationship to Maldor. I may not be exactly like you, but I am a Beyonder as well. I want to free you.*

Others have tried, the lurker conveyed. *When Maldor sends us on assignments, we are not at liberty to communicate. But here we are, not operating under active instructions. Ask your questions.*

Do you want to serve Maldor? Rachel asked.

We want one thing, the torivor replied, the slow words carrying heavy emphasis. *Our freedom. We yearn for home. We can earn our freedom through service, according to the covenant.*

Maldor bargained with you? Rachel asked.

Zokar instituted the covenant. He summoned us to this world and then subdued us. Where we come from, we need not die. Life is always. Here we are more vulnerable. We had to agree to the covenant or perish. Some of us chose oblivion. Most compromised.

If the agreement was with Zokar, how does Maldor control you? Rachel wondered.

The Myrkstone, the torivor replied. *Truth is a principle of our existence. We cannot lie. We cannot break our oaths. Our oaths were bound to Zokar and the jewel. Maldor used the Myrkstone to secure our cooperation. We are under no other obligation to serve him. Our allegiance was to Zokar. Yet while the jewel survives, we remain bound to this world. Restricted by our vows, we are powerless to harm it. Only by fulfilling our covenants can we escape its power. We often resist the will of Maldor. We do not relish servitude. But as we fulfill our promises as established by the covenant, we can escape the Myrkstone and return home. In the end, when he asks, we comply.*

Rachel thought about the command that had let her force open the burnished door. *What if I destroy the Myrkstone?*

Then we would be free.

What if you agree to a new treaty with me? A treaty that goes into force after I destroy the stone? A treaty with simpler terms. A treaty that will free you sooner than your other arrangement.

Our interest would depend on your terms.

How many of you remain?

Seventy and one.

Rachel tried not to grin. She looked over her shoulder. Nobody was coming for her yet. *I'm not sure how long I have. We had better start negotiating.*

CHAPTER 33

AN INTERRUPTED FEAST

The first sensation was of raindrops sliding down his body. The fat drops were sparse at first. He felt where each one kissed his bare arms, legs, or torso, and where the residual water traveled afterward. As the drops fell faster, they lost all individuality, spattering against his exposed skin and flowing in rivulets toward his naked feet. At first his loincloth absorbed some of the water, but soon it became saturated.

Next he became aware of the smells. The rain provided the dominant aroma, rich and humid, subtly shifting with the breeze and the intensity of the downpour. Lesser smells included wood smoke, wet stone, damp plants, and the beckoning allure of fresh blood. The layered scents were more vivid and intense than any sensory indulgence he had ever encountered. Was this how dogs experienced the world? He felt he could see with his nose.

His hearing was worse. Still acceptable, but not quite as sharp, muddied by unnatural echoes. The overlapping reverberations from the pattering rain masked nearly all other sound.

The pressure of the rope around his neck was constant, but it caused no pain. At least that had not changed.

Despite the absence of pain, the rainfall was not pleasant. Not because of the cool temperature. The more alert his mind became, the more the feel and smell of the water bothered him, like taking a bite of rotten meat or sipping spoiled milk. It felt *wrong*, smelled *wrong*, unsanitary, unwholesome, unwelcome. He resisted the urge to squirm.

Even with his eyes shut, Nedwin could feel that it was night. He breathed the moist air, unsure whether respiration remained necessary.

Nedwin opened his eyes.

He was dangling above the castle gate, strung up by his neck as an example for the kingdom to behold. They had not bothered to bind his hands or feet. No need, he supposed, when the man you were hanging was already dead. He felt a surge of triumph. He had died, but the goma worms he had swallowed while Copernum gloated had brought him back.

Ingesting the worms had been a rash action. It placed the entire world in jeopardy. Then again, if Maldor was going to rule Lyrian, maybe a plague-ravaged nightmare was what he deserved.

Nedwin had taken the worms from Ebera, just in case. Collecting rare specimens had been his main occupation for years. When he had been left alone with an infected corpse, he had found the temptation irresistible. He knew that none of his comrades would have approved, but the deadly sample had offered him a final, potent weapon to employ in the event of a worst-case scenario.

As the wind rose, the rain lashed at him. His body swung in the darkness, the wet rope creaking. Grinding his teeth, he tried to ignore the foulness of the water. He traced the scar where Copernum's sword had penetrated his chest. The worms had knitted it neatly, but his enemies had hung him too high for anyone to notice.

If Maldor had already won, unleashing the plague would be a beguiling temptation. Many innocent people would die, but under the tyranny of Maldor those same innocents were already doomed. The plague would be merciful for many, and it would leave Maldor with nothing to rule.

But Nedwin could not dwell on that line of thinking. He had to hope that Galloran would emerge victorious. He had to trust the prophecy. He had not taken measures to revive himself in order to destroy the world. He would be careful. He would use this second chance to accomplish a very specific objective.

The night was dark, but his intuition insisted that it had not been dark for very long. Maybe the suspicion derived from the temperature of the storm. Maybe from the amount of heat radiating from the nearby stones of the castle wall. Maybe he was influenced by some nuance of the smell.

Nedwin also instinctively knew that he had been dead less than a day. This was the night after he had been killed. Why was he so certain? Was he guessing based on how little his body had decomposed? After feasting on his blood, the worms would have set about repairing and preserving him. Perhaps the worms knew how much time had passed, and at some level the knowledge was transferrable.

Reaching over his head, Nedwin climbed the rope attached to his neck. It required little effort. His muscles felt stronger than before. Interesting.

Squatting in a crenellation between merlons, Nedwin untied the noose. The wet rope could have proven tricky, but his fingers were strong and nimble.

A guard was coming his way, walking along the battlements. A dutiful man. Most would seek shelter during a downpour of this intensity. They would keep watch, but they would wait until the rain relented to actively patrol the walls. Nedwin crouched low, trying to keep his pale, freckled flesh out of view.

The blood of the oncoming guard was the sweetest aroma Nedwin's nose had ever savored. It was an olfactory symphony. He hungered for it, thirsted for it. He craved that blood like he craved sleep, air, friendship, and peace. The blood promised to satisfy all urges and to heal all wounds, whether physical, emotional, or spiritual.

Lightning forked across the sky, jagged and close. Thunder crackled mightily.

The blood was off-limits. He had to remain in control of his urges. The worms had claimed his body. He could not let them have his mind. To taste that blood would spread the plague. To spread the plague would betray Galloran much worse than any of his previous failures. He had to resist. If he lacked the will to resist, he should have stayed dead.

Leaving eight fingers in view, Nedwin dangled from the wall and listened to the guard walk past. The guard did not pause. Nedwin pulled himself up, approached the guard from behind, seized him, and flung him over the wall. The man cried out before striking the ground. His armor clanged. The storm dampened the noise.

What next? Several stairways ran down the interior of the wall. Nedwin strode to the nearest one, hurried part of the way down, then leaped to the roof of a storage building. Working his way across the roof, Nedwin could feel the shingles creaking underfoot. He tried to be more careful and soon realized that he had lost some of his ability to move in silence. Was it due to a subtle reduction in motor skills? The loss of some instinct he had taken for granted? Interesting.

After hanging from the eaves of the storehouse, Nedwin

dropped to the wet paving stones, landing in a crouch. Drenching rain pelted down around him. He took cover behind some barrels under the eaves. The rain and darkness would help hide him, but he could take nothing for granted. A lanky, pale, mostly unclothed man in the yard of a castle would draw the eye even under inclement conditions. All it would take was a single vigilant guard and the light of a lantern.

He needed to reach the stables and the castle entrance hidden there, but any route he took would force him to cross open ground. He was currently shrouded in shadow, but light gleamed from many windows and lanterns. More lanterns would be lit if the heavy rain persisted.

Nedwin wished for a cloak or a blanket. With the rainfall he had an ideal excuse to hide his face and move quickly. There would be useful items inside the storehouse, but the sturdy door was locked, and without his tools he could not pick it.

As the downpour lessened, Nedwin realized that if he hesitated any longer, he might lose his best chance to reach the secret passageway below the stables. Risking open ground while the rain was heavy would be safer than risking open ground once the guardsmen resumed their regular patrols.

Nedwin crept from building to building, staying near walls and vegetation, taking cover wherever it was available. He found a soiled, sodden blanket in a handcart and wrapped it over his head and shoulders. It failed to cover his bare legs, but it provided a far better disguise than nothing.

The rainfall had become gentle by the time Nedwin reached the stables. They were dark and saturated with the odors of horses—hay, oats, wood, leather, mud, dung, hide, and especially blood. The allure was not nearly as strong as with human blood, but it smelled much more appealing than any meal Nedwin could remember.

Ignoring the scents, Nedwin found the hatch to the basement and then the disguised hatch to the subbasement. Down in the darkness, his fingers found a hidden catch, and he proceeded into a quiet hall.

The smells here were mustier—dust, stone, wood, rot, mildew, and rat droppings. Nedwin caught whiffs of the living rats, noting that rat blood smelled nearly as desirable as horse blood.

He could see nothing. Nedwin had no seaweed, and no way to light the torches stashed beyond the entrance. But he could smell his way easily. He could smell the walls as clearly as see them, just as he could smell the open spaces of the halls and rooms. He could even smell the locations of spiderwebs.

While prowling the black corridors, Nedwin noticed for the first time that his heart was no longer beating. He paused, feeling the lack of a pulse in his wrist, then his neck, and finally his chest. More than hanging from the wall, more than his enhanced sense of smell, more than his memories of the fatal injury, the lack of a heartbeat forced Nedwin to confront the reality that he was truly dead.

Nedwin rubbed his jaw. His life was over. He no longer belonged in this world. He was an abomination. His body housed the seeds of a horrible plague. If those seeds were planted in others, all of Lyrian would become like Ebera.

He had a final mission to accomplish; then he could rest. He would be careful. He would need the orantium. On his way to the hidden stash of twelve globes, he kept his ears alert. Hearing had been his sharpest sense for years, and it was frustrating to have it hampered. Even without perfect hearing, it soon became evident that a feast was in progress. If Copernum was in attendance, the meal might provide just the opportunity he needed.

Stealth had already failed him. This time Nedwin would rely

on overwhelming force. He would not survive, but survival was no longer a priority. He was already dead.

Nedwin found the orantium as expected, the twelve spheres bundled together in a sack, sawdust packed between them to help prevent an accidental detonation. He handled the sack gingerly.

By unseen passages Nedwin made his way to the dining hall. He climbed a ladder and peered out through a portion of tapestry that had been carefully thinned. Since he was looking from the darkness into the light, the colorful tapestry was almost transparent, affording him a good view of the roomy hall.

Nedwin stared in awe, hardly trusting his eyes. Not only was Copernum present, but so were the lords who had collaborated with him, including Dolan and the grand duke—more than forty conspirators in total. Who else had he expected to attend a feast sponsored by the usurper? Copernum was too smart to permit potential enemies near him at this early stage of the occupation.

Dessert had not yet been served, but the feast had obviously been in progress for some time. Many of the lords in attendance looked like they had already eaten their fill. Bustling servants shuttled away empty trays and plates. A large fire blazed in the huge hearth.

Nedwin could smell the food as never before. Beef, mutton, ham, chicken, turkey, and goose were present, with all their varied gravies, seasonings, and sauces. He smelled pea soup, chunky vegetable stew, mashed yams, fresh berries, pungent cheeses, buttered mushrooms, skewers of olives stuffed with garlic paste, and hunks of bread slowly growing stale.

Despite the diverse scents discernible in greater detail than ever before, the food did not smell appetizing. Not in the slightest.

All the aromas paled next to the intoxicating allure of fresh human blood.

Tonight the feast was not on the tables or in the kitchens. Tonight the feast was inside the diners, pumping round and round, warm and liquid and beckoning.

But Nedwin was not here to indulge his new appetite. No matter how brightly that desire burned, he must not heed it. He had a mission to accomplish.

He quietly unpacked the spheres from his sack, then replaced them without the sawdust for easier access. He practiced how he would hold the sack and how he would remove the spheres.

The secret entrance to the dining hall was concealed behind another tapestry, at the side of the room. It would not allow him to emerge near Copernum, but unless he was clumsy, it should be near enough.

Nedwin could not afford to wait. He needed to strike while Copernum remained. What if the head traitor excused himself before dessert?

Nedwin worked the releases and slid aside a cunningly constructed section of the stone wall. The section moved without much noise, disguised by boisterous conversation, clinking tableware, and hustling servants. The heavy tapestry still covered the gaping opening.

Thrusting the tapestry aside, Nedwin stepped into the dining hall. The fire in the hearth bothered his eyes, but not enough to slow him down. Most of the armed guards were clustered near the main door. The first orantium globe sailed their way. The second went to a nearer table. Both globes exploded in rapid succession, with white flashes and thunderous booms that echoed in the cavernous hall. The guards were thrown in all directions. One man lost his helmet. The table bucked and splintered, platters of food soaring into the air. Diners flipped and tumbled.

Startled faces turned his way. Nedwin saw shocked recognition in most of their eyes. All had professed loyalty to him and the crown. Smiling, he produced another orantium globe, tossing it at the guards near the table where Copernum, Dolan, and the grand duke dined. The explosion devastated the guards and overturned the table.

A quarrel hit Nedwin in the ribs. He observed it with mild interest. The projectile caused no pain and failed to hinder him. He rewarded the crossbowman for his accuracy with an orantium sphere that launched him, and others near him, into astonishing feats of acrobatics.

Servants were scattering, making for the doors to the kitchen. Nedwin threw a sphere there next, to dissuade people from exiting.

Some of the diners were pulling knives and drawing swords. Most were seeking cover. A hurled knife stuck in Nedwin's thigh, causing no significant harm or discomfort.

A group of nobles from the nearest tables charged Nedwin, forcing him to throw an orantium sphere closer than he liked. He felt the warm shockwave from the blast. The noise made his ears ring, and the flash left him dazzled. He staggered, but kept his feet. He could smell his own charred flesh.

Nobody was attacking him anymore. Most were pressing toward the doors. Nedwin threw a globe at the main doors and another at the doors used by the servants. The blasts claimed many lives.

"This is your reward for taking orders from a displacer!" Nedwin called, his voice strange in his ears. He threw a globe at some lords taking refuge behind an overturned table. A direct hit proved that orantium was much more powerful than wood.

Men screamed and moaned. Smoke filled the air. Nedwin stalked toward the table where Copernum was huddled. Their eyes met across the room. Nedwin had never seen Copernum looking bewildered or afraid. Tonight he saw both emotions displayed nakedly.

With three globes left, Nedwin hurled a sphere at another table where treacherous lords cringed. A few people were escaping out the doors. But not Copernum. Nedwin got close enough that he could not possibly miss, and demolished the table where Copernum cowered. Although it was heavier than the other tables, the orantium blasted it into kindling.

One globe remained.

Through the smoke, Nedwin saw Copernum scrambling away, his body bleeding and blackened. Dolan was dead. The grand duke was dead. Dozens of other traitors had perished.

"Wait, Nedwin!" Copernum cried, holding up a hand. His stunned eyes were desperate. Flecks of food had spattered his face and clothes. Splintered pieces of the table protruded from his body. "Wait! Kill me and Galloran dies. I have vital information!"

Nedwin shook his head. "Galloran has had enough of your help."

He threw the final sphere so that it shattered against the floor beside the disloyal chancellor. The glaring explosion did the rest.

Feeling oddly disconnected from himself, Nedwin looked around. The smoky room was still. Everyone had fled, had died, or was feigning death. He had succeeded. He had unnaturally extended his life for a purpose, and the task had been accomplished. The realization brought profound relief.

Just to be sure, Nedwin checked a few ragged pieces of his former torturer. After all, he was a displacer. But it was no trick. Copernum was not temporarily disassembled. He was extremely dead.

"You're even deader than I am," Nedwin mumbled.

How soon before more guards came after him? Any minute.

The thunder of the orantium would summon soldiers from all over the castle. Some of the guards might want to hesitate. They would hear what had happened from the survivors. They did not know he was out of orantium. And he was supposed to be dead. But not knowing that their leader had perished, they would also fear his wrath if they failed to act.

Nedwin walked toward the fire that still blazed in the hearth. He had deliberately not disturbed it with his barrage of orantium. He needed that fire.

Nedwin glanced at the secret passage. The dining hall remained still. He might be able to sneak away.

No. He had been fortunate. He had not only eliminated Copernum, but he had executed most, if not all, of the men capable of taking his place. Without the might of the giants, without treacherous nobles orchestrating the occupation, another revolution was inevitable. Justice had been served. The traitors had been punished. When Galloran returned, he would find allies running Trensicourt, not enemies.

Shuffling forward, Nedwin accepted that he would never see Galloran again. He would not be here to welcome his master home. But stories of this night would be everywhere. Galloran would find that his former squire had held true to the end, and that meant everything.

Nedwin paused near the hearth. The bright flames hurt his eyes. The warmth bothered his skin. Every instinct screamed for him to withdraw.

What if Galloran failed? What if the king never returned to his kingdom? If Maldor emerged victorious, Nedwin could unleash the plague and spoil the victory. Nedwin reconsidered a hasty escape. He thought about weeks of hiding, feeding on animals, waiting for news.

No. Too much could go wrong. For now, he felt certain that no worms had escaped his body. He had to keep it that way. He had to trust Galloran. But what if Maldor won? Nedwin bowed his head. He had no right to destroy the world. He had served Galloran to the best of his abilities. He must not sully his sacrifice. Bringing the worms out of Ebera had been his responsibility. Galloran had never authorized it. Every moment that Nedwin survived increased the risk of an accidental infection. The worms had to burn, which meant he had to burn with them.

It had been many years since Nedwin had feared death. He did not fear it now. The fire was not appealing. The blood promised fulfillment. He could smell it everywhere. The fire promised misery. He heard footfalls. Guards were coming. They were too late. Nedwin threw himself into the fire, squirming until he was settled at the heart of the flaming logs.

Everything inside him recoiled. Every instinct screamed that he must flee. He was not in pain. The worms, maybe—not him. The fire was everywhere. Warm, not hot. It had seemed bright and horrible, but now he found it almost relaxing. He smelled it consuming him. His eyes were closed. He was not dying. He was already dead. This was just the end of his worn-out body. He had stayed sane through it all. Sane enough, at least. He had done his duty. He felt certain that Galloran would be proud of him, and the thought gave him comfort. He could no longer smell the burning. He could no longer hear the logs crackling. His hardships had ended. No pain would haunt this slumber. At long last, Nedwin rested.

CHAPTER 34

BEYONDERS

It was a long wait before Maldor arrived.

At first the emperor sent servants. But no conscriptors or displacers were willing to enter the shadowy room to retrieve Rachel. Not while she stood ringed by torivors. She had listened as her enemies had discussed the predicament. They were afraid of the emperor's displeasure. They were eager for his approval. But every single one of them was more afraid of the lurkers. None of them even crossed the threshold.

Rachel would have lost track of time, but the lurkers kept her informed. Their negotiations had been concluded for hours. She did not engage them in casual conversation. According to the lurkers, the sun was already well above the horizon when Maldor appeared in the doorway.

He looked more like the smug gentleman who had visited her dream. He no longer appeared weary or infirm. No evidence remained of the facial paralysis. He wore dark, regal attire. The Myrkstone glittered against his chest.

Rachel wrung her hands. She was nearly out of time. This would be her only chance. She had to get it right.

"Such foolishness," Maldor fussed amiably. "You have placed yourself in grave danger, Rachel. Come out of there."

"I'm very comfortable," Rachel said from within her protective ring of torivors. "Could you have my bed brought here? And maybe some food?"

A torch in his hand, Maldor stared at her patiently. He did not cross the threshold. "I am impressed that you accessed this chamber. Getting past the guards required talent, but tearing out the door exceeded my expectations. The portal and the walls were all reinforced with Edomic."

Rachel was glad for the information. It confirmed that she had turned the stone to glass even though it had been enchanted. "I was determined."

"Why? Have you any notion of the peril you face? Inside that room I cannot hold the torivors in check."

"Do I look worried?" Rachel asked. "I have a lot in common with the torivors. We communicate with our minds. We're here against our will. And none of us belong to this world. We're all Beyonders."

Maldor chuckled condescendingly. "You have very little in common with them, Rachel. If you have let them convince you otherwise, there may already be no rescuing you. These are no frightened prisoners. You are among caged predators who would tear this world to shreds if given the chance. If you come out of there immediately, I may still be able to save you."

"They're not harming me," Rachel said.

"No matter what you imagine, Rachel, they are using you. Make no sudden movements. Walk to me slowly."

"No. I trust you less than I trust them."

"I'm sorry for the discomfort you suffered while trying to slay me," Maldor said. "You wield surprising power for one so young. I defended myself as gently as the circumstances permitted."

"You want to turn me into a freak, complete with displacer parts and a magic word that can destroy me."

Maldor raised his palms. "You are loyal to the losing side. You have not disguised the fact that you are my enemy and that you would harm me if you could. As much as I admire your talent and wish to see it increase, I must take measures to protect myself. Considering the circumstances, I believe I have been both generous and understanding. That will cease if you do not come out of there."

"What if I refuse?"

Maldor fingered his Myrkstone pendant. "I will order one of them to bring you to me. And then for the first time you will truly experience my displeasure."

"I'd like to see you try," Rachel said. "They don't have to obey your commands. Zokar was a different story. You don't have the same power over them. You can cause them suffering, and you can hold them bound until they fulfill their covenant, but the torivors are free to resist your demands. They can make you suffer too."

Maldor was no longer trying to appear kindly. "How dare you defy me in my own castle? Do you know where your brave Galloran is at the moment? Running. Fleeing with his pathetic host. My forces are pouring into the valley. They are currently reclaiming the empty keeps and mustering around Felrook, awaiting my orders. Your comrades cannot run for long. At my leisure it will be a simple matter to cut off all escape and destroy them to the last man."

"You think so?" Rachel asked.

"This is absurd. I have no need for a torivor to expel you. I need only deny you food and water and watch as you waste away. I will bring you the heads of the friends you might have saved had you been more cooperative."

"Wait," Rachel said. "Would you still spare ten of my friends?"

He gave her a flat stare. "I would if you provide the opportunity. Your comrades are running out of time. Even I cannot restore the dead to life."

Rachel hung her head, hoping she looked defeated. "I'm afraid to come out. You humiliated me. You hurt my mind; you hurt my body; you crushed my hope. You wounded my faith in my magic. I wasn't trying to anger you by coming to the lurkers. I just wanted to find a place where you couldn't touch me. A place where I didn't feel powerless. This was what I came up with."

Maldor's expression softened a degree. "An innovative option, but any kinship you have imagined between yourself and the torivors can only be based on a horrible misunderstanding of their natures. I mistrust this penitent charade, Rachel, but if you come out of there voluntarily, I pledge to forgive you. The cause you fought for is lost. Your people are on the run. The last rebellion has been crushed. It is time for you to choose a new cause. You fear what Lyrian will become under my rule? I offer you the position and power necessary to influence change. We need not be enemies. Come, Rachel, do not tarry in the shadows."

"Will we be alone? I want to talk more."

Maldor turned and made a gesture. "We will be alone."

"You'll still save ten of my friends?"

"If you emerge and provide the names, I will do everything in my considerable power to spare your favorites."

I will go to him now, Rachel conveyed to the torivors.

The tenebrous figures stepped out of her way.

"Will you back away?" Rachel asked. "You frighten me."

"Will you emerge if I depart?" Maldor asked.

"Don't leave," Rachel said, her voice quavering. "I want to talk. Just give me some space. I'm having a very hard day."

"Understood," Maldor said, backing down the hall.

Rachel walked forward to the threshold. She hesitated, waiting until he had retreated a good distance down the corridor. "Are you going to attack me with Edomic?"

"Not unless you attack me," Maldor said.

"I don't want to ever attack you again," Rachel said, stepping across the threshold. "But I do want to show you a command somebody taught me."

"Who?"

"Orruck."

His eyes widened.

Her mind felt clear. She had prepared for this moment for hours. Really, she had prepared for this moment ever since arriving in Lyrian. She had prepared by discovering her talent for Edomic. She had prepared with long hours of practice at Mianamon and elsewhere. Her will had been strengthened by those she had loved and lost. Her will had been reinforced through the stalwart examples of heroes like Galloran and those who served him. Her resolve had increased as she beheld the evil that Maldor represented. Her faith had been armored by the prophecy Jason had retrieved. Even her recent failure to defeat Maldor had helped her prepare.

Without pause Rachel put everything into the command. Her life depended on this moment. It was not hard to muster genuine emotion. All her fear, anger, and grief. All her hope, faith, and love. Her desire to live. All the strength of will that she could summon.

She focused on Maldor's pendant and uttered the command that would change stone to glass.

She felt the command succeed.

Maldor stared down in bewildered surprise.

The altered Myrkstone had a slightly different sparkle, but she could still sense power in it. Rachel had known the transformation alone might not be enough. She was ready.

Issuing suggestions in rapid succession, Rachel urged Maldor to lie down, to sleep, to run, to jump, to turn around, and to be silent. After he had almost obeyed her during their duel, Maldor had used that tactic on her, confusing her with multiple instructions. She knew that she was sharing the suggestions with greater subtlety and expertise than ever before.

Rachel saw Maldor struggling to resist her suggestions, but she did not pause to relish his temporary indecision. Raising her voice, using commands taught to her by Chandra, commands Orruck had forced her to practice in his presence, Rachel lifted the pendant off Maldor, slipping the chain over his head and into the air, then smashed it down to the floor.

The Myrkstone shattered.

Its quiet aura of power dissipated.

Recovering from the brief befuddlement of her suggestions, Maldor gaped at the particles and slivers of broken glass on the floor. Furious eyes found Rachel.

He barked a vicious command, drawing massive amounts of heat to her clothes.

Calmly, certainly, Rachel uttered the command he had used to disperse her fire attack. She had only heard the words once, but she had always been a quick study. Maldor crumpled as his command failed, clutching his stomach as he gagged and retched.

From his hands and knees, he glared at Rachel with enraged, bloodshot eyes. Then his expression changed, the fury melting into a terrified realization. Maldor was no longer staring at Rachel. He was looking over her shoulder.

She turned and saw a lurker emerging from the dark chamber,

as agreed, a sleek sword held in each hand. The lurker silently walked past her and tossed one of the weapons to Maldor. The emperor dodged aside, letting the sword ring against the stone floor. The lurker continued toward him unhurried.

Paying no heed to Rachel, Maldor looked from the lurker to the sword on the floor. Extending a hand, Maldor issued an Edomic suggestion, telling the lurker to impale itself. Rachel could sense that in his desperation he was pushing much too hard. When the command failed, the emperor dropped to the floor and vomited.

The lurker kept approaching with measured, fluid strides. Wiping his lips, Maldor looked up, crazed eyes full of terror. The lurker had almost reached him. The emperor raised both hands, palms outward, his lips moving hastily.

The blade sliced down on a trajectory to divide Maldor's head from his shoulders, but glanced away before reaching him. The torivor kept swinging. A barrage of potentially lethal strokes bounced aside as the sword struck a thin dome of energy that only flashed into view on impact. Each time the blade connected with the barrier, the dome gleamed blue white before fading from view.

The lurker kept swinging without hesitation. Maldor kept his palms raised, his expression concerned but determined, his gaze fixed on the lurker.

Rachel had expected the torivor to slay Maldor. But at least for the moment he was trapped. A brief, hysterical laugh escaped before her hands covered her mouth, tears warping her vision. Had she really done it? Would this hold him? Was she really going to live?

Maldor showed no sign of escaping. Blows rained down without interruption. The emperor didn't even glance her way.

Lurkers flooded from the chamber. Three stopped beside Rachel.

Well done, one of them conveyed.

Likewise, Rachel answered, struggling to regain her composure. *What will happen to Maldor?*

The attacker will not relent, the lurker pledged. *The defensive effort is taxing Maldor. He cannot hold out indefinitely. Escape is unlikely.*

You'll fulfill the rest of our agreement? Rachel checked.

We cannot lie, the lurker responded.

Then take me to Galloran.

CHAPTER 35

SACRIFICE

Tark surfaced inside the mine, gasping desperately. Luminous seaweed in hand, he crawled out of the water, his hair and pants dripping. He wore no shirt or shoes. He lay on his back, drinking in the earthy air. The swim had tested him to his limits.

Thanks to Ferrin, Tark had known exactly where to find the entrance to the mine and how far he would need to swim in order to reach the ancient air trapped inside. The entrance had been a long way down. Even with weights to aid his dive, the descent had consumed an alarming amount of time, the pressure building as he sank. Rocks clogged the entrance, but he had stroked through the gap Ferrin had made. For twenty feet it had been tight. Afterward, his lungs complaining, he had advanced along the underwater excavation until the tunnel finally elbowed upward and he had emerged here.

Not many men could have survived that swim. Ferrin had warned that it would be challenging, and the displacer had not been wrong. Tark sat up. His task was far from complete. All of Lyrian was counting on him.

By the light of his seaweed Tark saw the tools Ferrin had left. Multiple pickaxes, pry bars of varying length, rope, spare seaweed, and half a dozen orantium spheres, including one of the large gatecrashers. Ferrin had rehearsed the route that would take him to where the mine had been sealed off. The information had been shared not long before Ferrin was taken into custody.

Tark had informed Galloran how Naman had arrested Ferrin, but by the time Galloran confronted the commander of the seed-folk, the displacer had already quietly escaped. Ferrin had not been spotted since.

But Tark could not afford to dwell on that now. Led by Galloran, the retreat was already underway. Tark had to keep moving. The timing was crucial. According to Ferrin, the extensive tunnels should hold plenty of breathable air. The timing concerns involved the placement of Maldor's forces. Trying to warm himself, Tark briskly rubbed his arms. If he could hurry and detonate the vein of orantium while the vast host was massing around Felrook, the war might realistically end with a single blow.

Tark began gathering supplies.

Farther along the tunnel, a glow appeared beyond the reach of Tark's light. Ferrin held a newly lit length of seaweed in one hand and a large crossbow in the other. The crossbow was casually aimed at Tark.

"Ferrin?" Tark asked.

"Hello." He was frowning, his voice neutral. He looked weary and disheveled.

Tark had never seen Ferrin disheveled.

Tark's hand slid toward his knife.

"Don't touch that knife," Ferrin warned. "My finger is quicker than your arm." The displacer was missing his nose.

"What is this?" Tark asked, slowly raising both hands.

"What does it look like?" Ferrin asked. "After all I did, Naman arrested me."

Tark winced. "I know. Galloran was upset. He tried to intervene, but you were already gone."

"I believe he would have tried. But the time had come to take matters into my own hands. My captors left me a small opportunity to escape, and I took it. The experience served as a sobering reminder. If you detonate that vein of orantium, the Amar Kabal win. And the displacers lose. Forever."

Tark nodded. "You knew that from the start."

"But what were the chances we would actually succeed? Did you expect it?"

"I don't know."

"I didn't. Not really. But here you are, about to spill your blood down in the bowels of the earth to create a flash of orantium like the world has never known. I failed to give Esmira the proper credit."

"Seems she had a gift," Tark agreed. He glanced from the crossbow to Ferrin's eye. "Have you been toying with us all along?"

"I'm not sure what I've been doing," Ferrin replied. "I've been open about that with those who have bothered to ask. I'm not sure how I expected this to end. I certainly never thought I would find myself in a position to receive an imperial pardon."

"You really think Maldor would pardon you?"

"Naman seemed to think so," Ferrin said wryly. "The prospect once seemed impossible. I had crossed too many lines, burned too many bridges. But what if I were able to warn the emperor that Felrook had unwittingly been constructed on top of a mountain full of explosives? What if I could singlehandedly save his armies and his life? That would probably do the job."

"I can't believe this," Tark sighed. Everyone was counting on him. He could not fail! His mind frantically searched for a workable strategy. Ferrin would not miss with the crossbow. Even without it, Tark knew how well the displacer could fight.

Ferrin smirked. "It's amazing that this fortress didn't explode long ago. They could have tunneled into the orantium when digging the dungeons. The dungeons of Felrook are deep. A little deeper, and they might have had quite a surprise."

"You swore to uphold our cause," Tark said. "You swore to Galloran and Jason and Rachel."

"I did," Ferrin admitted. "Naturally, they all expected me to lie. It's what displacers do. Thanks to Naman, I've enjoyed some time alone to consider a new plan. Want the essentials? First, I shoot you. Then I inform Maldor that his fortress is built atop a mother lode of orantium. He wipes out the forces fleeing into the mountains, then chooses a new stronghold from which to rule for a thousand years. The smug seedmen fall. And I get pardoned. Nothing short of service this crucial would earn Maldor's forgiveness, but I expect this would prove more than sufficient."

"Maybe," Tark said, hoping to plant doubt.

"When I spoke with the oracle, she told me that before the end I would have the chance to decide the outcome. I didn't expect the opportunity to be so blatant. Perhaps neither did she."

"Don't do it," Tark said. "Galloran still has part of your neck."

"I appreciate the concern," Ferrin laughed. "I'm resourceful. I could get to Maldor before Galloran had any inkling of my betrayal. Some quick emergency graftings, and I would be fine."

"Why am I still alive?" Tark asked, aware that the quarrel could be loosed at any moment. "I can't stop you."

"Nobody can stop me. Today, right now, the future of Lyrian teeters on a knife-edge, and I get to determine which way it will fall. To side with Maldor will preserve my people and provide me with a long life as a noble lord. They might even grant me one of the few remaining displacer women as a companion." He paused, his eyes momentarily distant. "To side with Galloran would buy me death and grant victory to my ancestral enemies."

"You don't have to die," Tark said. "You could still try to flee."

"I will not flee. I've fled enough. If I kill you, I will have no reason to flee. If I let you destroy Felrook, I will remain at your side and see it done. If my people must fall, I will be man enough to fall with them. There would be no place for me in the world after that."

Tark felt a glimmer of hope. "Are you still undecided?"

"Not anymore. Funny. I came down here still uncertain, angry, all the possibilities dancing in my mind. I doubt anyone could have guessed what would sway my final verdict. Displacers have a reputation as selfish schemers, and my personal reputation is among the worst. But in the end I'll make this choice based on friendship. It's even surprising to me. I've never had friends before. Not real ones. Now I have three friends in the world, Tark. Three people who I truly love and respect. None are displacers. None serve Maldor. My friends are Jason, Rachel, and Galloran. In the end, with the fate of Lyrian in my hands, I'm not willing to let them down. I couldn't harm them and live with myself. They'll never know about this decision. They'll never know how much their friendship meant to me. But I'll know, and that's enough."

Ferrin lowered the crossbow.

"Really?" Tark asked. He had turned, offering his arm as a target rather than his chest. He had been braced to attack Ferrin after the quarrel hit. He had been braced to drag himself, bleeding, toward the orantium vein.

Ferrin gave a nod. "Naman made me angry. But I don't care about him any more than I care about Maldor. Why should either of them influence me? You treated me well when the seedmen came for me. Galloran, Jason, and Rachel have consistently treated me well. They wanted this, so they're going to get it. Besides, I gave Jason my word. Nobody has ever asked that of me. Not directly. Not knowing who I was. It pleases me to reward him for it." The displacer seemed to relax, as if uttering his intentions had made the decision real.

"If you're serious, we ought to hurry."

"Agreed. I know where the sealed portion of the mine begins, but it could still be a chore to reach the vein itself. Before Naman apprehended me, I had considered suggesting to Galloran that I join you, but I worried that he might object to my presence here at such a sensitive time."

Tark was already gathering gear. "Nobody can stop you now. I expect I'll be glad you're with me before the end. This is a weighty responsibility for one man."

Ferrin collected the gear that Tark could not carry. The displacer led them deeper into the mine, taking turns that Tark had memorized. After a long stretch down a straight tunnel, they reached a wall of rubble. Deep engravings etched the walls. Tark understood none of the writing. "Can you read this?"

"A variety of ancient languages are represented," Ferrin reported. "I can only read one of them. It warns intruders away. I checked all the tunnels. This was the only premature ending, and the only one marked."

"This might only be the first barrier," Tark said.

"I made the same guess," Ferrin replied. "But I decided I had better not investigate until Galloran got away. It would have been a shame to destroy our own armies along with Felrook."

Tark studied the wall of rubble, selected a pry bar, and went to work. After a minute or two he started giving Ferrin instructions.

Together they heaved stones out of the way. After most of an hour, Tark paused, panting, holding his seaweed into the high gap they were creating. "I can see the far side. The tunnel goes on."

Ferrin held up a canteen. "Water?"

"Don't mind if I do." Tark tipped his head back and drank. "I wonder if that will be the last I ever drink?"

"I don't think we're that lucky," Ferrin replied, wiping his forehead. Dust clung to his perspiration, and the action smeared it. "I expect we have more work ahead of us."

They cleared the remaining obstacles and brought their gear through the gap. The tunnel angled downward. They advanced until they reached an iron gate. The bars of the gate and its frame stretched from floor to ceiling, utterly blocking the way. Carvings decorated the walls.

"More warnings?" Tark asked.

"Everything I can recognize says to turn back," Ferrin replied. He rattled the gate. It had several locks. He peered at them. "These locks are corroded. I can't pick them. The iron still feels relatively solid. Orantium?"

"I would hate to risk a cave-in," Tark said, "but it might be our only choice."

"Where do we place it?"

Tark cut a length of rope and tied one of the smaller spheres near the center of the gate's hinges. They backed well away and flung rocks until the sphere shattered and the mineral inside exploded. The blast echoed down the long tunnel, the thunder skipping and rebounding as if the rumble were reaching for infinity.

Although damaged, the gate remained partially intact. A little work with their tools pried part of it open far enough for them to slip through.

Around a bend they encountered another wall of rubble. It

proved to be very thick, requiring more than an hour of heavy labor with pickaxes and pry bars complemented by two orantium blasts. The first orantium blast actually seemed to make matters worse, but the second helped considerably.

Once on the far side, Ferrin and Tark finished the last of the water.

"That may be your last drink," Ferrin said. "Unless we head back for more."

"This is already taking longer than I'd like," Tark said, running his tongue over his teeth. Even after the water, his mouth tasted gritty.

"Think of it as giving Rachel some extra time to get away," Ferrin said.

"Do you think she has a chance?"

Ferrin shrugged. "Part of the prophecy was meant specifically for her. We have good reason to trust that Darian the Seer knew his craft. I expect that means she has a good chance. Since I'll never know the truth, I prefer to assume she'll survive."

Tark and Ferrin proceeded along the tunnel. Up ahead, floor-to-ceiling bars blocked the way. They had an odd sheen, almost golden. Fifty feet beyond the hefty bars, the tunnel terminated. A white, pasty substance covered the end of the tunnel.

Ferrin rubbed the fat bars, then tapped his knuckles against one. "It makes no sound."

Tark hit a bar with a pickax. The impact was much quieter than it should have been. "What is it?"

"I have no idea," Ferrin said. "Some alloy. Something strong. It hasn't corroded at all. It looks to be anchored deeply in the floor and ceiling. There is no gate. No hinges. Nobody was meant to get past here."

Leaning on a long pry bar, Tark sighed. "Not only did they

conceal the location of the mountain. Not only did they submerge the entrance under a huge lake. Not only did they erect multiple barriers. Now this."

"That white coating at the end of the tunnel," Ferrin pointed out. "Do you suppose it is meant to seal off the vein?"

"I sure hope so," Tark said. "If the tunnel continues behind it, we could be in trouble."

Ferrin studied the wall of bars. "We could attack the stone. Blast it. Try to remove a bar that way."

"We could," Tark said. "I'm not optimistic. These bars are thick. They were put here to stay. They enter seamlessly into the natural stone. I think they may have been inserted using Edomic."

"The bars are spaced close together," Ferrin said. "Even taking it slowly, I don't think I could pass myself through piece by piece. But I can send my arms." They crouched. Ferrin detached one arm and passed it between the bars. Tark grabbed the other and placed it through.

"Hand me the smallest pick," Ferrin instructed.

Tark passed a pick between the bars. One of Ferrin's hands accepted it. His arms began working their way down the tunnel, moving like overgrown, fleshy inchworms. Before long they reached the end of the tunnel. The free hand probed the white substance on the wall.

"Feels like clay," Ferrin reported. One arm awkwardly tried using the pick. The hand without the pick tore away the white substance faster. Soon Ferrin dropped the pick and started clawing white clay from the base of the wall, one small handful at a time.

"If this is the last barrier," Tark said, "you might reach the orantium at any second."

"Wouldn't that be a happy surprise?"

"I wonder if we'll have time to notice."

"It might be quick, but I think we'll feel it coming."

Gripping the cool metal bars, Tark watched tensely as the minutes passed. The hands could not reach high, so they gradually excavated a tunnel at the base of the white wall. More minutes dragged by. "I wish I could help."

Sweat beaded on Ferrin's brow. "Me too."

Tark chuckled. "Want me to fetch water?"

"You might miss the blast."

"I think I'll notice."

"Sure, that would be nice."

Taking the canteen, Tark retraced their steps, clamoring through rubble and walking along manmade tunnels until he reached the place where he had entered the air pocket. He stared at the dark water. Did Ferrin really need his help? Tark glanced over his shoulder at the empty tunnel, then back at the water. What if he made a run for it? Might he get away? Probably not. The explosion should happen soon.

Tark shook his head. The musings were reflexive. He had run away more than once in his life. The thoughts were familiar, but today he had little desire to heed them. The displacer could not be trusted to finish the job. He had to stay and see this done. It was his chance to make things right, the chance he had always wanted.

Crouching, Tark lowered his lips and drank directly from the water. Then he filled the canteen.

On the way back, Tark thought about others who had sacrificed to make this moment possible. He thought about the members of the Giddy Nine. He thought about Tristan, who had died as they'd escaped Harthenham. He thought about Chandra, and Raz, and Dorsio, and the oracle. He thought about Drake. He thought about Io trying to protect Rachel. He thought about Ferrin, down here with him in the dark, digging toward a cataclysm.

When Tark reached Ferrin, the white tunnel at the base of the wall went back four feet. "You're a good man," Tark said.

"That might be something of an exaggeration," Ferrin replied, "but under the circumstances I'll take it."

Tark jutted his chin toward where Ferrin's arms were working. "I couldn't have done this without you."

"The thought had crossed my mind."

"You want a drink?"

"I'll need your help."

Ferrin knelt, and Tark poured water into his mouth. After pausing to let him swallow, he poured more. "Keep going?"

"Sure."

Tark shared water until Ferrin had drunk his fill. Down the tunnel, the hands and arms kept digging.

"Are you afraid to die?" Tark asked, taking a swig himself before setting aside the canteen.

Ferrin paused. Tark glimpsed something in his eye, a quiet struggle to remain in control. Maybe a hint of worry. "Yes, if I'm being honest. But we all have to go. I was trying to think of a better way than this. I couldn't."

Tark nodded. "I hear you. Ever play stones?"

"Sure."

"My father taught me the game. I'm no expert. Neither was he. But he taught me that sometimes you have to sacrifice a stone or two to gain a strategic advantage. He told me that sacrifice means trading something good for something better. It stuck with me. I guess it applies today."

Ferrin gave a nod. "I suppose it does. In fact, I find that a very rational way to look at it."

Tark sighed. "I feel like I've cheated death a lot."

"I could say the same. I suspect both of us have run out of extra chances."

"I hope so. For the sake of the battle, I mean."

Ferrin furrowed his brow. "What have we here?"

"What?" Tark asked, peering at the end of the tunnel.

"I think I've made it through the white stuff," Ferrin said. "There's something behind it. Something flat. Not stone. It feels like wood. Slightly spongy, though not as soft as cork."

"Can you tear it apart?"

"I'm trying." Ferrin winced. "Just tore a fingernail. Ouch, and another one. It feels pretty firm. Dare we hope this is truly the end?"

"Should we try orantium?" Tark asked.

Ferrin nodded. "It might be our only remaining option. I wish we could use the gatecrasher, but there is no way it will fit through the bars."

"A normal one might do it," Tark said.

"Let's find out," Ferrin said.

An arm came scissoring back to them. Tark handed it an orantium sphere, and the arm wriggled away.

"Use the crossbow," Ferrin said. "I want to get my arms clear, in case this doesn't work and we need more use out of them. I swear, Tark, if I have to cram myself through these bars piece by piece, I will see it done."

"I thought you said it would be too hard," Tark replied.

"It would be risky," Ferrin replied. "There are limits to how much of myself I can separate at once. If my displacement fields falter, I would become a big mess. Still, if all else fails, I'll try it."

Tark laid down on the ground and sighted with the crossbow. "It's too dark. I can't see the target."

"Throw a bit of seaweed that way."

Tark tore off a segment of seaweed and threw it through the bars. An arm moved to retrieve it. Tark settled back on the ground. After the arm put the seaweed at the back of the white clay excavation, Tark could see the globe perfectly.

"Give me a moment," Ferrin said as his arms retreated. "Want me to take the shot?"

"I can do it."

"I have two spare quarrels. With that bow at this distance, you'll want to aim about four inches high. No wind. The quarrel should fly straight."

Tark aimed as Ferrin described. The arms reached the bars.

"Do you want to attach your arms?" Tark asked.

"No," Ferrin said. "I'm missing an eye, an ear, my nose, part of my neck, even part of an artery in one arm. It's fitting that I should meet my end in pieces. We might still be hours away from a conclusion. Or this might be it." Ferrin turned slightly and looked right at Tark, giving him a nod. "You're a brave man, Tark. It has been an honor."

"Likewise," Tark said, letting his mind relax as he squeezed the trigger.

The quarrel sprang from the crossbow. At the end of the hall the orantium shattered. The mineral inside flared white and exploded. After a gasping rush of air, there came a second, stronger explosion. The second blast wave sent Tark rolling. Debris slammed against the bars. With a stronger rush of air, a third detonation followed. The last thing Tark knew was a sense of relief coupled with an intense white flash.

CHAPTER 36

THE FLASH

The sun was almost to the top of the sky by the time the lurkers delivered Rachel to Galloran. She found him in the western foothills, on the far side of a stony bluff. Having sensed the lurkers coming, the king reacted with apprehension at first, but soon Rachel explained how she had destroyed the Myrkstone and entrapped Maldor.

"You struck a bargain with the torivors?" Galloran clarified.

"Most are free to go," Rachel explained. "They can return to their home world. But three must unconditionally serve you until the day you die. It seemed fair, because three have attacked you with swords. And one must unconditionally serve Jason for as long as he lives and remains in this world, because they sent one for him. And one must unconditionally serve Farfalee, because one of them killed her brother."

"Unconditionally?" Galloran asked. "No limits? Not even Zokar attained that level of commitment."

Rachel shrugged. "I guess Zokar didn't free most of them."

"Will any serve you?" Galloran asked.

"One used swords to attack Maldor for me," Rachel said.

"He'll keep on him until the job is done. And the three that will serve you vowed to help me escape Felrook and bring me to you. That was all I really needed."

"So Maldor is pinned down by a former minion," Galloran mused, his mismatched eyes remote. "Yes, I can sense his Edomic exertions—potent, but strained. He seems both weary and unwavering, no doubt still holding off the torivor. A protective barrier such as he raised requires a great deal of power and concentration. As long as the lurker stays on him, Maldor won't have an opportunity to attempt any other commands."

"The torivors promised that the attack would not end until Maldor died," Rachel said.

Galloran shook his head and fixed Rachel with an intense gaze. "Do you know how many people have tried to undo the emperor? The attempts date back to the war between Zokar and Eldrin. Great warriors and wizards have failed." The king chuckled. "I privately feared he might find a way to escape the upcoming blast. Now I can rest easier. You have distracted and incapacitated him at precisely the right time. For years Maldor feared others with Edomic talent. Yet he insisted on you as his apprentice. That arrangement did not take long to unravel."

"I got lucky," Rachel said. "He was a much stronger wizard than me. The prophecy gave me the crucial hint. Orruck's command worked perfectly on the Myrkstone, turning it to glass. When I first faced Maldor, I noticed that an Edomic suggestion momentarily stunned him. So I hit him with a bunch of suggestions that slowed him long enough for me to smash the Myrkstone. Then he attacked my clothes with fire. When I had fought him earlier, he'd spoken words to quench my fire, and I memorized them. I guess he didn't expect me to remember."

"Fire is the quickest attack," Galloran said. "He was probably furious and reaching for a hasty victory."

"He didn't have much time," Rachel said. "By the time the fire had failed, the lurker was on him."

Galloran nodded. "He harnessed dark entities to do his bidding. That can lead to peril if the harness breaks. I am overjoyed that you survived, Rachel, and unspeakably proud of you."

"What now?" Rachel asked, blushing slightly. "What was the big weakness you discovered? You said something about a blast?"

"Felrook is built upon the mount where orantium was mined anciently. The mining was halted because they encountered a vein too large to extract. Tark is currently working to expose that vein."

Rachel covered her mouth. "Oh no."

"He was eager for the opportunity," Galloran assured her. "He volunteered without coaxing. The mine entrance was so deep underwater that he was the only man for the job. Maldor has founded a mighty empire. Even if he perishes, others could rise to finish what he started. But if the mountain erupts soon, his top leaders and his main fighting forces will be obliterated with him."

Rachel looked around. She almost didn't want to ask. "What about Ferrin?"

"Ferrin found the mine for us in the depths of the lake. After he explored it and shared the specifics with Tark, Naman, unbeknownst to me, took him captive to ensure he would stay out of the way."

Hot anger welled up inside of Rachel. "Where is he?"

"Ferrin promptly escaped," Galloran said. "He has not been seen since. He may have fled into the wilderness, but I suspect he went to the mine. If so, our future is in his hands as much as in Tark's. I still have a piece of his neck. If the mountain erupts, we'll know whether he was there."

"In the mine?" Rachel repeated numbly. "I can't lose him, Galloran. We've lost too many people. It's too much. Send a lurker. Send a lurker to retrieve him."

Galloran gave a nod.

Rachel sensed the king mentally communicating with one of the three lurkers. He made sure the dark figure knew who Ferrin was, then asked the torivor to fetch him.

Before the torivor could leave, the rumbling began, a brisk series of distant, mounting explosions. By the end of the thunderous crescendo, everyone had clamped their hands over their ears. A white flash seared the sky. Rachel heard the blast wave as it swooshed past, bringing the odor of scorched minerals, but the stony bluff prevented her from feeling the brunt of it.

The bluff also blocked Felrook from view. After the blast wave it was not long before rocks came hailing from above, ranging in size from marbles to houses. A meteoric boulder the size of a garbage truck shook the ground when it landed a couple of hundred yards away. The thumping patter of falling material persisted for many seconds.

By the time Rachel and Galloran had scrambled around the side of the bluff, Felrook and the soaring cliffs where it had rested were gone, replaced by an immense, charred crater, its dimensions larger than the former boundaries of the vaporized lake. While escaping, Rachel had viewed the armies occupying the keeps and assembling on the plains around Lake Fellion. Now it was like they had never existed. Everything near Felrook had been devastated—the keeps, the ferry town, the vegetation, the enemy armies. That part of the valley had instantly become a scorched wasteland. As Rachel stood silently beside Galloran, overwhelmed by the bleak sight, the sooty cloud overhead kept unfolding, creating a premature twilight.

Rachel became aware of people around her—drinlings, seed-folk, human soldiers—all with their eyes glued to the desolation left by the explosion. They moved like sleepwalkers, stunned, disbelieving. Some were injured. Most looked disheveled.

Rachel realized that most of the fleeing soldiers would not have known that Galloran had a plan to take down Felrook. They thought they were running from a vast army that would pursue and slay them. At best they might have hoped Galloran had some evasive maneuvers in mind that would lead their enemies on a long chase.

Now, without explanation, Felrook was gone, along with the enemy armies. In one inexplicable moment the war was over. Defeat had turned to victory as if by magic.

A trio of drinlings let out a cheer. Their enthusiastic outburst sparked other reactions. Rachel scanned what should have been a battlefield. Men threw down their weapons and raised their arms. A pair of seedwomen stood side by side, bows over their shoulders, one with a slender arm around the other, eyes wide and sparkling. A group of shouting drinlings dog-piled on top of one another, laughing raucously.

Everywhere she looked, Rachel found relief and jubilation. She witnessed celebrations great and small, demonstrative and quiet. These people had expected to die, but now they would live. They had come here hoping to free their homes from tyranny, and they had succeeded.

"He is gone," Galloran said softly. "I felt Maldor's Edomic right up until the blast. Now, nothing. Not a whisper of him."

Sighing, Rachel leaned against a boulder. She could hardly believe Maldor was gone. Could it really be true? Had they really stopped him? As she contemplated the miracle of their success, she felt profound relief. She tried not to think about Ferrin and

Tark. She tried not to dwell on all she had lost. She smiled when she saw a husky, bearded man running along with his arms flung wide, as if he were a soaring bird. She watched him grab a smaller man, perhaps a relative, and heave him over his shoulder. They had to be related. There was a resemblance, and a deep familiarity. Brothers, maybe. Or cousins. The bearded man spun, and the smaller man laughed, raising a fist.

Galloran came and leaned against the rock beside Rachel. His arm encircled her shoulders. His free hand stroked her hair. She leaned into him and wept.

Many miles away, Jason was hiking out of the Fuming Waste with Aram and Corinne. Something in his pocket felt cold and wet. He gingerly retrieved Ferrin's ear. It was clearly no longer connected to the displacer.

HOMEWARD BOUND

Rachel sat alone in an airy, striped tent. More than five years ago, the oracle of Mianamon had informed her of a certain day when she could return to her proper time. As was inevitable with such deadlines, that day had finally arrived.

She wore a nondescript dress of coarse gray fabric. It was not identifiable as coming from another world. Even soaked and dirty, it should hold up well.

A word spoken mentally brought a hand mirror across the room to her. Rachel tried to remember what she had looked like at age thirteen. Her eyes were the same, but her cheeks and chin were more sculpted. She was a couple of inches taller. Her parents would recognize her, but she was no longer their little girl. She would be nineteen soon.

A muttered word brought an empty glass to her hand. A casual phrase filled it with water from the air. As she drank, she wondered how she would feel to speak Edomic and get no response. It was hard to imagine. Edomic had become as natural as breathing.

During the past four months, Rachel had studied at the Celestine Library. She had made three other prolonged visits to the library since the fall of Felrook. In that time she had mastered hundreds of new commands and read about thousands more. With tutoring from Farfalee, Rachel had learned to decipher the two most popular forms of Edomic shorthand that scribes had employed over the years.

Farfalee had been reborn with her left leg paralyzed. She was optimistic that her next rebirth from her new, undamaged seed would fully restore her. Farfalee had insisted that there was currently too much to learn and do for her to lose another three months in the ground. But Rachel felt certain that part of Farfalee's reluctance came from worry about learning for sure whether the paralyzed leg would be part of life for the rest of her existence.

The charm woman and a handful of other adepts had joined them on the island jointly guarded by seedfolk, drinlings, and soldiers from Trensicourt. Rachel's extended periods of study had scarcely provided time to scratch the surface of the knowledge stockpiled there.

When it came to Edomic, none of the others could begin to compete with Rachel. Elaine could help tutor her regarding charms, but most of the rest Rachel had learned through reading and experimentation. Her abilities had grown exponentially.

But would she need to verbally summon fire in a world where the twist of a knob would heat a stovetop? Would she require telepathic communication when she could dial up a friend on a cell phone? For personal defense she could always carry pepper spray. She would probably not need it in the pleasant community where her parents lived.

Jason stepped into the tent, dressed like a prince on an adventure. "You look very generic."

"Thanks, I think."

"Mind if I come in?"

"Of course not."

"Aram just arrived. He brought his wife."

"I haven't seen her since the wedding!" Rachel said.

"We've missed you at Trensicourt."

"I was there most of the time," Rachel said. "It's only been a few months. I couldn't totally neglect the library. Farfalee would never have forgiven me. Besides, with my departure approaching, I wanted to make sure I learned all there was to know about getting in and out of Lyrian."

"Aram is the last," Jason said. "We're all here."

She nodded, setting down the mirror.

He was wrong. They were not all here. That was one of the big problems with Lyrian. It was full of ghosts. They had won the war, but at what cost? Chandra, Dorsio, Nia, Io, Nedwin. Tark. Drake. Ferrin. What good was saving the world if it meant losing your closest friends?

Rachel was grateful they had won. She was grateful for those who had survived. Nobody close to her had died since the day Felrook had been blasted into the stratosphere. Lyrian was free. Galloran had declined offers to become emperor, settling for restoring Trensicourt instead. But he could not prevent his legend from growing. Many kingdoms were rebuilding, and they all looked to him for advice and guidance.

The atmosphere in Lyrian had changed. For the first time in decades the future held real promise. The wizardborn were interacting with humans as never before. But Rachel suspected that for her, Lyrian would always feel haunted.

"You're still okay with going?" Jason checked.

Rachel tried to smile. "What other choice is there? One of us has to stay; one has to go. After all the things Darian got right, we can't really argue with him."

"He's much too dead for arguments," Jason agreed. "You kind of want to go anyhow, right?"

Rachel knew that Jason needed that to be true. He was too nice of a person, and they were too close. If he felt like he had forced her to leave Lyrian so that he could stay, he might feel guilty for the rest of his life.

"I feel the same way I've felt for a long time," Rachel said honestly. "I want my parents to know that I'm alive. I want to see them again. But I'll miss a lot of things. I'll miss all my friends here. I've grown used to Lyrian. It's hard to picture living elsewhere." She was worried about what her voice might sound like if she expressed her deepest concern. "I'll miss Edomic."

Jason nodded, his eyes serious. "Do you need me to go instead?"

Rachel wondered how much he meant it. Enough to say it, at least, which was worth something. "This has always been the plan. Besides, Darian mentioned your daughter visiting him, which can't happen if you aren't in Lyrian."

"He didn't warn that it had to happen," Jason said. "It might have just been a possible future. Who knows? Maybe my daughter could cross over like I did?"

"You've built much more of a life here than I have," Rachel said frankly. "You've gotten closer to people. You've gotten involved. You run a huge estate. You employ people. You're the Grand Duke of Caberton, along with your other titles. You could be chancellor if you wanted."

Jason shook his head. "Nicholas is better for that job. At least for now."

"Besides," Rachel said, "Corinne would never forgive me."

Jason had trouble hiding his grin as he looked away. "Did she say something?"

"I can just tell."

"We're just friends," Jason insisted.

"I know," Rachel said. "Good friends. No other guys get the attention she shows you."

Jason shrugged, still unable to meet her eyes. He had it bad. "You never know."

"Don't worry," Rachel said. "I'm going to leave, just like we planned. If it weren't for my parents . . . and the prophecy . . . but there's no point in thinking that way. I'm feeling better again. The anxiety comes and goes."

"It'll be strange without you," Jason said. "I'll be the last Beyonder."

"Except for the lurkers," Rachel corrected.

"I'll have to stay tight with Corinne for that, if nothing else," Jason said. "Even if Lurky Two does serve me, I don't like it in my dreams. I prefer to have a translator."

Rachel smiled faintly. She had often talked to his lurker for him. The lurker could understand Jason just fine when he spoke. It could even read his thoughts if he gave mental commands. But Jason couldn't hear acknowledgments or responses. He'd be all right. He had Corinne to help, and Galloran if needed. The king managed his three torivor bodyguards just fine. Without telepathy Farfalee and Jasher communicated well enough with their indentured lurker, getting help from Elaine as needed.

Everyone would be fine. With Trensicourt leading the way, Lyrian was becoming more prosperous and stable every day. Her friends would be safe. "I'll miss you."

"Give it some time. Eventually this will all seem like a weird dream."

Rachel shook her head. "I don't think so. Too much has happened."

"You'll deliver my letter?"

"And the jewels. And I'll develop the photos." She was returning with lots of photographic evidence. Most of the shots had been taken after the war. It was hard to take pictures while running for your life. She would keep most of the images private, but some photos would accompany Jason's letter.

"I'll miss you too, Rachel," Jason said gently.

Tears brimmed in her eyes. She looked down. "I'm doing this all wrong. I should never have allowed the rest of you to see me off. I should have gone through alone."

Jason pulled her to her feet and hugged her. She hugged him back. He was tall and strong. "We wouldn't have let you."

Rachel held him tightly. Could they have ever become a couple? If they hadn't known they would have to separate? Maybe. She certainly felt closer to Jason than to anyone. But it was pointless to think about. She was leaving. He was staying.

"If I hate it there, maybe I'll come back," she said. "I read a lot about ways between our worlds. It was my main emphasis these past months. There is no guaranteed way, but there are many tricks I could try."

"Darian told us that one of us had to stay and one had to go," Jason said. "He never said we had to go or stay forever."

Rachel nodded. "I'll keep telling myself that maybe I'll come back someday. That makes this more doable. I have to go. Not only because of the prophecy. I have to see my parents. I have to let them know I'm all right. I have to be with them again."

"I know. Listen, if you ever make it back here, you're welcome to stay at my enormous castle."

She pushed away from him, giggling. "Are you ever serious?"

"I'm serious! Caberton keeps getting better and better. I'll even lend you some of my servants and share some of my gold and jewels."

"What if I come back and hundreds of years have passed?"

"I'll remember you in my will," Jason assured her. "You'll always have a home at Caberton. If anybody doubts you, just point at the monument."

Rachel smiled weakly. Even kidding around, it was hard to think about the monument. It had been completed shortly before she'd left Trensicourt for the last time. The great square near the castle had been renamed Hero Square. There she had been immortalized in stone, her statue more than twice her actual height. The craftsmanship was exceptional. The sculptors were the finest from across Lyrian, including several of the Amar Kabal.

The statue of Rachel did not stand alone. Beside her were Galloran, Jason, Corinne, Farfalee, Jasher, Aram, Kerick, Halco, Andrus, Delissa, and Nollin. All of the delegation who had set out from the Seven Vales and lived.

The dead from the delegation were represented on the other side of the square, including the drinlings who had joined them at Ebera. Io, Nia, Raz, Dorsio, Nedwin, Drake, Tark, and Ferrin were all rendered in lifelike detail. Ferrin held his smiling head in his hand. The sculptors had argued that it made his heritage as a displacer too obvious, but Galloran had insisted for that precise reason.

Rachel loved that her friends had been memorialized there. She appreciated the plaques and fountains commemorating others who had fallen. She respected the sacred feeling the location inspired. But she could not look at her friends without sobbing. After the dedication she had only visited Hero Square twice more—once to take pictures and once to say good-bye.

"Hey, don't get like that," Jason said, giving her a squeeze.

"I'm all right," Rachel said, realizing that her thoughts must have been written on her face.

"Somewhere Ferrin is laughing his guts out that his statue stands in a place of honor."

"Drake, too," Rachel said.

"All of them, probably," Jason realized. "I can't imagine I'll ever get used to that statue of me."

"Whatever. You know you like it."

"What?" Jason asked, unable to resist a smile. "Maybe a little."

Rachel chuckled quietly. "I'm really leaving."

"Looks that way."

"I'm taking some treasure home. The necklace from Drake, of course, but some other stuff as well. I'm not sure if I'll ever try to explain any of it or cash in some of the gemstones, but I thought it would beat returning empty-handed."

"Good idea. You deserve some spoils after all you've done." He nodded toward the opening of the tent. "They have food prepared. Everyone wants to see you."

"I know. I've been stalling. I'm ready now."

The feast was held in a huge pavilion. There were grand announcements celebrating all Rachel had done for Lyrian. There were cheers and applause. But mostly she enjoyed seeing her friends. Corinne, who got more beautiful every year. How could Jason possibly resist! And Galloran, who would never again need to blindfold his mismatched eyes. Aram's lovely wife Brielle stood much taller than him, at least during the day. Rachel always found it strange to see the half giant dressed as a lord.

The meal was delicious, the praise generous, the conversations delightful, but everything felt fleeting. This was the end, and Rachel could not forget it. Regret and excitement warred within her.

The afternoon was waning when her closest friends escorted Rachel to the cave. They passed the guards and entered in silence. At one point they had to fall flat and slither forward. At last they came to a chamber where a clear pool hardly reflected the lamplight.

Rachel leaned over the side. "Look how far you can see."

"It's deep," Jason told her. "And cold. You'll sink until you think you might drown. But then you'll emerge in a farmer's field."

Thank you, Rachel, Galloran thought to her. *Lyrian will forever be indebted.*

You deserve more thanks than anyone, Rachel conveyed earnestly. *Without you, Lyrian would not have been saved, and I would not be going home. Trensicourt could not have a finer king.*

They embraced.

"Are you talking in your minds again?" Jason complained.

"Sorry," Rachel said. "It won't be a problem much longer."

"I don't know what I'll do without you," Corinne said.

"You'll be beautiful, and wonderful, and so happy," Rachel replied, embracing her friend. "I'm sorry for everything I'll miss. I'll think about you always."

She hugged and exchanged words with Farfalee and Jasher, Aram and Brielle, Elaine, Brin, and finally Jason.

"Take care," Rachel said. "Have a marvelous life."

"You too."

There was much more she could say, but it was already too painful. She turned to Brin. "You have weights for me?"

Brin showed her a pair of iron weights at the edge of the pool with loops of rope attached to them. "Just hold tight and you'll sink like an anchor."

Rachel smiled at everyone through her tears. "I'll make sure your letter reaches your parents," she promised Jason. "And those huge gems as well. I won't mess up the photographs."

"Good-bye, Rachel," Jason replied.

Rachel checked the pair of nondescript satchels over her

shoulders. Brin had waterproofed them. She grabbed the ropes connected to the weights, then nodded at Brin. "Toss them in."

Brin grabbed one weight; Jasher gripped the other. Both weights went into the pool, and Rachel went with them, letting their heaviness pull her forward and down. The water was shockingly cold, but she kept a tight grip on the ropes and sank rapidly. Rachel stared down into the darkness.

Farewell, Corinne, she conveyed.

Farewell, Rachel. The answer came faintly, as if from a mile away.

Rachel realized that if she let go of the weights, she could swim back up. Or had she already sunk too far? Would she drown in the attempt?

Can you still hear me? Rachel conveyed with all her might.

She sensed no answer.

Rachel tried not to panic as she ran out of air. Jason had warned it would be like this. She kept hold of the ropes, but it began to feel as if she was rising instead of sinking. Or maybe moving sideways. It was hard to stay oriented in the total darkness. The water seemed to be getting thicker, and it bothered her eyes enough that she closed them. Her speed seemed to increase. She collided with a yielding barrier, and suddenly she was on her back in a moonlit cornfield, spitting soil from her mouth as she gasped warm air into her starved lungs.

The scene was just as Jason had described, except he had arrived during the day. How late was it?

All her belongings had made it through with her. Standing, she tried to brush mud from her soaked dress with little success. She spoke words to extract the moisture. The Edomic command felt dead in her mouth. The water did not respond. She tried several commands. They all tasted like gibberish.

She had known this would happen, but she had not been

prepared for the reality of Edomic feeling and performing like nonsense. It was as if the law of gravity had ceased to function. It was comparable to amputation or paralysis.

Slowing her breathing, Rachel fought the rising panic. What would she do without Edomic? She was stuck here. There was no sure way back! She thought of her parents, and her panic receded.

Turning in a circle, Rachel spotted a glow that suggested a farmhouse. Leaving the weights behind, she started walking.

Some of the lights were on in the house. Rachel opened the squeaky screen door and knocked. A middle-aged woman answered. "Yes?"

"I'm sorry to disturb you," Rachel said. "I'm lost."

Looking Rachel up and down, the woman placed a startled hand against her chest. "Another one? How can—never mind—you poor thing! You're drenched! Come inside."

"Thank you."

"Don't tell me you lost your memory."

Rachel realized that she had better play it up. "Actually . . . I've felt really confused lately. Everything has been . . . hazy . . . disconnected. What year is it?"

The woman told her. Rachel nodded vaguely. It had been more than three years since she had disappeared. Rachel felt relieved that it had been long enough to explain why she looked older. The oracle had not let her down. "Can I use your phone?" Rachel asked.

The woman led Rachel to a telephone. Rachel had not punched digits into a phone in roughly six years. The number had not faded from her memory. She called her home. Her mother answered. The sound of her voice left Rachel momentarily frozen. Then, with a fluttering stomach, Rachel explained who was calling. Her mom freaked out, but in a good way. Rachel held the phone away from her ear during the worst of the shrieks and shouts. Soon her dad was on the line as well. Rachel could not resist her growing smile. Within the first thirty seconds their over-flowing relief and joy made the decision worth it. Speaking with them made Lyrian recede. Within minutes she felt much more firmly home than she had upon her arrival in the cornfield.

While she talked, Rachel fingered her satchel. Inside was the note Jason had let her read. Once she had developed her photos and made sure the appropriate pictures and valuables were bundled with the message and delivered to his parents, her obligations to Lyrian would be officially concluded. She did not need to open the letter to recall the contents.

Dear Mom and Dad,

You probably think I was eaten by a hippopotamus. I did jump into the hippo tank at the zoo, as I'm sure witnesses have reported. But the hippo did not kill me. This sounds unbelievable, but the hippo was a magical gateway to a place called Lyrian. I realize that no evidence can prove something so seemingly ridiculous, but I have included some jewels and photos to help.

My problem is that there is no sure way for me to travel back and forth between our worlds. I could come home, but it would probably mean never returning to Lyrian. I have built a good life here. I'm one of the leaders of the most powerful kingdom in this world. I have many close friends and important responsibilities. Lots of people count on me. I have a future here. And so I am never coming home from Lyrian. Instead, I am sending this message as both explanation and apology.

This is probably the last you will ever hear from me. I don't expect another chance to send a message. Please don't waste your energy looking for me. I am truly beyond your reach. I have risked my life many times to help save this land from a terrible threat. Several of my closest friends gave their lives. In the end we succeeded. As a result there is now so much potential here.

Please don't worry about me. I miss you, but I am also very happy. The first time I went to Lyrian was by accident. It was what really happened when I vanished. The amnesia was a cover story. I was never content after returning. This second time I came to Lyrian on purpose, and I am staying voluntarily. This is where I belong now. I love you both. My only regret about being here is that I will never see you again. Everything else is better than I could have hoped for.

There is no need to let others know about my true fate. It would just make us all look crazy. But I wanted you to know. Use your best judgment on whether to tell any other family members. If you talk to them, tell them I love and miss them, too. Please take good care of Shadow.

You are wonderful parents. I appreciate all you have given me and all you have done for me. I'm sorry if my disappearance seems ungrateful. Please know that after everyone I have met here, and everything I have gone through, I never could have been satisfied in our world.

Sorry if I come across like a lunatic. Sorry if this note somehow makes my disappearance worse. I sent this with good intentions. I had to try.

All my love forever,
Jason

ACKNOWLEDGMENTS

Wow! I can hardly believe I finished Beyonders. This was the first story I set out to tell as an author. I wrote the first draft of book one right after graduating from college. About four years later, the first book I ended up selling to a publisher was *Fablehaven*, and I wrote all five of those, plus *Candy Shop War,* before returning to Beyonders. By the time I got back to it, I had learned a lot as a writer, so I wanted to make some major adjustments, and my editor, Liesa Abrams, gave me a bunch of great suggestions that changed things even more. As a result, I totally rewrote the first Beyonders book, although I kept most of the same characters and problems. I feel lucky that the original version of Beyonders was never published, because I'm very pleased with how it turned out.

Thank you, dear reader, for sticking with me through this series. Your interest lets me do this for a living. Thank you for buying my books, for downloading my books, for telling people about my books, and for asking for them at the library. I love telling stories, and you enable me to keep doing it. I dedicated this book to you, and I meant it.

I need to give lots of thanks to Liesa Abrams, who worked

long and hard on this book with me. This was a big story, and this last book had more extensive edits than any other I've written. Liesa did tons to make this story better. Simon Lipskar, my brilliant agent, not only helps keep me employed, but also contributed some really smart ideas that improved this story.

I owe a lot of thanks to the whole team at Simon & Schuster. This includes Mara Anastas, Bethany Buck, Anna McKean, Fiona Simpson, Paul Crichton, Lucille Rettino, Carolyn Swerdloff, Mary Marotta, and the entire sales team. They got behind this book in a big way. Thanks as well to Lauren Forte, Lisa Vega, Jeannie Ng, and James Riley.

Other early readers who gave feedback include Mary Mull, Sadie Mull, Bryson and Cherie Mull, Pamela Mull, Summer Mull, Jason and Natalie Conforto, Chris Schoebinger, Liz Saban, Wesley Saban, and the ever-diligent Tucker Davis.

My family deserves special thanks. My job makes me travel a lot, and I often have to write long hours, but they're supportive and patient, and my wife helps me work through all sorts of story issues. I love them very much.

Beyonders is over, but I have more stuff coming. It won't be long before some new series begin. I have really exciting ideas for future stories, and I can't wait to share them. You can find out more at brandonmull.com, fan me on Facebook, or follow me on Twitter @brandonmull.

Don't miss Brandon Mull's epic new series:

HALLOWEEN

Weaving down the hall, Cole avoided a ninja, a witch, a pirate, and a zombie bride. He paused when a sad clown in a trench coat and fedora waved at him. "Dalton?"

His friend nodded and smiled, which looked weird since his mouth was painted into a frown. "I wondered if you'd recognize me."

"It wasn't easy," Cole replied, relieved to see that his best friend had worn an elaborate costume. He had worried that his own outfit was too much.

They met up in the middle of the hall. Kids streamed by on either side; some dressed for Halloween, some not.

"Ready to score some candy tonight?" Dalton asked.

Cole hesitated. Now that they were sixth graders, he was a little nervous that people would think they were too old to go door to door. He didn't want to look like a kindergartener. "Have you heard about the haunted house on Wilson?"

"The spook alley house?" Dalton clarified. "I heard it has live rats and snakes."

Cole nodded. "The guy who moved in there is supposed to be

a special-effects expert. I guess he worked on some big movies. It might just be hype, but I keep hearing amazing things. We should check it out."

"Yeah, sure, I'm curious," Dalton said. "But I don't want to skip the candy."

Cole thought for a minute. He *had* noticed some sixth graders trick-or-treating in his neighborhood last year. A few kids had looked even older. Besides, did it matter what anyone else thought? If people were handing out free candy, why not take advantage? They already had the costumes. "Okay. We can start early."

"That'll work."

The first bell rang. Class would start soon. "See you," Cole said.

"Later."

Cole walked into his classroom, noticing that Jenna Hunt was already at her desk. Cole tried not to care. He liked her, but not in *that* way. Sure, in the past he might have felt excited and scared whenever she was around, but now she was just a friend.

At least that was what he kept telling himself as he tried to take his seat behind her. He was dressed up as a scarecrow that had been used for archery practice. The feathered shafts protruding from his chest and side made it tricky to sit down.

Had he ever had a crush on Jenna? Maybe, when he was younger. During second grade, the girls went through a phase when they ran around, trying to kiss the boys at recess. It had been disgusting. Like tag, except with cooties involved. The teachers had been against it. Cole had been against it too—except when it was with Jenna. When she was chasing him, a secret part of him wanted to get caught.

It wasn't his fault he kept noticing Jenna during third, fourth, and fifth grades. She was too pretty. He wasn't the only one who thought so. She had modeled in some catalogs. Her dark hair had just the right amount of curl, and her thick eyelashes made her eyes look made-up, even when she wasn't wearing makeup.

He sometimes used to daydream about older jerks picking on Jenna. In his imagination, he would come along and save the day with a burst of bravery and action-movie karate skills. Afterward, he would be forced to suffer through her tearful thanks.

But everything had changed at the start of sixth grade. Jenna had not only ended up in his class, but by pure chance the seating chart had placed him directly behind her. They had worked together on group projects. He had learned to relax around her, and they had started to talk regularly and make jokes. She had turned out to be cooler than he had hoped. They were actually becoming friends. So there was no reason for his heart to pound just because she was dressed up like Cleopatra.

A graded test sat on top of his test, a circled 96 in red ink proclaiming his success. Tests waited on the other empty desks as well. Cole tried not to spy on the other scores, but he couldn't help noticing that his neighbors got a 72 and an 88.

Jenna turned and looked at him. She wore a wig of limp black hair with ruler-straight bangs. Dramatic makeup accentuated her eyes. A golden circlet with a snake at the front served as her crown. "What are you?" she asked. "A dead scarecrow?"

"Close," Cole replied. "I'm a scarecrow that got used for target practice."

"Are those real arrows?"

"Yeah, but I broke off the tips. Halloween or not, I figured they would send me home if I brought sharp arrows to school."

"You aced another test. I thought scarecrows weren't supposed to have brains."

"I wasn't a scarecrow yesterday. I like your costume."

"Do you know who I am?"

Cole scrunched his face, as if she had stumped him. "A ghost?"

Jenna rolled her eyes. "You know, right?"

He nodded. "You're one of the most famous ladies in history. Queen Elizabeth."

"Wrong country."

"I'm kidding. Cleopatra."

"Wrong again. Are you even trying?"

"Seriously? I thought I knew it for sure."

"I'm Cleopatra's twin sister."

"You got me."

"Maybe I should have come as Dorothy all shot up with arrows," Jenna said. "Then we would have matched."

"We could have been the sadder ending to *The Wizard of Oz*."

"The ending where the wizard turns out to be Robin Hood."

Laini Palmer sat in the desk next to Jenna's. She was dressed as the Statue of Liberty. Jenna turned and started talking to her.

Cole glanced at the clock. There were still a few minutes before class would begin. Jenna had a habit of arriving by the first bell, and Cole had coincidentally developed the same habit. More kids were coming in: a zombie, a vampire fairy, a rock star, an army guy. Kevin Murdock wore no costume. Neither did Sheila Jones.

When Jenna had finished talking to Laini, Cole tapped her shoulder. "Have you heard about that new haunted house?"

"On Wilson Avenue?" Jenna asked. "People keep talking about it. I've never really been scared by Halloween decorations. I always know they're fake."

"The guy who just moved in there supposedly did effects for Hollywood," Cole replied. "I heard that some of the stuff in his spook alley is real. Like, live bats and tarantulas and amputated body parts from hospitals."

"I guess that might be freaky," Jenna admitted. "I'd have to see it to believe it."

"It's supposed to be free. Are you going trick-or-treating?"

"Yeah, with Lacie and Sarah. You?"

"I was planning to go around with Dalton." He was relieved she would be out hunting candy as well.

"Do you know the address?" Jenna asked.

"For the haunted house? I wrote it down."

"We should check it out. Want to meet up around seven?"

Cole tried to keep his expression casual. "Where?"

"Do you know that old guy's house on the corner, with the huge flagpole?"

"Sure." Everybody in the area knew that house. It was one storied, but the flagpole was basically a skyscraper. The old guy looked like a veteran. He raised and lowered the flag every morning and night. "Meet there?"

"Bring the address."

Cole retrieved a notebook from his backpack and opened it. While he looked for his homework, his mind strayed. He had never hung out with Jenna after school, but it wasn't like they were going on a date. They would just be part of a group of kids, checking to see if a spook alley was actually cool.

Mr. Brock started class a few moments later. He was dressed as a cowboy with chaps, a big hat, and a sheriff's badge. The outfit made it tough to take him seriously.

Cole walked along the street beside Dalton, one foot on the curb, the other in the gutter. He was still a scarecrow bristling with arrows. The straw poking out from his neck kept tickling the bottom of his chin. Dalton remained a gloomy clown.

"She wanted to meet at the flagpole?" Dalton verified.

"Just near the house," Cole said. "Not on his lawn."

Dalton pulled back the sleeve of his coat and checked his watch. "We're going to be early."

"Only a little."

"Are you nervous?"

Cole shot him a scowl. "I'm not afraid of haunted houses."

"I don't mean the spook alley," Dalton clarified. "Haven't you always sort of liked—"

"No, Dalton, come on," Cole interrupted. "Be serious. It isn't like that. We're friends."

Dalton bobbed his eyebrows up and down. "My parents say they started out as friends."

"Gross, knock it off." Cole couldn't let Dalton say or do anything that might make Jenna suspect he thought she was cute. "I should have never told you I used to like her. That was forever ago. We're just doing this for fun."

Dalton squinted up ahead. "Looks like a big group."

He was right. They found Jenna waiting with seven other kids—three of them boys. She was still dressed like Cleopatra.

"Here they are," Jenna announced. "We can go now."

"I have the address," Cole offered.

"I know where it is," Blake said. "I went by earlier tonight."

"What's it like?" Dalton asked.

"I didn't go inside," Blake replied. "I just live nearby."

Cole knew Blake from school. He was the kind of guy who liked to take charge and talked a lot. He always wanted to be goalie at recess, even though he wasn't that good.

As they started walking, Blake took the lead. Cole fell in beside Jenna. "So what's your name?" Cole asked.

"Huh?" she replied. "Cleopatra?"

"No, you're her twin."

"Right. Want to guess?"

"Irma?"

"That doesn't sound very Egyptian."

"Queen Tut?"

"Sure, let's go with that." Jenna laughed lightly, then strayed over to her friend Sarah and started talking. Cole fell back to walk with Dalton.

"Do you think the spook alley will actually be freaky?" Dalton asked.

"It better be," Cole said. "I have my hopes up."

Blake set a quick pace. They marched briskly, passing a herd of little kids with plastic superhero faces. Most of the houses had halfhearted decorations. Some had none. A few had really elaborate jack-o'-lanterns that must have been carved using patterns.

Dalton elbowed Cole and nodded toward a doorway. A portly witch was handing out full-size Twix bars to a group of little kids.

"It's okay," Cole said, hefting his pillowcase. "We already made a good haul."

"Not much full-size candy," Dalton pointed out.

"A few little Twixes are just as good," Cole said, unsure about whether he had any in his bag.

"I heard they have some real cadavers," Blake was explaining. "Dead bodies donated to science but stolen to use as decorations."

"Think that's true?" Dalton wondered.

"I doubt it," Cole replied. "The guy would end up in jail."

"What do you know about it?" Blake challenged. "Have you been stealing corpses?"

"Nope," Cole said. "Your mom was too broke to hire me."

Everyone laughed at that one, and Blake had no reply. Cole

had always been good at comebacks. It was his best defense mechanism and usually kept other kids from bothering him.

As they continued down the street, Cole tried to think of an excuse to walk alongside Jenna. Unfortunately, she now had Lacie on one side and Sarah on the other. Cole had spoken with Jenna enough to feel fairly natural around her. Sarah and Lacie were a different story. He couldn't work up the nerve to barge in and hijack their conversation. Every possible comment that came to mind seemed clumsy and forced. At least Dalton was getting plenty of proof that he and Jenna were only friends.

Cole paid attention to the route. Part of him hoped Blake would lead them the wrong way, but he made no mistakes. When the spook alley house came into view, Blake displayed it to the others, as if he had decorated it personally.

The house looked decent on the outside. Much better than average. A few fake ravens perched on the roof. Webby curtains hung from the rain gutters. One of the jack-o'-lanterns puked seeds and pulp all over the sidewalk. The lawn had lots of cardboard headstones, with an occasional plastic hand or leg poking up through the grass.

"Pretty good," Dalton conceded.

"I don't know," Cole said. "After all the build up, I was expecting granite tombstones with actual human skeletons. Maybe some ghost holograms."

"The best stuff might be inside," Dalton said.

"We'll see," Cole replied. He paused, studying the details. Why did he feel so disappointed? Why did he care about the impressiveness of the decorations? Because he had talked Jenna into coming here. If the haunted house was cool, he might get some reflected glory. If it was weak, she would have gone out of her way for nothing. Was that really it? Maybe he was just frustrated that he had hardly talked to her.

Blake led the way to the door. He knocked while the other nine kids mobbed the porch. A guy with long hair and a stubbly beard answered. He had a cleaver through his head, with plenty of blood draining from the wound.

"He must be the special-effects pro," Dalton murmured.

"I don't know," Cole said. "It's pretty gory but not the ultimate."

The fatally injured man stepped away from the door to invite them in. A strobe light flashed nonstop. Dry ice smoke drifted across the floor. Tinfoil coated the walls, reflecting the pulsing light. There were webs and skulls and candelabras. A knight in full armor came toward them, raising a huge sword. The strobe light made his movements jerky. A couple of the girls screamed.

The knight lowered his sword. He moved around a little more, mostly from side to side, trying to milk the moment, but he was less menacing because he had failed to pursue his attack. Seeming to realize he was no longer very threatening, the knight started doing robotic dance moves. A few of the kids laughed.

Cole frowned, feeling even more disappointed. "Why did everyone build this up so much?" he asked Dalton.

"What were you expecting?" Dalton replied.

Cole shrugged. "Rabid wolves fighting to the death."

"It's not bad," Dalton consoled.

"Too much hype," Cole replied. "My expectations were through the roof." Turning, he found Jenna beside him. "Are you terrified?"

"Not really," she said, looking around appraisingly. "I don't see any body parts. They did a good job, though."

The clunky knight was retreating to his hiding place. The cleaver guy started distributing miniature candy, miniatures, but he gave everybody two or three.

Then an older kid with messy hair wandered into the hall. He was skinny, probably around college age. He wore jeans and an orange T-shirt that said BOO in huge black letters. Otherwise, he had no costume.

"Was this scary enough?" he asked nonchalantly.

A couple of the girls said yes. Most of the kids were silent. Cole felt like it would be rude to tell the truth.

The Boo guy folded his skinny arms across his chest. "Some of you don't look very frightened. Anybody want to see the really scary part?"

He acted serious, but it also could have been a setup for some corny joke.

"Sure," Cole volunteered. Jenna and a bunch of the others chimed in as well.

The Boo guy stared at them like he was a general and this new batch of troops might not be up to his standards. "All right, if you say so. Fair warning: if any of this other stuff was freaky at all don't come."

Two of the girls started shaking their heads and backing toward the door. One of them turned and buried her head against Stuart Fulsom. Stu left with them.

"Check out Stu," Cole muttered to Dalton. "He thinks he's Dr. Love."

"Why would those girls have come in the first place if they didn't want to get freaked out?" Dalton complained.

Cole shrugged. If Jenna had wanted to bail, would he have left with her? Maybe if she had buried her head against his chest, trembling with worry . . .

The remaining seven kids followed the Boo guy. He led through a regular kitchen to a white door with a plain br knob. "It's down in the basement. I won't be coming. You sure you want to go? It's really messed up."

Blake opened the door and led the way down. Cole and Dalton shared a glance. They had come this far. No way were they wimping out now. None of the others chickened out either.

Adventure awaits in the Five Kingdoms—
from the #1 *New York Times* bestselling author
of the Fablehaven and Beyonders series.

FABLEHAVEN

FROM *NEW YORK TIMES*
BESTSELLING AUTHOR

Brandon Mull